BLESSED TIME
©2021 CALE PLAMANN

Aethon Books
www.aethonbooks.com

Print and eBook formatting by Steve Beaulieu. Artwork provided by Fernando Granea

Published by Aethon Books LLC.

Aethon Books is not responsible for websites (or their content) that are not owned by the publisher.

ACKNOWLEDGMENTS

First and foremost I need to acknowledge my wife who has tolerated my long nights of typing and gamely tried to read the results even when they were pretty rough. I need to thank my father for loving the dumb stories and home brew roleplaying campaigns I've been concocting since I was a kid and pushing me to make the leap to writing as well as my mother and sister for their constant support.

I need to thank the Brittingham Crew (Brian, Ben, Adam, and Sean) for pushing me into writing my first flawed, choppy, novels and sticking with me ever since.

I also need to thank the discord communities over at The Silver Pen, Bad Cat Hangout and LitRPG Forum for helping me storyboard, workshop, and most importantly keep my sanity throughout the writing process. Including but not limited to (in no particular order): TheDude3445, Bri, Nulls, VeraAnne, Vowron, J. Pal, Traitorman, Origin, 4064, Fae/Kruos, NoDragons, MelasD, Vitaly, Necariin, Khend, Sam, Squirrel, Doom, and Fel.

I also want to acknowledge those who have been supportive and helpful in meatspace- Sarah, Liz, Jack, Eric, and Jerrie. I would also like to thank the support of Princess Charlotte, my cat. Sometimes, the perfect cure for writer's block is a small furry paw on the thigh demanding pets.

I would also like to thank everyone in the one creative writing class I took. Your collective advice was almost as terrible as your purple prose, but you inspired me to actually publish books to prove your dumb opinions wrong, so credit where credit is due.

Also- A big thank you to all of my supporters, but especially to Eli for being there since the beginning, Ari for stepping up to the plate and helping out so much, and Sesharan who has always been there with a kind word.

Finally, but certainly not least, I want to thank the wonderful team at Aethon. Without their hard work over the course of months, none of this book would have been possible.

SOCIAL MEDIA

If you enjoy what you read, please make sure to visit my website or reach out to me on twitter (where I talk about writing amongst other things) or join my discord where I almost exclusively talk about my existing books/what I'm currently writing.

https://www.caleplamann-author.com/

https://discord.gg/xzgycqtFNe

https://twitter.com/WritesCoco

https://www.patreon.com/CoCo_P

Want to discuss our books with other readers and even the authors like Shirtaloon, Zogarth, Cale Plamann, Noret Flood (Puddles4263) and so many more?

Join our Discord server today and be a part of the Aethon community.

·

PROLOGUE - A BLESSED WORLD

The Church of Luxos has long maintained that the blessings are proof that the gods love us. Without them, we would face a world filled with monsters, terror, and fell magic unarmed and naked. Cynics point out that without Ankros, there would be no need for the blessings. Humanity could easily survive without the magic, status sheets, and special abilities conferred by the Sixteen if the God of Night and Struggle didn't decide in his infinite wisdom to fill Karell with monsters and his warlike children, the Durgh.

This author, on the other hand, humbly disagrees with those cynics. We might be able to survive without the blessings and the monsters, but we would never thrive. Although the Durgh and monsters represent an external threat, kingdoms war with distressing frequency. Without blessings, we might not have the magic and martial arts to make such wars into the grand affairs they are today, but we also wouldn't have the magic to grow crops at a moment's notice or heal the wounded.

Plus, without attunements, what would we do for money? Some rural or poverty-stricken zones allow bartering, but not everyone possesses something that a merchant wants. If a man wants a loaf of bread and all he has to offer is jewelry, what is he to do if the baker has no need for jewelry?

Some of my contemporaries have discussed the concept of creating markers out of rare metals, disks, and triangles issued by the various kings with a set value. This idea seems manifestly unwise. Gold is rare and pretty, but what use does it offer to a merchant, warrior, or prince? Ultimately, it is but a few chips of a fancy rock that we've decided has an arbitrary value.

Attunement cannot be robbed from you and it is awarded by the gods themselves. What could be a fairer system? Although attunement can be transferred freely between individuals, an enterprising person can simply go and earn more by accomplishing the various tasks set out by the Major Gods. Each has their own goals for mortal life and growth that are reflected in how they reward us. Fighting monsters will earn you Night attunement from Ankros, God of Night and Struggle. Research, study, and learning new spells will earn you Moon attunement from Mursa, Goddess of Moon and Magic. Serving as a harmonious and productive member of society will earn you Sun attunement from Luxos, God of Sun and Growth.

Better yet, attunement is useful. Although classes help determine the amount of mana someone earns each level, attunement provides an important baseline for both mana capacity and regeneration. After all, each mortal has three mana pools, one associated with each attunement. Each pool is more useful for spells and martial arts closely related to the deity with whom the mana is attuned. Technically, you could try to use Moon mana to power an elemental fire spell, but even the most inexperienced scholars could tell you that Sun or Night mana would be significantly more efficient.

Of course, some of my contemporaries say this system is unfair. Not everyone receives a blessing. The forgotten don't have access to their status, making them unable to level or use magic entirely. Although they can still earn attunement, without their status, they don't even know how much they have, often leading to dishonest merchants swindling them. These disabilities, combined with a healthy amount of discrimination, often lead to the forgotten occupying the bottom rungs of society, mired in poverty and barely able to eke out a meager existence.

"Micah!" a voice called, causing a young boy to snap his head up from the dusty book he was reading. "The sun is starting to go down. You might want to finish your chores so that you can go home. You wouldn't want to miss your birthday tonight, would you?"

The boy slapped the book shut and slipped it onto the trolley he used to sort and file the library's books. Keeper Ansom was right. Today wasn't the day to be late.

A GOOD NIGHT'S SLEEP

Micah Silver ran home from the library the minute the sun dipped below the horizon. Keeper Ansom, startled from his slumber, rocked back in his chair at the library's front desk, just in time to take in Micah rapidly receding. The Keeper squinted his rheumy eyes against the brilliant orange and gold hues of the outside world before turning his head back to the magelight of his musty library. The old man chuckled fondly and stood up, his bones creaking in protest against their years of disuse, as he made his rounds of the library before closing up for the day.

As for Micah, he barely even noticed Ansom as he raced home. Today was the day of his sixteenth birthday. Tomorrow, he would awaken blessed, imbued with a unique power from one of Karell's sixteen deities. He would have access to his status screen and the ability to gain a class, levels, and experience. More importantly, he would be an adult, finally allowed to become an adventurer or learn a trade.

He didn't let himself think of the possibility that he could end up as one of the forgotten. Theoretically, it was an even chance; almost half of those born on Karell simply didn't awaken to a blessing. But it couldn't be him. Ever since apprenticing under Keeper Ansom at the age of thirteen, Micah had kept himself busy trying to develop the skills that might hopefully bring him to the attention of a capricious god.

From reading the Keeper's books while helping at the library, he'd learned the common belief that the forgotten were ignored by the gods due to their laziness wasn't entirely correct. It was true that the gods tended to choose those with skills and temperament suited to them, but it wasn't a sure thing. Many youths did everything they could to obtain a blessing, only to fall into the ranks of the forgotten. On the contrary, it wasn't unheard of for a lazy student to receive a blessing without earning a single skill before their awakening.

Regardless of the rumor's statistical accuracy, it drove Micah to work harder. Every weekday, he studied the tomes in the library, hoping to be rewarded with skill levels in spellcasting once he awakened. On the weekends, he practiced with the spear handed down from his older brother Trevor, repeatedly attempting to hit the sack of straw swinging back and forth from the plum tree in the family garden or practicing the basic forms that Trevor taught him.

Thinking about Trevor brought a smile to Micah's face. He'd been the first person in Micah's family to receive an Uncommon Blessing, the ability to throw a spear and have it return to his hand. Beyond his combat ability, Trevor was blessed with the innate knowledge of a previously unknown spear style. As soon as he received the blessing, Trevor had joined a midsized adventuring guild, the Lancers. After training for a year, he'd begun operating with a small party cleaning up the feral boars and small monsters that plagued the countryside around Basil's Cove.

Trevor wasn't high enough level to challenge a dungeon yet, but his team let Micah join them on some of their simpler missions. By the age of fifteen, Micah was able to kill a boar all on his own, a feat that earned him constant praise from his older brother. Although it wasn't much compared to the rest of their team's martial arts, it was an impressive enough achievement for an un-blessed youth.

Trevor was a vanguard, a whirlwind of stabbing and prodding spears that harassed and kept monsters at bay while Glenn and Meredith, the axeman and pyromancer of their squad, finished them off. Rounding things out was Renee, the team's archer, who provided non-magical ranged support for the rest of the fighters.

Micah would grudgingly accept being a warrior or vanguard like Trevor—he was good at it, after all—but that wasn't where his heart was. No, Micah wanted to be a wizard. He'd settle for becoming an elementalist like Meredith, specializing in one affinity of magic to the exclusion of all others, but his blood *sang* for proper spellcraft.

Ansom was a weaker wizard, only having low affinities in Earth and Wood magic. Still, even the old man's low-level rituals— twisting the two affinities together to make golems of stone and iron —absolutely set Micah's mind alight. From the first time he'd seen the creations helping Ansom move books around the library, Micah *knew* that spellcraft was his future. Never mind that most blessings came with limited to no magical affinity, forcing the adventurer to learn a martial art to channel their mana. Every fiber in Micah's being longed to make it happen.

On his way home, Micah stopped in the market to pick up some last-minute supplies before the benefits of his age faded. Luxos, the God of Sunlight and Patron of Humanity, commanded that all of his followers provide aid and succor to youths. All reasonable purchases and education were free until he became an adult, at which point the god would cut him off, forcing him to earn his own way in the world.

Well, not exactly free. Luxos provided Sun Attunement to the merchants, usually slightly above the market rate for whatever was purchased, to ensure that their "charity" didn't harm them in the long run. Tomorrow, if he wished to purchase something, Micah would have to trade slivers of his own attunement, the font of all mana production on Karell. Of course, once he was blessed, he'd be able to go out and earn attunement on his own by engaging in acts smiled upon by the gods.

Saying goodbye to Old Lady Jacobson, Micah loaded the sack onto his shoulder and headed back to his home. Trevor was out on a mission, wrapped up in important business and unable to come back for Micah's birthday, but that didn't mean that the rest of his family would let him celebrate alone.

Excitedly, he opened the door to his home, a midsized wooden building attached to his father's tailor shop. Immediately, the scent of freshly baked cake hit his nose, and Micah smiled. In the main room of the house, his father, Jon, stood next to his mother, Veronica, a hand affectionately draped over her shoulder. Meanwhile, Esther, his younger sister, bounced from foot to foot in excitement, her eyes fixed on the dinner table.

"Gods, look at you," Jon, a beanpole of a man just beginning to show gray in his beard and hair, said with a wistful smile on his face. "It seems like yesterday you were begging to apprentice at the library, and now you're of age.

"I keep forgetting how big you are," he continued, stepping around Esther to wrap Micah in a hug. "Remember, no matter what happens tonight, you'll always have a home here. Not everyone needs to have some sort of grand magical destiny, and I could always use another set of hands around the shop."

"Hush, dear." Veronica brushed his father aside before putting her hands on either side of Micah's face. "I know that you're special, Micah. All of my babies are. Trevor has his spear, you have your books, and Esther will find her own way. Don't let your father put the seed of doubt in your heart. You were born for greatness and I know it. Just call it a mother's intuition."

He smiled back uncomfortably. On his sixteenth birthday, his father had received a Common Blessing from Saborell, the God of Merchants and Craftsmen, that allowed him to measure and fit clothing with absolute accuracy. His mother was forgotten.

Officially, the forgotten weren't discriminated against, but many people whispered that the gods passed them over with their favors for a reason. Veronica tried to hide it, but every day, Micah could see how the sidelong pitying glances weighed upon her. Instead, she put every hope in her children. When Trevor was blessed with an Uncommon ability, Micah could have sworn that she was more excited than anyone else in the house, including Trevor.

As a forgotten, she faced daily struggles and would have had next to nothing on her own. Veronica was shunned in the marketplace and generally looked down upon by their neighbors. Unofficially, the forgotten weren't even allowed to rent or purchase homes in their family's comfortable upper-middle-class district.

Veronica was an exception and a sore point for their neighbors. Micah's father met her as a young man when she was selling flowers by the side of the road just outside the slums and took a liking to her.

Jon was a good man who could look past something as small as the minor magical blessings that most citizens didn't even use daily, but the same couldn't be said about the other craftspeople of Basil's Cove. Even on the day of their wedding, it had been impossible to quell all of the gossip about how she was marrying above her station, that the only reason a pretty girl like Veronica would marry a gangling man like Jon was his attunement and blessing.

To this day, Micah knew better than to bring up their wedding and neighbors around his mother. Mentioning her sister-in-law's toast in particular was a great way to get stuck weeding the family garden, only to eat bland steamed vegetables for a week.

"Get a good blessing," Esther ordered him, pressing her shoulder in between their mother and Micah so that she could wrap her arms around his lower torso. "Sandy says that you're only going to get a Common ability and that you'll never be as cool as Trevor. You need to get a good one so I can shut her up."

"With that motive," Micah laughed and tousled her hair, "how would I dare get something less than an Uncommon Blessing?"

"Good." Esther nodded curtly, a gleam in her eye as she adopted a serious air. "Now that you know, let's eat. Mom hasn't even let me touch that cake for almost an hour while we waited for you to come home."

After dinner, Micah lay down in his bed, mind racing. Sleep eluded him. It was paradoxical, really. As soon as he drifted off, he would learn his fate. He wanted nothing more than to sleep, but no matter what he tried—counting, meditation, reciting pages from Ansom's histories—nothing worked. Instead, Micah's nervous energy kept him unsettled, tossing and turning deep into the night.

Finally, he stood up and put on a set of nightclothes. Maybe some fresh air would help. It certainly beat stewing in nervous energy and worrying with his eyes closed.

He stepped out into the small garden that his mother maintained behind their house and made his way to a wooden bench fixed to his home's wall. Sitting down, he glanced up into the night sky. Even in the city, night was peaceful. Far away, Micah heard the bustle of the taverns and brothels, but in his neighborhood, there was nothing but the steady thud of the local constable's spear on cobblestone as he paced down the street.

Thud. Micah never really looked at the stars. *Thud*. Every morning, he was up with the dawn, working with Keeper Ansom until sundown. *Thud*. Then it was back home to eat a quick dinner before going to bed and repeating the process. *Thud*. Other boys his age spent time on boys and girls. *Thud*. Chasing after each other all day in order to play giggling, breathless games under the stars. *Thud*. They probably didn't stop for long to enjoy the night's beauty either. *Thud*.

Micah opened his eyes. He was someplace else. A dimly lit fog surrounded him, and the only object he recognized was the wooden bench that he had fallen asleep on. He stood up hesitantly, glancing into the murky abyss.

"Human," a genderless voice echoed through the emptiness of the space, "rejoice, for you have been blessed by the Sixteen."

Micah's heart started pounding in his chest. This wasn't how it happened for Trevor. His brother simply had a dream about how to use his ability and woke up able to see his status sheet with the name of the ability printed upon it.

"As more than one god wishes to select you," the voice continued, "the choice of which blessing to select shall be yours. You will only be told the name of the deity and the rarity of the gift offered to you. Choose wisely, as such an opportunity will never come again.

"Jiana, Goddess of Scribes, wishes to offer you an Uncommon Blessing," the voice intoned evenly. "Mursa, Goddess of Magic and Moonlight, wishes to offer you a Mythic Blessing, and Ankros, God of Darkness and Struggle, wishes to offer you a Rare Blessing."

Micah opened his mouth to respond. Clearly, he was going to take the Mythic Blessing. Mursa and Ankros were both Major Gods, their power orders of magnitude higher than the lesser deities that usually blessed humans. Even an Uncommon Blessing from one of them could outstrip a Rare or Mythic Blessing from a lesser god. Literally, the only blessing more powerful than a Mythic from a greater god would be to be made a Chosen, but each deity could only support one or two of those at a time.

"I apologize," the voice interjected, slightly amused. "It is unusual, but there has been a change. Ankros has heard the offer from Mursa and amended his own. Ankros is now also offering a Mythic blessing."

The empty, glowing fog sat in silence for a handful of seconds before the voice continued. "Please state the name of the god or goddess whose blessing you accept, and you will be expelled from this place to awaken with the power of their blessing in full force."

Micah's mouth flopped open, his initial answer caught in his throat. His pick of Mythic powers from greater gods. That was something out of a story, reserved for the rich sons of nobles born under auspicious stars. He marshalled his thoughts as he tried to make sense of the impossible situation. Having finally come to a decision, he opened his mouth to give his answer.

2

MYTHIC?

Micah woke up on the bench, the sun beating down into his eyes and his heart racing. Quickly, he sat up, trying to process the events of last night. He only knew one person with a Rare Blessing, and that was from an intermediate god. Stanley had been immediately recruited as an apprentice by Basil's Cove's archwizard.

He shivered in the chill morning air as he imagined what sort of favorable treatment he'd receive with a Mythic Blessing from a major deity. There was no question that the guilds in Basil's Cove would start a bidding war over his services. They might even send him to the capital to train with the high nobility. Images of dreamy princesses, heaps of magical items, looted dungeons, and slain monsters flashed through Micah's vision as he sat still, grinning like an idiot.

"Status," he said, unable to resist any longer. His vision blurred and the status screen came up, a light blue roll of papyrus covered in tight and efficient lettering just as Trevor had described.

Micah Silver
Age: 16

Class/Level - XP
HP: 10/10
Attributes
Body 5, Agility 5, Mind 9, Spirit 8
Attunement
Moon 5, Sun 2, Night 4
Mana
Moon 10/10, Sun 4/4, Night 8/8
Affinities
Time 10
Wood 6
Air 5
Blessings
Mythic Blessing of Mursa - Blessed Return, Ageless Folio
Skills
Fishing 1
Librarian 3
Spear 2
Spellcasting 2

Micah nodded to himself. More or less average physical attributes combined with a strong Mind and Spirit. About what he had expected. The only real abnormality was his affinities. Unlike other attributes and skills, affinities were more or less considered static. Although an affinity could be changed through powerful rites of magic, the difficulty and expense of such rituals meant that they were rarely performed.

Instead, a spellcaster was more or less defined by their starting affinities. That wasn't to say that a caster couldn't make do with weaker affinities, but affinities determined the mana efficiency of a caster's magic as well as the speed that they learned new spells. Theoretically, a scrappy spellcaster could make do with weak affinities and perseverance, but in practice, affinities served as a sort of soft ceiling on a caster's abilities. His affinities in Wood and Air weren't bad, slightly above average as dedicated spellcasters usually had affinities in the 4-5 range. The Wood affinity in particular marked him as a potentially above average healer. Useful, but not nearly enough to justify a Mythic Blessing.

The 10 affinity in Time was something else. According to Ansom's books, Time and Order/Chaos were the two primal fields of magic, much rarer and more powerful than their elemental counterparts, but poorly understood due to their rarity. Order/Chaos wasn't an unheard-of affinity, albeit usually only wielded at exceedingly low affinities by archwizards.

The only problem was that all of their spells were incredibly powerful and hard to utilize. Even with a 10 affinity, there was almost no way that Micah would be able to learn Time magic without years of experience and the levels that went with it. Worse, given the magic's rarity, the chances that Micah would find anyone able to tutor him in Time magic were just about nil. Although the strength and rarity of his affinity marked Micah as a potential prodigy, it existed just past his grasp, taunting him.

His attunements were much more standard. Awarded by the three Major Gods for acts done in their service, each attunement was associated with its own mana pool, the size and regeneration of which depended on a combination of Micah's level and attunement. Night, Sun, and Moon mana all had slightly different properties when applied to spellcasting. Micah's Moon mana worked well for all three affinities while the Night mana was only really useful for Air spells. As for the Sun mana? It was better than nothing, and he could use it as currency in a pinch.

Currency. Micah sighed. If he couldn't catch the eye of some noble with his Mythic Blessing, he'd need to find a way to earn attunement sooner or later. All exchanges required either a barter of goods or an exchange of attunement. Daily goods usually only cost slivers of an attunement, a tenth of a point or less, but expensive objects such as enchanted weapons easily ran into the dozens of points. Even if he could barely use Sun mana, Sun attunement was the primary currency in human kingdoms. At least there it could be some use to him.

Finally, Micah called up the descriptions of his blessing. His face fell, and his elation over his abilities left him like the water from a shattered pot.

Blessed Return
Casting time: 1 minute

The user casts their cognition through time back into their own body, five years in the past. Their level, affinities, and attunement are all set to the level they were at five years ago. Skills are not reset, allowing the user to travel back in time with their skills at their current level. This ability is only usable once every five years (subjective time). 1/1 uses available.

Ageless Folio
Bound Item

The Ageless Folio takes the form of a tattoo on the user's wrist. The user may freely withdraw the Folio, which takes the form of a thin book, at will. While holding the Folio, the user learns skills 20% faster and all of their thoughts are recorded automatically in their own hand. The Folio has an infinite number of pages and the user instinctively knows on which page any information rests. Notes taken in the Folio will remain in the Folio, even if the user utilizes *Blessed Return,* allowing the user to retain notes from a previous life. The Folio is blank when bestowed upon the user.

. . .

How in the hells was this Mythic? Clearly, the ability was powerful —anything that allowed someone to wind and coil time like a rope was insanely potent. Useful? That was a different question.

Theoretically, he could go back five years and train his skills, but Micah didn't even know how that would work. Humans only gained access to their status screen at the age of sixteen. If he were to travel to when he was eleven, he wouldn't even have any way of tracking his progress. Of course, he'd have to give up everything. His body, his attunements, any levels he'd earned. They would all be thrown away for the uncertain chance that the next iteration of his life would somehow yield a better result.

It was powerful in theory, but the idea of having to live his childhood once again drew a shudder from Micah. He needed adventure, to defeat monsters and conquer dungeons until his aura was fat and heavy with attunement. Returning to his eleventh birthday only to be scolded by his mother for every perceived misdeed was the exact opposite of what he craved.

He groaned, wondering what Ankros' blessing would have been. The God of Darkness and Struggle wasn't a popular subject in human kingdoms. The fact that he openly antagonized humans, sending monsters and barbaric Durgh after them so that humanity could "hone itself in combat" against his children didn't earn the god many friends.

Even that life of isolation and distrust would be acceptable if he had a proper Mythic Blessing. For every blessed individual, their blessing was the core of their identity. A unique ability or skill that set them apart from others and gave them an advantage in combat. In every story of legend, the hero's blessing was their signature move.

Rasdar the Bold had the Mythic ability to create a great dragon from flame that he could control with his mind. Nissia the Usurper could control the flow of all liquids, including the blood inside her opponent's bodies. Even an Uncommon ability would let someone ignore poison, summon a powerful bound weapon, or strike someone with their minds.

Micah? He had a book that helped him learn faster and an ability that he couldn't use without sacrificing everything. Admittedly, the book was useful as a utility skill, but its power was far from Mythic.

At least he had two skill ranks in Spears and Spellcasting. With a little bit of Wood and Air magic, he could become a neophyte battlemage and offer his services to an adventuring guild. Most of them were looking for people capable of casting healing spells, and Micah could already hold his own against low-level beasts, even without any magic.

"Micah!" Esther screamed, running out into the garden and jumping onto him, careful to avoid the tomatoes for fear of raising their mother's ire. "You weren't in bed! Did you get a blessing? Tell me what you have!"

He rocked back from her onslaught blankly before smiling wanly. It was true that his ability wasn't properly Mythic, but the book alone wasn't that bad. It was certainly better than the frequently mundane Common abilities.

"I guess Mursa spotted me studying magic all day, so she gave me a book." Micah did his best to crack a smile, summoning the Ageless Folio for Esther to see. It didn't look all that impressive. The book had cracked and battered covers, inlaid with basic geometric designs and wrapped around a handful of yellowing sheets of paper.

"Does it have spells or some sort of lost secret knowledge?" Esther looked skeptically from the book to Micah. "You promised that you'd at least get an Uncommon ability. I bet Sandy chores for a week. If I lose, you're going to be the one doing those chores."

"It is Uncommon." Micah's face strained under the weight of his forced cheer. "It gives me a 20% increase to learning skills and it has infinite space for taking notes. With this, I'll be able to save years' worth of research in becoming a wizard."

"You have affinities, then?" Esther's eyes were sparkling once again as she snuggled up against Micah.

"Wood 6 and Air 5," Micah said, nodding at her. Desperately, he wanted to tell her everything, pour out his grievances over his decent but underwhelming skillset, but he knew better. Anything he told Esther, her best friend Sandy would know within hours. The rest of the street would be in on the secret twenty-four hours after that. It had certainly happened before.

If Micah wanted to avoid everyone mocking him over his more or less useless ability, that was the only choice. Already he could hear it. "Mythic Micah." Gods, it even alliterated. He'd never be able to live a name like that down.

"Super cool, Micah!" Esther jumped up from his lap, narrowly avoiding the tomatoes. "I'll tell Mom and Dad right away! They'll be so excited. Two Uncommons. Wait until Sandy hears that!"

He watched her scamper away, all energy and excitement. There was something about her enthusiasm that wore away at Micah. For one brief second, he'd had the world laid out in front of him, only to have it jerked away. He sighed.

No. It was time to stop dreaming about being a hero. The Mythic title was little more than a cruel prank, but the goddess did provide him with the power and affinities he would need to carve a comfortable life for himself. He took a breath, reorienting his expectations. He would never be a champion of freedom and justice rubbing shoulders with the nobility, but it was well within his power to help the local guilds clear the nearby dungeons and retire to research like Keeper Ansom.

He smiled weakly to himself as he got up from the bench, smothering the dreams he hadn't dared to articulate even two days ago. From inside the house, his mother called out to alert everyone that breakfast was ready. His blessing might not be what he'd longed for, but it was certainly better than what a lot of people made do with.

He smiled weakly to the empty garden. Maybe if he kept repeating that to himself, he'd even start to believe it.

Micah glanced toward the door inside and thought of his mother. As disappointed as he was, at least he'd received a blessing. Sighing, he walked into the house, trying to make plans for his future.

3

A NEW LIFE

Trevor walked into the house, larger than life with his spear over one shoulder, covered in grime and streaming sweat. Micah was sitting next to Esther at the breakfast table as their mother brought over a plate of pancakes. Jon was absent, likely having eaten already and gone into the shop early.

"Micah!" Trevor shouted at him, dropping the spear by the door and punching him in the shoulder. "We just cleared out a scar wolf den, but I hurried over as soon as I could to congratulate you."

"Hey, Trevor." Micah smiled, rubbing at the bruise on his shoulder.

Trevor was around level 9 by now and, given his Vanguard class, his Body attribute was well over 10, making him roughly twice as strong as the average forgotten adult.

"What would you do if I didn't receive a blessing? That entrance really would've been in bad taste."

"I've seen how hard you work, Micah," Trevor snorted as he grabbed an apple from the table. "You sure as hell put more time and effort into your training than I did during my apprenticeship. If anyone was gonna get a blessing, I knew it was gonna be you.

"So," Trevor continued, flopping down into a seat next to Micah, "how's my little brother doing now that he's a man? Did you get anything good?"

"Uncommon and Mursa." Micah summoned the Ageless Folio. "It helps with my skill growth and lets me perfectly organize my notes. That plus Wood and Air affinities seems to peg me as a caster of some sort."

"How good are your affinities?" Trevor asked, trying to take the Folio from Micah, only for his hand to pass through the ramshackle book. "I might be able to get you into the Lancers if you're above 4 on one of them. We're always short on casters, and wizards are even rarer, even if you're only a dual affinity."

"6 Wood and 5 Air," Micah answered around a forkful of pancake, trying to ignore Trevor as his brother kept trying to poke the Folio while smiling like a madman as his finger slipped through the magical book. "I don't think I'm going to be a high wizard anytime soon, but it should be enough for me to hold my own in a city the size of Basil's Cove."

Trevor gave a low whistle before slapping Micah on the back again. "Hold your own?" He laughed. "With numbers like that and a little luck figuring out a ritual to raise your affinities, you could end up as a high wizard pretty easily. Affinities make things simpler, but with a high enough skill level, you can overcome a lot.

"Look." Trevor's face grew a little more serious. "You let your blessing be known and some of the bigger guilds in town will try to recruit you. Now the Lancers aren't a tiny guild, but we're hardly the Golden Drakes. I'd love for you to join my guild, but I'm not gonna push you. Anywhere you go, it's gonna be years of hard work, and a bigger guild could probably support your research better than the Lancers. Of course, if you join up with us, you'll get to hang out with me, and that's *got* to be worth something."

"If I had a Rare gift, I'd probably try to go to the capital or something." Micah chuckled as Trevor batted his eyelashes at him. "If I'm staying in Basil's Cove, I might as well join the Lancers. As you said, it's going to be a lot of work no matter where I go, so I might as well sign on with some people I like."

"That's the spirit, bro." Trevor laughed while Esther nodded earnestly. "You never stood a chance against my winsome personality and shameless begging."

"How do I sign up for the Golden Drakes again?" Micah rolled his eyes and ate another forkful of pancakes. "I'm sure I wouldn't get razzed as much over there."

"Nope!" Trevor shouted, standing up. "No takesies backsies. Look, I'm gonna take a bath. Why don't you finish breakfast, and then we can head down to the guild hall. I can get you registered and get you a class. You're gonna have to start earning attunements soon, no real reason to waste time."

Trevor rumbled out of the room, just as much a force of nature as when he'd arrived. For a second, there was only the clink of silverware on plates as Esther and Micah kept eating. Then his mother sat at the table and smiled at him.

"Uncommon and from a Major Goddess." She was beaming. Micah felt sick to his stomach as her pride showered on him. He couldn't even think of how his mother would react if she knew that his blessing was Mythic but largely unusable.

"I told you there was nothing to worry about, Micah." She tousled his hair. "All of my babies are destined for something special. I just know it."

Micah smiled back uncomfortably and finished his pancakes.

An hour later, he was standing next to Trevor as his brother flirted with a cute attendant working the front desk at the Lancers' guild hall. The building was a two-story stone edifice, ugly, squat, and long. The interior had some decorations, but by and large, it seemed to be a no-nonsense affair. The guilds were collections of mercenaries with charters granted by the local government to take commissions and fight monsters. The Lancers' main hall looked every inch the part. The furniture was crude but functional, the walls were covered with trophies from high-tier monsters, and almost everyone seemed to have a weapon of some sort strapped to their bodies.

Finally, the woman finished putting together Micah's introductory packet, a brief questionnaire regarding his abilities and goals. Quietly, he took a table and filled out the paperwork while Trevor kept chatting with her. After briefly writing down his abilities and signing a statement certifying that he hadn't overstated them, Micah returned the paperwork to the front desk, where it was slipped through a slot in the wooden wall behind the attendant.

Then he waited for almost a half-hour, sweating while Trevor tried over and over again to convince the attendant to go on a date with him. By the time a guild official walked into the hall to talk to Micah, the cheesiness of Trevor's pickup lines had reached the point that even some of the more hard-bitten mercenaries sitting around the front desk were struggling to keep a straight face.

"Silver," the woman snapped at Trevor, "leave Ashley alone. Other Silver." She pointed at Micah. "Follow me." The statement was clipped and dismissive, as the official had spun on a heel and walked down the hallway into the bowels of the guild.

Micah glanced at Trevor, confused. Trevor shrugged and made a shooing motion with one hand before turning away from the front desk and finally leaving Ashley in peace. Micah hurried to catch up to the official, almost reaching her by the time she turned into a side room.

Hesitantly, he stepped in after her, only to see that the official was already seated with a hazy white ball made from glass or crystal sitting on a pedestal on the table in front of her. Micah walked forward and pulled out the chair at the table before sitting down.

She let him sit for a while. A couple of times, he opened his mouth to say something, but stopped himself when he noticed her attention focusing on him. Finally, she spoke.

"Micah Silver." She spoke the words as if she was reading them, but his paperwork was nowhere to be seen. "Brother of Trevor Silver, a guild member of good standing. You have low levels of skill in both Spear and Spellcasting. It's true that you have two affinities with decent scores, but it would take a fair investment of time and money on our part to train your existing skills to a level where you could be useful. Tell me why our guild should invest that time in you."

Micah stared at her blankly for a second, his mind racing. All he knew was that he was supposed to join a guild. It was what you *did* if you had a blessing used in combat. Almost on its own, his mouth opened, desperate to fill the growing silence.

"Because I've secretly been adventuring with Trevor off and on for the last year?" Micah asked, hating himself for the slight stammer he heard in his voice. He knew that the Lancers should be thrilled to recruit him—wizards and healers didn't grow on trees, after all—but the official's brusque nature kept him off balance and already he was showing weakness.

"I mean"—Micah firmed his voice up slightly and straightened his back—"I've been studying basic spellcasting at my internship since I turned thirteen. If you ask Keeper Ansom, he'll tell you that I'm a diligent worker."

Micah paused for a breath. This wasn't right. He wasn't here to beg and plead for a job; he was here to show the Lancers that he belonged amongst them. They weren't going to give him attunement to be timid and hide himself away. He was here to learn how to fight, and he needed them to know it.

"More than anything, I've always wanted to be a wizard." His voice was steady, even. "If the Lancers turn me down, I'll find another guild. I know I'm going to have to work myself ragged if I want to be any good at this, but that's going to happen no matter where I go. I just figured that here there would be a couple more friendly faces while I put in that work."

For a couple long seconds, there was no reply. Finally, a smile broke out on the official's face as she jotted down a couple of notes on a piece of paper before her.

"Good," she replied. "I'm Zoe Daniels and I'm a deputy master here. Trevor might have told you about me because I'm the one in charge of his little band of misfits. He most *certainly* didn't tell me about letting his kid brother tag along on combat missions. I'll have to speak with him about that later."

"Oh," Micah replied sheepishly, scratching at the back of his head.

"I'm glad you followed up on your original response," Zoe continued. "There are plenty of people with talent on Karell, but over the years, our guild has found something out about talent. Do you know what that is, Micah?"

"Skills are more important?" Micah asked, grasping at straws while trying his hardest to sound confident.

"Close." Zoe chuckled before tapping her chest. "This is what matters. Determination. A talented individual who doesn't try isn't fit to hold the sword of a mediocre individual who works from sunup to sundown. Of course, talent still helps, but the Lancers aren't in the habit of recruiting the fancy noble types that will sit around talking about all the monsters they're going to slay but never leave the taprooms."

"Now, Micah," she continued, pushing the ball on the pedestal toward him. "If you put your hands on this class crystal, you'll be able to get a class, but you'll be locked into the Lancers for a decade. If you want to back out, now is the time to do it. You don't even have to give a reason. I don't even need you to elaborate. It can be as simple as 'the work sounds too hard,' 'you want to join another guild,' or even 'that you want to chase girls around town for a couple months before settling down.'"

Without saying anything, Micah exhaled, trying to calm his nerves before putting his hands on the sphere. An electric shock ran through his fingers, and his hands could no longer move. Quickly, the sphere heated up, burning his trapped hands as Micah fought the urge to try and rip his hands away. All the while Zoe watched on, disinterested.

"Analyzing skills and affinities," the same genderless voice from his dream spoke in Micah's head.

"Available classes are Wizard, Chronomancer, Aeromancer, Healer, Librarian, Spearman, Warrior." The voice rattled off the list without any emotion. "Please select an option to gain more information about it."

A specialist class for every affinity, a non-combat class, and two close-combat classes. Not a bad set of choices, but it wasn't that hard for him to narrow down. Micah knew better than to pick any of the specialist classes. Each provided a small bonus to his magic in that field at the cost of ever being able to cast spells of another affinity ever again. For example, if he became a chronomancer, he'd get a 10% boost to his Time magic, minimal increases per level to his HP, much greater increases to his per-level mana, and periodic attribute points added to his Spirit and Mind attributes.

Unfortunately, despite its power, chronomancy wasn't a real option. There weren't very many Time spells out there, and most of them were higher tier. If he specialized in Time magic, he'd have to work for years without access to any magic whatsoever until he leveled up enough to actually use a Time spell. That was, of course, if he was lucky enough to ever get his hands on the spell formula for one.

As for the combat classes, those would forever bar him from spellcasting in exchange for higher HP per level and periodic attribute points in Body and Agility. He could still learn a martial art and benefit from his affinity and mana in that way, but without access to a class that blended melee and magic, that selection would be tantamount to turning his back on spellcasting forever. No, there was only one choice that let him use all three of his affinities as well as his spear.

"I would like to be a Wizard," Micah replied, his teeth slightly gritted against the pain while Zoe nodded approvingly.

"Wizard—an advanced spellcasting class that allows the user to utilize and combine more than one affinity. Wizards gain Mind and Spirit attributes in alternating levels and have a high rate of mana growth. To unlock this class, the user must have at least 1 level in the Spellcasting skill and more than one affinity." The voice paused briefly after reading the description. "Would you like to confirm your selection?"

"By the Sixteen." Micah writhed as the heat increased on his hands. "Yes!"

The pain stopped and soothing white mist flowed over him. Micah could feel his body changing on a fundamental level as the energy washed through him, cleansing him and easing his pain. After a couple of seconds, it was all over and the hazy light in the sphere was gone. Micah glanced at it sheepishly.

"Don't worry about that," Zoe grunted, standing up and extending a hand to him. "It'll recharge in a couple of days and be ready for a new recruit then. For now, welcome aboard, Micah Silver. I hope you're ready to sweat, because we're going to work you hard."

4

BOOK LEARNING

The words ran together on the page as Micah tried to focus. He blinked and rubbed his face, trying to uncross his eyes. Gustav Borcher, his magic instructor, had lectured him on the basics of spell theory for most of the morning before handing him a copy of *Introductory Air Magic* and leaving Micah to his own devices.

Years of working in the library under Keeper Ansom's tutelage hadn't prepared him for the difficulty of learning spells. Much like skills, spells could level, with each level decreasing its mana cost and increasing its effectiveness. Complicating things further, as a spell's level developed, the casting time decreased.

On paper, this decrease was nothing but good news. After all, in the heat of combat, a fraction of a second decrease in spellcasting time could be the difference between life and death. In practice, however, it meant that Micah needed to memorize a spell and then memorize multiple iterations of the same spell. It was like renovating a house—some pillars were load-bearing, and removing them could cause the entire edifice to collapse. Others were helpful, but mostly cosmetic.

It was far from fun. After the third hour of learning which of the nonsense words and arcane hand motions were less important than the others, Micah was about ready to put his head through the table. Still, he restrained himself. Even if the various shortened forms of the same spell weren't useful at this exact moment, they would be vital eventually.

He sighed, turning back a page to the beginning of the *Air Knife* spell. He'd read through the spell form at least four times by now, but it just wasn't sinking in. The words and diagrams were clear, but he just couldn't get it all to come together into a recognizable whole.

Really, he was lucky that he had the Ageless Folio. The Lancers, understandably, were reluctant to let him take something as valuable as a magic primer home. Usually, this would have limited his ability to study, but so long as Micah willed it, the Folio would record every word that he read. Better yet, once he actually made sense of the swimming figures and diagrams, he could add his own annotations and notes to help his later study sessions.

The door opened and Gustav walked in. The wizard was significantly taller than Micah, a rail-thin man sporting a long, thin beard, but with eyes that burned intensely whenever the subject of magical theory came up. When Zoe first introduced him to Gustav, the elderly man had explained that his affinities were Earth, Air, and Water, but that his true passion was research and theory.

"All right, Silver," he said, his wheezy voice interrupting the small study room's silence. "Let's see if you're any smarter than your brother. I swear to the Sixteen, all that boy thinks about is his spear and girls."

"Instructor Borcher?" Micah questioned, looking up from his book.

"Call me Gustav." Borcher waved his hand. "I may be your instructor, but when it's just the two of us, there's no need to be all stuffy and formal. After all, the guild doesn't have a whole lot of wizards. It might only be two affinities, but you're a proper wizard and not some sort of halfhearted elementalist.

"You'll have to go through training like the rest of us." Borcher folded his angular form into the seat behind the study room's teacher's lectern. "The Lancers don't just give respect; we expect you to earn it. Still, if you can study a textbook the way your brother studies a waitress's rear end, you'll be a proper wizard before long, and that means a place of respect in the guild.

"We don't talk about it all that often," the tall man continued, brushing his wispy beard aside, "but not every class is made equal. True, you won't make it far as an adventurer without hard work, but certain classes just give more attributes per level. Elementalists get a point every other level, alternating between Mind and Spirit. That means that by the time they hit level 16, they will have gained 4 points in each attribute while you'll have gained 8. Hells, even outside of their slower growth, their mana pools aren't as big as yours."

"How do my attributes influence spellcasting anyway?" Micah asked, eager to try and distract Gustav from his struggles with implementing his introductory spells.

"Body and Agility," Borcher sniffed dismissively. "They barely matter. True, they'll improve your hit points and lend you the coordination you need to avoid getting struck in combat, but if you're close enough for that to be a concern, you've already screwed things up beyond repair.

"Now, Spirit," the old man continued, the gleam from their first meeting returning to his eyes. "Spirit is straightforward on paper. It increases your total mana. Each of your three mana pools is determined by a math equation. Namely, your level multiplied by your Spirit with that result multiplied by another number determined by your class. Then you add a flat amount equal to twice the attunement associated with that mana pool."

"That doesn't seem fair," Micah said, frowning. "That would just mean that rich people have more mana than the rest of us, especially at lower levels."

"Good!" The instructor grinned at him. "I knew you were smarter than your brother. You're completely right. It isn't fair. The heir to a noble house might have two or even three hundred attunement in each pool, giving them hundreds of mana at first or second level. That means that they can practice their entry level spells time and time again, gaining a number of skill levels without even having to encounter a beast or monster."

"How could Luxos let that happen?" Micah asked in confusion. "His priests always preach that he's created the optimal society for us. That doesn't seem all that ideal to me."

"Ideal according to whom?" Borcher chuckled. "The Church might play coy with ideas like equality and fairness, but in my sixty-eight years on Karell, I've seen nothing in their holy texts to actually show that Luxos believes in such things. No, I think the god is very satisfied with the present order. We don't live in a fair world, Silver. The quicker you recognize that and move on, the sooner you'll be able to progress as an adventurer."

"What about the Mind attribute?" Micah's brow furrowed into a slight frown as he tried to make sense of his instructor's hypotheses.

"That's a little more complicated," Gustav replied. "The Mind attribute helps with a lot of little things such as learning new spells and research. For day-to-day spellcasting, it more or less functions like extra spell levels. It reduces the spell's mana cost while increasing its effectiveness."

"What do you mean by research?" Micah asked. "I heard you talking about it before, but don't we just earn spells from dungeons or buy them from other spellcasters? What is there to research?"

"Silver." Borcher clicked his tongue, smiling as he shook his head. "Don't think I don't realize that you're trying to distract me. It won't work. Luckily for you, research is a weakness of mine. I'll answer this last question of yours, and then you're casting *Air Knife* on a training dummy. No more delays."

Gustav stood up and picked up a piece of chalk before walking to the room's blackboard. He wrote down three headings labeled *Rituals*, *Enchantments*, and *Spell Development*. Turning around, he smiled at Micah once again.

"Magic takes two major forms." The instructor's breathy voice became more formal as he began his lecture. "The first is what most are familiar with. Magic provided by the gods in the form of spells, martial arts, or blessings. Many aren't aware that there is another form of magic. Ritual magic and enchantments don't really use the system provided to us by the gods.

"Each casting needs to be meticulously researched," Gustav continued, writing on the blackboard as he spoke. "That doesn't mean once. Even if you've used a ritual or enchantment twenty times in the past, each new casting requires you to update it. You need to account for the season, the position of various celestial bodies, and other variables, such as barometric pressure and your source of power. This is partially a complex equation; most books on ritual magic contain intricate tables detailing how the magic is influenced by various outside events, but there is also the question of what variables will matter to the casting."

"That is the bulk of your research." Micah winced as Gustav's chalk squeaked and scratched against the board while he spoke. "Checking reference books to see how your predecessors handled similar experiments in the past takes time. A lot of time."

Gustav turned back around, a gigantic grin on his face. He leaned forward against the lectern, his eyes trained on Micah in the otherwise empty study room.

"The best part is"—the instructor winked at him—"sometimes the references are wrong. It's easy to miss a detail if it's obscure enough. Maybe there's a comet that only approaches Karell once every fifty years that changes the reagents used in a ritual. That isn't the sort of thing that's likely to be recorded, and if it is, it would only be in the most obscure of records. That's the fun of it—each and every time you perform a ritual, you run the risk that you overlooked something. Sometimes the casting just fails. Others? It's not unheard of for ritual casters to be sucked into a screaming void or turned into a fine dust by their own rituals."

"Normal spells don't do that, right?" Micah asked hurriedly, glancing at the textbook in front of him in concern.

"No," Gustav replied dismissively. "Magic that works through your affinities and status screen is tame. It can be cast quickly and repetitively without risking anything beyond the mana required to finish the spell. If you fail, you lose nothing more than your dignity and whatever you invested in the spell.

"On the other hand"—Gustav grimaced slightly before writing the word "limited" under *Spell Development* on the chalkboard—"traditional magic comes with major limitations. You must power the spells with your own mana rather than the life force and anima of a sacrifice, and those mana costs can become prohibitive. For example, right now, I am only teaching you tier-one spells. I hope within a couple of months to bring you to the point that you can use tier-two spells, but it will likely be a year before you are ready for tier three. As for tier four? You will need to earn many levels before you have the mana to even attempt them.

"In addition to mana costs," the instructor continued, writing the words "slow" and "not for combat" under the *Ritual Magic* category, "traditional magic has severe limitations based upon affinity. Primal, Wood, Fire, Earth, Water, and Air magic all do very different things, and there is a wide range of effects that you as the caster might want that don't fit into any of those categories. That's where ritual magic comes in. Each casting might take days to research and five or more minutes to cast, but with enough effort, you can theoretically do anything you want.

"Your level doesn't even matter." Gustav wheeled around, a manic glint in his eyes. "The energy for the ritual comes from the sacrifice of life force, usually a pig, goat, or particularly hardy plant. With enough preparation and knowledge, the very power of the Sixteen could be in your hands."

"What about enchantments?" Micah asked, enraptured despite himself by the instructor's enthusiasm.

"Oh." Borcher shook his head, wisps of white hair fluttering back and forth. "You're trying to get me worked up to get out of practice, aren't you? Enchantments are like rituals, but you imbue the power into an object. With the proper ritual inscriptions, an enchanter can use life energy to create a sword sharper than normal, a shield that moves toward incoming blows, or a monocle that lets you see in the dark. The same principles of research and preparation, irrespective of the caster's level, apply.

"Now, Silver." Gustav stepped around the lectern and waved a hand, his fingers twirling briefly while he muttered a handful of words. "Let me see your mastery of the *Air Knife* spell."

A figure made of soil quickly grew from a bin in the corner of the room, where loose dirt was kept on hand for the purpose of practicing Earth magic. Unsteadily, it stepped out of the container and into the center of the room between the lectern and the student seats.

"Quit dawdling." Gustav waved Micah down. "The only way you're going to learn is by trying."

Reluctantly, Micah walked to the front of the room, trying to replay the various hand motions and words to the spell in his head. Taking a deep breath, he looked to Borcher, who simply nodded at him.

He began moving his hands, the characteristic waves and flutters of Air magic defining the spells motions. The words spilled from his lips, the words pronounced awkwardly, their cadence stuttering and wrong.

For a second, it almost worked. Micah could feel the energy swelling up inside his chest. The air in between his hands swirled and compressed, forming a visible distortion in the shape of a ball before it began flattening into the shape of the titular knife.

Then, like the pop of a soap bubble, the spell shattered. The words fell dead from Micah's lips and the energy dissipated. He glanced to Gustav, embarrassment in his eyes.

"Good, good!" The instructor clapped his hands together. "That was one of the best preliminary attempts I've seen. No one casts a spell on their first try. Give it a week and I'll have you slinging Air magic with the best of them, Silver. You have the foundation. All that's left is practice."

5

NEWBIE

"Put some effort into it, Silver!" Cornell Dover, the leader of Lancer combat team "D," screamed at Micah. "I need this man up, in action, and drawing the monsters' attention in thirty seconds, or the front line is going to collapse and we're going to be neck deep in Charnel Horrors!"

Micah's hands were covered in blood, his heart racing, as he literally shoved his left hand into the wound, grasping a handful of torn muscle fiber and mouthing the words to *Augmented Mending* from the Ageless Folio that he held in his right hand. The muscles writhed and twisted like a cluster of snakes as they sought each other out and began reconnecting.

Then Micah ran out of Moon mana. Frantically, he switched to Night mana, but it felt like he was knee-deep in mud. Everything was slow, barely functional as the mismatches between the mana and the spell impeded him at every turn. The muscles wove together, making tenuous connections under his hand and growing stronger.

An arrow whistled past Micah's face, but he ignored it, knowing that he didn't have enough mana to complete the spells if he let himself be distracted. Distantly, he heard the arrow clatter against a wall behind him.

Pulling his hand out of the wound and propping the Folio into his armpit, Micah frantically began stitching the skin back together with the copper needle and thread he kept in a pouch at his waist. As soon as the hasty sewing job was done, Micah cast *Augmented Mending* once again, switching to Sun mana to avoid depleting his almost-exhausted reserves of Night mana.

The spell took and the wound closed, leaving nothing behind but an angry reddish-purple line. Micah pursed his lips. With more skill in *Augmented Mending*, he'd be able to perform an operation like this without having to manually manipulate the injured tissue or field-suture a wounded comrade. One day, he'd be able to cast the spell without leaving a scar at all.

The pig he was clutching onto squealed and ran away. Exhausted from stress and mana use, Micah stood up, still covered in its blood, as Cornell walked over to him nodding his head slowly.

"Not bad, Silver. I won't even have to deduct the cost of the pig out of your pay." The team leader threw him a wet towel. "*Augmented Mending* is a second-tier spell and you were able to cast it on a seriously injured target twice within thirty seconds. I'd still like you to get the casting time down on it, but you'll do for an emergency healer for now. Hamstring wounds like that can get really nasty if someone doesn't patch them up right away."

"Was the arrow really necessary?" Micah replied, wiping the blood from his hands and tunic. "The exercise was bad enough without you trying to scare the life out of me."

"That's why you need to get the casting time down, son." Cornell chuckled, walking over to a weapon rack on the nearby wall of the training room. "The exam says that I'm supposed to miss you with an arrow at twenty seconds. In combat, nothing is going to just sit there while you get a warrior back in the fight. They're going to target you."

"I passed, though, right?" Micah asked, trying to keep the weariness from his voice.

Cornell had made him do healing drills five days out of every ten, but they were by far his least favorite. *Mending* could cure bruises and abrasions, but to train in *Augmented Mending,* there was no other option but to… procure injured animals for Micah to heal. Usually, that meant Cornell surprising him in the middle of another activity, such as spear practice, with an animal that he would promptly injure in front of Micah, forcing him to stop what he was doing and heal it on the spot.

It was good practice; Micah was sure of that. In three months, his Spellcasting skill had risen to 5 and his skill in *Mending* and *Augmented Mending* had followed suit. Still, Micah longed for the day when Cornell certified him ready to join a combat team and he could leave the constant and grinding training schedule behind him.

"Yes, you did," Cornell replied with a smile, throwing him a spear. "You already know *Gale*, *Air Knife*, and *Wind Shield*. Gustav has certified you as an aeromancer, and with that test, you're certified as a healer. Now we just need to get you up to snuff with the spear and you'll be cleared for field work."

"Are you sure?" Micah caught the spear, glancing down at it dubiously. "I'm awfully worn out after all that spellcasting. I'm not sure I'll be all that useful right now."

"You know the rules." Cornell shot him a wink. "Make it five minutes without letting me hit you, or hit me once and you win."

"You're level 16, Cornell." Micah tested the pliability of the spear before taking up a guard stance. "There's no way I'll be able to even score one hit on you in a fair fight."

"Simple advice, then." Cornell twirled his spear. "Don't fight fair."

The rest of the afternoon was a bruising blur of constant fighting and Micah using the Wood spell *Refresh* to restore both of their stamina. Finally, for the first time in the hundred-plus spars spread out over the preceding three months, Micah managed to tag Cornell on the forearm with the side of his spear. Micah wasn't sure if the strike was luck, skill, or just Cornell deciding it was time for him to graduate. Cheerfully, the huge black man proclaimed his training over and told Micah to hit the sack early because he'd be teamed with a "newbie squad" the following day.

Lying down, Micah opened his status screen to take in the previous three months' worth of work.

Micah Silver
    Age 16
    Class/Level Wizard 1
    XP 0/50
    HP 10/10
    Attributes
    Body 5, Agility 5, Mind 9, Spirit 8
    Attunement
    Moon 8, Sun 3, Night 5
    Mana
    Moon 5/16, Sun 4/6, Night 1/8
    Affinities
    Time 10
    Wood 6
    Tier I - *Refresh* 3, *Mending* 3
    Tier II - *Augmented Mending* 2
    Air 5
    Tier I - *Gale* 2, *Air Knife* 3
    Tier II - *Wind Shield* 1
    Blessings
    Mythic Blessing of Mursa - Blessed Return, Ageless Folio
    Skills
    Anatomy 2
    Fishing 1
    Herbalism 1
    Librarian 3
    Spear 3
    Spellcasting 5

. . .

His attunement gains were modest, but that wasn't surprising. The Lancers didn't let him leave their guild hall to actually earn anything. Really, only the three points of Moon attunement were by his own hand.

It shouldn't have surprised him that Mursa would award his magical achievements with attunement; one for learning his first spell and one for each second-tier spell. According to Gustav, his magic instructor, that attunement would be limited to the first higher-tier spell per tier per affinity. Unfortunately, he wouldn't just be able to earn attunement by learning multiple higher-tier spells in the same field.

As for the point of Night and Sun attunement? Those were gifts from the guild. Loans, he was told. As a caster, they wanted to make sure he had enough mana to train with, but a full point of attunement was incredibly valuable. He'd need to pay those back as soon as possible or their interest would likely bankrupt him.

His spells were simple but useful. As for the Wood spells, *Refresh* cost very little mana but allowed him to restore stamina to a tired warrior, allowing them to retain their focus and continue fighting at peak efficiency. *Mending* healed bruises, sprains, and abrasions for a minor mana cost. *Augmented Mending,* however, was the spell he was proudest of. It was still at a low level, but for a hefty price in mana, he could close up even fatal wounds in a matter of seconds. Even without the other abilities, that spell on its own would make him a valuable addition to almost any adventuring party.

The Air spells weren't quite as impressive, but they still made Micah a useful addition to a combat team. *Gale* simply launched a gust of high-speed wind that could knock a target off balance, trigger a trap, or otherwise push something at a distance. *Air Knife* was a much more useful spell, allowing him to fire a small blade of compressed air to slash at a foe. It didn't do much to heavily armored foes, but a healer should be avoiding them anyway. *Wind Shield* was a useful but unimpressive spell. Micah could create a sphere of air that would deflect incoming arrows and gaseous attacks. According to Gustav, it was incredibly useful as a shield against archers, poisoners, and all manner of wispy or ethereal foes, but it just didn't seem essential to Micah.

Other than his increases in magic, Micah had already grown to appreciate the power of the Folio. Despite frequent bruising practice, his skill level in Spears had only grown by a point. In that same time, he'd learned Anatomy and Herbalism as part of his studies as a healer and gained 3 points in Spellcasting. Despite his earlier doubts about the blessing, Gustav was lavish in his praise over the speed with which Micah learned abilities when he had access to the Folio.

Internally, he wondered if his reaction on the day of his blessing had been too harsh. He hadn't told anyone that his blessing was actually Mythic, still ashamed of its fairly modest nature. That said, having perfect notes of his instructors' teachings to study each night combined with the 20% skill bonus served as a much greater boon than he'd given it credit for.

He blew out his candle and lay down. Cornell was right. If they were convening a newbie team, he'd have a big day tomorrow. He'd want to put his best foot forward when he met the people that in all likelihood would be his companions for the foreseeable future.

6

THE FIRST QUEST

Butterflies filled Micah's stomach as he walked into the training room to meet the rest of his team for the first time. As a spellcaster, he'd mostly been trained on his own by Gustav, but occasionally, when he sweated under Cornell's kind gaze, he'd see some of the Lancers' other candidates working in the training hall. Cornell never gave him a moment to talk to them, but Micah couldn't help but wonder which of them would be members of his new party.

As he walked into the room, Micah saw Cornell talking with another black man. Where Cornell was thin but well-muscled, focusing on agility and balance over brawn, the new man was a giant. He towered over Cornell, his bare torso covered in well-defined and bulging muscles accented by various tattoos. Complementing his mass was a gigantic single-bladed cleaver, almost as long as a short man's body, which the newcomer held over his shoulder with prac-ticed nonchalance.

Micah wasn't sure, but he could vaguely make out some Durghish features in the stranger. In addition to his size and skin tone, he had slightly wideset eyes and less prominent ears than the average human. Of course, this was all speculation. You didn't just *ask* someone if they had Durghish blood in them. Gods help you if they did. Everyone knew the Durgh were prone to violent outbursts, and inquiring about their ancestry sounded like the perfect way to discover the truth behind the rumors firsthand.

Nearby, two women whispered together. They were pretty, Micah supposed, in the same way that most young and physically fit women were. He was more interested in their equipment. Both wore robes inlaid with runes, obviously at least slightly magical. One had two shortswords strapped to her hips, as well as a bandoleer of thin, needlelike daggers crossing her chest. The other held a bow, currently unstrung, with a matching quiver on her back and a short-sword at her hip.

Both moved with a grace and fluidity while talking that stirred envy in Micah's gut. He was hardly clumsy—it was hard to be a proper adventurer with bad reflexes, after all—but both of them made him look like a newborn colt, all stumbling and knees.

Seeing him enter, Cornell stopped talking and waved him over.

"Silver, this is Drekt," Cornell introduced the towering bald man. "He's blessed by Ankros and pretty serious about it. I know that you aren't some sort of champion of Luxos, but I wanted to make sure there wouldn't be any sort of problem. He has seniority and I was about to make him your team leader. You can always turn down your team assignment, but that would just mean that you would return to training until another team becomes available."

"Nice to meet you, Drekt." Micah extended his hand. "I'm actually blessed by Mursa, but when I acquired my blessing, I also received an offer from Ankros. As long as you know your business, I'm not going to hold your patron against you."

"Good!" Drekt boomed, slapping his hand into Micah's with bruising force. "Ankros is woefully misunderstood in human lands. Most can't see beyond the stifling order that Luxos demands. They just see the dungeons and monsters created by Ankros and assume that those challenges make him evil. No one bothers to think that the mediocrity enforced by rigid laws is the real evil. Luxos prunes humanity like a hedge, growing us into a specific shape to match his desires. He never bothers to actually ask what form would be best for humanity as a race, instead just substituting his will for the natural order."

"You know the rules, Drekt." Cornell shook his head in exasperation. "No politics. Just because I was able to pull together a team without any ardent Luxos followers doesn't mean that they aren't out there. There are still plenty in the guild's hierarchy just waiting for you to fail so they can jump all over you."

Drekt opened his mouth to respond, a hangdog expression on his face, when the door to the training room burst open. A portly teen ran inside, huffing from exertion as he hastily tried to adjust a poorly fitted suit of chainmail hanging loosely from his bulging torso. In his hands, he awkwardly held a large shield and a small warhammer.

Micah winced as the newcomer jerkily shifted the hammer to his armpit, narrowly avoiding a gash on his forearm from the spike on the hammer's reverse end, before the stranger doubled over and began panting for breath.

"Now that all of us have finally arrived"—Cornell shot a withering glance at the struggling new arrival—"we can finally begin introductions.

"Some of you"—Cornell indicated Drekt and the two women with his free hand—"have served together in the past, but we do have a pair of new arrivals, so I think I should re-explain how this works. My name is Cornell Dover and I am in charge of D Company for the Lancers, which consists of three combat teams and a reserve team. Present in this room is our reserve team.

"As you are probably aware," he continued, his voice taking on a lecturing tone, "a combat team consists of between three and six individuals. Right now, the three combat teams in my company are full, but injuries and promotions happen often enough that all of you will get your chance once you get a few levels under your belt. Hells, if you do well enough together, you might all be promoted to combat status as a unit. Until then, you'll be dispatched on mostly low-profit missions in the hopes that you can hone yourselves enough to earn a spot on a combat team.

"Although I am your boss"—the tone of Cornell's voice put the last word in quotation marks—"your day-to-day operations and orders will come from Drekt here."

Cornell slapped the larger man on the back. Despite his comparatively slight stature, their difference in levels gave the blow enough force that the hulking man stumbled forward a step.

"Now that I've said my piece, why don't you go around the room and introduce yourselves, your class, and your blessing." Cornell smiled, his teeth a brilliant white in the training room's dim light.

For a second, no one spoke. Then Drekt rolled his mountainous shoulders and shuffled forward.

"I am Drekt Garrul," the large man said proudly, his voice a deep, clear bass. "I'm a Ravager, a class devoted to all-out attacks with heavy bladed weapons and some limited spellcasting ability, mostly related to enhancing myself. My blessing is from Ankros, and it allows me to ignore pain in combat and absorb a small amount of the skill levels of enemies that I kill without aid. From time to time, I may ask you to leave an opponent to me alone. I do not do so out of hubris, but instead out of a desire to grow stronger."

"Josephine Redflower," one of the two women said, stepping forward slightly. "Call me Jo; only my parents call me Josephine. I'm a scout. Most of the time, I'm finding our targets for us, but when I fight, I use stealth and agility more than brute strength. Well, that and I have a little Water affinity. My blessing is from Nysatress, Goddess of Water and Travel. It's nothing super impressive, but lets me walk silently. Useful for sneaking up on people, but not much else." She shrugged. "Not that I need it, given how much the rest of you tromp around and raise a ruckus."

"Sarah Redflower," the other woman said quietly but without a hint of nervousness. "I'm Jo's sister and the team's archer. My gift is from Tennema, God of Wood and Life. When I fire my bow, living things shy away from my arrows. Cover behind a tree or bush is more or less meaningless against me. I can also 'target' someone within sight and I won't lose track of their location as long as they stay within a certain range of me. A useful ability when Jo keeps trying to get the jump on me."

Jo smirked, a lively grin flashing across her face. "If you didn't throw a fit every time I dyed your hair in your sleep, I'd probably stop doing it."

"One of these days, I'm going to actually follow through on my threats and shoot you," Sarah responded, unamused.

"Your words wound me more than any arrow." Jo clasped both hands to her chest. "To think that you'd respond to my sisterly love and mild pranks with threats of violence."

Cornell cleared his throat, silencing the two women with a glare. Once he was sure that they were done with their digression, he motioned for Micah to continue.

"Micah Silver," Micah spoke up, trying to keep the catch from his voice as the entire room trained their focus on him. He'd never been all that great with crowds; that'd always been more of Trevor's thing. "Wizard and healer. I have affinities in Wood and Wind, and I'm told that I'm acceptable with a spear in a pinch. I'm blessed by Mursa with a book that lets me learn skills faster and take notes."

"Uh," the overweight young man stuttered slightly, "my name is William Grantly, but everyone calls me Will."

Everyone in the room stood, still looking at Will. The silence dragged on until Sarah clicked her tongue.

"What is your class and blessing, Will?" she asked curtly, a cutting tone barely concealed by her melodic voice.

"Oh, *oh*, sorry." Will blushed. "I'm a Vanguard, so I guess I, uh, stop people? My blessing is from Dunn, Goddess of Earth and Artifice, and I, uh, I get hard?"

"That sounds useful at parties," Jo snickered, punching her sister in the shoulder while Sarah just shook her head.

"What Will *meant* to say," Cornell interjected before things could get out of hand, "is that he has a *Rare* Blessing from Dunn. He turns his skin into stone, making him resistant to most damage and his strength almost doubles. He just received his blessing a little under a month ago, but there's pressure from the top to get him into the field as soon as possible. With a blessing like that, there's no use letting him languish away in a training hall. After all, with that ability, even if he screws up, it's not like he's going to get hurt."

With that introduction, Jo's snickering stopped and Sarah looked at Will appraisingly. Micah smothered a pang of jealousy. With a proper Mythic ability, that would've been him. He knew that he'd be better in the long run without the fawning and preferential treatment, but that didn't mean that some part of him didn't long for it. After all, what child didn't grow up dreaming of being special, a hero that could keep his community safe while being showered in attunement and praise?

"But what about us?" Drekt asked, a frown on his massive face. "His skin is made of stone, but what happens if he screws up and we get hurt?"

"Micah's a healer." Cornell waved vaguely in his direction, drawing a series of unwanted and curious gazes to him. "That's a lot more than most parties get, reserve *or* combat.

"Now," Cornell continued, pointedly ignoring the women's antics, "it's time to talk about your first mission. Our guild has a standing contract with Basil's Cove to keep the road to Westmarch clear. There's a nightwasp hive in the area that we periodically send combat teams into for royal honey, so we don't want to wipe it out if at all possible. Instead, we regularly send reserve teams to sweep the area and keep their numbers in check.

"It's a bit of a hike"—Cornell began handing out crude vellum maps of the area—"so you should probably set out fairly soon. We want you to stay in the field for three days clearing the area. You'll be rewarded with attunement for each stinger you retrieve, but remember: don't go to the hive. Even though individual nightwasps aren't terribly dangerous, they will swarm you and you will die. The guild has spent enough time and energy training you lot that we'd prefer it not all come to nothing."

Micah nodded as he looked over the map. Already he could feel the vague itching sensation in his wrist that signified that the Ageless Folio was automatically making a perfect copy of the drawing. Nightwasps were about a foot long, and although their poison wasn't fatal, it was incredibly painful. The perfect enemy for a new team of adventurers.

Plus, he'd heard from his father how the great swarms could drive away merchant caravans, interrupting trade. Even if the mission was a simple quest for beginners, it would tangibly help out Basil's Cove. Micah might not be a hero yet, but finally, after months of training, he was ready to begin doing his part.

7

ADVENTURE

The blade of condensed gas from Micah's *Air Knife* sliced through the nightwasp's wing, bringing it to the ground before it could close within fifteen feet of Will. He grimaced as he took in the overweight boy, swinging his hammer wildly at the wasps swarming him. He hadn't hit one yet, but it hardly mattered. His stone armor deflected all attacks, including Sarah's arrows, allowing her to shoot the nightwasps off of him with impunity.

Checking up on Drekt, Micah swore. At least three nightwasps lay bisected at the huge man's feet, but his oversized cleaver and bare chest did little to protect him. Two large lumps pulsed an uncomfortable red on his back where a pair of wasps had penetrated his defenses and stung him. Drekt was in the middle of a frenzy, likely unable to feel the effects, but Micah knew from his anatomy lessons that the venom would attack his nervous system with the potential to paralyze their victim's lungs and heart in large enough doses.

Ducking under a nightwasp that buzzed toward him, Micah ran over to the besieged Ravager. Quickly, he put his hands on the man's back and cast *Mending* and *Refresh* in quick succession.

Neither spell had quite enough power to cure the stings on their own, but *Mending* would cleanse most of the venom and *Refresh* would restore the towering man's stamina. At least at his current level, Micah didn't have enough mana to freely use his second-tier spells such as *Augmented Mending*. It wasn't a life-or-death situation, so slapdash first aid would have to do.

Drekt dodged backwards as another wasp swooped at him, knocking Micah to the ground as the big man almost accidentally rammed into him. Too enraptured by his battle frenzy, Drekt didn't even acknowledge Micah as he bounced off of the larger man's thick and tightly packed muscles.

Micah's head struck the ground, stars swimming across his vision. Ears ringing, he stared blankly at Drekt swinging the cleaver at a frantically dodging nightwasp. It slipped past the cleaver with almost depressing ease and dove toward Micah. From his back, he swung his spear awkwardly, barely managing to smack the cat-sized insect with its haft and knocking it away from his exposed torso.

The creature buzzed angrily, circling around toward Micah once again as he did his best to roll away from Drekt. Heedless of Micah beneath his legs, the big man stomped his feet into the ground, exerting all of his strength into another mighty swing of his cleaver at the weaving wasp. Desperately, Micah began summoning mana as he tried to cast another *Air Knife* to ward off the nightwasp.

A shortsword sheared through the diving wasp as Jo danced by. She twirled with a fluid motion, her blades flicking through the air and warding off one of its companions.

Micah pulled himself to his feet. Already he could see the angry lumps on Drekt's back beginning to fade as the healing magic continued to work.

Checking his mana reserves, Micah switched to his spear. He had enough for a couple more *Air Knives* or a single *Augmented Mending*, but as far as he was concerned, the job of a healer was to be prepared for a potential emergency. If someone on his team needed immediate care, he needed to be ready. Quick reactions could easily close an artery and save a party member's life. Micah wasn't as good with the spear as he was with Air magic, but it would have to do until his reserves regenerated.

He thrust with the spear, forcing a nightwasp that was weaving toward Drekt to dodge. Unfortunately, Micah just didn't have the agility or training to hit the tiny target. Luckily, Jo stepped in again, beheading the wasp as it tried to escape from Micah. He nodded to her in appreciation and then whipped around as he heard Will scream in pain.

There was only one nightwasp near him; the rest writhed on the ground with arrows lodged in them, but Will had run out of mana. He collapsed to his knees, hammer and shield forgotten, clutching his bicep and wailing as an angry red lump grew rapidly on his arm. Micah swore to himself once again, swinging his spear through the air and slamming it into the wasp. This time, the force of the blow cracked its exoskeleton, crippling the insect.

He ran over to Will and put his hands on the young man's arm.

"Make it stop!" Will bawled, tears streaming down his face as he begged Micah. "It hurts so bad. Don't just make it kind of better; fix it entirely!"

"But—" Micah began, only for Will to cut him off.

"It doesn't matter," he whimpered, rocking back and forth. "It feels like there are nettles everywhere under my skin. I don't care what you have to do, Micah, but make it stop."

A quick survey of the clearing revealed that Jo and Drekt were working together to bring down the last two nightwasps, functionally ending the encounter.

With a sigh, Micah gave in to Will's petulant demands, shifting his spell from *Mending* to *Augmented Mending*. The casting almost wiped out his reserves, but it did its work. Under his hand, the wound spat out a stream of black venom as Will's body expelled it. Before his eyes, the swelling and puncture wound faded away, leaving nothing but a slightly red lump on Will's pudgy arm.

Micah rocked back onto his heels, still crouching next to Will's huddled form, and sighed. This was their second battle against the nightwasps, and both of them had followed roughly the same pattern. Drekt struggled against the agile foes, but did his best, often at the cost of trading a painful sting for a clean blow on a wasp. The

Redflower sisters more than held their own, killing the majority of the insects with their precise, controlled attacks. Micah did what he could, killing a nightwasp here and there in between keeping the rest of the team on their feet.

Will was useless as anything but a target. Obviously, a warhammer wasn't the ideal weapon for attacking agile and airborne insects, but the way the young man swung it, Micah suspected that he hadn't even made it through basic training. He certainly wouldn't have been able to land a blow on Cornell without the instructor literally holding still. Even then, it would be a near thing. Wild and uncontrolled, Will whipped his warhammer back and forth without restraint, making it dangerous for Micah to even approach close enough to heal the young man.

"Clear!" Drekt shouted from his end of the clearing, wincing slightly as he leaned against the oversized cleaver.

"Clear," Sarah responded calmly.

"Clear," Micah chimed in as he used the butt of his spear to finish off the nightwasp he'd battered away to get to Will.

"I think that's enough patrolling for the day." Drekt glanced at Will's unmoving form with some concern. "Let's set up camp here for the night. Now might be a good time to check your status and reflect on what went wrong and right in those battles so we can make plans to improve."

Micah nodded, walking over to his backpack to unload his and Will's tent. He tried to ignore the Vanguard's unmoving body, but couldn't help but frown a little. He knew that the pain from the sting was mostly gone. *Augmented Mending* used up almost half of his mana, but it was a powerful spell. If anything, the young man was just suffering from the emotional aftershock from getting stung.

It hurt; Micah knew that from their first encounter, when he'd gotten careless and let a nightwasp get close. Spears were great weapons for keeping an enemy at a distance, but once a wasp got within his guard, all he could do was swing the pole of his spear futilely. He'd been able to fight and cast through the sting with some difficulty, but he didn't have any desire to repeat the experience.

He ran a hand through his messy and sweat-slick hair as he glared at the large man, still huddled in the fetal position. Inwardly, he acknowledged that his frustration with Will might be a bit unfair. After all, the main reason he'd been stung was Will's inability to draw the wasps' attention. Still, after casting *Mending* on himself he'd returned to the fight in short order without any of Will's moping or feeling sorry for himself.

Pulling out the heavily folded tent, Micah called up his status.

Micah Silver
　Age 16
　Class/Level Wizard 2
　XP 57/200
　HP 15/15
　Attributes
　Body 5, Agility 5, Mind 9, Spirit 9
　Attunement
　Moon 8, Sun 3, Night 5
　Mana
　Moon 2/27, Sun 9/15, Night 1/19
　Affinities
　Time 10
　Wood 6
　Tier I - *Refresh* 3, *Mending* 3
　Tier II - *Augmented Mending* 2
　Air 5
　Tier I - *Gale* 2, *Air Knife* 3
　Tier II - *Wind Shield* 1
　Blessings
　Mythic Blessing of Mursa - Blessed Return, Ageless Folio
　Skills
　Anatomy 2
　Fishing 1
　Herbalism 1

Librarian 3
Spear 3
Spellcasting 5

A level, then. Micah could certainly use the extra mana. As far as he could tell, he'd gained points equal to his Spirit upon level-up, hopefully a trend that would stay constant as he developed his class further. Even better, the level-up gave him a point in Spirit, further expanding his mana pools. His mana regeneration still wasn't exactly where he wanted it to be, but each level reduced his reliance on the spear.

"I gained a level!" Will shouted excitedly, animated now that Micah had taken the lead in setting up their tent, freeing the portly vanguard up to dawdle. "Guys, I'm level 2 already!"

"Good!" Drekt smiled, a giant toothy affair. Micah was pretty sure he spotted elongated canines amidst the slightly yellow snaggle of teeth that graced their leader's mouth. Yet another silent signal of his likely Durgh heritage. "A couple more points in Body and you'll be able to hold your own. For now, I think a celebration is in order."

The big man rummaged around in his backpack and came out with a skin full of some liquid. Drekt took a deep pull, shuddering for a second before throwing the skin to Sarah.

"Seniority," he said with a laugh, winking apologetically at Micah.

She drank briefly, grimacing and coughing as she passed the container on to Jo.

"Where in the hells do you find this stuff, Drekt?" Her voice was scathing as she smacked her lips in an attempt to clear its acrid flavor from her mouth. "Are you fermenting abandoned monster parts behind the guild hall, or are you just trying to level up your poison skill and using us as test dummies?"

"It isn't that bad, Sarah." Jo tossed the skin to Micah.

It landed in his open hands with a pleasant slosh, surprisingly heavy for its size. Micah looked at the skin hesitantly. Even from here, he could smell the strong, biting odor of cheap alcohol.

"It'll put some hair on your chest, Silver." Drekt laughed, a slight flush evident on his cheeks. "Think of it as a team-building exercise. Plus, you'll never get yourself a woman if you don't know how to cut loose a little."

Micah shrugged, lifting the cold metal of the skin's spigot to his lips. He almost gagged as the liquid splashed into his mouth. It felt like fire in his throat. He'd snuck some of his parents' wine before, but it tasted nothing like this. He felt himself starting to retch as the rotgut savaged his esophagus. Frantically, he screwed the cap back on the skin.

He coughed, doing his best to ignore his stomach performing backflips while Drekt laughed at his suffering. Already he could feel warmth rising to his cheeks. Micah was afraid to ask what proof the liquor was, suspecting that he'd actually just drunk their team's guild-supplied firestarter.

With feigned casualness, he threw the container on to Will. The young man looked at it dubiously.

"I don't think I'm allowed to—" Will began, a slight whining twang to his voice.

Micah rolled his watering eyes.

"We're in the field, so what I say goes," Drekt boomed, interrupting the younger man. "And I say drink up. After this, we'll start a bonfire. It'll ward away most of the unpleasant things that wander the forest at night, and we can tell some stories. Really get to know each other. Think of the drink as an icebreaker."

"He has a point," Jo drawled. "Anything that flammable has to be the natural enemy of ice."

Reluctantly, Will drank the vile liquid. Seconds later, Micah found himself using the absolute last of his mana to cast *Refresh* as the overweight adventurer threw up the entire contents of his stomach on the forest floor, much to Sarah's disgust and Drekt's delight.

"That settles it," Drekt cackled as he began stacking dry branches from the nearby forest for their upcoming fire. "Team rules; Will has to take the first watch tonight."

Micah smiled. He might be new, but he could sense the casual camaraderie from the team. It wasn't quite the welcome he'd expected, but already they felt like a congenial if dysfunctional family. He might as well get comfy with them. By all expectations, he'd be paired with them for a number of years.

8

BRUISES AND PROGRESS

Trevor's spear traced a half-circle through the air at a deceptively casual speed. Micah swore to himself as his *Air Knife* crashed into the visible distortion left by his brother's mana. An Uncommon spear martial art wasn't the most powerful ability Micah had seen at the Lancers, but it was more than enough to aggravate him, especially during a spar.

Drekt's cleaver swung down at Trevor, but with a quick sidestep and a tap of his spear haft on the side of the blade, Trevor redirected it safely to the side. With a flash of mana, Trevor's spear swung sideways faster than his muscles should have been able to propel it, the blunt wooden head smacking against Drekt's windpipe and stunning the larger man.

"Point," Zoe called out, gesturing at Drekt with a blue flag. "Throat strike. Drekt is injured beyond the ability of Red Team's Healer. Remove him from the exercise."

"Confirmed," Cornell responded from the other side of the room. "That spear blow was fatal. Take a seat, Drekt."

Micah didn't have the time to spare their coughing and sputtering leader as he stepped out of the training arena to nurse his injuries next to Sarah. One of the Lancers' other Healers ran over to help with the bruise, but Drekt gestured dismissively with one hand, the other still massaging his sore throat.

Glenn, the axe warrior from Trevor's team, danced just out of reach as Will swung his hammer with enough force to crack the floor. The battle between the two had been a stalemate from the beginning. Glenn couldn't harm Will in his stone battle form, but Will simply didn't have the skill to land a clean blow on the more experienced fighter, even when completely neglecting his own defense.

Unfortunately, Micah knew exactly how their duel would end. Eventually, Will would run out of mana and his transformation would end. Without the boost to his Body attribute, Glenn would easily avoid his hammer and deal blows the judges would find disabling or fatal.

An arrow bounced off of his *Wind Shield*, forcing a grimace from Micah. Renee, the opposing archer, alternated between firing training arrows at him and Jo. A lucky arrow to the face had knocked Sarah out of the fight early on, and ever since then, Renee had kept Micah honest and Jo off balance.

Of course, Jo wasn't going to be able to bail Micah out of his predicament. She was too busy dodging the wisps of *Fox Fire* that their Pyromancer, Meredith, coiled around herself. Every time Jo approached, a handful of the balls of blue flame would rush toward her, forcing the Scout to contort her body in an attempt to escape.

"Renee and Meredith," Trevor called out as he turned his attention to Micah, "I've got their caster."

Micah swore under his breath as Trevor threw his spear at him. Jerking to his side, he let the *Wind Shield* slow and deflect the spear just enough for his frantic movement to carry him past it.

Trevor reached out, and with a rush of wind, his spear sailed back past Micah and into his brother's hand. Grimacing, Micah grasped his spear in two hands and held it in the guard position that Trevor had originally taught him years ago. This close, Trevor wouldn't give him a chance to get off a spell. His brother knew better than that.

They approached cautiously, circling each other. Distantly, Micah heard the judges announce that Jo was disqualified due to a fatal hit, but he didn't have an opportunity to look away. His gaze was trained on Trevor's shoulders, looking for the subtle shift in weight that would precede an attack. Long ago, he'd learned to avoid the eyes— a spearman could feint with his eyes with a simple glance; shoulders didn't lie.

Micah was moving before Trevor began his thrust, but it was barely enough. The hafts of their weapons clacked three times as Micah was driven backward. The next stab came too fast for him to block, so Micah dropped to the ground and swung his weapon at knee level, hoping to trip Trevor.

Instead, Trevor leapt over Micah's strike and brought his own weapon down overhead on Micah's exposed shoulder. With a crack, Micah felt his collarbone snap. His left arm went numb and then red-hot pain flooded his body.

"Yield!" he shouted, trying to forestall a follow-up blow. "Trevor broke a bone; I can't fight any further!"

Trevor stepped back while Micah grabbed his shoulder and forced out the words to *Augmented Mending*. A second and most of his mana later, the pain dropped to more workable levels. He wasn't at full hit points, but the bone was more or less repaired and he could at least move without tearing up.

"Good job, everyone," Cornell called out, clapping his hands together as he walked into the center of the training room. "That went better than expected, but can we have everyone tell me what they did wrong?"

"You." Cornell pointed at Sarah where she was sulking in the waiting area. "You were eliminated first, so you get to start. Where did things go wrong?"

"Things went wrong when you had us spar with a full-blown combat team." Sarah threw up her hands. "We've only gone on a couple missions against low-level opponents. We just don't have the levels to compete."

"Redflower." Cornell shook his head, frowning at her. "I'm not sure what level you have to be to avoid getting shot in the face by an arrow, but it looked to me like you got careless."

"That isn't fair at all!" Sarah leapt to her feet, shouting at Cornell. "Renee used her blessing to curve her shot. How was I supposed to dodge it?"

"Shut up and sit down, Redflower," Cornell growled at her. "We are here for progress rather than excuses. Your Healer immediately cast *Wind Shield*. Micah took multiple hits from Renee without complaint while casting support spells. If you know you're fighting an archer, you need to take steps to defend yourself from arrows immediately."

"Well then, why didn't Micah cast *Wind Shield* on me?" Sarah complained, flopping back into her seat. "If he'd protected me properly, I wouldn't have been the first person eliminated."

"Redflower." There was a note of warning in Cornell's voice. "I told you to shut up. When I give you an order, you need to listen to it rather than throwing a tantrum."

"Silver." Cornell gestured to Micah with one of the flags he was carrying. "Tell me why you didn't cast *Wind Shield* on Sarah. Then tell me where you went wrong in combat."

"Uh." Micah massaged his still-hurting shoulder while trying to avoid Sarah's glare. "*Wind Shield* works both ways. It won't stop spells, so it's a good defense for casters, but if I'd cast it on Sarah, she wouldn't have been able to shoot out of it."

"Very good." Cornell nodded. "I'm glad that at least *your* lessons on squad tactics weren't wasted."

"Thanks, sir?" Micah responded morosely. Cornell's compliment sealed his fate. Sarah was going to be snippy with him for at least a week for "showing her up." "As for what I did wrong? I wasn't near enough to help Drekt with a healing spell. He was the one holding the team together and my ranged attacks weren't terribly effective against Trevor. At a minimum, I could have tried to flank Trevor and gotten a couple of spear attacks in."

"Drekt." Cornell nodded his agreement before pointing at the huge man. "What could you have done better?"

"My attack style is too wild," Drekt replied immediately and without hesitation. "Trevor is agile enough to dodge my attacks, and

I leave myself open to fatal counterattacks. The style is much more suited to smaller foes incapable of seriously harming me with a single attack."

"I wouldn't say it was that bad," Trevor cut in, a sheepish smile on his face. "A couple of those attacks were close calls. If I'd been a hair slower, it would've been you eliminating me out there. That said, I'd be happy to spar with you more one on one. Both of us could stand to sharpen our skills a bit before our next missions."

"Save it for the bar," Cornell replied, rolling his eyes as Drekt nodded slowly, accepting Trevor's offer. "As for Will? I'll save us the time. He can't fight. He's not at risk due to his blessing, but he'll need to continue lessons with his hammer. Even if he's capable of slamming that thing through a brick wall, it hardly means anything if he can't hit what he's fighting."

"Trevor and Drekt." Cornell glanced at Zoe, who nodded back at him. "You'll include Will in your training sessions. Both of you are decent combatants, but right now, Will looks like nothing more than a giant ball of wasted potential to me. He could use more than a little polish, and I expect to see some improvements by the next time we have one of these little get-togethers."

"I'm not sure that three people would work that well," Trevor cut in frantically, his lip curling slightly as he glanced at Will. "We won't have an even number of sparring partners, and I really don't know that much about training people in the basics. I don't really think that the sessions will be much help for Will."

"Stow it." Zoe walked over from where she'd been leaning against the wall to stand next to Cornell. "You agreed to have your squad train with and mentor your younger brother's team. This is mentoring them. I'm sorry if you don't like it, but this is where you can help the most."

"Thank you, Zoe." Cornell nodded at her before pointing his flag at Jo. "More reasonable Redflower, tell me what you did wrong."

"Honestly?" She smirked slightly at her sister. "I should have used Micah as cover before peppering their caster with throwing daggers. The arrows couldn't get through his *Wind Shield*, but I couldn't see anything similar protecting Meredith. If I'd managed to bring her down before she summoned more than three or four of those *Fox Fires*, it might have turned the battle around."

Cornell opened his mouth to respond before stopping. He gently tapped the side of his face a couple of times with the flag, then smiled.

"I still don't think that you guys would have won the fight." There was some mirth in his voice. "I really don't think that your team has a proper answer for Glenn and Trevor when they work together, but that certainly would have made things more interesting."

"Jo brings up a good point." Cornell's voice rose, taking on the tone he adopted while lecturing them. "Meredith's *Fox Fire* is powerful, but she needs to cast the spell multiple times before it's terribly useful. Their squad counters that slow start by having Renee pin people down with a barrage of arrows, usually using her gift early in the fight to curve arrows around defenses.

"If"—Cornell pointed his flag at Micah—"you have access to portable cover, use it. Between Micah and Will, you had two combatants that could more or less shrug off Renee's arrows. Sarah could have avoided disqualification by sticking close to either of them and quickly eliminated Meredith. After that, I think Renee would have been in trouble.

"*Unfortunately*"—he slapped the flag into his thigh for emphasis —"your team rushed into combat without a plan. You fought fairly well together, but you were outmatched and you should have known it. If you aren't able to outfight your opponent, you'd damn well better outthink your opponent.

"At this point," Cornell continued, nodding slowly, "I think you're almost ready to try an actual dungeon. We just need to work on your teamwork. As you may be aware, Basil's Cove is hosting a tournament."

"So you want us to enter the grand melee." Drekt nodded, grinning. "To learn to work together and win glory for Ankros. A spectacular plan."

"By the Sixteen." Cornell shook his head. "No. You'd get torn apart in seconds. Most of those fighters are over level 20, and fighting someone with a class specialization without one of your own is a terrible idea.

"You don't work together well," Cornell continued, chuckling lightly. "Right now, you fight like five individuals that happen to be stuck in the same room at the same time. I just want you to go to the tournament and have a good time. You need to bond as a team, and this is the best that Zoe and I could come up with on short notice."

9

THE TOURNAMENT

A cheer went up from the crowd as a great beast of fire rose up into the sky. Long like a snake with eight short legs and the head of a bear, it curled sinuously in the air. Opposite it, a shark made of water and ice, five times the size of any horse, materialized. It swam toward the fire serpent, snapping ice-dagger teeth the size of Micah's forearm.

The crowd oohed and aahed, blessed and forgotten alike pointing at the colorful magical spectacle. The serpent exhaled a gout of flame at the shark, which spun horizontally, preventing the flames from evaporating too much of its body at once. With a hiss of steam, the ice fangs of the shark tore into the side of the serpent, eliciting even more clapping and hollering from the bystanders.

"So," Jo said, elbowing Micah in the ribs as she nodded toward the magical display, "when do you think that you'll be able to do that? A giant bear made out of fire would be a pretty big help on patrol."

"He isn't even a fire caster, Jo." Sarah rolled her eyes. "He might be able to make a huge flower or something. I'm sure we could use a monstrous daisy to scare off all of the bandits on the road to Westmarch if need be."

"Those spells are third tier," Micah responded to Jo, trying to ignore Sarah's sarcasm. "It'll be a couple more levels before I can cast something like that, and even if I could, I doubt the guild would encourage it. Spells like that are for showing off. They aren't terribly useful in combat. Casters learn them to get laid, not conquer dungeons."

"Plus," Drekt said, nodding his head sagely, "I don't really know how useful your affinities would be for impressing the ladies and laddies. What are your options, a giant flower or a particularly dangerous-looking cloud?"

"Probably just the dangerous-looking cloud," Micah sighed. "Wood magic is good for healing and making existing plants grow, but it's incredibly inefficient if you're trying to create something from nothing. Maybe I could grow a vine into an interesting shape, but there's no way that I would have the mana to make a giant plant appear in the air."

"I'm sure you will find another way to get laid," Drekt responded, his mask of faux concern twitching as he tried to avoid laughing while patting Micah on the shoulder. "After all, it's not about the tier of the spell; it's about the skill mastery of the caster."

"I don't know." Jo grinned cheekily. "Sometimes a high-tier spell is nice too."

Micah opened his mouth to reply before closing it. Both Jo and Drekt struggled to avoid snickering at him. Really, he couldn't think of a response that didn't involve further ribbing from the two of them.

"Just out of curiosity," Jo asked suggestively, "what's the highest-tier spell you can cast anyway? We've all gotten a chance to see your *proficiency* with casting, but sometimes a girl likes to know what she's working with."

"Gross," Sarah answered for Micah as his mouth slammed shut and he turned beet red. Meanwhile, Drekt doubled over laughing.

"What's that wonderful smell?" Will asked, oblivious to the rest of his team's conversation. "It smells like they're frying something divine in bacon fat." He turned toward Sarah. "Will you go to that food stall with me? I need to have some of whatever that is."

Sarah sighed and followed Will as he scurried off through the throng. Luckily, the portly man couldn't move all that fast, but at the same time, it seemed like nothing was changing. Will was childish and impulsive, counting on the strength of his blessing to keep him safe from any threats, social or physical. Micah could understand why the Lancers would recruit the young man—his blessing had the potential to become extremely powerful—but at the same time, it seemed like the guild coddled him too much in an attempt to keep him happy.

"Isn't he supposed to be on a diet?" Jo asked Drekt, a frown on her face. "I know the guild doesn't usually get all that involved, but Will slacks off every time we do stamina training, and I seem to recall them limiting his food intake. Even if he has the most powerful blessing in the world, it isn't going to do us much good if he can't make it up a flight of stairs without needing a break."

"Yes," Drekt replied, the mirth gone from his voice. "The guild keeps giving me contradictory orders on Will. On one hand, they tell me that I'm 'too severe' and that I should 'take it easy' on him. On the other, I'm told that he isn't making enough progress. I don't know how they expect me to train him if I'm not allowed to yell at him when he slacks off. Especially considering how often he doesn't give training his entire attention."

"I don't suppose anyone told you to go easy on me?" Micah asked hopefully, a playful note to his voice. "As much as I love jogging up the hill outside of town over and over again until I'm ready to puke, I'd prefer to, you know... not do that."

"Well, your brother does drop in on me from time to time to talk about your training," Drekt said, smiling at Micah. "Of course, he just tells me to work you harder. According to him, 'no brother of mine is going to have a Body attribute below 6.' You should be happy that your brother is proud of you and pushes you to greater heights. He is a blessing from Ankros if I have ever seen one."

"Speaking about aggravating siblings," Jo cut in, glancing at the heavy crowd around them, "we should probably catch up with Sarah. I don't really want to watch Will stuff his face, but at a minimum, we should keep in contact with the two of them. Theoretically, this is a team-building exercise, and I suspect that Cornell is going to be annoyed with us if we lose half of the team barely an hour in."

Micah nodded and followed the two of them through the crowd. Drekt earned his share of angry looks and more than one harsh comment whispered angrily behind cupped hands. A tall black man with the barest hints of tusks stood out anywhere, and the memories of the most recent Durgh attack ran hot, even if it had been almost a decade ago.

He understood the sentiment. The Durgh host had lain siege to Westmarch for almost a month before the Pereston army, led by a contingent of Royal Knights, arrived to drive the Durgh back into the Great Depths. In that time, a lot of good people died or were captured by the Durgh, disappearing into the dark caves of the Depths with the attacking forces.

Even if the people didn't definitively know that Drekt was part Durgh, his size, skin, and "prominent teeth" hinted at his heritage. Micah didn't put much weight on it. Drekt was a friend, and busy-bodies would always find a reason not to like someone—their religion, heritage, or blessing. None of it really *meant* anything, but people used it as an excuse to justify being rotten.

On the other hand, Drekt seemed to have adapted to his status well. Micah might have politely put a hand on someone's shoulder and tried to slip by them, but the massive man seemed to realize that he would be a target of scorn regardless of his manners. Instead of pandering to social niceties to no avail, he simply plowed through the crowd, using his great muscled bulk to push people aside in his quest to find the food stands.

"There she is!" Jo shouted, pointing out Sarah standing next to a picnic table where Will sat happily shoving fried bits of something into his mouth. A pair of young men tried to talk to her as she tapped her foot impatiently, a look of disgust on her face.

They approached, the throng of humanity flowing away from Drekt's imposing form, and soon it was just the five teammates and the two oblivious interlopers.

"Come on, babe," one of them whined at Sarah. "I know you said that you came here with the fatty, but that's clearly a lie. If you don't want to go and grab a beer with us, we at least deserve to be told that to our faces. There's no need to insult us by saying you're interested in that."

The man pointed accusingly at Will, who had grease smeared all over his apple-red cheeks as he slid a full kebab of some unknown-but-deep-fried meat down his gullet. Happily, he reached for a pastry stuffed with sweet bean paste, not even paying the slightest bit of attention to the altercation behind him.

"Fine," Sarah replied, her voice icy. "I don't want to grab a beer with you. Now can you leave me alone?"

"That wasn't so hard, was it?" the man grumbled as he and his friend turned to leave. His eyes widened as he saw Drekt, and they both quickened their gait to clear the area.

"Will," Drekt sighed. "You aren't supposed to abandon your team. We were literally sent here to have a good time with the thinnest excuse imaginable. All we had to do was spend time together as a team, and you couldn't even manage that."

"But, Drekt"—Will looked up at him from the table, confusion on his face—"I was so hungry, and the food smelled really good. Plus, I knew you'd follow me here, so it wasn't really abandoning the team."

"You're hungry," Drekt said, massaging his temples wearily, "because you're on a diet. We're trying to get you in better shape by giving you well-regulated portions of meat and vegetables. How are you going to be able to fight off monsters if you stay fat? We all saw how much you struggled sparring with Glenn. It's not going to get any easier when you fight wild beasts, and their claws aren't going to be blunted and wood."

"It's fine." Will shrugged, his face shiny from grease and the mild heat. "Cornell keeps telling me that I'll get better with time. I just plan on waiting until I become a great warrior. Once that happens, it will be me helping all of you out! How exciting will that be?"

For once, Drekt was absolutely speechless, his mouth hanging open as he tried to articulate a response to Will's matter-of-fact idiocy. Micah raised an eyebrow in Jo's direction. She shrugged back at him, a half-smile on her face, and sidled closer.

"He's as pampered as a noble's fourth child," she whispered, shaking her head slightly. "Even with a Rare blessing, we're going to be stuck carrying his dead weight once we start fighting things closer to our level."

"That's a lot of dead weight," Micah observed, trying to keep his face calm. There was something about Jo standing this close to him that made the day even hotter than it already was. He didn't know whether it was the conspiratorial and intimate tone of her voice, or the way her fingers rested gently on his arm, but his heart was hammering in his chest.

She laughed. The dull thud of his heartbeat was in his ears now as Micah smiled back awkwardly.

"Come on," she whispered, "Drekt and Sarah are going to spend all day trying to keep Will out of trouble. I spotted some games of chance on the boulevard leading up to the arena for the grand melee. Let's slip out of here and see if we can find some trouble of our own instead."

Micah nodded, his mouth too dry to respond.

"Let's make things interesting," she said, winking at him. "The one that wins the fewest prize tokens has to donate them to the winner. I have my eyes on a new copper bracelet, but it's over two hundred tokens. Your contributions would be greatly appreciated."

With a tinkle of laughter, she was gone, slipping off into the crowd and leaving behind only the floral hint of her shampoo in the summer air.

10

_____

DUNGEONEERING

"**A**re you sure it's supposed to look like this?" Will huffed, his pudgy head swiveling about as he blinked at the stone walls of the dungeon. "It's awfully dark in here. How are we supposed to see the monsters?"

Jo stared at him as she pulled a torch from her backpack and wordlessly lit it. Turning to Micah, she thrust it into his free hand. He squinted at her in confusion.

"Support caster carries the torch," she said cheerfully before walking past him toward the tunnel. Micah turned to Drekt, a silent question in his eyes.

"Casters usually have a hand free to hold the torch," the large man supplied as he walked past the large stone arch that marked the mouth of the dungeon. "I suppose that's not really the case with you, given your insistence on using a spear, but most of the Time spell-casters only need one hand to cast spells so the other can be used for a light source. Most dungeons glow slightly on their own, so it's never completely dark, but for pureblood humans, it's still not a great environment to fight in."

"What about Jo?" Micah cocked his head, looking down the tunnel where their scout had disappeared into the gloom. "There's no way this torch is giving her any light."

"She can see just fine," Sarah cut in curtly as she walked past Micah, her bow strung and an arrow resting on the taut string. "Just worry about yourself, Silver. I don't want anyone dying because you're too busy gawking at your first dungeon to heal them in time."

Drekt patted him on a shoulder awkwardly, his massive cleaver held in one hand. Each blow from the man's massive paw staggered Micah slightly, causing shadows to skitter across the dungeon's walls as he stumbled forward.

"Don't worry, Micah," Drekt rumbled sheepishly. "She'll warm up to you eventually. Sarah can just be a little prickly to newcomers. I'm sure she's happy to have a fully trained healer on the team. Most squads our level have to rely on potions, and those are both uncommon and expensive."

"How am I a newcomer?" Micah inquired, cocking his head as he recovered from Drekt's accidental blows. "I've been serving with the team for almost six months now."

"Doesn't the guild just pay for potions?" Will furrowed his brow in confusion, ignoring Micah's question. "I don't understand why we would have to pay for them. The guild has bought everything else I'm using."

"Well," Drekt chuckled, taking his hand off of Micah's shoulder and switching to a double-handed grip on his cleaver, "not all of us have a Rare blessing. They fronted the attunement for me to buy my blade, but I have to pay them back in installments. Luckily, Ankros smiles upon dungeoneering and hands out Night attunement liberally for slaying new and powerful monsters. We have a lucrative profession, my friends—a good thing, given how blasted expensive all of our equipment is."

"What about Micah?" Will's tiny little eyes swiveled toward him. "He's the group's healer; doesn't the guild give him something? Everyone keeps saying that we don't have many full wizards and healers. Shouldn't the guild help him too?"

"Just an Uncommon blessing," Micah lied glibly, subduing his vague desire to confide in his team. "My dad's a tailor, so I have a fairly stylish set of traveling clothes, and the spear is a hand-me-down from my brother. He has a spear combat class and trained me. When he leveled up enough to get his own weapon, I got his old one."

"That doesn't seem fair," Will mumbled, mostly to himself, as he struggled to pull the giant hammer off his back. After months of training, he could lift and use the weapon when not transformed, but without any grace or fluidity. Any actual combat with it required his stone form. Really, despite his levels, Will was almost useless in his human form.

"How's Trevor doing anyway?" Drekt asked, ignoring Will's discontented muttering.

"I didn't know that you and Trevor were friends." Micah cocked his head at his commander. "He would always talk about friends from the Lancers, but he never mentioned any names around the house."

Before Drekt could respond, Jo burst into the hallway, sprinting silently toward them with her face split in a manic grin.

"Good news, guys!" she shouted, borderline cackling with mirth. "I found the first encounter! Bad news; apparently, cave adders can see in the dark, and slinking through the shadows to avoid them is pointless."

For a brief second, no one but Jo moved as the hiss of scales on stone filled the tunnel. Two dark gray snakes, each slightly longer than Drekt was tall, darted after Jo, pink tongues flicking out from their triangular heads as they tasted the air around them.

"Will," Drekt shouted as one of Sarah's arrows zipped past him, puncturing the hard scales of a snake, "transform and get into fucking position! Micah might be a healer, but I don't want to test the effectiveness of his antivenom. Cave adders are bad news!"

With a shove from Drekt, the portly man stumbled toward the injured snake, his eyes wide and the hammer trembling in his meaty fists. Fear froze the Vanguard as he stared helplessly at the monster rearing up before him. The snake pulled back its head to strike and Micah began chanting the incantation to *Air Knife*, focusing his mana and will on the coiled reptile.

He ran out of time as the animal lunged forward, snapping its jaws closed around Will's forearm and drawing a shrill and blood-curdling shriek from him. The *Air Knife* slashed into the creature's side, drawing a line of blood and causing it to withdraw and hiss in pain.

Will grabbed the creature, his now stone hands barely able to wrap around its girth, and squeezed. Frantically, it tried to bite him again, but its teeth were unable to find purchase in his heavy rock skin. Sarah slid forward, a frown on her delicate face as she held a nocked arrow half-drawn, waiting for an opening to shoot the snake grappling her party member.

Micah turned to the other snake just in time to see Jo pirouette out of the way, her body dancing past the lunging snake as a blade cut a line through its scales. For a moment, he couldn't help but marvel at her fluid grace and the ease with which she narrowly dodged the attack. Behind her, Drekt brought his cleaver down on the overextended reptile, cutting it in twain with an angry bellow.

Instantly, Micah felt the warm buzz that indicated an earned point of attunement. Returning his attention to the first snake, his eyes widened as he watched Will scream and clench his fists, stone fingers tearing through scales and pulping the monster.

Will dropped the snake, panting, and grabbed his forearm. His skin faded from gray to pink as he whimpered and fell on his rear.

Micah ran over, prying Will's free hand from the bite, and blanched. Each fang wound was gigantic, almost as big as a walnut and deeper than a finger. Already the flesh around them was turning a sickly gray, highlighting angry red blood vessels that pulsed away from the injuries.

"Fix it, Silver." Will's eyes were wide as his breaths came in short, quick bursts. "Oh gods, it feels like I stuck my entire arm in Granny's oven."

Micah cast *Mending*. At an almost-glacial pace, a drop of yellow ichor began to form over each puncture wound as Will's flesh rejected the venom. Frantically, Micah began mouthing the words again, holding Will still as the heavy man began to thrash under him.

As the second spell sank in, Micah didn't slow down, casting it a third time.

At some point, Will passed out from the pain. Sarah propped his head to the side with a grimace, trying to prevent the thrashing man from choking on the froth caking his mouth. Finally, after the fifth *Refresh*, venom stopped seeping out of the injuries and Micah took a second to wipe the sweat from his brow.

He glanced up to see the rest of the party surrounding him, frowning at Will's quietly twitching form. Micah cast *Augmented Mending*, running his mana reserves dangerously low as he closed up the snake's deep fang wounds.

For a second, there was no sound except Will's restless shifting and Micah's panting. Even if Micah really hadn't exerted himself, the tension and magic use was more than enough to completely exhaust him.

"Will should be fine," Micah said as he stood up, his muscles tight from stress. "I got to him in time to prevent the poison from getting to his heart, but that was a lot closer than I'd like."

"What kind of healer needs to wait until combat is over to fix a wound?" Sarah snapped at him, her hands clasping and unclasping nervously as she kept her worried eyes on Will's unconscious form.

"The kind that is on his first dungeon run with a newbie party, Sarah." Jo shook her head. "If it wasn't for Micah, Will would've already died."

"Just because you li—" Sarah began before slamming her mouth shut. For a second, there was silence, then she rounded on Drekt. "What about *you,* oh fearless leader? You just shoved a *boy* at a high-threat-level monster. How in the hells are you supposed to lead this team if you start sacrificing its members?"

"He should have transformed," Drekt said, shrugging. "Ankros says that the only way we improve is through struggle. He'll be fine in an hour or so, and maybe a little bit of pain will be good for him. Next time, when a monster attacks, he'll know to use his blessing right away. Don't underestimate the usefulness of negative reinforcement."

"Why in the names of the Sixteen are we here anyway?" Micah asked Drekt, trying to stave off another explosion from Sarah. Somewhere to the side, Jo chuckled at his transparent deflection. "I know the Lancers told us to come here, but why did they need us to raid this dungeon?"

"It's all part of Ankros' great plan," Drekt said, a smile on his face. "Without conflict, mortals become complacent and weak. We need constant struggle to become our most perfect selves. The dungeons are him providing that struggle. They provide danger to hone our reflexes and experience, and attunement and loot to increase our power."

"Loot?" Micah asked, cocking his head slightly.

"Yes," Drekt replied. "Just as the monsters in a dungeon respawn endlessly, the Sixteen provide appropriate rewards for those that can fight their way to a dungeon's boss room and defeat its champion. Sometimes it's as simple as a valuable bar of metal, but truly lucky adventurers can get their hands on enchanted items or even skill books detailing lost spells or martial arts."

"So we're just here risking our lives to make a profit for the guild?" Micah frowned slightly.

"Drekt likes to leave out the other side of Ankros' great plan," Jo said with a snort. "Each day a dungeon goes unraided, more monsters spawn. They fight each other and gain experience. Eventually, they start evolving. If you leave them alone for too long, they evolve beyond the ability of the dungeon to control and you have a break. Mutated and superpowered beasts roaming across the land, destroying villages, burning churches and raping livestock."

"... livestock?" Micah asked quietly, trying to gauge Jo's poker face.

"Ankros is the master of both the carrot and the stick," Drekt spoke over Micah's mumbled thoughts proudly. "He understands that we are motivated by both greed and fear, so he gives us both. Truly he's the most insightful of the Sixteen."

"What now?" Micah shook his head, unable to pierce Jo's

sardonic grin as she winked at him. "I mean, we just fought a couple of monsters. What comes next?"

"Well." Drekt nodded at Will's barely stirring form. "We wait for Mr. Grantly to recover from his unfortunate run in with the cave adders, and then we prepare ourselves. Dungeons are meant to test adventurers, and they aren't meant to be taken lightly. I'm sure Will is in a lot of pain right now, but with any luck, it will serve as a reminder to take all combat seriously. We've been fighting relatively sedate battles against weaker creatures up until now in order to gain levels. This dungeon will be our first real challenge and proof that we are worthy of being promoted from a reserve to an active-duty adventuring team."

"Glory, honor, etcetera." Jo rolled her eyes. "I'm mostly just in this to see what we're goin' to get from the boss. My gear is starting to get a little beaten up and I'd like an upgrade sooner rather than later."

11

ACCOMPLISHMENT

"Well" —Trevor wrapped his arm around Micah's shoulders, his cheeks flushed and the faint smell of brandy on his breath—"how does it feel to be a real adventurer?"

"I thought I already was an adventurer?" Micah mumbled back, his voice muffled by Trevor's bicep. "I've been hunting animals in the forest around town for at least six months now."

"But this is your first dungeon." Trevor's head moved up and down in an overexaggerated bob. "You popped your dungeon cherry and that makes you, officially, an active-duty member of the Lancers. *That* means we've gotta celebrate."

"I'm not even old enough to drink, Trevor," Micah protested, trying to squirm out from under his brother's arm. "Do you have any idea what Mom would say?"

"That hasn't stopped you in the field," Drekt interjected with a chuckle. "Remember that time we fought the bog horrors? Micah got so drunk, he ended up singing a duet with Jo."

Micah blushed, trying to wrench himself from Trevor's grasp as his brother laughed at his discomfort. Even drunk, Trevor's Body-based class was more than enough to casually overpower Micah's efforts.

"See?" Trevor staggered slightly into Micah. "Listen to tall, dark, and musclebound over there. If you're old enough to drink after killing a couple of bog horrors, you're old enough to drink in the Lancers' tavern.

"Plus"—Trevor winked at Drekt before leaning closer to Micah —"first time after you clear a dungeon, your drinks are twenty percent off. Mom raised us to be thrifty. It'd be a positive shame to pass a bargain like that by."

"Of course we want to hear another rendition of that lovely duet," Sarah snickered, elbowing her sister. "I think we recovered more than enough in monster parts and attunement from the dungeon to ensure that we can get Micah drunk enough for an encore. Possibly with some dancing on tables."

"I'll leave the dancing to Micah." Jo rolled her eyes at Sarah. "The last time I tried that, I got fined for damaging guild property."

"It is more or less a tradition for rookies at this point." Trevor nodded sagely, the faux seriousness of his voice betrayed by the drunken flush of his cheeks.

"Then it's settled." Drekt slapped a brooding Will on the back hard enough that the portly man stumbled. "We get the two newbies drunk enough to dance on the table. I'm sure I can justify it in our ledgers as a team-building activity."

"Let's build our team, then!" Trevor released Micah and veered toward the guild hall, leaving the rest of the party bemused outside of the entrance.

For a couple seconds, they stood in silence, all sharing glances. Finally, Will spoke up, a hint of frustration in his reedy voice.

"But he isn't even on our team?" His face was scrunched in confusion. "I get that he's Micah's brother, but why is he hanging out with us?"

"Don't worry about it." Drekt chuckled as he pushed open the door. "Trevor isn't a big hitter with the Lancers, but everyone likes him, mostly because he's one of the most sociable people in the guild. Mostly because of scenes like this. He just has a tendency to appear in the middle of parties and make himself the center of attention. Even if he wasn't Micah's brother, he'd probably find a way to sneak into our celebration. Just think of it as networking."

"Networking." Will puffed his cheeks unhappily. "Why should I have to talk to a bunch of people? They should already know that I have a powerful blessing. They should be getting to know me, not the other way around."

"Whenever you add a third person to a pair," Sarah replied over her shoulder dryly as she walked into the building, "things get political. Being high-level and powerful will let you ignore some of those concerns, but at the end of the day, people are going to have preferences. You don't have to bow and scrape, but it makes sense to be friends with as many important individuals as possible. You never know who the team will be paired with next month or which group might have news about a big score that they're keeping hush-hush."

"You should talk, Sarah." Jo brushed past Micah on her way into the guild hall, filling his nose with the scent of the lilac shampoo from her post-dungeon bath. "You spend half of these events drinking expensive wine by yourself, a quarter complaining to whatever pretty boy you manage to corner, and the final quarter drunkenly sobbing. If it wasn't for me, no one would talk to either of us."

Seeing Will puff himself up to respond again, Micah shook his head. Will's opinion of himself was as inflated as his waistline. He was an adequate fighter, mostly relying on the strength of his gift to make up for his lack of skill and instincts, but Micah had only talked with him a handful of times where Will hadn't made the entire conversation about himself. Sarah humored him, but Micah suspected that everyone on the team mostly just tolerated the arrogant fop.

"I'm heading in to make sure Trevor doesn't get into any trouble." Micah waved off Sarah and Will before one of them could say something that would annoy him. Sarah wasn't quite as bad as Will, but she certainly had a tendency to be hypercritical toward everyone that wasn't her, Jo, or Will. "Mom would kill me if he came home with a black eye for hitting on Zoe while drunk again."

Behind him, Micah heard Will sputtering something to Sarah,

but he did his best to ignore it. The world was hard and unfair enough without having to listen to Will invent more reasons why his relatively charmed life was the result of outside forces oppressing him.

Inside the guild hall, Micah nodded at the receptionist as he walked past the front desk toward the wing that held the tavern. It wasn't terribly large, a bar with one worker servicing a couple kegs of ale and several bottles filled with spirits of dubious vintage, but it was one of the most popular places in the hall. There was something about risking death fighting against Ankros' children on a daily basis that inspired the Lancers to revel in creature comforts.

As Micah entered the tavern itself, a wall of noise hit him. There was only one other party there—B company, squad two, Trevor's team. Most of them nodded or briefly hoisted a glass on Micah's entrance, recalling him from his pre-blessing days. He waved back, only to be interrupted by Trevor once more.

"There's one of the men of the hour!" Trevor slurred from the bar, where he stood next to Drekt and Jo. "Come on, Micah, let's get you good and sauced."

Micah waded through a crowd of back pats and formulaic congratulations from the other party to stand next to Trevor at the bar. Immediately, Micah's brother draped an arm over his shoulder, eliciting a snicker from Jo, and leaned toward the bartender, a grizzled older woman with a deep scar puckering the right side of her face.

"Marlene!" he practically shouted at her, likely unsure of his own volume. "This is my kid brother, Micah! He just finished his first dungeon run, so we're trying to celebrate in style. Get him a mug of brandy, please."

"I heard you the first couple of times, Trevor." Marlene didn't move from her spot at the bar, leaning back against a keg with her arms crossed. "What'll ya have, Micah?"

"It's a celebration." Trevor swayed into Micah as he spoke to Marlene. "He needs brandy! It's not a celebration without the good stuff."

"Can I have an ale, please?" Micah asked, his ears turning red as Jo practically doubled over laughing at him. "A red, if you have it."

"Come on, Micah." He had to reach out and stabilize Trevor as his brother lost his balance turning around while trying to speak to him. "This is a special occasion. If you don't like the brandy, at least try the juushk."

Micah blanched. Drekt had tricked him into drinking juushk once, the impossible-to-live-down "singing incident." Juushk was little more than millet, reduced to a mash and fermented. Spellcasters or alchemists were used in the process to ensure that the product wouldn't poison the drinker, but that was about all that could be said for it. Juushk tasted vile and left a hangover that lasted a full day.

"We'll save the juushk for Will," Jo intervened, snaking her arm through Micah's and pulling him away from Trevor. "I'm pretty sure he's taken a liking to the stuff."

Micah snorted, trying to contain his laughter as he let Jo lead him away. As bad as the drinking juushk had been for him, Will had spent most of that evening in a bush throwing up while Drekt watched on, laughing uproariously. Even the morning after, when Micah had lain curled in the fetal position beneath a tree barely able to drink water and wishing that healing magic worked on hangovers, Will had it worse. The man spent an entire day moaning, vomiting, and whimpering for hours in a puddle of his own fluids. Laundry the next day had been particularly vile.

As they left, Jo snagged two mugs of ale, both filled with a frothy red brew. He'd never had it before—being underage did have its drawbacks. Instead, he relied upon the rest of the party's recommendations. Well, the rest of the party other than Drekt. The crazy giant actively seemed to like juushk, to the point that Micah suspected that he had some sort of poison resistance as part of his blessing.

Jo practically pushed him into a seat in the corner before taking her own next to him. At the door, Will and Sarah walked through to another round of congratulations as Trevor talked animatedly but inaudibly with Drekt. Micah raised the chipped ceramic mug to his lips before taking a sip of the ale. It was sweet with a somewhat woody and bitter finish, but most importantly, after a long day of fighting monsters, it was cold.

He leaned back in his chair and sighed, enjoying the taste of the drink on his tongue and the wood on his back. Across from him, Jo chuckled.

"It's all a bit much sometimes, isn't it?" She finished her statement with a pull of ale, her gray eyes staring past him at the chaos near the bar. Micah squinted at her slightly. He'd never really noticed that she had gray eyes.

"I don't have something on my face, do I?" Jo cocked her head, brushing a stray strand of hair aside.

"No," Micah stammered, hastily taking a drink from his beer as he averted his gaze.

"Well then" —she set down her drink and placed her chin in her hands—"what were you looking at, Silver?"

He turned beet red, floundering for words as he wilted under Jo's gaze. She let him suffer for a couple of seconds before her laughter cut through the fog surrounding him.

"Gods, you're so cute when you get flustered like this." Her voice washed over him like cool water in a desert. "I've literally had your hands inside my torso as you healed a punctured lung while Drekt and Will fought off willow creepers an arm's length from your head and you didn't even blink, yet every time I try to flirt with you, you turn into a puddle."

"Wait." Micah's face twisted in his confusion. "You were flirting with me?"

"It's a good thing I don't mind them a little oblivious." Jo's laughter wrapped around Micah, filling him with a strange warmth. "All of the jokes in the field? Every time I found an excuse to touch your arm while talking over a scouting report? None of that ever registered with you?"

Micah shook his head helplessly.

"Well, that explains why the godawful drinking game didn't work," she said, almost to herself.

Micah cocked his head in an unspoken question, prompting her to continue speaking.

"That time Drekt gave us the juushk" —a brief, sour expression flitted across her face—"I figured that you were just shy and I hoped that a little liquid courage would push you to make a move. Unfortunately, we just ended up singing barroom ditties and earning skull-rending hangovers."

"Gods." Micah took a drink before setting his mug down and running a hand through his hair. "If I'd known, I would have said something. I just always thought you saw me as a friend, with all of the dirty jokes and teasing me."

"Well." She leaned toward Micah, her lips filling his vision. Almost absently, he noticed his Adam's apple bobbing as her face approached his. "I'm not leaving things up to chance and interpretation this time."

12

HALCYON DAYS

"**W**hy in the name of the Sixteen am I doing this again?" Micah hissed at Jo, his hands tightly gripping the rope tied around her waist.

She grinned up at him, wind whipping through her hair as she prepared to descend down the side of the mountain. Behind her, the early dawn light barely illuminated the crevice that Micah was in, bracing himself against a rock.

"Mostly because you enjoyed spending five hours climbing a rock face while staring up at my ass," Jo giggled back at him. "Also because you agree that hatching a cliff eagle egg and raising the chick as a pet would be super fun."

"I'm not sure about fun; raising a monster sounds like a lot of work to me," Micah grumbled, setting himself so Jo could use the rope he held to belay herself down the mountainside.

It wasn't a sheer surface; more in the range of a sixty-degree angle. Technically, Jo could handle the incline on her own, but it would be much safer for everyone if someone was on hand to provide a safety net just in case she were to fall.

That was the real reason he was here. Every minute with Jo was more vibrant. He just felt alive and *present* in a way that he didn't normally. That said, she would take risks. By the Sixteen, did she take risks. The bags under his eyes spoke to the unnecessary chances she took, dragging Micah along with her.

"You didn't deny that you agreed to come along in order to peek at my butt." Jo winked at him.

"You do have a fantastic butt," Micah agreed dutifully. "It was a bit hard to see given that you woke me up around midnight and made me climb a mountain in the dark, but I'm sure that it would have been breathtaking if I actually could have caught a glimpse of it."

"Maybe afterward." Jo grinned as she glanced down the incline toward the nest beneath them. "The mother eagle has left, and we don't have much time."

Micah grunted as the rope pulled against his hands. Almost immediately, he realized his mistake as the rope fibers bit into his tender skin. Gloves. There was a reason actual climbers used heavy leather gloves when doing rope work.

Luckily, Jo was fairly light, her slim form almost entirely muscle. Micah appreciated her dedication to diet and exercise for a multitude of reasons. A smile flashed across his face. He'd never thought that "supporting her weight while she made an idiotic attempt to steal a monster's egg" would be added to that list, but here he was.

Really, it shouldn't have come as a surprise to him. When Jo wanted something, she tended to speak her mind. Sometimes, what she wanted to do made sense. Others? It was little more than the excuse of an adrenaline junkie to get her next fix.

Micah was a little troubled that he didn't really seem able to say no to her. Sometimes, like this morning, he didn't want to follow along with her antics. He'd been tired and it was their only day off from patrolling.

She'd been willing to head out on her own too. It was just that when Jo explained to Micah what she wanted to do, he couldn't let her go alone. Jo might be fine with scaling a mountainside in the dark and sneaking up on a monster nest on her own, but the very idea gave Micah chills.

The idea of letting Jo go off on her "adventures," not knowing whether or not she'd return, terrified Micah. He knew for a fact that he'd just spend the entire night awake, worrying about her and wondering what more he could do to help.

Instead, here he stood. Worried for her safety but present, putting himself at risk to participate in the same idiocy that Jo insisted upon.

"*Shit!*" Jo's yell rocked Micah's attention back to the present. "Micah, *pull*. I got the egg, but its parents came back early."

He opened his mouth to respond, but promptly shut it as an incensed screech sounded from below. Leave it to Jo to land them both in hot water on their day off.

He did his best to ignore the way the rope jerked in his grasp, shaving off hit points as he pulled it hand over hand. The uneven surface of the hemp burned the flesh of his hands.

Micah bit his lip against the pain. He'd need to cast *Mending* sooner rather than later. There was no way that his abused fingers would be able to grasp on to the rocks of the mountainside with enough strength to make a descent.

"Get *away*, you overgrown chicken!" Jo shouted from outside the crevice. Squawking and wingbeats answered her.

Micah grasped the rope with both hands and pulled with all of his strength. It bit into his palms, pulling the softened flesh off his burns. Each jerk rattled his shoulders as Micah twisted his body, trying to give Jo as much support as possible while his hands left bloody prints on the rope itself.

She clambered agilely over the lip of the crevice, a grapefruit-sized tan egg tucked under one arm and a smile on her face. Behind her, a bird the size of a small pony screeched angrily as it swooped toward the entrance.

Swiftly, Jo stowed the egg behind a rock. One of her blades glinted in the dawn light as she swung it at the eagle, forcing it to arrest its dive and swerve away. Without asking questions, Micah cast *Wind Shield* over the cavern's entrance. It might not be enough to stop the bird if it was truly determined, but the wall of air pressure would slow or deflect any attempts to breach the cave.

"Wow!" Jo exclaimed before bursting into laughter. "That was wild. Did you see how close it got to me? I could feel the wind from its wings on my back as I made it over the edge there. Gods, that was close!"

She moved closer to Micah, one hand on his shirt and the other seeking his hand. Jo leaned in, her eyes bright and dancing as her lips parted slightly in anticipation of meeting Micah's own.

He winced as her hand touched his. She pulled back, looking down at the red stain covering her palm. Somehow, he heard the drip of his blood splashing on the cavern floor over the distant eagle attacking the spell protecting the crevice entrance.

"Micah" —she looked from her hand to his own—"you're hurt! Why didn't you say anything about being hurt? What happened?"

"You can be a little overwhelming at times, Jo," Micah winced as he picked a strand of hemp from his burned and raw hands. "You didn't give me a second to let you know I was hurt before you bounded over here."

"But how did you get hurt?" Concern filled her eyes as she looked at his mauled hands. "You should've just been safe in the cave the entire time."

"Rope burn," Micah hissed, pulling more of the rope threads from his hand. Healing would cause his skin to grow over the wound, but he'd be in for even more pain if he didn't clear the injury of foreign matter first. "You were in danger and needed me to pull faster. I don't know how I'd be able to live with myself if you got attacked on the mountainside and weren't able to defend yourself from the eagle. If it took a little pain to get you back to safety, that was a price I was willing to pay."

"That looks like more than a little pain, Micah." Jo frowned, guilt flashing behind her eyes. "Are you saying that you suffered through all of that because you thought I needed help with the cliff eagle?"

"Didn't you?" Micah replied, pouring a splash of juushk from his kit over his newly cleaned wounds to sterilize them before spellcasting. "I mean, it hurt like the hells themselves were twisting in my grip, but it's easier to heal my hands than the entirety of your back. The talons on that bird aren't a joke."

"No!" she blurted out before biting her lip and chewing it in frustration. "Well, yes. I really couldn't have fought it properly on the mountainside. It just doesn't seem fair that you're the one getting hurt for my idea."

Micah cocked his head slightly, smiling sadly as he spoke the words to *Mending*. His hands dripped blood as they went through the pantomime the spell required.

"Maybe you shouldn't have come?" Jo mused out loud, pacing back and forth and ignoring the irate bird of prey outside the cave. "This was all my idea and you only got hurt because you followed my lead. I know that sometimes I insist on adventures that could get dangerous, but I never meant for anyone to get hurt. I should probably leave you back in Basil's Cove the next time I try something like this."

"But that reckless streak of yours is why I need to come with." Micah sighed in relief as he flexed his newly healed hands. "You live in the moment. It makes everything about you exciting and new. Unfortunately, you just don't take danger all that seriously, Jo. If I wasn't here, not only would you have been attacked while making your way back to the cave, there wouldn't have been anyone here to heal you."

"The eagle was supposed to be hunting for prey." She sulked slightly. "I've watched it off and on for two weeks now and it always takes at least an hour to return. I prepared for everything. It wasn't supposed to come back for at least another half-hour."

"It did, though." Micah smiled slightly. "It's hard for you to say that you've prepared for everything when I'm literally looking at evidence to the contrary in the form of an eagle circling the entrance to our cave."

"I know, but" —her eyes flashed back to his newly healed hands, distress clouding her face—"I didn't think that you would get hurt. You have to understand, that's never what I wanted."

"Jo," Micah laughed, "I don't think you're a monster. It's just that sometimes you don't think. I still love the vibrancy and excitement of your adventures; they can just be a bit much sometimes. Seriously, I don't even know when you sleep. I can barely keep up with you."

"I'm sorry, Micah." She glanced down at the floor of the cave. "I guess I've just been doing what I wanted and not really considering you. I… I'll have to think about how to change that."

"Don't worry about it, Jo." Micah put a finger under her chin, angling her head up so she could look at him through damp eyes. "Look, let's just give this egg back to the eagle and get out of here. The idea of trying to scale our way back down the mountain and then making an almost-full-day trek back to Basil's Cove while being attacked by an angry bird doesn't really have a lot of appeal. Plus, I don't want to kill a monster just because it's trying to protect its young. That doesn't sit right with me."

"Fine." Jo smiled weakly. "I suppose it's the least we could do."

13

AMBUSH

"Come on, Micah, think of it as an adventure," Trevor quipped, spear over his shoulder as he walked next to Micah. "Unless there's a raid, the guild never sends out multiple teams after the same objective. This will probably be our only chance to work together unless there's a dungeon break."

"Can you at least show some concern, Trevor?" Sarah took a brief break from scanning the nearby forest to scowl at him. "Westmarch reported Durghish scouts sniffing around and then went silent. For all we know, the entire contingent deployed there is already dead or twisted into warbeasts."

"Lighten up." Trevor laughed, winking at Sarah. "Westmarch is a citadel. There might only be five hundred soldiers there, but they're all over level 7 and well-trained. Plus, I've seen those walls. They were raised by a team of high-level Earth wizards almost a hundred years ago. Granite, five times a man's height tall and about one-fifth as thick. Even if the Durgh have a veritable army, they aren't getting in there anytime soon."

Sarah scowled at the both of them, drawing an aggrieved flicker of expression from Micah. Trevor was always like this, brimming with chatter and opinions regardless of how appropriate they were. Most people learned fairly quickly that he was immune to shame. Any attempt to scold him would be answered with a laughing wink.

Instead, they took it out on Micah, as if it was his business to keep Trevor in line. He sighed. Of course, it could be that Sarah had it in for him. She'd never been his biggest fan, quick with a dirty look or a biting remark, but ever since Jo—

"Say, Micah," Trevor interrupted by purposely bumping into Micah's shoulder. "Your ex-girlfriend's sister is kinda cute. Do you think she likes me?"

Micah turned to Trevor, his mouth open to say something, but the words just didn't come out. Jo had dumped him almost three months ago. Honestly, it was for the best. When Jo knew what she wanted, she just reached out and took it. Where he would spend days debating merits and consequences of his actions, Jo would act.

Before long, their relationship had turned into her doing things while Micah followed along. Once the initial novelty wore off, their reckless behavior began to nag at him. He'd tried to suppress his fretting and indecision in order to go with the moment, but Jo noticed. She always noticed little details like that.

She'd been nice about it, pointing out that he wasn't happy and that he was forcing himself. She'd even left the door open to dating him again if he could get past his passive nature.

That was almost the worst part. The breakup would have been much easier if she'd been insensitive or cheated on him. Instead, he couldn't help but agree with her. Even if he had trouble admitting it to himself, dating her had worn on him near the end. It only would've been a matter of time before one of them snapped at the other and said something they couldn't take back.

He still cared for Jo, but they were better as friends. As much as he liked spending time with her, whenever they were together, he felt like he was being overshadowed. They'd spent all of their time on spontaneous "adventures," breaking minor laws and incurring unnecessary risks for the thrill of it. Micah didn't care for the adrenaline rushes that Jo obviously craved; he much preferred spending his time reading grimoires or stories of past heroes.

"Micah," Trevor interrupted him, concern on his face, "I'm just messing with you. It's been a couple months since you and Jo broke up. You've spent this entire time moping. I was just hoping for some kind of reaction out of you."

"Look" —Micah smiled weakly at his brother—"I'm fine. This is all for the best. We need to be able to work together as professionals. She saw that things were turning toxic and she ended it. We're still friends. I just have to shake off a bit of a funk and I'll be good to go."

"You know what's great for shaking off a funk?" Trevor asked conspiratorially. "Now that you're eighteen, I can take you to the Rose Petal House and buy you some liquor and a girl to take your mind off of your ex. Trust me, it does wonders."

"By Mursa's quill, we are *not* having this conversation," Micah groaned, blushing furiously. "It's not about sex. I just miss her, but at the same time, I know I'm better off with how things are."

"If it's not about the sex" —Trevor winked at Micah—"there's no reason not to go to the Rose Petal House. We're going to make a fortune off of this raid; we may as well use it on something entertaining."

Micah paused, trying to think of a way to change the subject. His eyes flitted over the rest of their column. Combat teams from three different guilds, all fitted with the eclectic but well-maintained gear that differentiated them from royal or noble soldiers, trotted down the packed-dirt road toward Westmarch. Nine teams, three each from the Lancers, Mystic Hammers, and Steel Shrikes. Forty experienced men and women, each of whom had fought and bled in the dungeons around Basil's Cove making names for themselves.

He didn't know all of them personally, but everyone in the convoy knew of each other. Basil's Cove was a city, but it wasn't a large one. There were only so many active combat teams. Between bards' tales, bragging over drinks, and a series of good-natured rivalries fostered by the guilds, word spread fairly quickly about each and every adventurer capable of contributing in a proper dungeon run.

"Why do you think we're getting paid so well?" Micah asked Trevor in an attempt to distract his brother from loudly talking about

Basil's Cove's most infamous brothel. "This is just supposed to be a scouting mission. They'd only send this many adventurers if they were expecting things to get rough."

Before Trevor could respond, a woman began yelling. "Contact!" Micah whirled toward where she was shouting, panic in her voice. "The Durgh are in the ground—"

The rest of her sentence was cut off as a pyromancer triggered an explosion, blowing up a good chunk of the nearby forest and raining streams of fire down on the convoy. Quickly, Micah cast *Wind Shield*, protecting those around him from the falling embers as the condensed air diverted the flames aside. Up and down the trail, magical defenses and blessings launched into the air to protect other adventurers.

Wordlessly, Trevor turned and ran over to his squad, his jovial nature melting away the second the situation demanded concentration. Drekt and Will positioned themselves between the rest of the party and the area of the explosion, each activating their gift as they prepared themselves for combat.

The rest of the raid party did the same, breaking down into its nine composite teams. A fireworks display of magic and gifts lit up the trail. Every melee class in one party began glowing gold as a protective field from their caster settled in. Another party was surrounded by a waist-high spiked bulwark of steel.

A hail of javelins flew out of the forest. One blurred straight through the still-active *Wind Shield* and struck Will in the throat. Micah flinched back as the allegedly impenetrable stone armor exploded into a shower of gravel. He blinked. That wasn't possible.

Will fell to the ground bonelessly, his rocky body cracking the beaten earth of the path. The spear, fashioned from the lacquered spine of some monster, quivered in Will's still form. Micah stared blankly for a second before the road erupted into chaos as various adventurers returned fire. Sarah fired an arrow at a shape darting out of the forest as Micah mouthed the words to *Augmented Healing* and placed his hand on Will's collarbone.

Nothing.

He was gone.

A bellow from Drekt pulled Micah back into the world. The huge man swung a cleaver at something that had once been a hound before it was subjected to the Durgh's twisted alchemy. The blade practically bisected the creature, but there were more behind it. Many more.

Micah cast *Root Spears*, a second-tier Wood spell. His breath came out in short, panicked bursts as stakes of wood grew out of the ground, stabbing into some of the charging horrors and forcing the others to evade. A chorus of panicked screams erupted from the other adventurers, barely drowning out the sound of jaws tearing flesh and snapping bones as they tried and largely failed to defend themselves after the decimation of the javelin attack.

Then the Durgh themselves strolled out of the forest. Each of them was half again as tall as the humans they fought, thick with heavily corded muscles. Their black skin was littered with tattoos, each glowing with a fell pale green light. Two of them walked toward their party, moving casually as adventurers fought and died in front of them.

"Sarah, support me!" Drekt shouted as his cleaver finished off the last of the hounds in his vicinity. "Jo and Micah, deal with the other one!"

Micah glanced at Jo. She gave him a quick smile that set his heart aflutter before throwing a stiletto at the advancing Durgh. It waved a hand indifferently, catching the tiny blade on the heavy metal of its thick-bladed gauntlets.

She sighed theatrically at Micah and drew her shortswords, sprinting toward the giant. Micah launched a pair of *Air Knives* over her shoulder. The Durgh didn't even try to block, just letting the spell trace shallow lines of blood across its muscled abdomen as it focused on Jo.

Micah ground his teeth in frustration. The only spell he had that would even injure a Durgh was *Sonic Bolt*, a second-tier Air spell, but there was no way he'd be able to get it off without hitting Jo. He gripped his spear with both hands and cautiously approached the two.

Jo moved with the grace of a dancer, slipping just under punches from the Durgh's gauntleted fists, only to slash upward, drawing deep, bleeding wounds on the creature. It didn't seem to care. Despite the blood flowing freely from its forearms, it acted like the cuts were merely superficial.

Then it stomped the ground, activating a blessing that knocked both Micah and Jo from their feet as the ground bucked beneath them. Micah scrambled back to his feet just in time to watch in horror as the Durgh punched Jo. All of her evasiveness meant nothing in that moment of imbalance and she flew backward, grunting as the blow connected solidly.

His vision went red.

Without thinking, he unleashed a *Sonic Bolt*, draining almost all of his remaining mana. For the first time, the Durgh looked alarmed as the attack bypassed its leathery flesh and attacked soft tissue directly, shaving off a good chunk of its HP. It stumbled and fell to one knee, blood dribbling from its ears.

Micah charged, thrusting his spear into its back just below the shoulder. It wasn't the most logical plan, but after Will and Jo fell, he wasn't thinking. The Durgh stood back up and took a faltering step toward him, its balance clearly off due to its ruptured eardrums. Micah stabbed it again, sinking the spear into its gut all the way to the crossbar.

It backhanded him. There was a flash of pain, and then Micah was insensible. His right arm shattered as the blades from the gauntlet bit deep into his flesh. Almost in slow motion, Micah hit the ground and bounced.

He blinked at the afternoon sky, his vision narrowed to a tunnel. Distantly, he knew that he should get up and do something, but he couldn't really understand the urgency. He didn't even know what it was he was supposed to do. Far above him, a bird flitted between clouds.

A Durgh's face, eyes wild with hatred as it gnashed its tusks, appeared above him. Micah knew he should fight or resist as it reached for him with its gauntleted, bloodstained hand, but he could barely lift his arms.

The Durgh's head jerked back as a stiletto sprouted from its cheek. It turned from Micah just in time for Jo to jump off of his spear, still lodged in its gut, and plant another pair of stilettos in its eyes.

Micah blinked again. She looked like hell. Her robes were torn and stained with blood, and the entire left side of her face was bruised beyond belief, but at that moment, she was the most beautiful thing Micah had ever seen.

Then the blinded Durgh grabbed her. Even through the haze of his head injury, Micah heard the pop of bones shattering as it squeezed and she went limp. It took hesitant a step toward Micah before dropping Jo's body right next to him. It wobbled and fell to its knees, finally running out of hit points as the blood loss took its toll.

Micah turned his head to look at Jo. She was still breathing shallowly, blood gurgling past her lips. Hazily, his anatomy skill identified a punctured lung. The only treatment was an immediate and invasive application of three castings of *Augmented Mending*. Even if he'd been at full mana, he didn't have the strength to cut her chest open and cast the spell on her wrecked organs.

"Hey, Micah?" She coughed as she spoke, blood staining her teeth.

"Jo," he replied. Everything was dark and distant.

"I'm sorry, but I don't think I'll have the opportunity to give you a second chance." The coughs transformed into a ragged jag as she began choking on her own blood, unable to clear the fluid from her throat and lungs no matter how much she hacked and heaved.

A hand grabbed Micah by his collar. In a brief tumult of motion, he felt himself slung over a man's shoulder. Looking down, he made out Trevor.

"I've got Micah!" Trevor was screaming at someone, but it sounded like he was in a windstorm. The words were muffled and hard to make out. "Josephine's gone. We need to move before the Durgh come back for us!"

He winced as his brother's shoulder jolted up into his injured torso. He was running. Drekt led the way with Sarah flanking them, stopping occasionally to fire an arrow backward. From far away, he heard the baying of hounds.

Micah didn't know how long they ran. Then Trevor jerked and pitched forward, spilling Micah to the forest floor. A huge dark fist grabbed Micah and slung him over Drekt's shoulder. Trevor lay unmoving, a black-lacquered harpoon made from a monster spine quivering in his back.

Then they were moving again. Mercifully, Micah blacked out, unconsciousness protecting him from the grief and pain.

14

RESET

The walls were going to fall. Micah cast *Root Spears*, doing what he could to slow the Durgh host's advance. He felt his XP ticking up as the swarm of warbeasts simply overran the area of his spell, ignoring the damage inflicted by the knee-high punji sticks the spell thrust from the ground in their frenzy to reach Basil's Cove.

This wave would be the small ones. Mutated wolves, pack animals, and men, twisted by the dark alchemy and rituals that made the Durgh pariahs in civilized lands. The next wave would be the real monsters, the gargantuan beasts that roamed the tunnels of the Durgh's underground kingdoms, ritualistically melded into engines of destruction.

Next to him, Sarah fired arrow after arrow, barely bothering to aim as the density of the attackers guaranteed her hits. It hardly mattered. Her eyes were dead, and Micah didn't blame her.

Drekt stood by grimly, his cleaver planted in the battlements while he did his best to ignore the hostile stares from the other defenders. The rest of the soldiers manning the wall didn't trust him, suspecting that he was at least partially Durgh. They weren't wrong —after months of goading, Micah had gotten the huge man drunk enough to admit that his grandfather was a full-blooded Durgh.

Whatever his birth, he was manning the wall next to them, ready to bleed and inevitably die at the hands of his estranged relatives. It was more than most of the nobles could say. They'd fled Basil's Cove almost a week ago, just after Westmarch fell to the Durgh incursion. Ostensibly, they were retreating further into the Kingdom to try and raise support for a counteroffensive, but everyone from the guilds knew the score.

Even if help was coming, it wouldn't come in time. Westmarch had been slaughtered, with only a handful of sorry, broken refugees managing to trickle back to the alleged safety of Basil's Cove shortly after their expedition returned.

It had been an absolute massacre. Only a few adventurers had survived the frenzied retreat. Of the initial survivors, many were hunted down by hounds and harpoon-wielding Durgh as they ran for almost an entire day and night through the forest.

Micah ran a hand through his greasy and unkempt hair as he glanced to the side, at the spots on the wall where Jo and Will should have stood. The entire operation had been a trap. The Durgh knew that humanity wouldn't let Westmarch fall unavenged, and they'd lured the guilds away from the city's walls and defenses to decimate the defenders.

Even now, as he hurled spells at the attackers, Trevor, Jo, and Will flashed before his eyes. Trevor and Will both still had the Durgh spears sticking out of them, but Jo stood slightly distant, blood trickling down her chin as her body was racked with a wet, repetitive cough. None of them said anything. They just watched his futile struggle on the walls of Basil's Cove, as if waiting for him to fall and join them.

Micah chuckled. It wasn't like he'd have to wait too much longer for that. He turned his gaze from the oncoming horde, barely slowed by the defenders' magic and ballistae. Glancing down, he winced at the crude arm carved from living wood that grew from the mangled stump of his right shoulder. He could move the prosthetic, but without any of the agility or grace he was accustomed to. Despite constant healing spells, deep down, Micah knew he would never be able to use a spear again.

A thud drew his attention to the main gate. A warbeast, grown from one of the great subterranean worms, twenty feet tall and covered in spikes and scales, slammed its clublike tail into the thick wood once again. Spells sparkled around it as the defenders struggled to even hurt the massive creature, but the Blessed capable of fighting something of that power had already fled Basil's Cove. It wouldn't be long now.

He closed his eyes to hide their burning dampness. Soon he'd be able to join Jo and Trevor. Below him, the small warbeasts reached the wall. Halfheartedly, he threw an *Air Blade* at a twisted cat monster as it dug its claws directly into the fortification and began pulling itself up toward him.

With a hiss of exertion, Drekt and a soldier upended a cauldron full of pitch on a cluster of warbeasts, scalding and killing them. A halfhearted cheer sounded from their section of the wall, only to be immediately extinguished when another swarm of warbeasts immediately took their place, scrabbling over the bubbling corpses of their comrades.

The front gate thudded again, a dull booming sound that almost drowned out the clatter of claws on the wall in front of them. The assaulting worm was aflame; a high-level pyromancer running her mana dry to sustain a barrage of spells that blanketed the creature. It simply ignored the fire as it pummeled the gate. Micah didn't know whether the fire wasn't damaging the monster or if the Durgh had just made it immune to pain.

It hardly mattered. Even if the fire was harming it, the gate would fall before the flames brought the monster low.

Micah created a squall of wind, exhausting a good 20% of his mana reserves to throw the warbeasts off his section of the wall. They landed on their backs, misshapen messes of limbs that squirmed to their feet. He'd bought the archers a little more time to thin the swarm, but even as feathers sprouted from the monsters' soft undersides, he knew it wouldn't be enough.

He could already see the Durgh warriors silently walking out of the nearby forest in formation, standing just behind the final wave of advanced warbeasts. Their front row carried heavy tower shields to protect them from arrows, but it was hardly needed. The defenders didn't have the time and energy to spare on the real threat.

With a signal from a Durgh clad in shiny silver armor, the final wave of warbeasts rumbled forth from the forest toward the wall, the Durgh themselves following shortly thereafter. Already Micah spotted at least three of the mutated worms.

Maybe if the strongest among them had remained, there would be some purpose to this fight, but the Golden Drakes had fled along with the nobility and the elite of the militia to "seek help." It was a cowardly retreat, made all the more damning by the Council's final edict commanding that the remainder of the guilds and the militia hold the city to the last. They hadn't even let the civilians evacuate with them.

Micah, his friends, and his family were nothing more than a sacrifice. They were only meant to delay the Durgh long enough for those who truly mattered to make it to safety.

Hells, the Durgh probably wouldn't even occupy the city. As strong as they were, they knew better than to challenge the Royal Knights. No, in all likelihood, this raid was for nothing more than slaves and plunder.

True, the bards would likely sing songs of "the butchers of Westmarch" and "the heroes of Basil's Cove," fighting nobly to the last man, but it would be propaganda. Nothing but a recruiting tool tailored to lure more starry-eyed young Blessed into serving the very nobles that abandoned Micah. He snorted; the nobles would probably even commission the song.

Tears stung Micah's eyes as he watched the Durgh fall into formation with deadly precision. Despite his childhood dreams of being a hero, he just hadn't been strong enough. He'd tried and he'd bled, but Jo and Trevor were gone. Worse, from what he'd heard about the Durgh, his parents and Esther would be lucky to die in the sack of the city.

The fate of Durgh slaves wasn't pretty. Some toiled hard to produce food for the host, some became food for the host, and perhaps the most unlucky were twisted by foul rituals into the very warbeasts that clawed at the walls below him. He'd warned his father and given him a knife. Micah could only hope that he'd have the courage to use it.

Micah stood on the wall, the weight of his regrets rooting him in place as he watched his world come crashing down around him. If only he'd worked a little harder. If only they'd found out about the Durgh incursion early enough to call the Royal Knights to Basil's Cove. If only his damn gift had been enough.

No. Micah gritted his teeth. His gift *was* enough. He'd just been too scared to use it. He'd let childish fears about losing the levels and attunement he'd gained stop him from traveling back and learning the skills he needed to hold his own. If he'd treated being an adventurer seriously from the beginning, rather than as some sort of silly game, none of this would be happening.

It was funny. He'd fought for a little over a year and a half to become a level 11 wizard, and now that he was here, his path was clear. He'd throw it all away in a second for Trevor and Jo to come back. Mursa must have known what was coming, and she'd given him a second chance, both to improve himself and fix the mistakes and laziness that had brought him here.

He laughed to himself, tears streaming down his face. Beside him, Sarah glanced at him and simply clicked her tongue before she resumed firing arrows into the enemy. Drekt paused as he hefted another cauldron full of pitch, giving him a look drenched in pity.

Saying a quick prayer of thanks to his rarely acknowledged goddess, Micah stepped away from the battlement and took a quick breath.

"Blessed Return." When he spoke the words to activate his gift, they took on a voice other than his. They were poetry. Melodic, a song almost. Then mana began to swirl around him, building toward a crescendo. Across the field from Basil's Cove, the Durgh howled,

obviously sensing the huge vortex of mana condensing around Micah, but unable to reach him in time to interrupt the spell.

The mana swelled and reality fractured. It was as simple as that—for a fraction of a second, everything froze, and then it shattered into a million glittering shards, revealing the exact same scene as before.

Micah felt himself being pulled backward, step by step retracing his actions in reverse. At first, the pace was faltering but inexorable, but the speed of his observations increased with each second until everything was a blur, a riot of color and mana. Then he slammed into something soft, his back bouncing off of his childhood bed with the force of a catapult.

He jolted out of bed, his body small and frail. Looking down, he noticed that his arms were pale, unmarked by the scars and muscles he'd earned as a Lancer. Outside his bedroom, he heard Esther's childish voice as she called for their mother to fetch a toy for her. Micah began laughing, a shrill, tinny sound from his young throat. It worked. He was thirteen once again.

15

ONCE AGAIN

Micah swung his feet out of the bed, marveling at the way they barely touched the ground. He'd been scrawny at thirteen, going through a late growth spurt just before his fifteenth birthday to fill out his gangly frame.

He stood up, hissing slightly as his bare feet touched the cold wood of the floor. He'd forgotten how icy his room got in the fall before the wood stove in the kitchen properly heated up the entire building. Micah wobbled slightly as he tried to take the first step with his awkward new body. The limbs were too long, all elbows and knees, throwing off his precarious balance.

He stopped, his hand on the simple wooden door leading to his bedroom. This was the moment of truth. Without a blessing, no one could view their status screen. They would still have stats and attunements; they just couldn't use them for anything. The question was whether he'd still retained his blessing after traveling back in time. Hesitantly, Micah tried to call up his status.

Micah Silver
    Age 13 [ERROR] / 18
    Class/Level-XP

HP 8/8

Attributes

Body 4, Agility 3, Mind 9, Spirit 8

Attunement

Moon 4, Sun 1, Night 2

Mana

Moon 8/8, Sun 2/2, Night 4/4

Affinities

Time 10

Wood 6

Air 5

Blessings

Mythic Blessing of Mursa - Blessed Return, Ageless Folio

Skills

Anatomy 6

Fishing 1

Herbalism 4

Librarian 3

Ritual Magic 2

Spear 5

Spellcasting 10

A wide smile blossomed on Micah's face. Whatever magic powered his status and blessings clearly didn't know what to make of his return.

Despite its confusion, it still worked well enough. His class was gone and his attributes and attunements were trash, but years of training with the Folio had given him the skills of an experienced adventurer, and the Folio itself contained the spells and ritual formulae he'd need to regain his power quickly.

It wouldn't be easy to avoid the coming storm, but with those skills and the time to hone them further, this was doable. For the first time in weeks, hope began to bloom in Micah's chest.

"Miiiiicaaaaaah!" Esther screamed, slamming open the door and almost running into him. "Momma said to wake you up. Breakfast is ready and she didn't want you to be late for your apprenticeship with Keeper Ansom again."

"Well, I'm certainly up." Micah chuckled, ruffling her hair as he walked out of his bedroom. A wave of nostalgia washed over him as he smelled the ham sizzling away in the kitchen. Constant fieldwork had kept him from his mother's cooking for most of the last year in the previous timeline, and only now did he realize how much he'd missed her homemade meals.

After a brief but hearty breakfast, Micah began the walk to Keeper Ansom's library. Around him, the comfortable morning sounds of Basil's Cove tried to lull him into a sense of normalcy.

The bell from the docks announced to the stevedores that a new ship was pulling into harbor for unloading. A cluster of children ran by shouting the names of the "blessings," play acted in their games of tag. All of this was complemented by the quiet babble of petty merchants as they sold all manner of knickknacks and food from small stalls lining the city streets.

It was all so mundane, in sharp relief to the terror and adrenaline of the Durgh invasion. Micah couldn't help but smile as he quickened his pace, trying to arrive at the library just as it opened.

He was almost on time, drawing a mirth-filled admonishment from Ansom as he gasped for breath in the darkened building's vestibule. Silently, he vowed to take up jogging. Even if his younger body lacked the muscle definition and endurance he was used to, a short run shouldn't leave him winded and heaving. If he really planned to make a difference in five years, that would need to change.

"Keeper Ansom," he said between deep breaths, sucking down the morning's humid air, "I was talking with some of my friends about Blessed and none of us could figure out how they get their classes. James said that they just get them along with their blessings, but that doesn't sound right to me."

"That's why you're working for me and James is apprenticing as a butcher," Ansom replied with a chuckle, buying Micah's lie.

"Classes are bestowed by something called a class crystal. Really, it's not much more than a chunk of quartz enchanted and imbued with a point of attunement. They aren't terribly hard to make; it's just that spending a point of attunement on them is expensive. Most of the adventuring and crafting guilds have a couple on hand that they let their protégés use in exchange for an exclusive contract. It's the same story with the military and civil government. Heck, I'm a decent enchanter myself. I could probably make one if I wanted to."

"How does the crystal select your class, then?" Micah questioned, doing his best to sound like the inquisitive youth he remembered himself to be.

"They analyze your skills, affinities, and blessings," Ansom replied, moving over to a pile of books by the side of his desk. "Most people end up with fairly simple classes because it's hard to amass the necessary abilities to earn an uncommon or rare class before they turn sixteen. Technically, you don't need to select a class right away, but it's difficult to earn attunement without one, so most people don't bother with waiting. Still, some scholars have studied the process.

"Here." Ansom passed a musty tome to Micah titled *On Classes and their Assignment.* "About a century ago, the royal house of Kerrakan commissioned this work. As far as I understand, the purpose of it was to help them design rigorous training regimens to ensure that their children would earn more rarefied classes than those available to you or me. Once you finish your work, you can take it to the reading room."

Micah nodded, grabbing the book from Ansom and clasping it to his chest before scampering off to an eventful day of sorting and reshelving books. Every once in a while, the Keeper would need him to engage in the tedious drudgery of copying by hand a damaged passage in an older grimoire, but usually, Ansom gave him only simple organizational and filing work. The end result was Micah having half of almost every day to read through whatever might take his fancy.

In his previous life, that had included an embarrassing number of books about heroes and knights rescuing fair damsels. Sure, he'd also read some more practical works on spell theory, but there hadn't been any focus or drive behind his actions. This time, Micah passed by the histories and propaganda entirely. As soon as he finished his work for the day, he began poring over *On Classes*.

It was fascinating. No one in the Lancers really talked about the theory behind receiving a class. As far as they were concerned, you just touched a crystal and got your options. There wasn't even a cursory attempt to understand how and why an individual received the options they did.

On Classes treated class selection with the same scientific rigor a botanist would plant classification. Known classes were laid out by category, rarity, and benefits provided to the recipient. There was even a table cross-indexing the classes by the skills needed to unlock them.

Apparently, wizard was an uncommon class because it required multiple affinities as well as a skill. When Micah compared it with the more common elementalist spellcasters, he noticed the difference immediately. Only elementalists specializing in the primal elements, Time and Order/Chaos, earned an attribute per level. Of course, their classes were also considered uncommon due to the rarity. Every other spellcaster specializing in only one element provided much less mana per level and only 1 attribute point every other level.

Semi-angrily, he paged toward the end of the book, looking for more advanced spellcasting classes. Some were a matter of luck—such as sorcerer, which required affinities in both primal elements—but many were simply more advanced versions of wizard. High wizard required a Spellcasting skill level of 10, doable but well beyond the capabilities of most commoners, especially if they were unprepared. Magi needed two affinities and a Spellcasting skill of 5 along with a skill level in Ritual Casting. Adept also demanded two affinities, a Spellcasting skill of 5, and a skill level in Enchanting.

Each of those classes granted a point in both Spirit and Mind per level, doubling a wizard's attribute growth. What truly caught Micah's eye, however, was the thaumaturge class. Only one royal son had ever managed to earn it, and he'd been quickly killed during a dynastic dispute lest he turn into an unstoppable despot. The details on its acquisition were spotty, but it was rumored to require three or more affinities, and 10 skill levels in Spellcasting, Ritual Casting, and Enchanting.

Of course, the class was as useful to the recipient as it was difficult to acquire. In addition to increased mana growth, the class gave a point in Spirit, Mind, and an attribute of its user's choice each level. The book had an afterword, theorizing the existence of even more exalted classes that would put their users on par with the saints themselves, but Micah simply ignored the baseless speculation.

Micah closed the book, a gleam in his eyes. That was true power. He'd always known that nobles were more powerful than a guild Blessed. The insufferable pricks never shut up about it after all. He'd always just chalked it up to the absurd amount of attunement they inherited, letting excess mana subsume any difference in skill the two might have.

The book changed things. The nobility were powerful, but their secrets weren't entirely beyond his grasp. With proper training and preparation, he'd be able to claim a rare class and unlock his potential in a way that would *force* them to listen.

The next day, after finishing his normal work, Micah cracked open a book on enchanting. He wouldn't have the time to become a thaumaturge—after all, it took him almost three constant years of spellcasting to earn his way to 10 ranks in that skill—but with the time he had, it shouldn't be impossible for him to learn enchanting well enough to make a class crystal.

Once he selected a class, most likely Magi, he'd be able to use his spells again. Then, it was just a matter of sneaking out at night to practice spells and gain levels. If he became powerful enough, one of the larger guilds would have to take notice of him. That would be his chance to pass on the warnings about the Durgh incursion.

Mentally setting the Folio to take notes, Micah dove into the book on enchanting. It was like crossing calculus with calligraphy. Each rune etched onto an item created an effect and altered the item on a fundamental level. Every rune needed to be custom-tailored to the object that it was being inscribed on, with slight changes to the composition or even metaphorical significance of the object being enough to cause an enchantment to fizzle. Worse, each subsequent rune required the enchanter to account for the changes made to the magical fabric of the object by previous runes.

He ended the day with a headache, a skill level in Enchanting, and a point of Moon attunement as a reward for his diligence. For almost a month, he did nothing but study enchanting at the library and follow up on his studies from the notes inscribed in the Folio at home.

Fairly quickly, he made it to the second skill rank in Enchanting before his growth tapered off, likely due to his reluctance to actually practice the skill. After all, every attempt at enchanting, whether or not it was successful, cost attunement. At least until he turned sixteen, he had almost no way to regain any attunement he spent.

Finally, a couple days after Trevor's sixteenth birthday and blessing and just before Micah's fourteenth birthday, he reached the third level in the skill. Reluctantly, Micah went to the market and acquired a decent-sized chunk of quartz from a curio shop. The milky crystal had some use in enchanting, but it was a common enough mineral that no one second-guessed a boy claiming he wanted it to "make jewelry" for his mother.

That night, he snuck out into the garden with the necessary reagents to enchant the quartz: a small amount of silver dust, a chisel, a kitchen knife, and a live chicken he'd fed a sleeping draught. Once he was sure the rest of his family was sound asleep from another dose of the sleeping drugs that he'd slipped into their dinner, Micah began the process.

Sprinkling a pinch of the dust over the quartz, he recited a ritual spell of consecration to prepare it before quickly slitting the chicken's throat and letting its blood soak the stone. Theoretically, a chicken wasn't needed, but any ritual or enchantment needed energy. If lifeblood or some other easily accessible source wasn't provided, it would simply take it from the caster. A simple two-rune enchantment like this wouldn't kill him. Probably. It certainly would sap his vitality, making him frail and more prone to injury or disease.

As the blood soaked into the stone, it grew warm in Micah's hand. Quickly, he began inscribing the runes into the quartz, careful to follow the detailed instructions and mathematical proofs laid out in the Ageless Folio. After what seemed like hours, Micah leaned back breathing heavily, his body drenched in cold sweat. The rune was done. There was only one final step.

He cut his hand with the knife and let his blood mingle with that of the chicken on the stone. A primal force slithered into his mind and asked him a wordless question. Three clusters of light appeared, one as white as the sun at noon, another a pale gray, and the final one a single point of starlight in a field of darkness. Micah focused his attention on the sun and indicated his acceptance.

With a crackle of energy and the smell of burning flesh, a tremendous amount of energy transferred from his body into the crystal. His entire body felt weaker, like he'd run for hours without rest or water, and he knew instinctively that he was now one point of Sun attunement poorer.

The dried blood flaked off the sides of the crystal. Where once the quartz had been a rhombus, now Micah held a perfect sphere, slightly smaller than his tiny fist. Before his eyes, it began to grow with an inner light.

New life and energy flowed through his body as he was awarded a point of Moon attunement for his achievement. Apparently, Mursa approved of his first forays into enchanting. Micah chuckled and held the sphere up to the starlight. Now he only needed to let the crystal charge for a couple of days, and he'd be ready to resume his work once more.

16

RECLASSED

While waiting for the class crystal to charge, Micah spent all of his free time at the library studying ritual magic. Really, the apprenticeship was a lucky break on his part. The library was technically owned by a collection of Basil's Cove's richest families. On paper, Keeper Ansom only curated and maintained the books, but the nobles of Basil's Cove knew better than to remove the old wizard. The library was such a disorganized sprawl that without the Keeper, no one would be able to find any of the tomes they needed.

The fact of the matter was that no one family could easily afford all of the books in the library, and usually, each noble house only wanted one or two at a time. While a novel or history book might be cheap, possibly even mass-produced by a printer with the appropriate blessings, grimoires containing spells or other valuable knowledge were rare, often by design. It was obvious, really. It wasn't any harder to print a book containing valuable information on classes, monsters, or spell theory. The rich and powerful just controlled the production of such texts in a mostly successful effort to keep a monopoly over them.

The more Micah thought about it, the angrier he got at himself for how he'd misused his time in his first iteration. With most of

Basil's Cove's theoretical knowledge just sitting around him, most of which was restricted to people of his class, instead, he'd read children's stories. Admittedly, he was a child at the time, but still. It was almost as foolish as his instinctive rejection of his blessing. Mursa gave him the ability to travel to the past for a reason, and he'd be an absolute idiot not to take advantage of that gift.

As for his studies? Ritual magic had always fascinated Micah. Like enchanting, it didn't require an affinity, but by the same token, it wasn't terribly useful in combat. Rituals could be used to see great distances, summon fell creatures, enhance someone's body, change the weather, or any number of things.

Theoretically, the only thing that mattered in a ritual casting was the skill level and experience with the specific ritual of the caster. Unlike spells, they didn't require mana. Casting a ritual was more a matter of scholarship and calculation. Every factor needed to be accounted for, from the phase of the moon to the position of the stars and, more importantly, the processing of the reagents.

Technically, even a first-level ritual caster could use the most powerful rituals devised. In practice, the complexity of even simpler rituals tended to overwhelm any caster without a double-digit Mind attribute and years of research spent on developing the skill.

The results of a failed ritual were much more serious than a fizzled spell. With ordinary spellcasting, either the spell worked or it didn't, but miscast rituals could work in ways unforeseen by their casters. The guidebook warned of teleportation rituals that lodged the user into solid walls, or summoning spells that released eldritch horrors upon the world, as well as more mundane failures that simply stripped the caster of their vital energy and left behind a mummified husk. Micah wasn't sure if the book was overstating the risks as a warning, but he wasn't inclined to push his luck.

Finally, the crystal was charged. Once again, Micah waited for his family to go to sleep before sneaking out to the garden and placing his hands on the sphere. The heat built as the voice entered his mind.

"Error," the genderless voice stated without any inflection.

"Prospective user is under the age of majority. No class can be assigned at this time."

"Override," another feminine voice, clear and beautiful but speaking from a great distance, interjected. "Designate prospective user as temporal anomaly and reanalyze."

That was new. Micah frowned, trying to ignore the way the crystal continued to heat up under his hands. None of the books mentioned anything like this.

"Prospective user is eighteen solar years," the original voice responded. "Adjusting internal records and analyzing skills and affinities.

"Available classes are Magi, Adept, High Wizard, Wizard, Chronomancer, Aeromancer, Healer, Doctor, Herbalist, Surgeon, Librarian, High Spearman, Spearman, Warrior." The voice recited the list emotionlessly. "Please select an option to gain more information about it."

"Magi," Micah choked out through gritted teeth. The interlude while the voices argued had let the heat in the crystal build to an almost-unbearable level.

"Magi," the voice responded. "An advanced class that allows the user to utilize and combine more than one affinity. A focus on ritual casting gives the user bonuses to learning and successfully casting rituals. Magi gain one point in their Mind and Spirit attributes each level and have a high rate of mana growth. To unlock this class, the user must have at least 5 levels in the Spellcasting skill, 1 level in the Ritual Casting skill, and more than one affinity." The voice paused, casting Micah into a pit of agony as the smell of cooking flesh wafted up from his palms. "Would you like to confirm your selection?"

"Yes," he hissed out. Magic flowed into his body, but with the sound of a windowpane breaking, the crystal shattered, rapidly breaking down into a fine white dust. Micah didn't know or care why it happened, instead clutching his still-smoking and blackened hands.

Through a haze of pain, he cast *Augmented Mending* from memory, not even thinking that his status sheet currently didn't show him knowing the spell. Perhaps by a miracle or some intercession of Mursa, it still worked, consuming all of his mana but ending the pain in his hands. Blacked skin chipped and began falling off his palms, revealing pristine pink-white flesh underneath.

Micah looked at his hands in wonder. That shouldn't have happened. Spells took weeks of practice to perfect; even if you knew their words and formulae, you couldn't just cast them. The inflection of the chant and the flow of mana through the caster's body were both delicate skills that couldn't be acquired overnight.

Even if he knew the spell, he didn't have enough mana yet to cast *Augmented Mending* at level 1. Like skills, spells gained levels that altered both their mana cost and effectiveness. At level 1, *Augmented Mending* should have been ruinously expensive and barely enough to heal a serious cut.

He checked his status, face breaking into an immediate grin. He'd gained a point of Moon attunement from "learning" his first second-tier Wood affinity spell, and *Augmented Mending* was already at level 7, exactly where it'd been when he threw himself into the past. Apparently, *Blessed Return* treated spell levels as skill levels.

Even if his mana levels were pitiful due to his low-class level, Micah's high skill level in spellcasting and basic combat magic would be enough for him to start venturing outside the city walls to gain levels. Really, it was only a matter of finding low-level enemies such as feral boars and kobolds until he gained the levels and mana needed to use the entirety of his magical arsenal.

Once he leveled up a couple times, even if his body was nowhere near as rugged as it used to be, the extra Mind and Spirit points from his enhanced class would be enough for him to quickly surpass his previous life.

Quietly, Micah swept up the dust from the crystal and went to bed. He still needed to get up early enough to go to the library and continue his study of ritual magic. His skill level wasn't high enough yet, but he'd already made note of a teleportation ritual and one that would halve the amount of sleep he needed in a week.

Part of Micah was concerned that his master plan involved

fiddling with the very fabric of the cosmos in order to sneak out at night, but at the same time, he couldn't come up with another solution. He could create an energy draught with his Herbalism skill, but it wouldn't be anywhere near as effective as the ritual, and it had some nasty side effects and addictive properties if he used it too often. Plus, the guards would certainly notice if he went to and from the city frequently without a proper explanation. The last thing he needed was to be labeled a spy.

The next two weeks went quickly. During the day, Micah studied ritual magic and astronomy, incrementally improving his knowledge toward the two selected rituals. At night, he cast his spells one by one, unlocking them as he prepared for his eventual sojourn outside the city walls.

Finally, Micah considered himself ready. He'd learned enough enchanting and ritual magic to create a beacon, a target for the teleportation ritual to lock on to. If he was going to train at night, he needed to create a beacon outside the walls, someplace secluded where monsters and travelers wouldn't come upon him.

Greeting the guards, Micah left Basil's Cove early Saturday morning. They didn't inspect him that closely—after all, youth were exempt from the city's tolls per Luxos' edict. They'd probably care a little more when he came back, just to ensure that he wasn't carrying contraband, but even then, most of the guards in his past life hadn't taken their jobs all that seriously. Their actual job was to scare off wandering monsters and bandits, not to regulate the flow of dream leaf into the city. After all, Basil's Cove was a fairly prominent port. Dream leaf, divine tears, drake resin—all of them were smuggled off of visiting ships and into the houses of ill repute in the slums.

Technically, the narcotics were illegal, but the city didn't put a large amount of effort into policing them. So long as users stuck to their ramshackle drug slums in the forgotten districts, the Council didn't even bother to send the militia to arrest them. They kept the forgotten high and complacent regarding their social stature. Frankly, Micah had always wondered if some of the noble houses that made up the Council were actively part of the trade.

Micah looked up at the cloudless sky, enjoying the crisp air of the sunny morning. The hardened dirt of the road crunched under his boots as he walked for almost a half-hour before summoning the Ageless Folio and checking local landmarks. Spotting the lightning-struck pine tree towering above the local forest, he smiled and veered from the path, humming a fast-paced ditty.

Using his spear as a walking stick, Micah made his way through the forest, occasionally checking the Folio for references to landmarks. Once he got turned around—a tree that was felled during his original journey still stood—but before too long, he came upon his target, a mound of boulders and rocks, almost twenty feet high. When he'd first discovered it, four years in the future in his previous timeline, Micah and Drekt had speculated that it was the result of a high-level Earth spell. After all, how else would a pile of boulders appear in the middle of an otherwise flat but densely forested plain?

Walking closer, he spotted his goal: a small circular cave, just shy of six feet tall and wide. As an adult, Micah might struggle getting in and out, but for his current slight stature, it would be perfect.

Kneeling down, Micah smiled once again. He traced his finger around the large pawprint embedded in the moist forest soil. When he and Drekt came upon this place in the future, it'd been the home of an adult dire stoat. From the size of the track, it looked like the stoat, currently a juvenile, had already moved in. A perfect source of experience for a young Magi out and on his own for the first time.

17

THE PLAN

Micah crept to the edge of the cave, pausing to listen for the stoat. For a moment, he heard nothing but the twitter of nearby birds. Then he made out the quiet sound of fur brushing against stone. Perfect.

Sneaking back out of the clearing in the forest around the outcropping, Micah positioned himself with his back to a nearby tree. Dire stoats weren't incredibly dangerous if you could see them coming, but they were fast and liked to attack from the flanks. The last thing he needed after all of his work over the last couple of years was to be killed by an overgrown weasel because he got careless. He summoned the Folio and tucked it under his arm as he planted the butt of his spear against the tree.

"Wake the fuck up, you overgrown hamster!" Micah screamed, wincing as his voice cracked. Going through puberty for a second time was going to be fun. "By Ankros' night, get your tail out here so I can send you back to whatever hell he dragged you up from!"

It was an established fact that the beasts Ankros created were more intelligent than their more mundane brethren. Some even understood Common. Micah didn't know if the dire stoat understood him, but if it could, getting it extra pissed off wouldn't hurt. Even if it couldn't, raising a ruckus outside of its den was sure to grab its attention.

The stoat stormed out of the cave, its elongated furry torso waist-high on Micah's current body, but just over knee height on a proper adult. It wrinkled its nose at him, its white muzzle prominent against its reddish-brown hide. It paused for a second at the threshold of its cave. The oversized weasel cocked its head at Micah, trying to make sense of him.

He cast *Root Spears,* feeling the exhaustion wash over him as the second-tier Wood spell sank into the forest floor. A second later, a series of two-foot-long sharpened wooden spikes exploded from the ground in a large area around the dire stoat. The lengths of wood stabbed in all directions, creating a jagged tangle of undergrowth with the monster at the center.

It squealed as two stakes punched into its side, penetrating fur and flesh to draw blood. The creature squirmed and tried to escape by pulling its body off the spikes, only to widen the injuries. Micah didn't even pause to see the effects of his first spell. He began mouthing the words to *Air Knife* as soon as he'd recovered enough from *Root Spears* to cast again. A blade of air rushed away from Micah's outstretched hand, exhausting his mana and opening a gash on the monster's shoulder.

Quietly, he tried to center himself and focused on refilling his mana pools. For the moment, the stoat was stuck in the center of the *Root Spears* effect, making movement a difficult and painful process. A good thing, because casting the second-tier spell followed by *Air Knife* had almost emptied his reserves. If the animal were to free itself, he wouldn't have much of a choice but to try and fend it off with his spear. An uncertain process at best, given his childish muscles.

After a minute or so, its struggles began to abate as the stoat lost blood. Once it managed to pull itself from the two staves impaling it, Micah tensed his grip on his spear, waiting for the injured animal to charge. Instead, it slipped while trying to climb the blood-slick wood, falling onto another spike.

Micah didn't move from the tree, slowly watching as his mana recovered. He probably had enough for another *Air Knife*, but he wanted to save it in case the stoat made a move once *Root Spears* ended or the creature escaped.

Finally, it stopped struggling altogether. Shortly thereafter, the five-minute duration on *Root Spears* ran out and the wood grew brittle, cracking and falling apart. Micah released the breath he hadn't even realized he'd been holding, the tension leaving his shoulders. The fight was over, but it would take a while to get used to how helpless his tiny body was.

As weak as a dire stoat was, he was level 1 and just shy of fourteen. He needed to temper his usual confidence as an experienced adventurer. If it hadn't been seriously injured by the *Root Spears*, Micah would have struggled to fend it off, let alone come out on top. Still, the spoils of battle were his: one damp, poop-filled cave and enough stoat blood to enchant a beacon.

Micah grabbed the dead monster by its short tail and dragged it into the cave, struggling to move its surprisingly heavy form. Once he made it to the cave, he reached into his backpack and pulled out a large garnet and a smooth stone bowl. Quickly, he filled the bowl with the stoat's blood and dropped the pre-prepared garnet in it.

Wrinkling his nose, Micah brushed away the filth that clogged the cave's entrance before using a small hammer and chisel from his backpack to carve a circle into the floor of the cavern. Dragging the stoat over, he cut it again and used the weight of his body to wring enough blood from the dead animal to fill the circle.

Reciting the precise words of the ritual, Micah removed the garnet from the bowl of blood. It was warm to the touch, and as soon as he removed it, the blood burned with green flames. Standing in the center of the circle of blood, he recited another incantation and placed the gemstone in the exact center of the circle. The circle roared to life with green flames as well, trapping Micah inside as he continued reciting the nonsense words and atonal yelps of the ritual.

Sweat began to pour down his back from the heat given off by the flames as he continued the casting. One wrong word—hells, even the right word but facing the wrong direction—and everything would be wasted or worse. Still, he'd practiced the incantation recorded in his Folio countless times. Micah was confident that he could complete a ritual this simple, even if he were drunk or drugged.

Ten minutes later, it was over, the only evidence that something untoward had happened being the barely visible silver circle etched in the floor of the cave and the charred corpse of the stoat. It was for the best that no one knew about the ritual. Although ritual casting wasn't officially illegal, the Church of Luxos tended to frown upon it and watched those capable of performing the rituals. After all, an incorrect casting could rip a hole between dimensions and unleash a swarm of monsters or a virulent plague, or reverse gravity altogether.

Packing up his hammer and chisel, Micah took note of the shattered bowl and sighed. Apparently, the heat from the flames was too much for the simple implement. He'd just have to make up a story about breaking the bowl when he got home and accept punishment from his mother. She'd probably ground him again.

Not that "sending him to bed" would be all that effective anymore. He fished a second garnet out from the backpack and smiled at the faint red glow deep in the stone. It was the sister of the gem used in the ritual, split from the original rock with the very hammer and chisel he'd used to etch the circle.

The teleportation ritual itself was nowhere near as hard as creating the beacon. So long as he had the garnet, it was really just a half-hour of casting and the sacrifice of the life energy contained in a potted plant.

Of course, there was still the matter of getting back inside the city walls. He'd need to capture a creature large enough to power another ritual but small enough that he could smuggle it back into Basil's Cove. Only then could he create another circle in his bedroom to allow himself to teleport back home once his activities for the night were done.

Walking out of the outcropping, Micah propped his back up against it and pulled out the sandwich he'd packed for himself that morning. Biting into it, he called up his status menu once again.

. . .

Micah Silver

Age 13 [ERROR] / 18

Class/Level Magi 2

XP 51/200

HP 12/12

Attributes

Body 4, Agility 3, Mind 10, Spirit 9

Attunement

Moon 11, Sun 0, Night 2

Mana

Moon 30/30, Sun 0/0, Night 13/13

Affinities

Time 10

Wood 6

Tier I - *Refresh* 10, *Mending* 9, *Plant Weave* 7

Tier II - *Augmented Mending* 7, *Root Spears* 4

Tier III - *Heal 2*

Air 5

Tier I - *Gale* 7, *Air Knife* 10, *Air Supply* 4

Tier II - *Wind Shield* 5, *Sonic Bolt* 4

Tier III - *Updraft* 1

Blessings

Mythic Blessing of Mursa - Blessed Return, Ageless Folio

Skills

Anatomy 6

Enchanting 3

Fishing 1

Herbalism 4

Librarian 3

Ritual Magic 3

Spear 5

Spellcasting 10

. . .

Apparently, there were some benefits to fighting monsters above his level alone. The early levels were the easiest to gain, but even then, it was a bit of a pleasant surprise to earn enough XP for a level after just one kill. Ankros must have awarded him extra experience for his feat.

Glancing over the rest of his status sheet, Micah nodded in approval while chewing the sandwich thoughtfully. His mana growth remained the same from his previous life. Twice his attunement plus 1 for every point of spirit per level after the first. Slightly worriedly, Micah noted that his zero Sun attunement from creating the class crystal prevented him from gaining any Sun mana on level-up. Still, all of the bonus Moon attunement he'd gained from relearning second- and third-tier spells, creating his first enchantment, and casting his first ritual more than dwarfed that loss.

It was unfortunate that he couldn't cast *Sonic Bolt* without drawing attention. As its name implied, the spell generated a lot of noise. Since he'd learned it about a year ago in his past life, the spell had quickly become one of Micah's favorites, launching a ripple of air vibrations at a high enough frequency that eardrums ruptured and soft tissue hemorrhaged. It wasn't the most powerful second-tier spell available—there were plenty of Earth and Fire spells competing for that title—but it was by far Micah's most powerful single-target spell.

Even though the Lancers taught him a pair of third-level spells when he made it to his tenth level, neither really helped him right now. *Updraft* produced an upward gust of wind that would cushion a fall or help Micah jump higher. Theoretically, at higher levels, it would let him fly after a fashion, but the spell was a mana hog and tricky to use. In short, he hadn't found the opportunity to properly level it yet.

Heal was more useful in general, but not to a solo operator like Micah. In a team, it allowed him to heal his companions with a potency comparable to *Augmented Mending* but at range. He certainly appreciated being able to fulfill his role in a party without risking himself overly much, but for self-healing, *Augmented*

Mending was just as good, a cheaper mana expenditure, and higher level.

Finishing his sandwich, Micah stood up and stretched the kinks out of his back before grabbing his spear. Now to begin the next phase of the plan. Basil's Cove's city council didn't listen to the midsized guilds like the Lancers. They might respect them in the same way they did a collection of skilled artisans or craftsmen, but the way the city had fallen in the first timeline made it obvious that the smaller guilds weren't respected.

The only people with political power in Basil's Cove were the noble families that sat on the Council and the Golden Drakes. The Kingdom was more than powerful enough to beat back the Durgh; the only reason for the disaster in the last timeline was a lack of warning. Properly alerted, the nobles could scout out the Durgh and appeal to the King to send in a contingent of Royal Knights, high-level Blessed loyal to the crown.

Micah's only question was how to convince the local nobles and the capital to take the threat seriously. All he could think to do was reveal himself and some of his abilities. This time, if he showed up at the door of the Golden Drakes and revealed his affinity for Time magic as well as an unnaturally high level and skillset, hopefully they'd believe him when he said he had a message from the future.

With a high enough level, he would even feel comfortable revealing that his blessing was Mythic. If nothing else, a Mythic blessing associated with the primal element of Time would get their attention. Maybe then they'd believe that his gift included a "message from the future."

There was plenty of room to go wrong, but it wasn't like Micah had another choice. Even with only sleeping half of the night and constantly fighting monsters outside of Basil's Cove, he'd be lucky to reach level 20 by the time the Durgh arrived. The leaders of the midsized guilds that led the defense were all in their mid-forties, and at least one of them had died without fanfare in the first clash with the Durgh. Micah had no way of knowing how powerful the leaders of the incursion were, but he wouldn't be able to fight them on his own.

As uncertain a prospect as going to the Golden Drakes—a generally arrogant and elitist guild in his previous life—was, it seemed like Micah's only option. He just needed to make himself look like a valuable enough asset that they would drop their veneer of haughtiness to invest in him. After all, Micah thought darkly, the Golden Drakes were well acquainted with looking the other way for some of their more unsavory candidates so long as they showed enough potential to justify such discretion.

Slinging his backpack over his shoulder, he started off into the forest once more. He would need blood sacrifices to create the second teleportation beacon, and he had limited time before the sun set.

18

PRODIGY

M icah walked back from the library. Once again, it was his sixteenth birthday, but this time, there wasn't any tension. Briefly, he relived the moment from his previous timeline. It had seemed so pivotal then; his very future hung on events outside of his control. For some reason, he'd wanted to hurry them forward rather than take a couple minutes to enjoy his last day as a youth.

He chuckled slightly to himself as he took in the setting sun. He already had his blessing as well as enough skill levels to impress any recruitment officer. The past couple years had given him enough time to hone his skills and gain the levels he'd need to prevent being overlooked. Even Micah's body had filled out, his solo escapades giving him the tone and definition that he'd lacked in his last timeline. Already, even with his extensive time in the library, his Body and Agility attributes were at 6 each.

Home was just as he remembered. Trevor wasn't there, occupied on some sort of mission beyond the city walls. His family threw a small party. Also, as he remembered, Esther was excited for cake and his mother pushed him too hard while his father hinted that he'd accept Micah no matter what. It was a touchingly nostalgic moment.

Even though he'd relived this timeline for the last three years, it never seemed as real as the first. The party unfurled like a play, scene by scene mimicking his first time through, almost to the point where he could recite his mother's speech before she said it. The entire experience felt surreal, almost like a dream. His responses were the same, but he felt disconnected, like he was miles away from his family's kitchen.

Micah didn't know when he started thinking of his "new" family as placeholders for his "real" family, but it'd happened. Maybe it was the constant training. He just didn't have the same free time to spend with his family as he'd had in his previous life. Micah knew that his beliefs were irrational and unfair to them, but that didn't mean he could slack on his training. He vowed, probably for the tenth time, to make it up to them once this timeline was fixed and the Durgh attack was averted.

He went through the motions, eating dinner while pretending to be excited and nervous about his blessing. His family bought it. They spent the entirety of the dinner reassuring him rather than noticing that Micah's actions were slightly off. Even if they did notice, they clearly just chalked it up to nerves and didn't mention it out of politeness.

Really, he just wanted to get everything over with. He never loved being the center of attention, and his mother's investment with his blessing bordered on desperate. Finally, Micah escaped and went to bed. Relief filled his body as the starchy cloth of the sheets surrounded him. He fell asleep almost as soon as his eyes closed.

"Micaaaaaaaaaaaaah!"

He woke up the next morning to the sound of Esther screaming at him and jumping on his bed. Somehow she'd gotten his door open without waking him, and now he had a squirming younger sister whipping the pillow out from under his head and beating him soundly with it.

"WakeupwakeupwakeupWAKEUP!" she shrieked at him in elation as he tried to roll over to avoid her blows. "Tell me what your blessing is. Luxos says you have to tell me. I'm still a youth."

"Hold on," Micah croaked out, shielding his head with his right arm as he tried to rub the sleep from his eye with his left hand. "Just give me a second here. I'm still basically asleep."

Esther scurried back on his bed, giving Micah some room to get his bearings, but still holding on to his pillow. He suspected that any efforts to fall back asleep would be swiftly thwarted. Out of options, he shook the last of the sleep out of his system and smiled at her.

"My blessing?" he asked, feigning confusion. "I do recall having some sort of dream about that, but I can't put my finger on it…"

He dodged the pillow thrown at his head and leaned forward to ruffle Esther's hair. She wriggled out of his grasp with snake-like agility and jumped out of his bed, pouting and stomping a foot on his bedroom floor.

"Micah." She put her hands on her hips, mimicking their mother's favorite scolding pose. "You promised."

"I'm not sure I did." He chuckled, pulling the blankets off of himself and letting his feet dangle onto the cold floor. "But I'll let you know anyway. Mythic Blessing of Mursa. She granted me limited power of prophecy, some decent affinities, and a book that has notes and the story of a possible future. Better yet, I got a class and 10 levels. I'm already higher leveled than Trevor."

This time, lying to Esther barely even fazed him. If he was going to join the Golden Drakes, he'd need to demonstrate the rarity of his blessing. Of course, they didn't need to know about the actual time travel. That seemed like the sort of thing he should keep secret just in case it came in handy. Prophecy was a good compromise. Powerful, useful, and given the fact that he'd just lived through the future, not entirely wrong.

"What?" Esther's eyes grew into dinner plates. "Wait until I tell Sandy!" She sprinted out of his room, not even closing the door behind her.

Micah chuckled to himself and walked into the kitchen. His mother was mixing the ingredients for their morning pancakes, but for once, Micah was up early enough to see his father chewing away thoughtfully at his morning eggs and toast.

"You're up early." Jon chuckled, brushing some crumbs from the toast from his bushy mustache. "I take it from your sister's reaction that she had something to do with that?"

"She didn't want to wait to hear my blessing." Micah pulled out a chair and sat down across from his father. "Strange that she's more excited about it than I am."

"Well," his mother called from where she was preparing the pancakes, "don't leave us in suspense either. Tell us what the Sixteen saw fit to give you."

"It's a Mythic Blessing from Mursa." Micah winced at the sound of his mother dropping her cast-iron pan on the floor. She loved that godsdamned pan. "Limited prophecy in the form of a book that details possible futures along with a starting class, 10 levels, and some pretty good affinities."

"Mythic." Micah's mother lurched forward toward the wash basin, her knees giving out under her as she clutched at the counter to avoid following the pan to the ground. "My boy has a Mythic blessing. This changes everything. There's so much to do. I, I have to tell someone."

"Are you certain, Micah?" Jon set down his toast, focusing entirely on Micah. "You don't seem all that excited about your ability. Please tell me you didn't just make something up to get your mother excited. You know she's sensitive on this topic."

"The goddess was quite clear." Micah shrugged, glancing guiltily at his mother as her babbling segued into sobbing with joy. "I just know that a Mythic ability from a Major Deity is going to come with its own problems. There's no way I'll be able to join the Lancers with Trevor, and there's a good chance that I'm going to be sent to the capital for training. I'm not exactly excited to leave everything I know behind."

"Trevor was excited to try and rope you into the Lancers," his father replied with a chuckle. "He was trying to be cagey. He didn't want to pressure you into it, but it sounds like you've picked up on his plans anyway.

"You've got the right of it, though," Micah's dad continued. "Everyone looks at the greater blessings as a gift, but they come with their own share of responsibility. You'll likely end up with your fair share of wealth and fame, but the King is almost certainly going to want to make you a Royal Knight. I don't think I've heard of a common-born with a Mythic gift that hasn't been snapped up by a noble house or the royal family."

"I know," Micah replied. "I don't think I have a choice but to get wrapped up in court politics, and I barely know what's going on. It's like being forced to play a game, but nobody has bothered to explain the rules."

"Another apt description." His dad chuckled. "It's hard to go wrong with the royal family. They have most of the power around here and a pretty decent system for developing new talents. You might be able to get better benefits for yourself by joining a noble house, but it's too easy to piss off the kind of people you can't afford to annoy. If you go that route, it will be all too easy for you to make the kind of enemies that you just can't afford to make. I certainly don't know enough to advise you.

"Don't worry too much about your brother," Jon continued, edging a slice of egg onto his toast before bringing it to his mouth. "He'll understand. As heartbroken as he'll be that you have to leave, he'll be twice as proud for you. I say you join the Golden Drakes. They're a high-tier adventuring guild headquartered in Basil's Cove, but they have ties to the royal family. They'll get you the training you need without ruffling some noble's feathers."

"Thanks," Micah replied sincerely, slightly surprised at the depth of his father's knowledge and analysis. He'd never really thought about it, but Jon made some of the finest tailored suits in Basil's Cove. He likely rubbed shoulders with the same elite that Micah would be dealing with shortly on almost a monthly basis.

"What about Mom?" he asked, eyes flickering back to his mother, who was still mumbling to herself on the floor. "She's taking this a little... differently than I expected."

"Don't worry about her either," his dad said with a chuckle. "You should probably grab some fruit or something for breakfast before you head over to the Golden Drakes' guild hall. I don't see your pancakes being done anytime soon. Other than leaving you to starve, she'll be fine and bragging about your gift to the neighbors in a couple hours."

Smiling and whistling a tune, Micah grabbed two slices of fresh bread and an apple before setting out. The sun was barely up and the regular morning noises of Basil's Cove were rather muted. He took advantage of the lack of foot traffic to cut through the usually busy market district.

The Golden Drakes' guild hall stood right at the border of the Noble Quarter. You didn't need a letter of recommendation to get past the nobles' guards, but they certainly watched Micah like a hawk as he walked up to the door.

Registering with the Golden Drakes was a very different experience. Micah was given roughly the same questionnaire as the Lancers, but after turning it in, he was left to cool his heels for almost four hours. Finally, a plump man, sweat beading on his face and wearing a cloak embroidered with gold thread, entered Micah's waiting room.

"Mr. Silver." The stranger pulled out a handkerchief and blotted his damp forehead. "I've been assigned to talk to you about your application. You've indicated that you have a Mythic gift for prophecy and 10 Time affinity. Obviously, these abilities are incredibly powerful. It isn't uncommon for people to fake having a powerful ability in order to gain wealth and acclaim."

The man sat down in a chair across from Micah with some relief. During his entire rippling descent, Micah couldn't help but notice how very *pink* this man was. Whoever he was, he certainly wasn't accustomed to missing a meal or traveling outdoors.

"At this time," the man continued, "you can withdraw or modify your application without penalty. Be aware that I am a certified Truth Seer. If you refuse to withdraw your application and you are found to be lying, I will be quite cross and the penalties will be very strict."

"I understand." Micah nodded. "Just tell me what I have to do."

"Simply put both hands on the table," the man replied, slightly breathlessly. Apparently, he struggled for oxygen after the simple act of pouring himself into the chair. "I will need to hold both of your wrists while you recite your abilities, and I will be able to tell if you're telling the truth or not. Very simple."

Micah extended his hands. The stranger took them in his own and muttered something. Micah felt his arms goosebump as a static charge went up them. He shuddered briefly from the sensation before making eye contact with the stranger, who nodded at him.

"My name is Micah Silver." He chose his words carefully. "I have a Mythic Blessing from Mursa, Goddess of the Moon and Magic. Part of that blessing includes a 10 affinity in Time magic and limited knowledge of future events, specifically in the next two years. I am a level 10 Magi. I also have a book that aids me in learning new spells and abilities. This book contains details about the spells I have learned."

"Truth," the man replied, his mood lightening considerably. "Please state your other affinities for the record and I'll send in the next inspector."

"Before I state my affinities," Micah continued, steeling himself, "I feel obliged to let you know that there will be a Durgh incursion in about two years. I believe they are amassing now, but when they come, their numbers will be sufficient to overwhelm both Westmarch and Basil's Cove. As for my affinities, Wood is 6 and Wind is 5."

"Truth and truth." The man frowned. "Unless your actual gift is one related to deception or hiding your abilities, you believe in all of the statements you've made today. Obviously, I am not in a position to make a decision on your prophecy, but I will escalate your claim. You can be sure that a committee will investigate its veracity as soon as possible."

19

WITH GREAT PURPOSE

Micah thrust his spear into the shade ogre's chest, sinking the head deep through the tightly coiled muscles to its heart. The creature bucked against the daemons holding it steady once or twice and died, slumping in their grip. One of them leaned forward, sniffing the ogre with its great wolflike head before releasing the inert body.

"Very good, Micah," Brenden complimented, the slight hint of an accent clipping his voice as he nodded approvingly. "You slightly overextended on *Gale Thrust*, but that was a superb exercise in mana control."

Micah planted the butt of the spear in the ground and held it vertically, leaning against the weapon as he panted, sweat streaming down his face. The other daemon prodded the dead shade ogre, whining softly. Both of them were Onkerts, the weakest of the five known daemon breeds. Resembling gorillas with the head of wolves, they were by far the most summoned daemon due to their "low" energy costs.

He shuddered remembering that cost. Four pigs. A half-hour per daemon per life, cut and bled in accordance with the ritual and cast into the flames. The Church of Luxos disapproved of daemon summoning, but they'd never gotten around to banning it entirely.

The summoned daemons were too useful to the ruling class, both as shock troops and magically enhanced laborers.

Their weakness was relative. Ritual magic could be used to summon other lesser creatures such as elementals or spirits. The spells were easier and the costs were lower. Of course, someone as arrogant as Brenden would never stoop to such half-measures. The difficulty of the ritual, price, and unruliness of the creature were half of the point behind summoning daemons. It was almost a status symbol to the man.

"Now, Mr. Silver," Brenden said as he continued down the dungeon's hallway, motioning for Micah to follow him, "for the next target, I want you to disable it using *Paralytic Sting*. We need to make sure that your Wood magic doesn't fall behind. We both know that the actual goal is for you to earn enough mana to cast fifth-tier spells so you can start learning Time magic, but there's no reason for us to neglect your Spellcasting skill and weaker affinities."

"Sure, Mr. Thrakos," Micah agreed, trotting to keep up. "I still think it'd be quicker to let me fight the monsters."

"You"—Brenden Thrakos turned, an eyebrow raised, and snorted at Micah while looking him over dismissively—"are an investment, Micah. You're level 12, but we're in a level 15 dungeon. I'm not even sure if you'd be able to solo any of the monsters in here, let alone beat them in a timely fashion. No, we need you to gain levels so you have the mana for Time magic. You'll land the killing blow on each monster as we've been doing up until now."

"But what about my skill levels?" Micah frowned. "If I'm only delivering killing blows, I'm only going to gain levels. Sure, my mana pools will increase, but that'll be it. I won't gain any skill levels in Spellcasting, let alone in a specific spell."

"Micah." Brenden whirled on him, a flash of annoyance in his eyes that he quickly buried under a cake-sweet smile. "This is how all of the nobles do it. You learn skills until you earn a good enough class. Then you gain experience until you level up enough to have the mana to train your martial arts and spells. It might not be how the stories talk about it, but trust me. This is how everyone serious does it."

Ahead of them, the Onkert tackled another shadow ogre; the hulking creature's ability to hide their presence was entirely useless before the daemon's acute noses. One of the Onkert wrestled the crude greatsword from the ogre's hands while the other twisted its arms behind its back. By the time Brenden and Micah came into the room, one of the daemons had kicked its knees from behind, bringing the almost ten-foot-tall monster to its knees. The other drew its head back, exposing its throat to Micah.

"Now," Brenden continued with the air of someone explaining advanced mana theory to a goat, "use *Paralytic Sting* to disable it and then finish it off with a *Sonic Bolt*."

Micah cast *Paralytic Sting*, coating his right hand in a glowing green sheen of mana. He stiffened his fingers and jabbed the hand into the side of the struggling ogre's neck. The spell discharged into the monster, causing its eyes to cloud and its motions to quiet. The spell didn't do any damage, but even at a fairly low skill level, it could utterly paralyze a monster below level 25 for almost a minute.

It had better, Micah thought as he gritted his teeth. *Paralytic Sting* was a third-tier spell and used a good portion of his mana to cast. Seconds later, after a nod from Brenden, Micah unleashed a *Sonic Bolt* at close range into the ogre's skull. Blood began to flow from its nose and ears, but it continued breathing.

"Again," Brenden said impassively, motioning with his hand. The Onkert holding onto the ogre's head gripped it by the hair and lifted it up, closer to Micah.

"This doesn't feel right, Mr. Thrakos." Micah looked down at the paralyzed helpless ogre, bleeding and immobile before him.

"I believe my hearing must have been scrambled by your use of a sonic spell in an enclosed space," Brenden replied, his voice dangerously calm. "I told you to use the spell again, and I thought I heard you questioning me."

Gritting his teeth, he cast the spell again, killing the creature and emptying himself of Moon mana. Checking his reserves grimly, Micah noted that he still had a little bit of Night mana left.

Whatever he'd thought the Golden Drakes were, his training had been something else. As soon as his abilities were verified, they'd given him a lavish suite and luxuries he'd only dreamed of while working for the Lancers. A couple days later, they'd brought in Brenden Thrakos, a talented wizard and martial artist with affinities in Wood and Air.

Training under Brenden was completely different than his time with the Lancers. He hadn't been assigned to a team or sent on any missions where he might ever be in danger. Instead, the guild "power leveled" him. Brenden had taught him a couple additional spells and a martial art, the Wind Spear, but after that, it was just a matter of sending him through the same level 15 dungeon over and over again.

It had done wonders for Micah's experience and levels, but it was a remarkably hollow endeavor. He didn't really have any friends at the Golden Drakes guild, instead spending almost all of his time with Brenden. There wasn't any camaraderie or risk, just the day-to-day chore of landing the finishing blow on a monster he would ordinarily struggle with. Honestly, if it hadn't been for the knowledge of his previous life, Micah suspected that he wouldn't even know how to fight right now.

Even Wind Spear was a bottom-tier martial art that he practically had to beg out of the Drakes. It was evident from their dismissive response to his requests that they just didn't see much value in him learning combat abilities. The handful of skills and spells they'd taught him seemed more like an attempt to placate and humor him than actually make Micah a more powerful spellcaster. As long as he kept gaining skill levels in Spellcasting and levels in Magi, none of the supervisors really cared what he did.

The entire system was cold and impersonal, but as he'd been informed at least a half-dozen times in the last six months, the Golden Drakes were a big business. They only treated him well because he had the potential to be a high-level Magi in a rare affinity. Beyond Micah's Time magic, decent Wind and Wood mages were a dime a dozen to a guild like the Drakes. They still likely would have hired him, but he would have spent the first five years of his training protecting miners seeking ore in the Great Depths to prove his worth, a thankless and dangerous task.

Only then would they have bothered to put him in a combat team and send him to the dungeons to earn money and gain proper levels. The higher echelons of the guild could compete with the lower tiers of the Royal Knights, but pretty much everyone else was a foot soldier or support staff, and that hierarchy had been made clear to Micah from day one.

"Good." Brenden nodded at the dead ogre. "We have two more before the boss fight and I want to make sure you've recovered what mana you can just in case we need you for an emergency heal. Take a five-minute break; we'll be working on your spear form from here on out."

Micah grunted back at his instructor, more than anything wishing to return to his days on the Lancers when it was just Drekt, Jo, Sarah, Will, and him. They'd never managed anything worthy of a bard's song, but he still had plenty of fond memories.

Sometimes they'd been victorious, sharing a toast as they looted the junk-filled packs of a clan of kobolds. Others, they'd ended up running for their lives, puffing for breath as they fled a cave or ruin they'd been exploring. Surprisingly, some of his most cherished memories were of them fleeing, Jo and Drekt cackling like madmen while they were pursued by monsters well over their level.

All of their adventures hadn't mattered all that much in the long run, but they'd certainly made Micah feel alive, like he was part of something greater and that his daily efforts mattered in some small way. Even if he didn't accomplish all that much, there was something to knowing that each level and point of mana was something that he'd struggled and bled to earn.

Still, as dissatisfied as he was, at least the Golden Drakes listened to his prophecy. Almost immediately, they'd dispatched scouts to the Great Depths outside Westmarch to verify his prediction. If it would save his friends and family, Micah was more than willing to put up with the Drakes leeching all excitement and joy out of being an adventurer.

"Your five minutes are up, Mr. Silver." Brenden began walking ahead. "Try to avoid overextending yourself this time."

Clenching his jaw, Micah stood up and followed the man to the next room. If he was lucky, they would finish early and he'd have some time at the guild hall to himself before his afternoon exercises. He was almost never lucky.

That night, a knock on Micah's door dislodged him from his study of ritual magic. Brenden had insisted that the rituals would eventually become a key part of his Time magic repertoire once he leveled up enough to use fifth-tier spells. Micah hadn't complained. The topic was interesting; certainly more fun than spearing restrained monsters, and it reminded him of happier days working with Keeper Ansom.

"Come in," he called, slipping a felt bookmark into the grimoire before closing it and turning in his seat to face the door.

Brenden stepped in, stiff and formal. He glanced over Micah's room, taking in its neat state and the stack of books by his reading desk. The gaze dissected every imperfection, looking for a reason to scold him. Finally, after finding none, Brenden grudgingly nodded his approval.

"I've come to check up on your studies, Mr. Silver," he stated, his tone clipped under the weight of his accent. "I see that you're reading *Taraken's Intermediate Mutations*. How are you progressing on your transference rituals?"

"Fairly well." Micah nodded, summoning the Folio from his wrist. "I've been more interested in the summoning and translocation rituals. I keep running into references of using an inert metal like lead to offset the energy spikes caused by a recent meteor shower, but I haven't been able to figure out how the lead would interact with Akh, Tel, and Bo runes."

"Immaterial." Brenden shook his head, annoyance flashing through his eyes. "You were told to focus on transference rituals, specifically energy transference, as it is a key component of Time magic. Tel and Bo runes aren't used in transference rituals, so learning them is a waste of your time."

"But I've hit a bit of a wall on transference," Micah answered, trying to hide the hint of a whine from his voice. "Both translocation and summoning use transference to fuel their rituals. I figured a practical application of transference might help it all make sense to me."

"Mr. Silver." Brenden crossed his arms, clicking his tongue at the younger man. "I've had people with the Deceit skill try much better excuses than that on me. It's not going to work. Get back to studying what I've told you to study. It'll be for the best in the long run."

"Sure," Micah replied with a sigh, flipping the pages in the Folio until he was looking at his notes on transference. "It's not that hard, just exacting and time consuming. I really think that I'd be better motivated if I had a more practical discipline to apply the transference to."

"You will soon," Brenden said, his face a mask of boredom and vague annoyance. "The guild leadership has verified the prophecy you revealed when you joined the guild. The Durgh are massing. Already the call has gone out for the Royal Knights. Together, the Knights and the Golden Drakes are going to crush the nearby Durgh outposts to put them on the defensive and head off any attack."

"You mean I'll finally get to battle with the rest of the guild?" Micah jumped up from his chair, barely noticing the pile of expensive tomes tumbling off the table from the force of his movement.

"No," Brenden replied, the faintest hint of a sneer curling his lip. "You will be going to the capital for further training now that the extent of your gift has been revealed. A seer is *far* too valuable to risk in the front line."

20

GOODBYES

The market bustled around Micah as he followed Brenden. The older man strode imperiously through the crowds, forcing them to part around him. A few people shot disgruntled glares in his direction, only to look away upon noticing the sigil of the Golden Drakes on his lapel.

The insignia might protect the two of them from any overt reactions to Brenden's imperious behavior, but it did nothing to silence the angry muttering. No one said anything definite, but for every face that turned away after realizing the forces Micah and Brenden represented, there was another voice grumbling indeterminately just behind their backs.

Finally, Brenden stopped in front of an upscale boutique specializing in high-end adventuring gear. Looking the well-decorated, midsized building up and down, Brenden clicked his tongue and sighed.

"Quit dawdling, Mr. Silver," Brenden called over his shoulder, annoyance on his face. "This store is barely adequate, but it'll have to do. There's hardly anything better in this hamlet."

"Basil's Cove is a city," Micah corrected halfheartedly. He knew that Brenden didn't actually care, but it still rankled him that the older man would try to denigrate his home in such a petty way.

"There are over thirty thousand people living here, and we handle almost all of the trade up and down the Horn Coast."

"Thirty thousand?" Brenden sneered back at him, stopping in the doorway to turn around and face Micah. "The capital has over a million. The Kingdom itself has almost ten million citizens. Maybe thirty thousand is more than a hamlet, but I don't know why it even matters. It's little more than a rounding error. The difference between Basil's Cove and a real city is infinitely larger than the distance separating this provincial 'city' from a hamlet."

"Why are we shopping anyway?" Micah asked, trying to change the subject and deflect Brenden's temper. "I never get to leave the compound, and then suddenly out of nowhere, you tell me we're going to the market."

"Simple." Brenden turned back to the shop and walked in, finally letting the pair of people that had been waiting to leave while he ranted at Micah slip out. "The Sixteen have heard my prayers, and in their mercy decided to deliver me from this rural hellscape. You are being transferred to the Golden Drakes' home office in the capital, which means that I am free to return to a city with actual restaurants, bards that know how to tune their lutes, and theaters that will run performances with more sophistication than constant pratfalls and fart jokes."

"No one said anything about this." Micah's forehead furrowed as he followed his irritable mentor into the store.

"I just said it now." Brenden didn't even bother to look back as he swept through the store before stopping in front of a display of robes and travel packs. "Consider yourself both in the loop and informed. Now get over here so we can get you fitted for your travel apparel. I don't want anyone to accuse me of breaching my contract with the Golden Drakes because you showed up to the capital without appropriate equipment."

Brenden snapped his fingers above his head, drawing a series of frowns from other shoppers, but summoning an attendant that hurried over. She was young, pretty, athletic, and wearing a skirt that was cut mere inches from immodesty. Obviously, her employer had hoped that adventurers would spend more time looking at her than the prices of the wares they were purchasing.

Loneliness washed over Micah as his memory flashed back to his previous life with Jo. She'd been a little too wild for him, prone to dragging him away at midnight to sneak into a temple for a tryst or an active dungeon for a date. Jo was a consummate adrenaline junkie, but in that timeline, only near the end did he grow out of being a shy librarian's assistant.

Things never would have worked between them. She wanted more excitement and adventure than the Micah of that timeline could provide, but when things were good, they'd been almost perfect. There was just something pure about fighting monsters all day before returning to camp and giggling at dumb inside jokes while the moon filled the sky.

Even after Jo had suggested that they break up, he'd held those memories close. She was right—once the infatuation of the early relationship had worn off, it became harder and harder to keep up with her. Micah had liked spending time with Jo, but the idea of climbing a cliff at midnight just to dangle their feet off the edge started to seem less "romantic" and more like a dangerous chore that would leave him exhausted the next day.

After the breakup they'd remained friends. At first, Micah had been hurt and remained fairly quiet to avoid starting drama in the party, but eventually, he'd realized that it was for the best. Although there was an unmistakable chemistry between Jo and him, they'd just met at the wrong time. He had neither the energy nor the maturity to keep up with the woman. Then again, neither did the slew of men she'd dated after him.

His stomach dropped. Knowing it was for the best didn't change how he felt. The fact that Jo could date who she wanted didn't make it any easier to see her laughing with someone else.

He took a deep breath, the air shuddering in his throat. Brenden glanced at him and promptly dismissed Micah's concerns as beneath his notice.

By the time he'd reset the timeline, they'd settled back into being friends once again. Their relationship never became physical after the breakup, but Jo had become a confidante. They'd shared their fears, concerns, and plans under the starlight, and things between them had been almost like before. There'd been no one on the team that he trusted more than Jo. He knew that if need be, they'd have died for each other.

Micah sighed, forcing his hands to unclench. She had. A lot of people had.

Brenden sniffed at the attendant dismissively, drawing Micah's attention back to reality.

She blushed before speaking hesitantly. "Welcome to Haarvash's Emporium, kind sirs." Her voice trembled slightly as her gaze fixed itself to the Golden Drakes badge on Brenden's collar. "My name is Miranda. Please let me know if there's anything I can do to be of assistance."

"My ward"—Brenden nodded toward Micah, not even bothering to look at him—"needs travel clothing. I don't know the first thing about fashion or attire in this area, but he can't be an embarrassment to me. Outfit him with travel apparel and a pack full of clothing and bring him back to me."

"You do know that my father is a tailor, Mr. Thrakos?" Micah asked, not really expecting Brenden to acknowledge him. "If all we needed was to get me fitted for clothing, we could have just visited him."

"Enough, Mr. Silver," Brenden said, cutting him off. "It's unacceptable for my ward to be clad in provincial hand-me-downs. If we're forced to acquire your attire here, I'll be damned if you're clothed in anything less than the best that Basil's Cove has to offer."

"Silver?" Miranda's eyes brightened as she looked at Micah once again. "As in Jon Silver? We carry his work here. His embroidery is to *die* for."

"Whatever." Brenden rolled his eyes and turned away from the both of them. "So long as he doesn't end up looking like a farmer in an ill-fitting suit. I know I'm not giving you that much to work with, but do your best."

The door chimed, causing Micah to look up. His breath seized in his throat as he saw Sarah and Jo Redflower walk into the shop. She was just as beautiful as he remembered, laughing at some joke from her sister as she brushed some hair from her face.

"Cute, aren't they?" Miranda chuckled as she approached Micah with a tape measure. "Both of them come in here shopping at least once a week. I can introduce you, if you'd like."

"I just feel like I know them." Micah smiled weakly. "But it can't be real. Like they're from a dream or something."

"Miranda!" Jo shouted, waving to flag the attendant down as she power-walked over. "Did you get any of the new scabbards in? I need something that will accent that armor I bought last month."

Brenden stepped in front of her, frowning with his arms crossed. Jo stopped short, barely avoiding plowing into his chest.

"Your friend is occupied, young lady." Brenden scowled down at her. "She's currently helping outfit my ward. You can gossip with her once she's finished with her work. Until then, amuse yourself elsewhere."

Jo opened her mouth to say something, only for Miranda to shake her head. Micah did his best to avoid eye contact. Even without Brenden's arrogance, he didn't feel ready to see Jo again.

His emotions swirled as she glared at the both of them. Her gaze focused on the insignia on Brenden's shoulder, transforming her mouth into a thin line. Her eyes flashed as she shifted her attention to Micah and Miranda.

"Fine," Jo replied, turning back to Sarah. "If they give you any trouble, Miranda, just let me know. Not everyone is afraid to stand up to the Drakes."

"Your friend is safe," Brenden snorted. "Don't overvalue yourself. I'd take her if I wanted, and there's nothing you could do about it. It just isn't worth sullying my reputation on a dalliance with a provincial trollop."

Jo turned red, her mouth opening to issue an ill-advised response. Sarah grabbed her sister's wrist, interrupting her and shaking her head. Brenden smirked and walked away, clearly dismissing the two of them.

"Sorry about that, Miranda." Micah smiled weakly at her. "It's probably for the best if we get to shopping. The sooner we buy what we need and get out of here, the lower the chance that someone aggravates Brenden enough to make him lash out."

The actual shopping was fairly quick. Miranda efficiently took his measurements, periodically slipping him sympathetic looks. Afterward, she brought a selection of outfits for him to peruse. Micah was hardly a talent on his father's level, but he knew a fair amount about the proper cuts and stitching of fabric. Between Miranda and him, they were able to put together a full ensemble of clothing and travel garb that would hopefully stand up to the capital's scrutiny.

Brenden barely looked at it before escorting Miranda to the front desk to make the purchase. Micah stood awkwardly, his hands stuffed in his pocket, waiting for the entire transaction to be completed. A woman cleared her throat behind him, prompting him to turn and see Sarah standing next to Jo.

"Excuse me," Sarah said, an uncharacteristic smile on her face. Jo scowled at him.

"Uh, yes?" Micah responded.

"I couldn't help but notice that you appear to be a member of the Golden Drakes." Sarah extended her hand, a far cry from her usually judgmental and sarcastic self. "My name is Sarah Redflower and this is my sister, Josephine Redflower."

"Micah Silver." He took her hand; Sarah's calluses from constant combat contrasted with his own soft digits. "It's a pleasure to meet both of you."

"Why were you harassing Miranda?" Jo jumped in suspiciously. "Even if you are rich, you can't just bother a girl like that. It's not like she's a piece of property that you can go out and purchase. She's her own person with rights."

"Silver!" Brenden shouted impatiently as he walked toward the door. "Quit flirting with your girlfriends; we need to get moving if you're going to catch your carriage."

He smiled weakly at both of them. Melancholy swept over him as he realized that in this timeline, he'd probably never see either of them again. As much as he wasn't ready to see them again, he wasn't nearly ready to let them go. There was so much he hadn't processed, so much he hadn't said, but there was nothing for it. The hands of fate were pulling them apart with a force that couldn't be denied.

"Goodbye," he said sadly, smiling slightly. "It was nice to meet you. I feel in a different life, we could have been friends."

21

THE CAPITAL

Bitollan, City of Lights and Spires, was as majestic as its name sounded. Even at night, magelights of a dozen colors illuminated the soaring buttresses of the city's towers. Micah tried to enjoy their splendor as he rode the carriage in, but his excitement was tempered by the knowledge that he was missing the battle for Basil's Cove at that very moment.

Deep down, Micah knew that it was all worth it. As much as he wanted to be on the front lines, elbow-deep in combat and risking his life side by side with his former friends, he didn't have any real basis for that desire. Still, he couldn't help but compare himself to the nobles and Golden Drakes members that had fled Basil's Cove in his previous timeline. The fact that he had sacrificed everything to keep his family safe didn't make him feel like any less of a coward.

He jolted slightly as the carriage rolled over a rut in the road. Micah sighed and closed the window. He'd have plenty of time to gawk at Bitollan later. For now, he just needed to focus on the advanced ritual book Brenden had given him when they'd parted. He'd been reading it for most of the weeklong journey, and by this point, Micah was convinced that the book was on the Church of Luxos' "burn on sight" list.

Where most of the books on rituals he'd been introduced to up until now walked a fine line of acceptability, this one focused entirely on the transfer of anima. True, every ritual or enchantment needed anima, the life force behind a living being, to power it. Up until now, the portions of the rituals related to anima had been fairly perfunctory. The caster sacrificed an animal, presumably and hopefully livestock or a monster, and its life force was added to the ritual.

This book, *On Life and Energy* by Karin Dakkora, was decidedly more in-depth. Micah's inner bookworm found the ruminations on the nature of the soul fascinating, but the appendices to the book were concerning. Where normally a book on theory would simply opine and try to make sense of observations, *On Life* contained descriptions of detailed experiments. Ones that involved captives being used as batteries until everything vital was drained from them, leaving the victims as little more than empty, drooling husks.

The fundamental point of the book was that ritual and primal magic could feed upon anima to empower them. More than half the book was devoted to finding ways to improve on the drawing and transference of anima as part of ritual casting. The author was disdainful of most recorded spells and rituals, decrying them as the safe dabbling of the mediocre. Micah did agree that rituals spelled out in the last third of the book by Karin were much more exciting, but in the "these might rip a hole in reality" sense rather than anything he was eager to try.

Frowning, he pulled out the Ageless Folio and searched for Karin Dakkora's name. Thanks to the magic of the Folio, he found her almost immediately. One of Keeper Ansom's records had detailed a noble party of heroes defeating a dark archwizard that swore loyalty to no god.

Apparently, her collection of summoned daemons had raided nearby cities indiscriminately, and all of the Sixteen had joined together to request that their greatest champions rid Karell of her plague. The record went on for pages about how her fell powers spat in the face of the natural order and threatened the entirety of Karell with some sort of unknown incursion from "the outside." It didn't detail what "the outside" was, but Micah got the distinct impression that it wasn't a friendly or happy place.

He closed the book with a sigh and dismissed the Folio. *On Life* was almost certainly a banned book. He wasn't entirely sure why Brenden had insisted that he study it, but his time with the Golden Drakes had taught him that asking that sort of question was frowned upon. Hopefully, someone in the capital would be more willing to shed light on the situation.

Micah closed his eyes, trying to will himself to sleep. Bitollan was still miles away. As striking as the city was at night, there'd be plenty of time to gawk at its sights and get answers tomorrow.

At first, sleep eluded him, the occasional ruts jolting him to wakefulness, but before long, he slipped off into a dreamless slumber. Occasionally, he'd return to wakefulness as the carriage rumbled over rocks and ruts in the road, leading to a rather fitful slumber.

He awoke to a callused hand shaking his shoulder. Micah sat up, blinking against the harsh white magelights that illuminated the coach driver in the carriage's open door.

"Come now, milord," the man spoke with a thick country drawl. "Let's get you inside and into a comfier bed so I can unhitch the horses."

"Milord?" Micah cocked his head at the man. "My father was a tailor. Last I checked, I was fairly far from being nobility."

"Whatever you say, milord," the driver responded with a chuckle, climbing out of the coach to give Micah access to the doorway. "I'm a forgotten, so even having a trade smells a bit like nobility to me."

"Plus," the driver continued, "if I'm dropping you off at the right place, I'm definitely calling you milord on account that I don't wanna get beaten by a palace guard for disrespect." The man jerked his head, indicating the twisting marble towers behind him that glowed in the magelight.

Micah stepped out of the carriage, craning his neck to take in the massive building. Absently, he noted that his jaw was slack, but he couldn't help himself. Mammoth walls of smooth stone surrounded the building, their gem-inlaid runes practically humming with energy.

The building itself looked like an artist's rendition of a castle, only stretched to twice its normal height.

Internally, Micah balked. No building of stone could be that thin and that high. Even though he *knew* that magic was being used to lighten and strengthen the stones, part of him recoiled, expecting the towers to collapse under their own weight at any moment.

"That was my reaction the first time I saw it too, milord." The driver removed Micah's luggage from the rear storage shelf on the carriage. "Course, I grew up on a farm. Most magic we saw was the local lord's elementalists, cleanin' out the kobolds before they could run off with that year's harvest. Here in the capital, there's magic on every street corner. Hells, the buildings themselves are practically works of art."

"Where—?" Micah tried to recollect his thoughts. "What is this? I was just supposed to be transferred from the Basil's Cove Golden Drakes' branch office to headquarters in Bitollan."

"This here's the Royal Knights' headquarters." The coach driver set down Micah's luggage next to him with a dull thud before holding his hand out slightly expectantly. "Far as I can tell, it's mostly administration, training, and research here. Field soldiers are housed a good grip away."

"As for the Golden Drakes?" The man shrugged indifferently. "They have connections to the royal family; everyone knows that. I don't know why I was directed to bring you here, but I know you're expected. They'd have impounded my carriage the minute I drove it into the Royal District if you weren't."

"Milord." The driver coughed slightly, glancing down at his empty hand. "The Golden Drakes settled up your bill, but it's been a hard couple of winters. The tab itself barely pays for what I owe on the carriage. If you'd be so kind as to spare some attunement, I've got three little ones and a fourth on the way."

"Oh." Micah shook his head, trying to clear the fog of drowsiness and wonder. "Of course. What kind of attunement would you prefer?"

"Sun would be great, milord." The coachman beamed at Micah,

displaying a pair of missing teeth. "Name's Gheblan, milord, but my friends call me Gheb. You look like you're in a bit over your head, so I thought I'd throw a little advice your way. Folks like me? We try and stay away from the rich and powerful sort. Sometimes things work out like in the fairy tales for the little ones, but more often than not, we step on toes we shouldn't step on and hurt feelings that can't be hurt.

"Not to say you're clumsy, mind you." Gheb frantically waved his hand. "No, the rich just have their own way of doing things. It's too easy to say the wrong thing to the wrong person and *pfff*... You're gone." Gheb waggled his fingers, a serious note in his eyes. "Happened to my cousin Reggie. He saved a count's prized horse from having to be put down after it threw a shoe. Count brought him out to his estate. Had a feast in his honor and everything. Then Reggie had a couple too many drinks and complimented the wrong young lady. Count's son killed him in front of everyone to win back her honor. At his own feast."

Gheb crossed his arms, shaking his head. "You stay alert and you stay careful. You didn't know where you were going until you arrived? Well, that's a surprise, and surprises aren't accidents in Bitollan. You're playing a dangerous game, and it sounds to me like someone else is already a couple moves ahead of you."

"What should I do?" Micah asked him worriedly, touching Gheb's bicep to transfer the Sun attunement to him. "I could not drink. Try to avoid saying something I shouldn't to the wrong person."

"Wish I could help you more." Gheb shrugged. "Not drinking might show a lack of trust or hospitality. Could be an even worse insult than talking about someone's grammum."

"You there!" a voice shouted from the gatehouse as a tall, well-built man wearing sparkling silver chain armor and carrying a halberd began walking toward them. "Move the carriage or we'll have it impounded for loitering."

"That's my cue." Gheb chuckled, hopping back up onto the carriage with an agility that belied his husky frame. "If you're ever in a spot of trouble, head on down to the Charcoal Ox in Soap Town and ask for Gheb. Doesn't smell the best down there on account of the rendering plant, but that just means we don't have to deal with as many guards. I can't promise much, but if I were you, I wouldn't be trusting any promises right now."

With a whistle and a flick of the reins, the horses started trotting away, their hooves clacking against the cobblestones. Micah turned as he heard the sound of the guard's footfalls approaching him. The man looked him up and down impassively. Micah shifted self-consciously as he compared his battered travel linens to the guard's gleaming armor and helm.

"Are you Micah Silver?" the man asked, leaning forward slightly to squint at Micah's face. "I was told you'd have a spear."

"Oh." Micah coughed nervously, motioning toward the oilskin-wrapped spear that leaned against his suitcase. "Yes, I'm Micah Silver."

"Good, we've been expecting you." The guard nodded, satisfied with Micah's response. "Let's get you inside and settled in." He turned around and began walking back toward the gatehouse.

"Wait." The guard stopped abruptly, forcing Micah to twist his body to avoid running into him. "That coach driver didn't bother you for a tip, did he?"

Micah nodded uncertainly.

"By the Sixteen." The guard shook his head angrily. "Pests, the lot of them. He was paid in full at the outset of your journey. He probably took you for an easy mark and ran a grift on you."

22

ACADEMY

The next morning, Micah was woken by a sharp and officious knock on his bedroom door. Struggling to clear the sleep from his eyes, he yawned and dragged himself out of bed. He padded in silence across the bedroom's plush carpet, his feet sinking almost to his ankles in its soft embrace.

A second before Micah reached the door, it opened on its own, revealing a tall, rail-thin man wearing an immaculately pressed formal suit. He ran a stern glare over Micah's rumpled bedclothes and clicked his tongue.

"Of course you don't have proper attire." He sniffed irritably. "I don't suppose you've even seen a doublet before."

"I know what a doublet is." Micah cocked his head, trying to make sense of the mostly bald stranger critiquing his wardrobe at the crack of dawn. "My father is a tailor after all. I just wasn't told that I would need formal clothing. I was just told to grab my adventuring gear and report to the carriage post for a trip to the capital."

"Good." The man threw up his hands. "His father is a tailor. I'm sure that will impress the Third Princess and the Duke of Essenbrox's second son. You can inform them that your crinkled and out-of-style drapings are actually a fashion statement of some sort. They'll be quite impressed."

"Well, what am I supposed to do about it?" Micah snapped back at him, annoyed at the older man's one-person community theater routine. "I came in after midnight, haven't had a full night's sleep, and no one bothered to tell me formal wear was apparently an essential component of my wardrobe. Who in the name of the Sixteen are you anyway?" Micah asked incredulously before continuing in a calmer tone. "I have a couple dress shirts, but nothing more formal than that. Unless you can scare up something else for me, we'll need to make do with what I have."

"My name is Martin Osswain." Martin squinted down his nose at Micah. "The Royal Academy has assigned me to be your batman. It reflects on me when you show up to morning classes unprepared and looking like a particularly disheveled turnip salesman."

"Aren't batmen supposed to show more deference?" Micah let some of his annoyance bleed into his voice. "I literally don't know why or what I'm doing here and already I'm catching guff from you."

"Hmmf." Martin stepped past Micah into the bedroom before looking around and crossing his arms. "The batmen for the children of full nobles or knights might show respect in honor of your parents, but you as a person aren't anything special yet. At the moment, you're nothing but potential, hormones, and trouble. If you get knighted, I will be the first to insert a deferential 'ser' before your name. Until then, you're just another talented cadet that I have the unfortunate duty of trying to keep out of trouble. Do you know how many of those the Academy sees?"

"I'm assuming that you're about to tell me a very high number," Micah responded dryly, walking over to his luggage and laying out a dress shirt and pair of trousers.

"Well." Martin paused, slightly nonplussed. "Yes. The Academy accepts over twenty scholarship students with a Rare Blessing from a Major Deity, Mythic blessing from an intermediate deity, or one of the rare Chosen from a lesser deity each year. In addition, there are approximately five high-class scholarship candidates like you that are either the Chosen of an intermediate deity or the recipient of a

Mythic Blessing from a Major Deity. Of those twenty-five, about eight to nine make it to graduation. The rest fail their exams or become too crippled to continue."

"What about the nobles?" Micah asked, donning his shirt and fiddling with the ivory buttons. "Surely they aren't crippled and killed at the same rate. I would presume that their families would have something to say about that."

"Of course not," Martin snorted, eyeing Micah's clothing dubiously. "They're from established brands. Most of them aren't seeking full knighthoods anyway; simply a well-rounded education from the best tutors available. For you? Knighthood is the only way for a scholarship student to graduate. I would advise you to take your studies seriously."

Micah opened his mouth to speak, but Martin interrupted by saying, "Wait, is that *boar* tusk you're using for buttons?" He snatched Micah's hand away from the shirt, bending down to peer more closely at the shirt. Disappointment and disgust warred with each other in his eyes.

"Yes," Micah snapped back. "I know that it isn't in fashion, but once again, I wasn't told that formal clothing was required, and even if I was, I simply don't have the money to invest in more valuable ivory and cloth. Unless the Academy is going to pay or clothe me, these shirts are simply going to have to do."

"Fine." Martin released his hand, pacing back and forth through the room's thick carpet. "You'll make a laughingstock of me, but apparently selfishness is all your kind knows. I'm sure you'll enjoy treading upon thirty years of my honor like it's a cheap rug thrown on the floor of your family's hovel."

Micah frowned at Martin and opened his mouth to respond, only for the older man to keep speaking, ignoring Micah's unhappiness altogether.

"Your first class is Introductory Enchanting." Martin didn't even look at him while reciting the itinerary. "Enchanting will last about four hours on Mondays and Wednesdays. On Tuesday and Thursday mornings, you will study Intermediate Ritual Magic. Every afternoon, you will continue to work on your spellcasting. Fridays and Saturdays will be devoted to level growth in the Academy's captive dungeon. You will have Sundays to yourself to *socialize*." Martin practically spat out the last word.

"Socialize?" Micah asked, frowning in Martin's general direction. "What is there to do around here?"

"You'll hardly have the time, boy." Martin sniffed at him. "Your betters might be able to find a moment to visit the botanical gardens, restaurants, museums, and zoos attached to the campus. As for you? If you want to make Knight, you'd better put aside any childish dreams about having a fun and rewarding school life. You're here as an investment, not to play foolish games."

Unwilling to argue with the ornery older man, Micah finished dressing himself under Martin's disdainful gaze. Given that he was still unsure of his surroundings and the social order he'd been thrust into, a wait-and-see approach seemed best. After all, he wasn't an expert on noble etiquette, but as far as he could tell, servants weren't supposed to chew out and mock their masters. Whatever was happening, it wouldn't be too late to stand up for himself after he learned whether he could safely do so.

Class went about as well as Martin had predicted. Honestly, Micah wondered if some of the nobles had blessings related to sight, because one of them simply looked at him when he stepped into the classroom and stated "boar tusk" despite being over forty paces away. After that, none of the noble cadets even looked at him, and Micah ended up seated with the other scholarship students in the back of the lecture hall.

Their section of the classroom was silent, following the professor's words as best they could yet largely unable to ask questions. Whether it was how far back they were or another example of class stratification, Micah was simply ignored both times he raised his hand to follow up on something the professor said. Quickly, he learned his lesson.

In the front of the room, it was a very different story. The professor would promptly answer any questions asked of him, likely afraid of the powers behind the students. As for the cadets, some of the nobles paid attention, but most of them simply chatted quietly with each other.

Micah had no idea how much, if anything, they were actually picking up from the lessons. On the other hand, he also didn't know how much it mattered to them. As far as he could tell, they were simply at the Academy so that they could later brag about their graduation as an achievement. Learning was a distant second to networking.

Despite his chilly reception, to Micah, the class was a dream come true. The professor went in-depth over many of the more troublesome equations related to basic strength enchantments, including some that still troubled Micah. Although he took notes of his own to help cement the lesson in his memory, he was thankful for the Ageless Folio. The itch on his wrist was distracting, but he knew that it was taking down all of the lesson word for word.

Lunch was more of the same. Micah didn't even bother trying to sit with the nobles. Their section of the cafeteria was a minefield. From one glance, Micah could tell that their seating arrangements betrayed a complex web of social and political alliances and rivalries.

In short, the cafeteria was the game board for a complicated and deadly social game. Even if he'd been welcomed at one of the tables, he probably wouldn't have taken the offer. It presented too great of a risk of annoying someone else important.

Instead, he sat in the corner with the rest of the scholarship students. They ate in silence. Even when Micah tried to ask them questions about their affinities and classes, most of them just grunted in response. Only one even bothered to talk to him, a rather lonely boy named Bart. Eventually, Micah just gave up on speaking to anyone else. He wasn't at the Academy to make friends, and Bart's rambling stories about how much he missed his dog and fishing would have to do.

That afternoon, each student was assigned their own mentor for their mana-related classes. Some of the cadets that focused more on physical combat practiced their martial arts rather than spellcasting, but the model was the same for all of them. The instructor would force them to wear items enchanted to stimulate their mana regeneration. Then they kept casting spells at a series of dummies and targets until they ran out mana entirely. As soon as he was unable to cast any further spells, his instructor tossed Micah a practice spear and forced him to repeat basic spear forms until his muscles screamed.

It was hardly an interesting way of training, but it allowed the students to safely and efficiently raise skill levels in their respective spells and martial arts. With everything else going on, it was strangely therapeutic. He didn't need to think about his future or what was happening around Basil's Cove. All Micah needed to do was try and shorten the chant to *Air Knife* as he cast it over and over again.

The next morning was a repeat performance. Micah attended his intermediate ritual magic class, only to be snubbed by a different and more advanced set of nobles. Again, his wardrobe gave enough clues about his social status to strangle any socialization before it could begin. With a slight smile on his face, Micah went to the back of the room once more in order to find an open seat near the scholarship students. The middle-class cadets kept to themselves while the professor gave a very in-depth lecture on the role of lunar phases in ritual casting.

Friday and Saturday involved Micah going into a dungeon while Martin supervised him. Surprisingly, the fussy old man was a level 44 Aquamancer, more than capable of defeating any of the monsters in the dungeon. It was possible that Martin's advanced level had something to do with his dismissive attitude, but Micah suspected that the old man was just an asshole.

Unlike Brenden, Martin actually let Micah fight the monsters, occasionally giving his spear form or spellcasting a halfhearted compliment. Really, Martin looked bored more than anything. The one or two times Micah got himself into trouble against monsters above his level, Martin stepped in, but the rest of the time his "servant" seemed more focused on reading the small paperback book he brought into the dungeon with him.

Micah's head hit the overly stuffed pillow. One week of school at the Royal Academy was in the books and it certainly could be worse. True, the training regimen assigned to him was grueling and there were more than vague hints that he could easily be crippled or killed at the Academy if he didn't live up to his potential, but other than a cold shoulder from the nobles, no one had mistreated him. He wasn't a target for scorn; simply a non-entity until he proved himself.

He suspected that things would have gone worse if he'd tried to force the issue and sit with some of the nobles. Still, the lack of friends was a bit concerning. Micah worried that years of training with no one to talk to but Martin would crack his psyche like an egg.

He closed his eyes. He'd have to get in touch with Bart and spend some time relaxing. If he'd learned anything about the difference between the Golden Drakes and the Lancers, it was that the Lancers knew the importance of downtime. He'd have to think of something to do. Bart was earnest, but he certainly wasn't imaginative.

23

SETTLING IN

"Why don't you just ask your batman for help with your homework?" Bart asked quizzically. "Whenever I struggle with a concept, I just ask Davis for help. He grumbles a lot, but I've found his guidance much more useful than the hands-off teaching and theory we get around here."

Micah glanced at him, a slight frown on his face as he debated shushing the man. They were in the Royal Academy's library, a massive wood-paneled room lined with stained glass windows to let in light. When the sun set, staff would ignite magelights behind them, ensuring that the room was constantly lit in a rainbow of colors. The bookshelves around them were silent, the only sound being that of pages turning as other students tried to study.

"I don't think Martin would do that," Micah whispered back. "He doesn't really strike me as the helpful sort. He mostly just makes fun of me and threatens me. Any time I try to talk to him, it always just ends up with him reciting statistics about how many candidates fail Knight training."

"Davis doesn't even bother." Bart shook his head. "We all knew the risks when we signed up. Even if the odds are against me, earning a knighthood and entering the nobility is just too big of a prize to turn down. I mean, what are our other options? Risk our lives daily as adventurers in a minor guild? We might get a little bit of attunement, but they wouldn't have the resources the Knights do. You might end up with a couple more levels than the average person, but eventually, you'll grow old and slow."

"I wasn't given a choice." Micah pushed away the tome he was studying, resigning himself to unproductivity. "I joined a fairly prominent guild in my home city. After training me for a while, they stuffed me in a carriage and I ended up here."

"But they tell you everything when you sign up for the scholarship?" Bart asked. "After you get your blessing tested, they tell you the odds and how much help they'll give you. I barely understood the contract they had me sign. I didn't even know the first thing about how much attunement I'd need or what exclusive access to trainers and a beginner dungeon meant."

Bart blushed. "I needed my dad to help. He was scared of Davis, but the two of them talked it out. They explained to me that I could always join a guild controlled by the throne rather than the Knights, but that I would end up fighting monsters right after my introductory training. I don't know the first thing about fighting. Even with the strict testing here, it seemed like better odds for me."

"But what about the constant threats of maiming and dismemberment?" Micah asked, the beginning of a frown on his face. "Martin barely even talks to me, but when he does, he absolutely will not shut up about how I'm an embarrassment that will end up crippled or dead within the year."

"Martin." Bart tapped his chin for a second. "Wait, is your batman Martin Osswain?"

In response to Micah's nod, the other student shook his head, eyes going wide. "Why in the name of the Sixteen would you accept a sponsorship from Knight Osswain?"

Micah winced as Bart raised his voice. Apparently, in his surprise over Micah's response, he'd forgotten that they were in the Academy's library.

"Knight Osswain was one of the prime actors in the Elven Purges," Bart whispered furiously, library decorum all but forgotten.

"He was caught hoarding forbidden books and experimenting on captured elves. The senior knights spared him for his service to Pereston, but he's been taken off of active duty in disgrace. It was the talk of the Academy last year."

"First of all"—Micah made a shushing motion, trying to ignore the eyes of the other students drawn by Bart's voice—"I didn't pick anything. I already told you that I was told to get into a carriage, and the next morning, Martin was tearing into me. Second, since when are you plugged in to Academy gossip? Third, what do you mean Martin's a Royal Knight? I thought he was just a tutor or something?"

"All of the batmen are either knights or senior squires assigned by a knight." Bart shook his head, whispering excitedly. "They told us all of that at orientation. A knight needs to sponsor a scholarship candidate for them to get into the Royal Academy. The order rewards the knight based upon their scholarship candidate's achievements. A lot of knights will take a year or two off of actively adventuring to hone their craft and train promising disciples. Davis said that most scholarship students don't become squires or knights because their sponsors don't support them." Bart patted Micah's hand sympathetically. "He says that if you're prepared, there shouldn't be trouble. The Academy doesn't recruit students with weak blessings. They just want to make sure that we apply ourselves and prove our loyalty to the Kingdom."

"What happens if your sponsor doesn't help you?" Micah asked, leaning back in his chair and closing his eyes. "I think Martin's even showed up to my dormitory drunk once."

Bart frowned at him, confusion warring with unease on the man's face. He closed his book, tapping the cover quietly for almost ten seconds before he responded.

"Knight Osswain is notorious." Bart bit his lower lip. "He has enough seniority that no one else is going to take you under their wing, but even before he was disgraced, the other knights would talk about how he was a bit of a bully. Now? I can't imagine how bad he is. If you're on your own, all I can say is study hard. The other scholarship candidates don't talk much, but there's supposed to be a give and take. The work here is hard and there are risks if you fail, but at the end of the day, we're getting a once-in-a-lifetime chance to break into the upper classes. The Academy is a dangerous opportunity, but all of us are here by choice."

"Not all of us." Micah sighed, chewing on his lip as he looked at the closed book in front of him. Once again, he toyed with the idea of telling Bart more about his situation. Ultimately, he held back. Talking too much had already stripped him of his freedom. Micah might trust Bart more than anyone else at the Academy, but that didn't mean he should spill his secrets to the boy.

"Worry about what you can control." He smiled weakly at Micah, his mouth barely visible in the dim library. "If your sponsor isn't going to go above and beyond to help you, I guess the only thing you can do is work hard. We're not supposed to talk about the tests," Bart whispered, licking his lips nervously, "but they can get pretty bad. You should be all right if you take things seriously and don't just assume that your blessing will carry you through. Plenty of candidates with more potential than you or I have failed out because they got complacent."

"What happens if you fail anyway?" Micah asked thoughtfully, leaning back in his chair as he focused on his skittish companion. Bart's eyes were practically bulging out of his head as they swiveled back and forth, searching for anyone that might overhear their conversation.

"Bad things, Micah," Bart muttered. "It's all decided by your sponsor. If they like you and you fail by a hair? You get punished. With Knight Osswain as your sponsor? Don't fail. Your tests will likely be harder than anyone else's, and the punishment won't be anything to play around with. Just don't."

Micah frowned. This was probably the most serious he'd seen Bart. Usually, he was a little much, an attention-starved bundle of energy talking Micah's ear off at every opportunity. It was more than a little jarring to see him like this.

"I guess I just have to study twice as hard as everyone else, then."

He smiled at the agitated boy unconvincingly. "If my only options are success or whatever unspeakable punishment Martin wants to inflict on me, I'm going to choose success."

Bart chuckled, a strained titter as he looked away. Micah sighed. Whatever their earlier conversation, the other boy was too on-edge now to talk freely.

Micah picked up the hefty book he'd been reading earlier and opened it. The words on the page seemed to run away from him as Micah tried to make sense of them, his mind spinning. The individual letters were hard to read, written in spidery hand and faded after the passage of years. He simply stared at them insensibly in the library's dim light.

As much as Micah needed to study, the focus just wouldn't come. Mentally, he shrugged and began flipping through the pages of his book, consigning its contents to the Ageless Folio. He could catch up on his reading later. For now, he had an entire library at his fingertips and the ability to seamlessly record anything he saw. It would be a shame not to use it.

24

SCHOOL LIFE

After two weeks, Micah truly started enjoying his time at the Academy. As upsetting as his time with the Golden Drakes had been, especially when Brenden would simply tell him to drop a course of study because it wouldn't benefit his "build," the Academy felt like it was going to make it all worthwhile. The nobles might be snobs, and the scholarship students might be too terrified to bother with, but finally, he was actually learning something.

Of course, that didn't mean that Micah wasn't trying to make some friends despite his handicaps, however ill-advised that might be.

"Micah, look!" Bart shouted, his eyes wide as he pointed at the bored and vaguely malnourished-looking tiger.

Micah felt for the creature. It was just trying to get some sleep while Bart and a handful of entitled noble children shrieked at it from just outside the enclosure.

"I see the tiger, Bart." Micah tried to smile, hoping that his overly enthusiastic friend wouldn't notice how forced the expression was. "Tigers certainly are majestic creatures, but there's no real need to get overly excited. We are at a zoo, after all; there are plenty of animals on display."

"You don't understand, Micah." Bart turned back to him, joy written across his face. "You grew up in the country and actually had a chance to adventure before you were sent to the Royal Academy. I'm from the city and my dad's a stonemason. Other than horses, I've never gotten a chance to see anything larger than a dog."

"What about leveling?" Micah frowned slightly as he asked the question. "Don't you have to delve into your dungeon with your batman too? I'd expect you to encounter all kinds of fantastic creatures down there."

"That doesn't count." Bart's happiness disappeared like a snuffed torch. "Reginald scares the hell out of me and keeps threatening to kill me if I don't meet his benchmarks. He won't even tell me what the 'benchmarks' are. Plus, everything down there is trying to kill me. It just isn't the same."

"How about we go to the HJ Thiel Aquatic Exhibit next?" Micah asked, trying to rekindle Bart's earlier excitement. "Basil's Cove is by the ocean; we don't have access to many freshwater biomes. From what I've read in the pamphlets, there should be a bunch of species that neither of us have seen there."

"That sounds splendid, Micah!" Bart's smile lit up his face before he led the way toward the indoor aquatic exhibit. Apparently, the water needed careful temperature regulation provided by enchantments, meaning smaller, enclosed and indoor exhibits.

Quickly, he caught up to Bart, a slight smile on his face despite himself. Micah wasn't entirely sure how Bart had picked up a Mythic Blessing from an intermediate deity; the man was slightly dumber than the average pile of bricks. Still, the larger man was earnest, friendly, and sported an infectious laugh.

Under ordinary circumstances, he probably wouldn't have even befriended Bart. A simpleton was far from his speed. That said, he was glad he'd taken the time. There was something straightforward and sincere about Bart, like a large, friendly dog.

Whenever they spent time together, Micah didn't have to watch his every word. Mostly because Bart was too stupid to actually blackmail him, but also because Bart was loyal to a fault. As far as Bart was concerned, they were friends and that was the end of it. Through thick and thin, they'd have each other's backs.

Micah suspected that the world wouldn't let them off that easily. The Royal Academy was the sort of place that ate naive and trusting souls like Bart alive, but at least for now, he was a friend and a refuge from the constant stress of their training.

"Look at him go." Bart whistled in awe as Micah walked up behind him. For some reason, Bart had made a beeline past the merfolk, kelpie, and diamondfish exhibits, instead standing enraptured before the tank devoted to a family of river otters.

One of the sleek mammals darted past, catching one of the silvery fish loaded into their tank by the keepers. Quickly, the creature surfaced, rolling over onto its back to eat its treat while making eye contact with Bart and Micah.

"They're beautiful animals, aren't they?" Micah nodded in the otter's direction, barely able to draw Bart's attention as the other man pressed his face against the glass of the cage.

"Just look at their little paws, Micah." Bart looked back at him, a slight wistful smile on his face. "Do you think that the Royal Knights will let me get a pet otter when I make full Knight? I know that's a long way off, but all the Knights are rich, powerful, and respected. I don't really know what I'd do with all that attunement... Maybe buy my family a better house, but I want something for myself. I just didn't know what it was until today."

"Sure." Micah tried to keep the emotion from his voice. It was hardly a sure thing that either of them would survive to graduation, let alone be in a position to demand exotic pets. "Once you become a full Royal Knight, a pet otter probably won't be a problem at all."

The rest of the visit to the zoo progressed smoothly, ending with both of them paying more attunement than they should for some sort of well-seasoned grilled meat on a stick. He enjoyed the meal, but Micah couldn't help but worry about the future. Half of the reason he spent time with Bart was to avoid thinking about the topic.

As for his actual combat capability, Micah made steady progress. Slowly, but still at a rate that raised Martin's bushy white eyebrows,

Micah's skills ticked up month by month. He grew in level at a slower rate now that he wasn't simply killing monsters immobilized by Brenden, but the levels did come, bringing more mana in each of his pools that allowed Micah to cast more spells and with greater force.

Finally, when he reached level 19 deep in the Academy's captive dungeon, Martin motioned for him to stop. Micah leaned against the wall, sweat pouring down his body due to his exertion and the dungeon's elemental fire theme. He'd heard that the nobles had access to dungeons whose themes didn't make the actual act of delving in them physically uncomfortable and sweaty, but Micah did have to admit that the shorter line for the fire dungeon was a boon when he wanted to do as many runs as possible in his limited time.

"Micah." Despite being on the third floor of a dungeon, Martin's voice was as stuffy as ever. "Now that you're level 19, we need to talk about your first class specialty. You've been surprisingly thoughtful to date for an individual of your experience, but this is a decision that impacts your entire future."

"I've heard other students mention specialties," Micah huffed in between taking a drag from his waterskin, "but no one really talks about them in any real detail. All I know is that they're a big deal and they happen at level 20."

"That makes sense." Martin nodded thoughtfully. "Most noble families treat their research into class specialties about as seriously as they do initial classes. As far as I know, you get one every twenty levels, with the power of the specialty raising significantly each time. Depending upon your class and skills, different options will be available. It's fairly common to get an upgrade to a martial art or field of magic, but there are rumors that some of the noble houses have figured out how to unlock esoteric specialties that grant bonus attributes at each level.

"Not all of the specialties are fully explored," Martin continued, his dry voice washing over Micah. "We have some ideas about the more basic specialties, but my goal isn't to grant you a bonus 2 HP per level or the ability to speed the research of your own spells. If you're going to earn a knighthood, you'll need Time magic.

"You've learned well over these months," Martin grudgingly acknowledged. "Your Spellcasting skill is at the level that you could earn a class specialty in Chronomancy, allowing you to use those spells much more freely. Unfortunately for you"—Martin smirked, quickly flashing his teeth at Micah—"the rules for getting an elemental specialty are well-known. All you need is to know one Time spell when you level up.

"Of course"—Martin's unpleasant smile spread across his entire face—"the lowest-tier Time spell that I'm aware of is in the fifth tier. Although you can cast some fourth-tier spells, the limit between four and five is a fairly serious one. Actually, casting a fifth-tier spell is a daunting task for anyone under level 30."

"But how do I learn one?" Micah frowned. "I've been trying to make it to fifth-tier magic for almost a full year and I still have a ways to go. I suppose I can keep practicing fourth-tier spells until my Spellcasting skill levels up enough, but that seems awfully slow."

"One year to cast fifth-tier magic and he's complaining," Martin snorted. "Boy, I can only cast sixth-tier spells. The fifth tier took me a decade. Being a prodigy gives you some shortcuts; it doesn't let you circumvent the entire race."

"How am I supposed to learn Time magic, then?" Micah cocked his head to the side. "Everyone keeps telling me that there aren't any known spells below the fifth tier, but there has to be some way to earn the class specialty."

"That's true," Martin agreed. Glancing about, he cast a quick spell, creating a bubble of water around the two of them that blocked out all ambient sound. "Has anyone told you the tale of Karin Dakkora?"

"No," Micah replied slowly, his memory flashing back to the almost-certainly illegal book "gifted" to him by Brenden. It was still in the bottom of his travel luggage; Micah hadn't dared to bring the book out since his arrival at the Academy. After all, what was the need when the Folio retained a perfect copy of any book he read?

"It's not a tale that the Church would tell." The usual boredom and arrogance in Martin's voice were replaced by reverence. "Karin was the greatest ritual caster that this planet has ever seen. Her research was absolutely revolutionary. She posited that the magic given to us by the gods was little more than a weak and feeble thing. A toy or bauble that you'd use to distract a child to stop them from accidentally putting their hand on a hot stove. She created rituals of a magnitude and elegance that they could've changed the world and ushered in a new golden age.

"But." Martin spat on the ground. When he looked up, his eyes burned with a dangerous zeal. "The Sixteen grew jealous of her, fearing that her power had begun to rival their own, and sent their champions to lay her low. Despite a simple Rare Blessing and fighting alone, she struggled with the divine champions for a decade while she sought the ritual that would finally allow her to defeat them once and for all. Unfortunately, despite holding out for all that time, she was finally defeated.

"And yet"—Martin practically hissed the word as he stepped closer to Micah—"some of her works survived. Collected by her followers and those interested in *true* power." Martin's smile didn't reach his eyes as he said, "She created a ritual. One that lets a caster draw power from the life of another in lieu of mana. Right now, all that stands between you and the fifth tier is mana, right, boy?"

Micah nodded uncomfortably. The sweat pouring down his back had little to do with the heat.

"Good." Martin's eyes flashed with a predatory gleam. "I know that you've been focusing on ritual magic. I'm going to teach you that ritual and you're going to use it to cast a fifth-tier Time spell the next time we venture into this dungeon. And if you don't?" Martin snapped his fingers, causing the sphere of water to pop like a soap bubble around them. "You'll have confirmed my suspicions about you—that you've been wasting my time for these past six months. By the Sixteen, boy, if you can't make this work, I'll kill you myself."

25

THE RITUAL

Micah shook his head as he read over the spell formula for *Foresight*. It was more than just mana; the diagram for a fifth-tier spell was exponentially more complex than a fourth tier. Even then, he struggled with casting *Healing Wave*, the only fourth-tier spell he'd managed to learn so far. The worst of it was that there wouldn't be any extra chance to cast the spell. He'd have one chance to use the excess mana from the ritual to bridge the gap and cast it. If it fizzled, they might have the materials for a second try, but that'd be it. Without the mana, he was doomed to fail.

Spells weren't something you'd cast on your first time through. Each of them involved a complex set of nonsense words combined with precise body positioning and hand motions. Maybe a caster could succeed with a first-tier spell on their first try, but each tier became significantly more difficult. His third-tier spells all took two to five attempts before Micah mastered them well enough to cast them consistently. *Healing Wave* took a week of daily exercises, failure after failure followed by the long wait as he bided his time waiting for his mana to slowly recharge.

Theoretically, *Foresight* was the simplest known Time spell. It would let Micah see shadowy outlines of what would happen over the course of the next second. The spell used an insane amount of mana and only lasted for five seconds, but during those five seconds, the caster was next to invulnerable. Any reasonably fit person could dodge almost any blow simply by knowing exactly where it would land.

He closed the book he was studying from and glanced at the door to his bedroom. Ever since he and Martin returned from the dungeon, his batman had informed the Academy faculty that Micah was "feeling ill." He'd spent almost the entire week locked in his bedroom with Martin patrolling outside, preventing any external contact.

Micah withdrew the Folio from his wrist and went over the conditions of the ritual once again. At least that was one spot where he was fairly confident of success. He'd taken advantage of his week of forced solitude to closely study the materials provided by Martin and Brenden.

The ritual itself wasn't terribly advanced; it just involved the removal of certain limiters designed to prevent an ordinary energy transference casting from running out of control. The book contained some worrying hastily scrawled notes with words such as "explosive" and "spontaneous combustion" describing what happened to casters who didn't use one hundred percent of the mana provided by the ritual.

He could see why the Church warned people against using the ritual. It provided extra mana, but it took almost twenty minutes to prepare for each casting. Once the ritual was completed, the caster needed to immediately use the mana channeled into them by it. Casters couldn't hold on to any of the mana past the immediate casting of a spell, making it only useful in very specific situations such as sieges, where a spellcaster had adequate time to prepare. Worse, the chances of miscalculating the mana granted by the ritual and accidentally magically crippling yourself were astronomical.

Still, it wasn't like he had any options. Martin hadn't been joking when he threatened him. Frankly, Micah wasn't sure that Martin really joked about anything, and his next scheduled foray into the dungeon was tomorrow. For better or worse, in about twenty-four hours, he would be using a dangerous ritual to fuel casting a spell far beyond his capacity, all while a murderous assistant watched his every movement.

Maybe if he hadn't gone through Cornell Dover's training in his first life, the task would appear even more daunting. The Sixteen knew that neither the Golden Drakes nor the Academy had prepared him to cast spells under pressure. Luckily, Micah had his fair share of experience casting spells beyond his capability in high-stress situations.

For what felt like that twentieth time in the last six months, he reflected upon the different training philosophies of the Lancers and the Golden Drakes/Royal Knights. The crux of it was that the Lancers had cared the most about his willingness to push himself to the limit while training. After that, they'd put him in dangerous situations that they considered within his capabilities in order to teach him how to operate under fire and stress. Their guild might not recruit the same quality of adventurer as the higher-tier guilds, but each and every one of them, no matter how base their gift, were given a fighting shot to actually make something of themselves.

The higher-tier training regimen of the Academy and Drakes, on the other hand, seemed strangely inefficient. His entire time with the Golden Drakes, Micah had been coddled beyond belief. He'd learned spells from books and slew bound monsters. Only when he'd reached a decent level had he been sent to the Royal Academy, where he actually got to fight, but even then, he'd only learned a limited number of spells and martial arts, all in peaceful classroom environments.

Now, he was given a do-or-die test. He'd always wondered about the numbers of crippled and dead candidates that Martin quoted at him. It didn't seem to make sense that scholarship cadets were dying en masse, given how sterile and safe the training was.

With the new "test," everything locked into place. His fellow scholarship candidates' silence and haunted eyes. The prodigious casualty rate. His casual dismissal by the noble and knight heirs.

They might be in the same school, but the methods used on the scholarship students were much rougher. Martin, with the Academy's tacit endorsement, sought to push him beyond his limits. If Micah succeeded, he'd have access to Time magic at an incredibly low level, hugely increasing his power. If he failed, in all likelihood, he'd be a burned-out husk, discarded and incapable of serving the Kingdom any further.

Maybe then the nobles would recognize him as someone worth befriending. After the cold shoulder he'd received, Micah wasn't sure he'd trust any of the nobles, but as he sat staring blankly at the Ageless Folio, it made a depressing kind of sense. Until he completed his tests, Micah was an unproven product. More likely to die or be discarded back into the massive pile of common citizens he'd been drawn from than to amount to anything.

He returned the Folio to his wrist and started preparing for bed. Maybe he should have panicked, wasted the last week trying futilely to escape from the Academy, only to end up hyperventilating in the corner when he failed. It just all seemed so useless to him. At this point, worrying about factors outside of his control wouldn't help him. He had enough skills in Ritual Magic and Spellcasting to give him a credible shot at success. There just wasn't much more he could do. A good night's sleep and maintaining a positive attitude tomorrow would do more to ensure this success than any more last-minute studying.

Closing his eyes, he focused on measuring his breathing. He counted his breaths in and out as he worked on stilling his racing heart. As his body calmed and his thoughts slowed, Micah smiled slightly, his eyes still closed. He couldn't help but reflect on how this all began, insomnia keeping him from sleep at his parents' house. Once again, his future was out of his hands, and all that was left was to wait for sleep to take him.

The next morning, he ate a full breakfast and performed some basic calisthenics in the privacy of his shag-carpeted bedroom. He briefly reviewed the textbooks and star charts, making a handful of last-minute notes and adjustments to the ritual's formula. Finally, Martin knocked on his door, opening it a second later.

"It's time, Silver." The older man tossed Micah his spear before shifting the bag containing the ritual's components over his shoulder. "This time, I'll clear all of the monsters until we get to the boss room. He'll be the sacrifice to power the ritual. I don't want you wasting any of your mana. You'll need to be in peak condition if this is to have any chance of success."

Micah nodded, not bothering with a verbal reply. He had any number of witty and biting responses, but ultimately, what would they do for him? Martin was over twice his level and could cast sixth-tier combat spells. Escape was an impossibility. His only chance at survival was success, and antagonizing his bodyguard cum executioner didn't seem like a wise course of action.

They walked in silence through the halls of the Academy toward the basement's dungeon entrance, Micah's eyes burning a hole into Martin's back the entire time. Finally, they stood before the double iron doors that marked the beginning of the dungeon, and Martin turned back to Micah.

"I know you hate me, Silver." His tone didn't contain any sympathy, just a dry recitation of facts. "You know that I was Commonborn, right? Years and years ago, I stood exactly where you are now. A talented kid, full of arrogance and vinegar. I hated my batman when he put me through my tests. This is just how things are done. A candidate can't grow properly without stress, without a threat forcing them beyond their limits. Don't expect any mercy from me. If you fail, you die. I just want you to understand that you are walking a path that hundreds of great men and women walked before you, and it is a large part of what made them into the Knights that they eventually became."

Martin shrugged indolently. "I don't have anything like confidence that you'll succeed. I actually expect you to fail, to be frank, but you will be given your chance. Each of the tests are a necessary gateway, separating those that have a powerful blessing from actual warriors."

"Each of the tests?" Micah asked incredulously, frustration dripping from his voice. "How many more times will you have to threaten my life?"

"I don't know." Martin opened the gate to the dungeon, motioning for Micah to follow. "Did you think that I was the one that planned all of this? No, the Academy isn't anywhere near that haphazard. Each scholarship student's tests are personally handed down by the Master of Curriculum. If you make it past this, I'm sure she'll tell me what the next step is. *If.*"

The journey through the dungeon was almost unbearable. Floor after floor, the tension just kept building. Micah didn't even have a meaningful battle to release the stress knotting up his shoulders and back. Martin simply batted aside monsters Micah had struggled against last week, summoning giant pillars of water to crush them into dust against the dungeon's walls. They didn't even slow their advance until, finally, Martin and Micah stood before the large stone archway that signified the door to the boss's lair.

Martin only paused for a second, ensuring that Micah was still behind him, before the old man walked into the chamber. The boss, an eight-foot-long salamander that clung to the ceiling and spit streams of fire that could melt a metal shield to slag, didn't stand a chance.

Martin raised both of his hands above his head, shouting an eldritch incantation. Eight tentacles of water reached out from Martin, pulling the surprised creature from the ceiling with an audible pop before binding its legs, tail, and snout. Martin strolled leisurely into the lair to admire his handiwork before dumping the sack full of materials into the center of the room and tossing a wickedly curved knife to Micah.

"The moment of truth is upon us, Silver." Martin stepped back, finding a pillar to lean against as he observed the entire chamber. "Use the ritual to cast the spell. It's too late to run and you know the price of failure. There's only one path for you, boy, and that's forward."

Micah bit his lower lip, jogging into the room. Quickly, he began scratching the runes into the dungeon's stone floor, periodically checking his notes to ensure that the inflections were correct. Next came the reagents, dusts made from gemstones, and the ground-up bones of powerful monsters. Each rune flared briefly as the correct mixture filled it. Finally, he placed the symbolic catalysts at their positions, embedded in the runic circle that would channel the spell.

Almost twenty minutes to set up the circle, slower than expected. Micah's heart began pounding in his chest as he looked at the dagger in his hand. He began reciting the words of the ritual, enunciating each word as he motioned with the dagger, trying his hardest to maintain his sweat-soaked grip while he engaged in the frenetic hand motions required by the ritual.

The power built slowly, taking the form of a sense of dread growing like a tumor in the back of his mind. Finally, Micah stepped forward, the knife flashing briefly, opening a cut on the salamander's throat. Blood poured into his cupped hands.

He brought them to his mouth, struggling to avoid gagging at the heavy, salty taste. After drinking the required mouthful, he cupped his hands once more beneath its neck, collecting another handful.

Quickly, Micah scrambled back into the center of the circle, letting the blood dribble from his hands onto the circle's runes. One by one, they began glowing with a green light, clearly visible in the dim chamber.

The salamander struggled against its bonds, croaking in distress. Its eyes snapped open and revealed the same green glow as the circle. Visibly, it shrank, shriveling before Micah's eyes as power poured into him in great, unrelenting waves.

Frantically, he pulled out the Folio and recited the words to *Foresight* as the mana caused his reservoirs to swell like balloons. On an instinctive level, Micah knew that if he didn't act soon, his mana pools would overextend and pop. He didn't know exactly what would happen, but from the warnings in the ritual's description, he'd be luckiest if it simply erased from creation.

The spell formula grew in his mind, each nonsense word and arcane motion adding definition to its misty shape. Mana began to pour from him into the spell, relieving the bloating that threatened his very existence.

With each second, he enunciated the words with more force, and Micah's hand motions became more defined. Vague rainbow shadows began to extend from everything around him, showing him hints as to where they might be in the next moment.

Then he misspoke. The syllable *Harr* came out *Hark*. The magic shuddered around him. Micah stumbled slightly, his left hand barely out of position as he tried to recover from his mistake.

The soap-film images of the future faded into nothing as the spell fizzled into the smoky air of the dungeon. Micah fell to his knees, gasping. The spell didn't even have the dignity to explode or spray a shower of sparks when failing. It just worked one second, and then the next, it was gone.

He looked up at Martin in fear. For the first time since changing timelines, Micah realized that it wasn't going to work out. That small part of him that "knew" he was going to be a great hero had lied to him once again. He'd gambled everything, but now it was all over.

He closed his eyes. It wasn't a complete loss. Images popped up unbidden of Trevor, Esther, his parents, Drekt, and Jo. Even if he were to die here and now, he'd done something good in saving Basil's Cove. A tear hissed as it splattered against the dungeon's overheated floor.

"As expected." Martin clicked his tongue in disappointment. "Luckily, there's a contingency. Don't ever say that I've done nothing for you, boy."

Micah looked up from the rough rocks of the dungeon's floor, confusion on his face. Brenden strode into the room with a cocky smile and a wriggling sack over his shoulder. Micah's old mentor nodded at Martin before walking up to him and dumping the sack next to the ritual circle.

"Good to see you again, Thrakos." Martin smiled slightly. "Now, Silver, Mr. Thrakos has so graciously provided you with a second chance to complete the ritual and cast *Foresight*. You won't get a third."

"But it won't be enough," Micah spoke questioningly, barely daring to hope. "The ritual requires an incredible amount of energy to operate. Nothing that size will have enough power to actually fuel the spell."

"That's certainly true for non-sapients," Martin agreed, grinning at Micah. "You haven't inspected the gift that Mr. Thrakos brought you. Don't be so quick to dismiss it out of hand."

Horror burning in Micah's chest, he reached down and pulled the burlap sack off of the wriggling form. Staring up at him in terror was Bart. The man silently screamed at him, muffled by the gag wrapped around his face.

"Your friend there already failed his test." Martin motioned mockingly at Bart. "But here at the Royal Academy, we don't believe in waste. His failure is your second and final chance."

26

GRADUATION?

"**D**o you mean—?" Micah glanced up at Brenden and Martin and motioned at the sacrificial knife. Bart shook, trying to free himself from his bonds, his eyes fixed on the blood-stained knife.

"You could always just sit there pissing yourself like a scared puppy," Brenden sneered back. "Being an adult means making tough choices. Even if you hadn't failed today, it was just a matter of time. Let me tell you a secret, Silver. Everyone fails a test. If you pass? We just keep giving you another until you do. Eventually, you'd be where you are today."

Brenden spat on the ground next to Bart's struggling form. "No one gets knighted without getting their hands dirty. The Royal Knights aren't an organization for idealists; that sort of emotional weakness will get people killed on the battlefield. We do good work. Necessary work. But for every job the bards sing about, there are three more performed in the dark. Assassinations, poisonings, and diplomatic deals that would turn a man's stomach, but they keep people safe. Without us, the common people of the Kingdom would've been killed ten times over."

"But I thought you were with the Golden Drakes?" Micah's eyes widened. "Why were you my mentor there if you're a Knight?"

"He's not a Knight yet, boy," Martin interjected. "Brenden is a squire. Once the Drakes sold you to us, I sent him over to handle your early education. He let me know when it was time to accelerate your training and sent you to the capital. Now, are you going to sit there mewling about how the world has wronged you, or are you going to actually try to make something of yourself?"

"The Drakes sold me?" Micah cocked his head to the side, blinking rapidly as the room spun around him.

"As soon as you revealed you had the power of prophecy." Martin chuckled. "That's the sort of blessing that's very useful to a ruler but relatively useless to a guild. The Golden Drakes have some connections to the Second Prince, and they know better than to hold on to recruits that might be strategic assets. We paid a baron's ransom in attunement for you, boy. I still think it was a waste, but who knows. You might prove me wrong yet.

"Now"—Martin pointed at the knife in Micah's hand—"no more dawdling. Get on with the ritual. Either you'll succeed or you won't. Either way, I want a resolution so I can get out of this armpit and take a shower."

"Was Brenden telling the truth?" Micah asked, stalling for time as his thoughts raced, trying and failing to find a way out of his dilemma. "Is this really necessary? Is going through with the ritual actually going to teach me something that will help me protect my family?"

"Aye." Martin's voice took on a contemplative tone. "I still don't think you're fit to be a Knight, boy, but the one thing I will say about you is that your heart is in the right place. The Knights need to be ready to do things under the cover of darkness that we aren't terribly proud of, but it's all for a purpose. We protect people like your family and that port city you're from. We make the sacrifices that they're too timid to consider in order to keep this land civilized.

"Enough dawdling, boy." Martin's eyes snapped back to Micah. "Perform the ritual or die next to your friend. It really doesn't matter to me."

Micah looked down at Bart shivering against the bonds. They'd never been close, but Bart was what passed for Micah's best friend at the Academy. He stared up at Micah, pleading with his eyes.

Micah gritted his teeth, trying to will his weakness away. Martin wasn't lying. He could see the glee in the older man's eyes when he talked about murdering Micah. If this didn't work, Martin would use a water tendril to smash him against the wall with enough force to break every bone in his body.

He closed his eyes, the dagger weighing heavily in his palm. It all wouldn't matter soon. This timeline wasn't nearly as bad as his first, but there was no way Micah was going to live out his life under the Knights' thumbs. If they were going to make him kill another student just to "show his loyalty," it was only a matter of time before they escalated the atrocities expected of him.

Maybe he didn't have the makings of a Royal Knight, but after hearing the nonsense spewed by Brenden and Martin, that sounded like it was for the best.

Really, when he thought about it, Bart was barely even a person. This entire timeline was doomed to fade away the minute he reverted. In a couple of months, Bart would cease to exist, even if he survived today. Micah wouldn't feel *good* killing him, but at this point, his choice was stark and clear.

The justifications rang hollow even as Micah repeated them to himself. Every word felt like ash in his throat as he inwardly mumbled the excuses. He knew right from wrong, but survival was survival.

Micah began reciting the words to the ritual. Brenden and Martin's visible approval damned him almost as much as Bart's frantic struggling. Once again, the incantation went off without a hitch. The only moment of doubt came when Micah struggled to choke down the ritual mouthful of Bart's blood. The salt and iron burned his mouth, and Micah felt the bile begin to rise in the back of his throat.

With an act of will, Micah ground the nails of his right hand into his palm, using the pain to distract himself from his barbaric actions.

He scattered the second handful of blood into the circle, activating the runes once more.

Mana surged into him, more than he ever thought possible. Bart's life gave him easily two to three times as much as the dungeon boss, quickly swelling his reserves to the breaking point. Without breaking his focus, Micah began casting *Foresight*.

This time, the spell was almost perversely easy. Maybe it was the advantage of having attempted it once before, or maybe it had something to do with Bart's sacrifice, but each word and motion came like he'd rehearsed them a hundred times. Almost in a trance, Micah finished the final incantation and rainbow smears—aura-like projections of the potential future actions of everything around him—snapped into place.

With perfect clarity, he watched Brenden slouch over to Bart's desiccated body to dump him in a flaming brazier almost a second before the actions actually occurred. Some aspect of the spell allowed his focus to split perfectly, tracking every discrete moment between the present and a second in the future simultaneously. The rainbow blur of motion should have distracted Micah, but instead, he was oddly fascinated by it.

"Well," Martin spoke a second in the future, "that was a pleasant surprise."

"It surprised me too," Micah replied, too enthralled with the multicolored blur of future possibilities laid out before him to notice that Martin had just opened his mouth.

"Maybe we should wait to continue this conversation." Martin smiled slightly. "You seem a bit overwhelmed by your cosmic significance at the moment."

Micah nodded absently, staring around the room. All too soon, the spell came to an end, the probability arcs shortening until they disappeared entirely. Suddenly, Micah was fully grounded in the present once more. Brenden looked vaguely nonplussed over not being allowed to murder Micah, but Martin was strangely happy.

"Good." Martin smiled, his eyes roaming over Micah like he was a prime cut of meat. "You've proven yourself worth the investment the Royal Knights have made in you. Now we just need to get you leveled up to 20 so you can claim a class specialty. Then we can begin on your advanced studies and transform you from a confused young man into a proper warrior."

With a hiss, Bart's body began to burn in the brazier. Micah's gaze snapped back to it, watching the acrid black smoke begin to fill the room. Almost immediately, everything began to smell of charred meat. He wrinkled his nose in disgust. Even if this timeline was a dead end, he wouldn't forget what he'd been forced to do today. Next time, he'd know better than to trust the Royal Family and their knights.

"Oh, stop moping," Brenden said, wiping Bart's blood from his hands onto the dungeon boss's corpse. "He was dead anyway. He needed to make a breakthrough as an Enchanter and he was given three chances. Even if you took some sort of moral stand and refused to perform the ritual, he'd have joined you in the fire anyway. The Knights will make you wealthy, powerful, and famous so long as you're useful. If you aren't useful? Well. No use wasting resources."

Micah hurried to catch up to Brenden and Martin as they left the dungeon. The following week, he was excused from every class. Instead, the three of them went into the dungeon as often as it reset. Micah killed monsters held still by Martin's water tendrils or Brenden's daemons over and over again.

As he gained experience, the accomplishments felt hollow. The skill and progress that he earned weren't his. They were nothing more than tainted gifts, given to him by the Royal Knights at the price of Bart's life.

Finally, he hit level 20. Withdrawing his spear from the imp's chest, Micah heard a chime that rose steadily in pitch until it became an omnipresent droning whistle. His vision blurred and the floor rocked under him. He sank to a knee, shaking his head to try and clear his senses.

The noise faded away, prompting Micah to open his eyes. Around him was nothing but dimly lit mist. The floor felt the same as before, but it was the only touchstone of normalcy. He couldn't see Martin anywhere. He might still be in the dungeon, but at this point, his location was more of a guess than anything.

"Congratulations, Blessed," the familiar voice from his class selection emanated from the mist. "You've reached your first milestone and are eligible for a class specialty. A series of options will be presented to you based upon your affinities and skill levels.

"For your achievements in learning the martial art, Wind Spear, you may upgrade the martial art to Uncommon rarity, increasing the effectiveness of all abilities associated with that martial art." The voice continued its even tone and measured cadence, unperturbed by Micah's bewilderment. "Due to your increased physical fitness, you may specialize as an athlete and gain additional hit points upon each level-up. For following The Path of the Spear, you may specialize as a spear adept, making you more effective in many small ways with a spear. For your achievements in Wind magic, you may specialize as an Aeromancer, decreasing the mana cost and increasing the effectiveness of your Wind magic. For your achievements in Wood magic, you may specialize as a Healer, decreasing the mana cost and increasing the effectiveness of your Wood magic. For your achievements in Time magic, you may specialize as a Chronomancer, decreasing the mana cost and increasing the effectiveness of your Time magic. For your knowledge and achievements in ritual magic, you may specialize as an Occultist. For your knowledge and achievements in enchanting, you may specialize as an Enchanter."

The voice paused as Micah blinked rapidly, inundated with information.

"Be aware that you may only select one specialty or improvement of a specialty every twenty levels," the voice said, its tone unchanged. "Please select one of the previously listed abilities or request that they be repeated for you."

"Chronomancer." Micah tried to prevent his voice from cracking. Martin had been clear: Any other specialty would not result in his survival.

"Granted," the voice replied, the mist fading away to reveal the chamber of the dungeon he'd been standing in before. Martin stood nearby, attempting to rub some monster blood from the hem of his outfit.

"Congratulations on your level, Micah." Martin's voice didn't carry any warmth. "Now that you're done staring vacantly into space, it's time to move on to the next step of your training. Moment of truth once again, Mr. Silver." A water tentacle snaked out from behind Martin's back. "You should be close to full mana right now. If you picked Chronomancer as we agreed, you'll be able to cast *Foresight*. Otherwise…" He shrugged.

"The Royal Knights are fairly keen on following orders," Martin continued, the water tentacle snaking near Micah. "We aren't interested in accepting rogue elements into our ranks."

Micah glanced toward the tentacle and bit back a sarcastic response. As much as he didn't enjoy the constant threats, he knew they were genuine. Now wasn't the time to goad the malevolent killer that held his life in his hands.

He cast the spell, only stumbling once but quickly catching himself. It consumed over half of his mana, but by his projections from before he'd gained the specialty, it should have taken over 130% of his available mana. The world faded into the rainbow blur of probabilities around him.

Micah's eyes widened. He ducked a full half-second before the water tentacle—its tip flattened into an axe head—swung at his neck, traveling at barely visible speeds. He rolled to the side as a hypersonic disc of water drilled through the dungeon floor.

He pulled himself up into a crouch and raised his spear. Just as he was about to charge, he paused, literally seeing his future-self get pulled apart by a lattice of water blades that sprouted from nothingness around Martin.

"Good, good!" Martin clapped his hands together, grinning maniacally at Micah. "A Magi managed to dodge two high-speed attacks and avoid rushing into a defensive trap. I'd say that's proof positive that you had *Foresight* active."

"That" —Micah's teeth chattered as cold sweat ran down his back—"that was all just a test? You could have killed me!"

"*Would* have, boy." Martin clicked his tongue at him in disappointment. "Sometimes I wonder about your Mind attribute. No matter how much we tell you that the Royal Knights aren't a place for the weak, either physically or emotionally, you never seem to properly take it in. You're more or less one of us now." Martin began walking out of the dungeon, motioning for Martin to follow him. "If you can cast a fifth-tier spell before your eighteenth birthday, no matter how you got there, you're qualified to be a junior squire. If you've learned anything from me during these past eight months, I want to be clear on the most important lesson. You're going to have to toughen up. It takes a lot to survive in our organization, but the rewards are more than worth it. Right now? You've only gotten your foot a couple inches inside the door."

27

SQUIRE

"**A**nd this will be your room, Squire Silver." The servant opened the door to a midsized room about twelve stories up in one of the towers. "You've been assigned to Ser Osswain for your apprenticeship. Squire Thrakos will be by soon with your first assignment."

"Do you know when Squire Thrakos plans to visit?" Micah asked, taking in the snug but well-appointed apartment. "Do I have time to draw a bath?"

"I would not presume to know what a squire does with their time." The servant still refused to make eye contact with Micah, instead staring at his immaculately polished shoes. "I do know that it is best not to make a knight wait. The punishment for doing so is quite harsh."

"Understood," Micah replied glumly, walking into the room.

The door closed behind him with a click as the lock engaged. He sighed. They'd inducted him into the Royal Knights. Micah Silver, Squire Third Class.

According to Martin, he should be proud. Usually, the Master of Curriculum required test after test, constant proof of skill and loyalty before a Blessed would be made into a squire. Apparently, the magnitude of his achievement and the rarity of his Time affinity allowed

Micah to sidestep years' worth of classes to ensure his "political reliability." As it stood, Micah had been brought into the Royal Knights at one of the youngest ages in recent memory.

It didn't come without a cost. The locked door confirmed that he wasn't trusted, and even five minutes of conversation with Martin provided ample demonstration that the older man didn't respect him. He might be part of the Knights, but there wasn't any sense of belonging.

Even if they'd made him a member, they'd conferred none of the rewards normally associated with joining the organization. The Knights considered him useful, an asset and nothing more. Martin had so much as told him that any escape attempts would be punished with either death or dismemberment.

Micah walked over to the reading desk built into the wall of his apartment. The arrangement was quite cozy; a bookshelf stocked with tomes on magical theory and ritual magic sat just to the left while a magelight hung from a gossamer thread above the table. He only needed to tap it to turn the light on, illuminating the room without any need for the dangers of an open-flame candle.

On the desk lay a book, its cover weathered and yellow to the point that he could barely make out the title: *Time and Its Uses*. He opened the book gently, careful not to pull or tear at its ancient binding. The book was a treatise on magical theory, specializing in Time magic with a handful of spells scattered throughout its length.

He lost himself in the grimoire. It divided the study of time into two major fields: transferring one's thoughts and perception forward or backward in time, and the actual energy related to the passage of time itself. Perception was the easiest field to learn, with *Foresight* and *Time Echo* being the two most discussed introductory spells.

Time Echo was intriguing. Although a fifth-tier spell, it was a much easier spell to learn and use than *Foresight*, hinting at Martin's barely concealed antipathy toward Micah. Where *Foresight* allowed a glimpse into the near future, *Time Echo* focused on the past events that had occurred at a specific location.

The user could cast their sight and hearing into the past,

rewinding events at up to ten times their normal speed, only limited by the hefty per-second mana cost of the spell. At his current level, Micah could only rewind his vision of a location by a couple hours, but he almost immediately saw how the spell would aid either a diplomat or a spy.

The sections on temporal energy were even more interesting, albeit borderline useless. Temporal energy was just too powerful and difficult to tame. There were ways to recreate it with mana, but they were simply too energy-intensive to exist as anything more than theories for the scholars to debate.

The book contained a powerful spell, *Temporal Transfer,* that allowed a caster to create "age" with mana or to draw "age" from a target into the caster. It was just that it took a full mana pool to create even a month of age, and drawing time into oneself predictably aged the caster.

With a single knock on the door, Brenden strode into the room. He glanced around briefly before smiling at Micah. It was an ugly thing—his lips were pulled back tight, displaying a mouth full of teeth without a single ounce of mirth.

"Squire Silver." Brenden walked over to Micah as he placed a cloth bookmark in the grimoire and set it down. "It's good to see you so studious now that we're both squires to the same knight and all. Ser Osswain sent me to get you. He has a task for you, but first, he wants to show you a surprise to commemorate your induction into the order."

Micah followed Brenden, thoughts flitting through his mind as he speculated as to the nature of the surprise. Neither Brenden nor Martin were sentimental sorts. Anything they gave him would come with a price tag, usually one far above and beyond what the gift was worth.

Brenden opened the door with a mocking flourish. Inside was a well-appointed dining hall with five sumptuous meals set out on a beautiful table carved from a single old-growth tree. Micah's breath caught in his throat.

"No," he whispered as Esther bounded around the table toward him, flinging herself into the air to wrap him in a hug.

"Martin thought you'd like to catch up with your family," Brenden said with a laugh and a wink. "Once you're done with lunch, we'll have them escorted to their new living arrangements and you can begin your project."

"You mean—" Micah's eyes went wide with horror.

"Squire Thrakos invited us to live on the estate of the Royal Knights," his mother interjected excitedly. "Apparently, people have tried to use the families of Royal Knights as hostages against them in the past. These days, it's standard practice to pay their family a generous stipend to relocate so that we can't be used against you. Of course, we couldn't turn down such a generous offer, especially if it had the potential to put your work at risk."

"Hostages?" Micah turned back to Brenden, his eyes wild.

"Tragic, really." Brenden's eyes danced while he tried to adopt a dour tone. "Families killed and tortured just because a knight wouldn't cooperate with their captors. These days, we try to do everything we can to prevent such a sad recurrence."

Brenden left the room, Micah's eyes still trained on him. A slap on his back returned Micah's attention to his family. Trevor's hand was on his shoulder as the big man leaned in for a hug, engulfing Micah almost entirely.

"By the Sixteen, you're huge now." Emotion choked his brother's voice. "You're only seventeen and you've probably already passed my level entirely."

Trevor grasped Micah's shoulders, pushing him back a step so he could look him up and down. Micah noticed the shine of unshed tears in his brother's eyes.

"You don't know what the past year has been like, Micah." Trevor's smile only wavered slightly. "You didn't get to come home from the Golden Drakes, so we never really got a chance to catch up, but I've been so proud of you. Plus, the minute they announced you were being transferred to the Royal Academy... Well." Trevor smiled sheepishly, wiping away the moisture pooling around his eyes. "I just couldn't shut up about you. I think I told everyone at the Lancers about 'my younger brother, the Royal Knight candidate' at least twenty times."

"It's good to see you too." Micah smiled back, trying his hardest to make the most of the moment with his family. "They've been working me so hard that I haven't had a chance to come home and visit. It'll be nice to have you all close at hand."

Trevor shooed Esther away before leaning in close. "What about your boss, that Brenden guy?" Trevor whispered to him conspiratorially. "He's pretty cute in an overly authoritative sort of way."

"What?" Micah sputtered. "By the Sixteen, no. Never. Gods above, I thought you liked girls."

"I do like girls" —Trevor winked at him—"but that doesn't mean I can't like boys too. I never really spoke up about it back in Basil's Cove. It's a smaller city and they frown on alternative lifestyles there. You saw how the housewives treated Mom. Can you think of what they'd do if either of us did anything other than settle down with a nice human girl? Hells, I wasn't about to date an elf, boy or girl. There'd just be too many rumors."

"Here" —Trevor smiled, slapping him on the shoulder once again —"things are different in the capital. I don't know if I'm going to talk to Mom or Dad anytime soon. I know they're pretty keen on grandkids, but if the right guy comes along..." Trevor shrugged.

"Squire Thrakos is *not* the right guy." Micah shook his head empathetically. "Please. Anyone associated with the Knights should be considered off limits. There's a lot going on behind the scenes that I can't talk about, but just don't. *Please.*"

"Spoilsport," Trevor replied at a normal volume, pulling away from Micah with a laugh. "Come on, lunch is getting cold and it sounds like you still have an assignment this afternoon."

After the meal, Brenden led the way to Martin, constantly trying to draw Micah into a pointed and passive-aggressive conversation. Micah knew better than to engage. Brenden just wanted to bait and taunt him about his family. The older man couldn't help but target Micah's every weakness. He couldn't really make out whether

Brenden didn't like him, or if the older man was just an asshole. Either way, he wasn't keen to start an argument he couldn't win.

Together they walked into a laboratory, books and reagents meticulously stored up against its vaulted stone walls. Martin absently waved them in as he put the finishing touches on a ritual circle. At its center, a swarthy man wearing only ragged undergarments struggled against metal bonds holding him to a steel slab. Micah squinted at the man, whose face vaguely triggered a thread of memory.

"Micah!" the man shouted as soon as his eyes fell upon him. "You gotta tell these guys that it's all a mistake. Whatever they says I've done, I didn't do it!"

"Who?" Micah cocked his head to the side, trying to ignore Brenden's damning smile at his side.

"It's me!" The man rattled his wrists against his bonds. "Gheb! The carriage driver? I brought you from Basil's Cove to Bitollan."

"This man is a criminal, Micah," Martin replied indolently, motioning to Brenden, who quickly gagged the struggling man. "He's a senior agent in the Resistance. Under interrogation with a Truth Seer, he admitted to gathering information and passing it on to dissident forces. He's already been found guilty of treason."

"The Resistance?" Micah asked, frowning slightly. "What are they resisting?"

"What indeed." Martin smiled, walking over to a chair within arm's reach of Gheb and seating himself. "Everything, really. They're a group of forgotten. Their stated purpose is to acquire 'equal rights' for the forgotten, but really they're nothing more than a bunch of rabble-rousers, trying to create chaos and benefit from the suffering of others."

"What is he doing here, then?" Micah asked slowly, his eyes flicking from Gheb to Martin and back.

"The same thing you are." Martin smiled. "Serving your purpose in the greater scheme of things. You see, Micah, Brenden told me you've begun reading up on the spell *Temporal Transfer*. What the written grimoires don't speak of is the theoretical breakthrough made by Karrin Dakkora. Unfortunately, she didn't have any Time affinity, so she couldn't act on the theory, but she created a theoretical ritual to amplify *Temporal Transfer*. One that would allow a caster to transfer years from one target to another."

"Every nation has an organization like the Royal Knights." With a nod from Martin, Brenden handed Micah a sheaf of papers containing the formula for a ritual. "The problem is that it takes years to get soldiers to higher levels. I've spent most of my life working my way to level 44. Enough to make me a full Knight, but I know my limits. I don't have enough time to make it past level 60 in this lifetime."

Brenden grabbed a censer full of incense and placed it at Micah's feet as Martin kept speaking. "Battles between kingdoms are decided by powers between levels 60 and 90. The problem is that anyone at that level is too old. Often pneumonia is more likely to claim their life than an enemy's arrow.

"But"—a mad smile occupied Martin's face—"what if Dakkora's ritual works? What if we can transfer years from an old man like me and give them to refuse? Then we can put our malcontents and prisoners to work while giving the elite of the Kingdom a second life."

Understanding dawned on Micah's face. This was why he hadn't been put through propaganda classes extolling the virtues of the Royal Knights. His absolute loyalty only really mattered if they planned to let him do unsupervised field work. Holding his family hostage would be more than enough.

Micah was never going to be allowed to leave the Royal Knights' headquarters. He'd been treated differently from the beginning, because this had been the plan from the beginning. He might become a Knight at some point, but it would be in name only. In reality, he'd be nothing more than a piece of equipment, tuning up and maintaining their top agents' peak physical condition for years if not centuries to come.

"I know my place." Martin bowed from his chair with a self-deprecating flourish. "I'm an old man that's getting close to his limit. I'm useful to the Kingdom, but if I die, it won't be crippling. I am our test case. Your job is to get that formula to work. Once you succeed with me, you'll return the truly powerful to the full glory of their youth.

"Then"—Martin's eyes shone with an unhealthy fervor—"the Kingdom will stand tall. Pereston will finally have a Blessed above level 100. Once their classes evolve, they'll practically become demigods. None of our neighbors will be able to stand before us. We'll unite the continent in a generation."

Micah looked down at the formula before glancing at Brenden. The older man was standing in front of the door. His only escape would be when the cooldown on his blessing ran down. Until then, he could only grit his teeth and try to survive this bleak timeline.

28

THIRD TIME'S THE CHARM

The spell worked. It took four tries for Micah to get the feel of the ritual and how it interacted with *Temporal Transfer*, but it worked. Each attempt left him sick to his stomach. The one time Micah actively wanted a new spell to not live up to expectations, it performed flawlessly.

Gheb screamed and begged Micah through his gag the entire time, but there wasn't anything he could do. Brenden stood just outside of the circle, a summoned daemon at his back just waiting for Micah to hesitate. There was no question in Micah's mind that any failure on his part would spell the death of his entire family. Micah's only option was to grit his teeth and count down the days until he could use his blessing again as Gheb deflated before his eyes, the Time magic wilting him like a week-old bouquet.

The spell "only" stole a year of Gheb's life for Martin, but that was enough for it to be declared an unqualified success. Performing the ritual and *Temporal Transfer* in the laboratory became Micah's new world. Each day, Brenden would escort him to the room, where a new prisoner would be waiting. Some truly deserved to have years ripped from their lives: murderers, kidnappers, and rapists. Many were political prisoners, members of the Resistance, or even just outspoken individuals that annoyed the wrong noble.

The first month was mostly devoted to "treating" Martin, performing the spell over and over again until Martin shed his age like a used overcoat. The difficulty of the casting steadily pushed up his Spellcasting and Ritual Magic skills until Micah was able to transfer two to three years at a time.

He didn't dare voice his suspicions, but after the third or fourth use of the ritual, it became obvious to Micah that this wasn't about "testing" the magic. Each time, Martin looked at the prisoners with an off-putting sense of hunger, but he always insisted that the spell needed more "fine-tuning." The spell and ritual worked fine.

Given the secrecy of the project, the way Brenden constantly prevented Micah from talking to anyone in the Royal Knights except for his family, there was only one conclusion: Martin was just trying to reclaim his youth before someone else in the Knights learned the significance of the ritual. Finally, once Martin looked to be in his early twenties, he announced the project a success.

The next day, Micah vaguely hoped for a period of rest, but once again, Brenden retrieved him from his apartment. When they walked into the laboratory, it was practically humming with tension. Martin stood in the center of a cluster of older, well-armed men, showing off his new body.

"Squire Silver," he called out as soon as Brenden brought him into the room. "The man of the hour is here."

Micah's breath left his body as all six of the other men turned to look at him. Every one of them carried a palpable aura of power, a weight of energy and gravitas that demanded respect. They stared at him with vague disinterest, cataloging and immediately dismissing him as beneath their notice. Micah would bet his last point of attunement that all of the newcomers were above at least level 60. He was a rabbit, shivering and alone in the midst of a pack of wolves.

"As I was discussing, gentlemen," Martin said with a hint of nervousness as he draped an arm over Micah's shoulders, "this here is Squire Silver, the Time Magi that performed the treatments on me and restored my youth. It should just be a matter of time and effort for him to do the same for you."

Their gazes intensified, but no one responded. A cane clacked on the stone floor, and the men parted, making way for a wizened old woman who slowly approached Micah. She was almost a foot shorter than him, her hair a stringy tangle of white and gray, but her rheumy blue eyes didn't miss a thing. Micah couldn't look away. She glowed like the sun. A corona of power leaked off of her, her very aura creating heat mirages in her wake.

"You've kept him at level 20?" she asked Martin, her voice the crackle of paper crumpling.

"Yes, M'lady Ikanthar." Martin hastily bowed at the waist.

"He's compliant, then?" Ikanthar continued, peering at Micah's shaking form. "You haven't treated him too badly, I hope? I don't want a spy or saboteur working on me."

"Yes, M'lady," Martin responded unctuously, his eyes flashing a threat at Micah. "He was discovered by the Golden Drakes, a high-tier adventuring guild, where he demonstrated the power of prophecy. They sold him to us and we've been training him ever since. Squire Silver has a perfect 10 affinity in Time, so we've been able to train him to use Time magic and the ritual at a much lower level than would otherwise be expected. He's already gotten his hands dirty on my orders several times and his family is being held against his good behavior."

Micah twitched slightly as Martin laid out his entire life story, describing him as an auctioneer would a prize head of cattle.

"Good." Ikanthar hobbled to the seat next to the restrained prisoner. "If this works, your research into the black rituals will be forgiven, Knight Osswain, and you will be rewarded. If this doesn't work, you knew the risks when you began your research into Dakkora's rituals. They are forbidden for a reason, but as you know, success forgives all sins."

"Success forgives all sins," all of the Knights reverently repeated in unison, as if it were some sort of talisman or prayer.

Martin flinched at her words, his usual bluster gone and a haunted look in his eyes. Apparently, he wasn't nearly as important as he'd led Micah to believe. A good thing to know.

"Now"—she waved a wrinkled and veiny hand in Micah's direction—"boy, work your dark magic on me, but be aware, if you fail or try to harm me, you and everything you love will learn the true depths of human misery in exquisite detail."

"Archmagus Ikanthar isn't prone to idle threats, Silver." Martin turned to him, his face deadly serious. "I'd suggest trying your hardest."

Micah coughed nervously, very aware of how dry his throat was. He approached, smiling weakly and not even looking at the political prisoner he'd be draining today. Micah found that it helped. Their screams still haunted him, but at least he didn't have to look into their eyes as the age flowed into them. He still saw Gheb staring at him every time he tried to sleep.

He traced the circle, placing the ritual's reagents and components, his hands shaking slightly under the gaze of the powerful Knights. Now that he'd had a moment to calm down, he recognized almost half of them from the bards' tales. Noble men, renowned for their valorous deeds and service to the Kingdom. Men he'd grown up respecting and wanting to emulate. All waiting to kill him if he didn't perform an unnatural act of magic on a defenseless prisoner.

Micah enacted the ritual, once again using his body as a conduit to transfer the monstrous power of age and authority built up in Archmagus Ikanthar's elderly and twisted body. The temporal energy passed through him toward the prisoner, but for the first time, he felt something new in its wake, a vague sense of the weight and majesty that the temporal energy represented.

With Martin, it'd simply been a chore, channeling a massive amount of energy from one spot to another. The ritual and spell were little more than an equation in which he was a variable. He played his part, but there was a lack of vital understanding. He knew that the temporal energy existed and that it was powerful, but he couldn't harness or control it.

It wasn't mana. Temporal energy was something more than that, much closer to the anima used in ritual magic. Primal energy that moved outside the safe boundaries of regular magic, only restricted by the natural phenomena of the universe itself.

His mind went back to the ritual he used to graduate. As the energy passed through him, he could see how the spell forms and reagents would interact with it, transforming it into something that he could begin to use. It wasn't a complete thought, just the beginning of a concept.

There wouldn't be a way to use it as mana; the energy was too wild for that. It would overwhelm the limits of magic almost immediately and backlash on Micah, consuming him in a moment. He squinted his eyes, trying to see the shape the ritual would take.

Then the spell was over. Absently, Micah realized that he'd fallen to both knees, gasping as sweat poured down his back. The prisoner had aged visibly, wrinkles appearing around the corner of his eyes and gray gathering at his temples.

Archmagus Ikanthar stood up from the chair, stretching her back briefly. The room's silence became electric. The various Knights grasped the hilts of their weapons, each training their eyes on Micah, waiting for any signal from Ikanthar of his betrayal. She waved her hand, a ball of fire forming in her palm without her chanting a single word to the spell. Quickly, it turned into a writhing snake and wound in between her fingers.

She snapped her thumb and index finger together, dissipating the tendril of flames. She turned to the crowd of Knights and nodded with a quick smile.

"You've done our Kingdom a great service, Knight Osswain." She inclined her head ever so slightly at Martin. "No one else thought to harness the black rituals in this way, molding an untrained talent into the vehicle of our Kingdom's rebirth. For this, you will be removed from your duties at the Royal Academy and rewarded greatly. From this day forward, Squire Silver will be entrusted to my care."

Micah started blankly at Martin as the older man opened his mouth to respond, then closed it bitterly. His entire fate had been decided before his eyes without even a second glance. Like he was a bolt of cloth or a loaf of bread to be sold at the market.

"Yes, Archmagus," Martin replied, the reluctance audible in his voice. "It shall be as you command."

The hour or so after meeting was a blur. Micah was ushered away by the Archmagus' servants. Soon he found himself in a new, slightly more luxurious apartment with the notable addition of bars on the windows. Any slight chance he'd had of crawling out the window and using *Updraft* to cushion his fall was long gone. Even if he chose to abandon his family, he was truly and completely trapped.

Micah pulled out the Folio and began sketching his thoughts on the new ritual. He'd need more experience transferring temporal energy to perfect it, but if he had to guess, temporal transfers looked like the entirety of his near future.

He just hoped that Archmagus Ikanthar wasn't the type to destroy her tools once she was done with them so that no one else could use them. He only had about four months left before the cooldown on *Blessed Return* finished off. It would be a painful kind of irony if she simply killed him right before he was able to use the blessing to escape this bleak timeline.

Luckily, those four months passed quickly and productively. Ikanthar literally never spoke to him during that time. Servants would fetch him and ensure that Micah was dressed appropriately before ushering him off to a much larger laboratory, where he would perform the same ritual time and time again. At some point, when Ikanthar was a beautiful and vibrant young woman, she stopped appearing, and one by one, Micah found himself casting the spell on a series of geriatric senior Knights.

Transferring energy for the Knights wasn't nearly as beneficial to his research as the times he'd performed the ritual on Ikanthar herself, but it hardly mattered. By that point, Micah had already created most of the theoretical framework for a ritual to harness the temporal energy. He wouldn't be able to cast the ritual before reverting the timeline—too many eyes were on him at all times—but the Knights provided ample research material he needed to polish off his final draft.

He didn't know for sure what the difference between Ikanthar and the Knights was. Maybe it was her total level eclipsing theirs or her status as a Chosen of Katton, God of Fire and Forge, but for some reason, the energy flowing from her was just on another level. He hoped that when the time came, it wouldn't matter, but really there would only be one way to find out. In his next life, he would need to do everything he could to avoid falling into her grasp once again.

He looked up at the ceiling of his room. It was two hours past midnight, and the moon was high in the night sky. Hopefully, Mursa would be looking down on him—a minute was a long time to wait while trapped amongst enemies. The guard had long since changed and none were nearby. Just in case, he'd pushed one of his bookshelves in front of the door.

"*Blessed Return.*" The voice, not his own, issued forth from Micah's mouth and time began to blur.

29

RITUALIST

Micah opened his eyes. He was thirteen for the third time.

Rolling over, he buried his face in his pillow and screamed out his frustration until his tiny frame was breathless and red. Two years of biting his tongue and serving as a slave for the Golden Drakes and the Royal Knights. Two years of smiling at his family while Brenden's mocking eyes bored into his back. Two years of betraying everything his parents had raised him to be on a fundamental and systematic level.

He rolled over and looked at the wooden ceiling of his childhood bedroom, his breath coming in ragged sobs. Those last few months when he'd been treated as nothing more than a piece of meat had tested him. It had taken everything Micah had in him to not mouth off. Maybe he'd even have gotten lucky and one of the Knights would have killed him. Only the knowledge that he had a way out of his servitude had kept Micah going.

This time, things would be different.

He stood up, stretching his scrawny limbs and shuddering in the morning air. Weak. Defenseless. With a creak, the bedroom door slid open and Micah whipped around, his heart pounding in his chest. Esther's hand, pudgy with baby fat, was barely visible inside the entryway.

"Come on in," he said, relaxing slightly. Mentally, Micah made a note to act more like an actual thirteen-year-old. Emotionally, he might be twenty-three, but everyone would expect age-appropriate behaviors.

Shyly, Esther slipped into the room, her eyes on her socks. When she spoke, her voice was soft, the consonants stretching out in a childish lisp.

"I heard you yell." She shuffled her socks across the hardwood floor. "I wanted to make sure there wasn't a mouse or spider scaring you."

Micah smiled at Esther as he crossed the small room to meet her. Whatever else may come, this was what he was fighting for. These little islands of normalcy in an uncaring ocean of chaos and danger.

"And what would you do if there *was* a mouse?" Micah asked, reaching down to tousle her hair. "That would be pretty scary."

"I'd get Trevor!" Esther exclaimed proudly. "He's big, and he said that if there were any kids being mean to me or any monsters, he'd fight them. He's going to be an aven shurer."

"What about me?" Micah feigned outrage. There was just something about Esther's attempts at heroism that melted the years of stress and nightmares. "I'm pretty strong and I'm going to be an adventurer too."

"But Trevor beats you every time you race or wrestle," Esther replied dubiously, inspecting his stick-thin arms. "Even Becky beat you last week when you tried to race her, and she's a girl. I think I'll call Trevor if there's a monster."

Micah winced as Esther wriggled from his grasp and ran out of the room, apparently satisfied that there wasn't a spider or rat in his bedroom. He'd forgotten that Becky, the tomboy daughter of a neighbor, had been his rival until he began working for Keeper Ansom. Of course, the word "rival" overstated Micah's role in the relationship. Becky trounced him fairly thoroughly every time they tried to compete.

Frowning slightly, Micah pulled out the Folio and paged to his previous memories of Becky. Sure enough, she received a combat-related blessing and became an adventurer for the Sword Disciples. They were a mid-tier guild like the Lancers, and as of the end of his first timeline, she'd been put in charge of a low-level team. Even with a Mythic Blessing, she'd managed to one-up him once again.

Closing the Folio, he sighed. He truly did have the build and reflexes of a spellcaster. Both Trevor and Becky grew up with the muscle and agility of melee combatants, but even after all of his work in the previous timeline, he'd barely reached an above-average physique. It seemed that leadership escaped his grasp once again. After all, it was hard to earn the respect of an adventuring party casting spells from the back line.

Once again, he'd have to go through all the awkwardness of puberty while working out and trying to temper himself. He certainly wasn't excited about another four years of body aches, hormonally destabilized moods, and cracking voices.

Still, having to start from scratch was better than being trapped by the Royal Knights. Micah had learned his lesson there. Without backing, if he revealed the extent of his gift, some powerful force would swoop in and exploit him. He couldn't let that happen again. This time, he needed to find a way to defeat the Durgh alone.

It was time to see what tools he had to work with this time around. Micah called up his status.

Micah Silver

Age 13 [ERROR] / 23

Class/Level-XP

HP 8/8

Attributes

Body 4, Agility 3, Mind 9, Spirit 8

Attunement

Moon 4,Sun 1, Night 2

Mana

Moon 8/8, Sun2/2, Night 4/4

Affinities

Time 10
Wood 6
Air 5
Blessings
Mythic Blessing of Mursa - Blessed Return, Ageless Folio
Skills
Anatomy 7
Enchanting 6
Fishing 1
Herbalism 5
Librarian 4
Ritual Magic 14
Spear 7
-Wind Spear 2
Spellcasting 20

He tapped his chin contemplatively. His skill levels were high, even for someone at the 20th level. As awful as the Knights were, their methods were effective. Being forced to repeatedly cast rituals and spells that should have been beyond his abilities had done wonders for his skill growth. In fact, he was fairly close to the skill requirements for becoming a Thaumaturge. He just needed to upgrade his Enchanting skill by 4.

Summoning and opening the Folio once again, Micah turned to the page detailing Karin Dakkora's ritual on energy transference and his theorized permutations to it. The three major uses he'd speculated on were using temporal energy to fulfill some or all of the attunement cost in enchanting, using temporal energy to fulfill some or all of the life force requirement for a summoning, and trying to find a way to weaponize *Temporal Transfer*.

The final method was well beyond his meager store of mana at the moment. After all, he'd need at least enough mana to initiate *Temporal Transfer* in order to begin siphoning temporal energy into a target. That said, the other two might be just what he needed to fight off the Durgh incursion.

In his last life, Micah had focused on ritual magic, but he had managed to develop enough of a base in enchanting at the Academy due to the similarity of the two fields to know that attunement was an enchanter's primary problem. Almost every enchantment took at least a half-point of attunement, with more powerful enchantments taking multiple full points.

He could gain a point of Moon attunement fairly quickly by "learning" a first-tier spell, but beyond that, as a thirteen-year-old, Micah didn't really have a good way of gaining more attunement. Goods were given to youths for free, but by the same token, no one in their right mind would buy an object from him lest they incur Luxos' wrath for undermining the monetary system.

If he was going to become a Thaumaturge, Micah would need to gain 4 points in Enchanting without earning a single level. That meant perfecting his modification to the temporal transference ritual. The only way he would be able to gain those skill levels was by dramatically decreasing the attunement cost of new enchantments.

Sighing, Micah closed the book. The worst part was that he'd need to do all of this while maintaining a normal schedule. His family would wonder if he didn't get an apprenticeship, so it would be off to Keeper Ansom's library once again for him.

Despite being productive, the following months left bags under Micah's eyes. The library contained the basic books on ritual magic and enchantment theory he needed to finish adapting the ritual, but beyond that, they were more or less a waste of time. He'd already learned most of what he needed at the Royal Academy, and almost everything he hadn't already committed to memory was safely transcribed in the Folio.

The nights, on the other hand, were of great use. Almost casually, he set up teleport beacons in his bedroom and at the dire stoat's cave, the large weasel posing almost no threat to him. *Air Knife* wasn't a particularly powerful spell, but at his level of Spellcasting and skill level in the spell, even with the meager handful of mana available to

Micah as a classless Blessed, he easily murdered the creature from a distance.

Defeating the dire stoat and reclaiming the cave was tedious rather than a challenge due to Micah's skill levels. Once he set himself up in the cave, Micah began procuring the animals he'd need to further his experiments.

Night by night, he accumulated creatures, either by catching them in a series of live traps or by purchasing them at the market and ferrying them out to the forest. They weren't powerful magically, generally being young and inexperienced, but with practice, he was just barely able to touch the temporal energy in them.

Surprisingly, he gained an extra point of Moon attunement the first time he successfully performed the transfer ritual. Somewhere out there, Mursa was watching and rewarding Micah for his research.

It wasn't as much of a success as he'd hoped, dropping the price of enchanting a bolt of his father's cloth to make it more lustrous and durable from one-third of an attunement point to one-tenth of a point, but Micah took it as a sign that Mursa smiled upon his efforts. Strange, really—he'd expected a more negative response from the stories told about Karin Dakkora.

After that, he replicated the ritual as often as possible, transferring the age and experience from his collection of geese and raccoons —two months at a time—into enchanting a series of knickknacks.

Without a class, Micah didn't have the mana to make anything truly powerful, but that didn't mean that his efforts were fruitless. After almost two months, he'd gained 3 points in Enchanting and developed a collection of costume jewelry and cheap blades that could perform minor but useful effects.

Nothing too powerful, but enough to catch a merchant's eye if Micah could risk the attention. A ring that would pulse in the presence of poison. A belt buckle that would aid digestion. A necklace that created a bubble of air around the user's head on command, letting them breathe underwater for a period of time or avoid gaseous attacks.

Unfortunately, Micah had a problem. He was beginning to run

low on attunement, having burned through most of the points he'd gained from successfully "learning" ritual magic and enchanting. He couldn't afford to waste more attunement on minor enchantments powered by inefficient transfers of temporal energy from younger creatures.

Luckily, he had a goal. In a nearby grove lived a great stag. Once upon a time, it must've been a king of the forest, chasing any other buck from its does with ease, but now, age had caught up with it.

Its former red-brown coat was gray, fur falling off in clumps due to sickness and malnutrition to reveal the wrinkled skin beneath. It was more than a match for Micah physically, but then again, what wasn't? With the aid of his magic, Micah hoped to capture the creature in order to use its temporal energy in a grand enchantment that would push his skill level up to 10.

The Saturday of the hunt began like any other, with Micah making an excuse to Trevor and Esther about why he couldn't play with them despite being off work at his apprenticeship followed by performing the teleportation ritual out to his cave. Almost immediately, he began working on a very particular ritual, one he'd seen Brenden perform dozens of times but had never tried himself.

Regretfully, he dragged over the cages he'd made for the pair of badgers that he'd trapped almost a month ago. He preferred using temporal energy to the more traditional way of performing rituals, but the first time through a dangerous casting wasn't the time to substitute. After all, if this didn't go perfectly, he would almost certainly die without someone on hand to protect him.

Opening the Folio, he began the ritual, slashing open his forearm to drop blood all along the outside of the circle. His voice took on a strange resonance as it began to mix and interact with principles far outside the visible world. A strange pressure began to build around Micah, and reality *thinned*. For a brief second, he glimpsed into a formless and chaotic beyond, just a sideways step from Karell, but Micah closed his eyes and refused to let it distract him.

Then it came time for the sacrifice. He plunged the dagger into one badger after another. Over the past month of him continually rejuvenating the animals, they'd become tame, almost pets. It pained him to betray them, but a ritual of this magnitude called for blood and life. The weak souls of the badgers wouldn't provide much of an anchor, but they were by far the best medium he had on hand.

The darkness of the page parted like a curtain as a large, hairy hand reached out from somewhere else and grasped onto empty air. With a bestial howl, it pulled itself forward, staggering onto its hands and knees. The gap in existence winked out behind it as it stood up, almost nine feet in height. The Onkert daemon was just as he remembered it, with the snarling maw of a wolf placed on top of the huge and well-muscled body of a gorilla.

Micah sighed, only to quirk his mouth slightly when he received a point of Moon attunement. The ritual was successful, and the Onkert would follow his every command until its anchor—the anima of a pair of badgers—faded.

He had between fifteen and twenty minutes. He'd have to hurry if he planned to catch the stag that quickly.

30

A THIRD CLASS

Micah gasped for breath as he tried to follow the galloping Onkert daemon. He'd gotten close enough to the stag to wound it with an *Air Knife*, slashing open its leg and leaving a blood trail for the daemon to follow, but his tiny body couldn't keep up. The Onkert barreled through the forest, digging its armored knuckles into the soil as it shouldered past old-growth trees and trampled underbrush.

Already he was only following his summon by sound and its path of destruction. The Onkert was far ahead of him, occasionally howling as it sought its injured quarry. Micah stopped for a second to catch his breath, his rail-thin arms and legs trembling from exertion. Idly, he hoped that the sound of the Onkert barreling through the forest scared away whatever else might be nearby. His tiny, sweat-soaked form wasn't in any shape to fight off a particularly aggressive rabbit, let alone a boar, wolf, or monster.

A howl of triumph interrupted Micah's panting. With a grunt, he pushed off of the tree he'd been resting against and began jogging down the trail left by the daemon. Hopefully, it would follow its commands and only subdue the stag. He'd never seen the Onkerts disobey Brenden, but this was also his first summoning. Only the

Sixteen knew if the incantation binding its will was done completely correctly.

About four minutes later, Micah staggered into a clearing, sweat streaming down his body and his breath coming in short, ragged bursts. The daemon held the stag pinned to the forest floor, its slavering wolf jaws whining and snapping at it, but Micah's will held it back. No matter how it tried, the daemon was unable to harm the majestic but aging creature.

Mentally, he assessed the time and sighed. There wasn't energy left in the summoning ritual to drag the stag back to his cave before the Onkert dissipated. Micah began quickly pulling ingredients out of the backpack that had become the bane of his existence on the jog over. He didn't look forward to it, but he would need to make a priority out of cardio once again. Getting winded from even this minor piece of exertion was downright embarrassing.

As efficiently as possible, Micah set up the transference ritual around the stag. It had given up struggling, exhausted from the chase, but now it was still, trapped under the Onkert's weight. It eyed him warily as Micah traced a circle of quartz dust around it and began placing the reagents. He made his adjustments on the fly, judging the time of the ritual from the angle of the sun and hoping that his calculations were correct. Rituals weren't meant to be performed without hours or even days of preparation, but Micah would only have one chance at this.

One minute left. Micah threw his spear into the center of the circle. He needed to enchant something, and it was all he had on hand. Hopefully, it would serve as a proper medium for the massive torrent of energy he planned on drawing from the stag. He'd prefer it if his enchantment didn't end in an explosion and singed eyebrows.

The words came easily. With a dab of blood from the stag's injured leg on his index finger, Micah rapidly traced the necessary runes onto the haft of the spear. Another smudge of blood, and he traced the other set on the weapon's glittering metal head.

The spell reached its crescendo just before the Onkert dissipated. Micah's hand on the stag pulsed as he mentally reached into the core of its being. Unlike the smaller woodland creatures, it had gravity and purpose to go with its age. The temporal energy was just under the surface, clustered around the creature's withered muscles and poorly healed wounds.

With the help of the ritual, Micah drew the energy from the stag, pouring it into the hasty runes inscribed in the animal's blood on the spear. For a second, the blood glowed white-hot before evaporating and leaving behind intricately patterned char marks on the spear. Temporal power built in the weapon, contained for now by the ritualistic bindings he'd inscribed on it.

Then the Onkert faded, turning translucent and immaterial in the blink of an eye. The stag, partially rejuvenated by Micah's magic, stood up and bounded out of the clearing, but he didn't have the time to look at it. The entirety of Micah's focus was concentrated on the small chisel in his hand. Almost in a trance, he layered inscription after inscription on the weapon as the temporal energy *thrummed* down its length, waiting for a mistake to release it in a fiery blast.

He worked on, blind to his surroundings, grabbing reagents from the backpack absently as the layers of enchantments on the spear deepened. Finally, with the sun low in the sky, Micah sank a full point of Moon attunement into the spear, finishing his work. Without the stag, this project would have cost him at least 5 full points, functionally crippling him as a spellcaster.

For a brief second, nothing happened. Micah cursed himself as he stared at the inert weapon. He didn't have the spare attunement to waste on failed projects. Then, starting with the butt of the spear, his rune carvings began to glow. Slowly, greenish-gold light traced up the intricate curves and whorls until they hit the head of the spear, which burst to light in a strobe of white energy.

Micah fell back, an invisible wave of force knocking him off his feet. He stood up with a manic grin on his face, ignoring the persistent pain in his lower back, and picked up the spear. It was lighter, pulsing with latent energy.

Setting himself, he performed a simple thrust. He felt a small portion of his mana flow into the weapon and a focused jet of air shot out from it, boring a hole into a nearby tree deep enough to reveal the plant's pale wood. It wasn't as powerful as his *Air Knife*, but the enchantment gave him a ranged option while using the spear.

Walking up to the tree, Micah placed his thumb in the hole. It was still warm from the friction of the air against the tough bark, but the scar from the Wind Spike was almost deep enough to get his entire finger into it.

Micah nodded in satisfaction before taking a step backward. This time, he swung the haft of the spear horizontally at the tree, like a staff. It pulled more mana, and the weapon writhed, wrapping itself around the tree before hardening once again. Micah gave it a quick, exploratory yank, but it held firm.

Flexing his will, the spear softened, released the tree, and hardened once again into its traditional shape and length. It looked like the enchantment had been a complete success. In addition to the usual minor strengthening and sharpening runes, he'd managed to infuse the weapon with two low-tier elemental effects. Wind Spike and Vine Capture weren't the most powerful or useful enchantments that he'd learned in his time at the Royal Academy, but they were the only two that he thought he could pull off unclassed and at his present skill level.

Of course, if he were willing to sell it, the spear would probably be worth between 12 and 20 attunement. A small fortune to someone as impoverished as Micah, but to a warrior, a weapon was their life. Adding magical utility abilities that the average Blessed soldier wouldn't have the affinities to access except through an enchantment made enchanting a lucrative art.

Checking his status sheet, Micah smiled. Whether it was the rushed circumstances of the casting or the complexity of the enchantment itself, he'd reached 10 in the skill. Now it was only a matter of returning to his cave and utilizing the class crystal that he'd stored there. Once he had a class, he could start earning levels and unlocking his higher-tier spells. Given the liberal rewards Ankros gave for clearing dungeons and killing monsters, especially without assistance, Micah would be on track to earn back the attunement he'd spent on Enchanting in no time.

He began walking back, spear over one shoulder and a much lighter backpack slung over the other. Behind him, the sun began to dip below the horizon, spurring Micah to move faster. Even if the forest hadn't been dangerous after dark, he needed to get home by sundown or his mother would be upset.

Really, given his mental age, it probably should have bothered Micah that his mother would still scold and ground him, but instead, he found it endearing. Having to pretend to be a child once again helped keep his focus on what truly mattered and motivated him.

Adventuring was more than watching numbers go up on his status sheet. The average people, the forsaken, and those with common blessings, they too deserved a chance to live their own lives free from the constant risk of death. Society needed people like his father just as much as it needed the "legendary heroes" of the Royal Knights.

It would be too easy to become enraptured in gaining power just for the sake of growing stronger. Some of the adventurers in the Lancers, and almost the entirety of the Golden Drakes and Royal Knights, fell into that trap. As far as Micah could tell, they only bothered with gaining levels and skills to become more powerful than their rivals.

They'd lost their way. They didn't answer Mursa's call to increase knowledge and learning. They didn't follow Luxos' command to improve society as a whole. The only god they even theoretically supported with their constant petty struggles was Ankros, and even then, their growth was more a matter of posturing than actually pitting themselves against the champions of other nations.

Micah's thoughts were interrupted by the cold and wet tip of an animal's muzzle pressing against his cheek. He jumped, whipping around with the spear at ready. The stag from earlier cocked its head at him in bemusement, its great antlers flashing in the orange afternoon light.

He frowned slightly, noticing that despite the animal being noticeably younger, its fur was snow-white rather than its previous brownish gray. It snorted at Micah before walking slowly toward him. Without showing any fear, it nuzzled his shoulder once again.

Micah lowered the spear and stroked its muzzle. Its fur was softer than expected, a rich white mat that tangled around his fingers. The stag stepped backward and pawed lightly at the forest soil before snorting again, shaking its head in the general direction he'd been walking.

"Fine." Micah chuckled. "I'll lead the way."

He couldn't be sure, but the stag clearly wasn't an ordinary deer. It wasn't an unheard-of phenomenon for an ordinary animal to receive a deity's blessing and gain an affinity. It didn't happen as often as with humans, elves, and the Durgh, but when it did, the blessing was usually coupled with an increase in intelligence. Either way, he wasn't going to get rid of the stag without attacking it, and given his current lack of class, combat didn't seem like the best choice available to him.

Finally, he reached the cave. He stepped into the cavern's mouth, his new companion following him fairly closely. It stopped and wrinkled its nose in disgust, likely at the unappetizing scent of the caged animals inside. The stag snorted once before exiting and walking around the crag in which the cave was situated. It looked at him one more time before beginning to eat grass in disinterest.

"Fair enough." Micah shrugged, chuckling slightly at the animal's almost-instant dismissal of his "base." "I didn't pick it because it's pretty."

He walked inside, passing by his food stores and the cages of the raccoons and squirrels. In the bowels of the cave, he fished a burlap sack out of an alcove in the wall and removed the class crystal hidden inside. Seating himself on the hard floor of the cavern, he placed both hands on it before diving into the misty realm of whatever force governed classes.

About fifteen minutes later, he stood up, stretching some of the soreness out of his body. This time, class selection didn't carry with it any of the drama or uncertainty. As soon as he'd heard that Thau-maturge was an option, Micah had selected it. Gaining a point of Mind, Spirit, and one point that he could assign anywhere per level was reward enough, but the noticeable increase in per-level mana growth confirmed his choice.

The class selection still burned his hands slightly, but other than that one minor setback, all that was left was to see how far this supposedly legendary class could take him.

31

SOLO? LEVELING

Micah's *Air Knife* slipped under the shadow ogre's guard, scoring a hit in the tough flesh of its torso. It bellowed its frustration at him, swinging a clawed hand at neck-level. Micah brought his spear up and willed mana into it to wrap the weapon around the ogre's fist. His toes left the ground as he let the momentum of the attack transfer through the spear's haft and carry him back a handful of paces, safely outside of the monster's reach.

It dumbly looked down at its hand, the hardened wood of the spear curled around its forearm. Experimentally, it tried to punch him again, only for Micah to jump into the air once more. It cocked its head, growling at its captured arm.

Another *Air Knife* hit it in the face, shaving off a couple more hit points. This time, it yanked backward with its bound hand, trying to pull Micah toward it. He let go of the spear and allowed the momentum of the ogre's action to pull it off balance. Stepping closer, he unleashed a *Sonic Bolt* into it at point-blank range.

It staggered and listed to the side as the spell burst its eardrums, sending the room spinning around it. Micah was well-acquainted with the feeling. Over the past couple of years, he'd been forced to use a *Sonic Bolt* in enclosed spaces more than once, and each time his balance just wasn't the same until he healed himself.

As the ogre fell to the ground, he grabbed the shaft of his spear and sent a pulse of mana into it to return its shape to normal. Withdrawing the weapon, he set his feet in the first stance of the Wind Spear art and unleashed a *Gale Thrust*, jamming the weapon up through the chin of the disoriented ogre and into its brain.

The critical hit using the martial art did the trick, finally killing the monster. Heaving a sigh out of his aching body, Micah turned to check the status of the rest of his party. The Onkert daemon he'd summoned before entering the dungeon struggled to hold down a shadow ogre while the stag rammed its horns repeatedly into the struggling monster's sides.

Micah frowned slightly, noting the blood oozing from a quartet of gashes on the stag's back. Clearly, the ogre had managed to rake the deer with its claws. Mumbling the spell quietly, he cast *Heal*, wiping out most of his mana reserves to close up the wounds at a distance.

Cautiously, he approached the trio of creatures, waiting for an opening and then thrusting his spear into the ogre's thigh. Even with all his strength, the weapon barely made it an inch or two past the monster's tough skin before it was stopped dead by its densely packed muscles.

He withdrew the weapon and stabbed once more, knowing that each point of HP and drop of blood he drew from the monster would bring it one step closer to dying. Finally, the ogre weakened enough for the Onkert to pull back its torso and expose its chest and neck to the stag. The beast promptly gored the struggling ogre, removing a good portion of its throat.

The monster stubbornly clung to life, thrashing against the Onkert's steady grip for almost a minute before blood loss claimed it. The daemon let the body slump to the floor, then casually sniffed it before losing interest.

Micah walked over to the stag and collapsed against it, exhausted. The warmth of its white fur and the steady movement of its chest as it inhaled and exhaled calmed him. Its wet nose poked into his cheek. Without looking, Micah reached up and began stroking its muzzle.

Over the last two years, the stag had become his constant companion. The week after he earned his class, it had joined him in a run through a beginner's dungeon. Between the two of them, they'd made short work of the leaflings and pygmy dryads. As he grew in level, Micah had begun using the stag's temporal energy to summon an Onkert, slowly restoring the animal's youth. It might not be able to speak, but in the intervening years, it'd shared dozens of life-and-death struggles with Micah.

Between his work at Keeper Ansom's library and his constant sojourns to the forest to level, Micah had begun to suspect that he spent more time with the stag than his parents and Esther. Still, the stag understood him.

They both wanted to grow stronger. Every time he drew temporal energy from it, Micah could feel the primal energy in its body accumulating from their adventures. It was only a matter of time before it evolved, and he couldn't completely restrain a pang of excitement as he tried to figure out what the stag would turn into.

It wasn't common for a blessed animal to evolve, but it wasn't unheard of either. According to Micah's reading, evolution was to blessed animals what levels were to the mortal races. Once the creature gained enough experience, it would enter a trance and mana would course through it, changing it on a fundamental level. Given the almost-constant fighting he and the deer had engaged in over the past two years, it made sense that the stag would evolve sooner than it otherwise might.

Two years. A bitter smile flashed across Micah's face as he leaned back into the stag's soft hide. He'd be turning sixteen next weekend. Then it'd be time to officially "announce" his blessing so that he could devote all of his time to leveling.

Micah still hadn't decided what to do. His first instinct to conceal the depth of his abilities was clearly the right one. Being enslaved by the "benevolent rulers" of the Kingdom in his last timeline had more than proven that point. At the same time, he didn't know how he could get the outside assistance he'd need to fight back against the Durgh incursion without revealing himself. Even joining a guild like the Lancers seemed problematic. He'd have to slow down his own leveling in order to avoid revealing the depth of his abilities.

Sighting, he called up his status sheet. He had time until his mana recovered, so he might as well go over his options once more.

Micah Silver

Age   15 [ERROR] / 25

Class/Level   Thaumaturge 14

XP   1,740/15,000

HP   290/290

Attributes

Body   10,   Agility   10,   Mind   26,   Spirit   25

Attunement

Moon   9   Sun   1   Night   8

Mana

Moon   103/455,   Sun   159/439,   Night   132/453

Affinities

Time   10

Wood   6

Tier I - *Refresh* 10, *Mending* 9, *Plant Weave* 9

Tier II - *Augmented Mending* 8, *Root Spears* 8

Tier III - *Heal 4, Paralytic Sting* 2

Air   5

Tier I - *Gale* 7, *Air Knife* 14, *Air Supply* 4

Tier II - *Wind Shield* 6, *Sonic Bolt* 6

Tier III - *Updraft* 2

Blessings

Mythic Blessing of Mursa - Blessed Return, Ageless Folio

Skills

Anatomy   7

Enchanting   11

Fishing   1

Herbalism   5

Librarian   5

Ritual Magic   16
Spear   10
-Wind Spear   7
Spellcasting   22

The increased Body and Agility had certainly helped Micah's solo adventures, but as soon as he'd hit 10 in each of them, he'd focused the remainder of his free attribute points on Mind and Spirit. Mind increased the effectiveness of spells while decreasing their cost, but the biggest impact from the Thaumaturge class was on his mana. Every level he gained added about 26 mana to each pool, precisely 125% of his Spirit attribute.

Already, at level 14, Micah had almost as much mana as he'd had at level 20 in his previous life. Given that each point added to Spirit also retroactively adjusted the mana gained from previous levels, Micah fully expected to have the mana to cast his fifth-tier Time spell well before level 19 without having to resort to a dangerous ritual.

Still, those were just numbers. The Thaumaturge class made Micah much more powerful than any of his peers, but it was still far from sufficient if he planned on challenging a being of true power.

On the horizon, the Durgh incursion lay like an ink stain, spreading ever closer to the present as each grain of sand passed through the proverbial hourglass. In spite of his efforts, they represented an insurmountable obstacle. Unless Micah revealed himself and surrendered his freedom to garner the attention of the Royal Knights, he had no way of beating them.

Sighing, Micah stood up, the stag snorting behind him at being disturbed by his movements. His mana had recovered enough for another fight, and he only had a couple hours left on the Onkert's summon. Clearing the boss room without the daemon was a laughable prospect, meaning he'd have to hurry if he wanted to make it all the way through the dungeon. Any dawdling and he risked losing out on the bonus XP and gear from the boss fight.

The rest of the dungeon was straightforward. The Onkert took the lead, and Micah healed it whenever it set off a trap. If they encountered a creature, the daemon would help subdue it while Micah and the stag finished off their enemies. For a normal party, this would've been a war of attrition, a race to finish the dungeon as the wounds built up on the Onkert, but Micah made sure to heal them almost as soon as they were inflicted.

The dungeon wasn't designed to accommodate something of the daemon's power. So long as Micah made sure to heal it quickly, the regular foes might periodically pose a challenge, but never a proper threat. It was a bit strange, he reflected—in all of the stories he'd read about heroes and legends, the tale had always been about a warrior or a spellcaster, never a summoner. Despite that, daemons were incredibly useful tools, granting him the ability to raid dungeons well beyond his level.

Maybe it was simply the Church of Luxos altering the histories to minimize the impact of summoning; he certainly wouldn't put it past them. Or perhaps it was because most summons required a serious sacrifice, something that he could circumvent by removing a couple months of age from the stag. Of course, it also might be a cultural blind spot. Stories about a summoner hiding behind a horde of magical creatures weren't nearly as compelling as those of a valiant knight slaying a fell beast.

Micah snorted, shaking his head at the situation. Hells, he wouldn't be surprised if summoning were at least partially frowned upon because it allowed a skilled user to overwhelm a much higher-leveled foe so long as they had time to prepare. He suspected that the Royal Knights wouldn't be keen on allowing that sort of threat to their power to develop.

It was something worth considering. He'd already discovered methods to allow him to lower the cost of summoning a daemon. It might be worthwhile to see if he could find a way to improve his methods further. After all, a squad of daemons that lasted for days would let him challenge even higher-ranked dungeons.

Finally, they reached the boss's room, and Micah stopped. Dungeons changed their layouts slightly, shifting the location of traps and the content of rooms to keep adventurers on their toes, but he'd never heard of them making major structural changes.

The main doorway to fight the boss was still there, an imposing edifice of iron and stone, but next to it was a smaller door marked with a yellow crescent symbolizing Mursa's moon. One that wouldn't accommodate a daemon or a stag.

He walked forward, almost in a trance, and laid his hand on the door. An electric tingle ran up his arm. Micah turned back to the stag, his hand still on the frame of the door and an unasked question lurking just behind his teeth. The stag walked up to him and nudged him gently with its muzzle, pushing him in the direction of the smaller door.

"You're really okay with me leaving you behind?" he asked it softly.

The stag snorted, nudging him with its snout toward the doorway once more.

"Thank you." Micah smiled at the deer. "I don't know what it is, but it's calling to me. I think I need to go in."

It snorted again and turned to leave, its hooves clopping against the stone of the dungeon's floor as it made its way toward the exit. Micah took a deep breath and turned the doorknob, stepping through and into a world of dimly lit mist.

32

DIVINE REVELATION

Micah clutched his spear, squinting into the mist that spread out before him, unable to make out anything but vague and diffuse white light. Behind him, the door closed of its own accord. With a portentous click, it promptly began fading out of existence. He frowned slightly, but didn't otherwise visibly react as his only escape route disappeared.

"Congratulations, champion," a genderless voice stated without any noticeable expression. "By raiding a dungeon above your level without the assistance of another sapient Blessed multiple times, you have been selected for an additional challenge. Your patron, Mursa, has taken note of your bravery and selected a suitable reward."

"But first," the voice continued, cutting off Micah's burgeoning sense of elation, "you must prove yourself worthy of the goddess's attention and reward. Rather than the dungeon boss, you will be fighting a challenge personally selected for you by the goddess. Defeat it and grow."

"Do I get a choice in the matter?" Micah asked, glancing around the mist-filled expanse looking for the source of the voice.

"You already chose," it replied emotionlessly. "You made your decision when you embraced your curiosity and entered this place. Now prepare yourself. It approaches."

"It approaches," Micah mimicked, his voice a singsong lilt as he gripped his spear and stared into the empty mist. "Very helpful."

A heavy footstep echoed throughout the desolate space. Somewhere nearby, a large animal snorted. Micah tightened his hold on the spear.

Wind blew across the expanse, carrying away the mist. Micah swore under his breath. He was in a grand arena, almost as large as the central market in Basil's Cove. The walls seemed to be carved from one mammoth slab of gray granite, seamless and impossible to climb along the entirety of the boundary. Above the barrier, mist still hung heavy over the arena's stands, concealing great and illogical shapes that moved occasionally, half=seen. Micah's mind rebelled as he tried to make out what lay in them, his thoughts refusing to dwell on the tantalizing and alien silhouettes.

More pressingly, at the other end of the arena, stood a gigantic red lizard. Frankly, it looked like one of the dragons from Keeper Ansom's records and legends except for its lack of wings. It was just taller than Micah at its shoulder, but its torso was the size of a house without even including its head or tail. Those almost doubled its already colossal length.

Its tail, a long, sinuous affair covered in densely packed burgundy scales, ended in a forearm-length blade of sharpened ivory. The beast flicked it from side to side with a speed and agility that brought sweat to the back of Micah's neck. If the monster got close enough to use it, that blade would be almost impossible to avoid.

The creature's head, an ugly mix of jaws and bone spikes, sat at the end of a long, curving neck as it stared down at Micah with the reptilian eyes of a predator. The entire arena shook slightly when one of its gigantic, clawed feet came down, digging into the sand that formed the floor. It snorted again before inhaling and arching its neck backward.

Micah threw himself to the side, cursing the uncertain sand footing of the arena floor as it slowed him. The beast exhaled a beam of light that slammed into the ground where Micah had been standing with the force of a trebuchet. The sand exploded into the air, spraying him with molten droplets that rapidly whittled away Micah's hit points.

He rolled to his feet, patting out the areas where his cloak still burned from the hissing liquid beads of sand. Behind him, the ground clicked as it cooled and hardened into a misshapen crater of black glass.

"Well," he mumbled to himself as he used *Mending* to restore the hit points lost in the attack, "I guess that rules out peppering it with attacks from afar and using a *Wind Shield* to protect myself."

The monster dug its claws into the sand, digging deep furrows before it launched itself into a great, rumbling leap toward Micah that cleared almost a third of the distance between the two of them. It quickly settled into a sprint that covered an uncomfortable amount of ground with each stride.

Micah frantically tried to cast *Plant Weave* as it charged, hoping against all odds that he'd be able to find dormant plant life beneath the sand of the arena floor.

The spell reached out, searching for any signs of life to latch on to. The monster managed to take another two steps before the *Plant Weave* snagged a handful of roots dwelling conveniently close to the surface.

Immediately, Micah forced mana from the spell into them, magically inducing the dormant vegetation to grow. He completed the casting by implanting the spell image—his mental conception of what the completed spell would look like—into the roots. In his mind, they twisted together into a densely woven snare that stealthily slipped out from the sand and grabbed one of the monster's ankles.

It'd do. It had to.

Micah held his breath, watching as the noose of roots crest from the sand just as the creature approached. With a burst of energy from him, it lunged upward, catching the right-front foot of the lizard.

For a second, everything worked perfectly. The lizard's leg yanked against the vegetation and pulled it off balance. It planted its other leg and strained to pull itself toward Micah.

Then the plants ripped, the overwhelming momentum of the

multi-ton monster more than a match for a handful of hastily grown roots and vines.

Micah's eyes widened as he began stuttering out the chant to *Updraft*, hoping that he could get the third-tier spell off quickly enough that he would be able to jump past the charging monster. It wouldn't be in time. The scaled monstrosity was moving too fast, and he'd tried the stunt with snagging its foot too close. He could already practically feel the creature's hot breath on his face.

Its clawed foot missed the ground. The *Plant Weave* had thrown off its gait by a fraction of a step, and the lizard was moving too fast to recover.

Micah could see the surprise in its eyes as it tumbled forward, planting its shoulder into the sand of the arena floor. He finished the chant to *Updraft*, jumping over the body of the colossal reptile as it slid past him, disoriented but mostly unharmed. He stabbed downward with the spear and triggered one wind spike after another that sparked off its thick scales. They might have damaged the lizard, but Micah doubted it.

Landing, he spun and thrust his spear, launching another wind spike into the softer scales of the creature's stomach. This time, rather than sparks, Micah was rewarded with a trickle of dark blood as the enchantment on his spear barely cut through the creature's armored hide.

It flicked its tail in Micah's direction, forcing him to throw himself face-first onto the sand as the blade whistled overhead. Whispering the words to *Root Spears* with his mouth pressed into the floor, he was rewarded with a bellow of rage. The wooden stakes thrust upward from the arena and into the unprotected underbelly of the monster.

Standing up, Micah used the moment of distraction to run toward it, firing an *Air Knife* into its lower torso as it tried to pull itself to its feet. Another blast of light disintegrated a chunk of the arena's wall as the monster tried to twist its head toward him. Silently, he thanked his foresight in investing attribute points in both Body and Agility.

They might not directly improve his ability to cast spells, but without them, he'd have been annihilated by that breath weapon. Twice.

Up close, he unleashed a *Sonic Bolt* at the monster's head as it tried to stand. It stumbled, head drooping closer into Micah's range as the vibrations rattled its skull. He cast the spell again, causing the monster's eyes to blank entirely while its body dropped bonelessly to the sand.

Smiling grimly, he sprinted to its head and was glad to confirm his suspicions. The colossus had thick scales to ward off conventional weapons, but sonic attacks tended to ignore defenses like that. Despite not doing as much damage as a sword or a spear, their vibrations ruptured veins and damaged organs with almost no regard for the armor covering those soft tissues.

Adopting a ready stance of the Wind Spear style just in front of the monster's head, Micah planted his feet and prepared his mana for the martial art. He stabbed forward with all of his strength. The *Gale Thrust* punched deep into the lizard's unseeing right eye, hopefully drilling the spear into its brain.

It jerked its head up, the pain from the spear lodged in its head waking it from the *Sonic Bolt*-induced stupor. Micah gritted his teeth and held on to the spear with both hands, feeling it jostle back and forth deep in the creature's skull as his weight wrenched the weapon to the side. Hot blood sprayed across the arena as it screamed defiance at him, roaring at a volume and range that promised he would need an *Augmented Mending* to repair his eardrums later.

Before Micah could complete the *Sonic Bolt* spell he was mumbling, the monster whipped its head to the side. The spear lodged in its eye shifted with a sickening *squelch* sound before it caught, stuck in the lizard's eye socket. It jerked in Micah's hands, but the combination of momentum and blood slicking the haft of the spear was too much.

The slick wood slipped from his hands and Micah went flying. There was a brief moment of weightlessness before he struck the arena wall with an audible crack of breaking bones. Immediately, a sharp, burning pain erupted from his shoulder and stars filled his vision.

Micah stood up, doing his best to ignore the sharp throbbing from his left side. The creature was staring at him, its remaining eye clouded with rage while the other wept tears of dark blood around the spear. Its head pulled back as it prepared to exhale once again.

Micah sprinted toward it, ignoring the jolt of electric pain coursing through his shoulder with each jarring step. Dodging to either side would be futile at this range; it could simply adjust its head to the left or right by a fraction of a degree and he'd be nothing more than a charred addition to the arena floor. His only hope lay in the fact that every breath attack to date had been telegraphed by the creature first rearing its curved neck back before lunging forward to exhale.

It wasn't a given, but it might be possible to get close enough to the creature that it couldn't angle its head downward quickly enough to reach him. The only other alternative was to try and find a way to deflect the blast, which was patently impossible with his current spell selection.

The head thrust forward and Micah threw himself into a rolling skid, trying futilely to keep only his good shoulder in contact with the sand of the arena. He gasped in pain as his body weight pressed down on the broken shoulder, blanking his mind. Almost in slow motion, white light erupted from the creature's maw, tracking a line in the sand toward him.

He stared at the advancing beam insensibly, the pain radiating from his shoulder stealing his breath and preventing rational thought. It cut out some five paces from Micah and left a trail of burbling, red-hot molten glass in its wake.

The lizard wobbled, a spattering of scalding blood raining down on the sand around Micah from its wound. Staggering to his feet, Micah put his good hand on the creature's chest and unleashed a *Sonic Bolt* directly into its torso.

Its head snapped at him drunkenly, the loss of blood and depth perception from its missing eye giving Micah enough of an edge to scamper away. He cast another *Sonic Bolt,* this one from close range into the back of its skull. The part of his mind that was detached from the fight noted his dipping mana pools.

With a crash, the monster slammed to the ground next to Micah. The impact of its fall knocked him from his feet and onto his injured shoulder once more. His world flashed black, and stars filled Micah's vision.

Micah blinked. His entire world was pain. Beyond the red-hot poker lodged in his shoulder, his body was covered in bruises and abrasions. In the supernova of agony, time was meaningless. He might have been lying on the arena floor for a second or five minutes.

Each breath lodged a molten spike of pain into his shoulder, the air hot in his lungs as it rasped past his ragged throat. His heart beat in his ears, and a low moan unconsciously rose from his chest.

Without caring about the consequences, he cast *Augmented Mending* on himself twice, the first setting his shoulder and the second clearing up most of the internal bleeding. Micah rolled over and pulled himself up to his hands and knees, coughing up blood. At some point, at least two of his ribs had broken and punctured a lung. One or two inches deeper and the bleeding would've been too much. He would have never woken up from being knocked out.

Pulling himself to his feet with a wince, Micah looked over at the monster. Its chest still moved up and down shallowly, but it was clearly unconscious. He limped over to it and cast *Plant Weave,* creating a rope of braided roots right in front of its head. He picked up the rope, gritting his teeth in pain as his body screamed at him for bending over.

With one smooth motion, he yanked his spear from the creature's injured eye and shoved the length of roots into its place. The other eye opened hazily as agony shocked it back to awareness. Micah stared it down, smiling grimly.

Without moving, he cast *Root Spears* on the rope. It erupted in wooden thorns up and down its length, shredding the soft tissue and brain inside the gigantic reptile's head. Blood poured from the wound and hissed as it stained the arena floor. Its tail twitched once, and then the breathing stopped.

Micah let himself slump to the arena floor, focusing on deep, calming breaths to avoid panicking now that the wave of adrenaline fled his body.

Mist rushed into the arena, cooling Micah and quickly obscuring everything. The diffuse light around him grew to an almost-blinding intensity. Micah brought his hand back up to his eyes, shielding them.

A second later, it was all gone. There was no mist, and he was sitting in the room outside the boss's chamber in the dungeon. The only signs that the entire encounter hadn't been in his imagination were the bruises and scrapes covering his body and the ornate wooden box sitting on the stone floor in front of him.

Gingerly, he opened the box. Inside were the fruits of his labor, the rewards of a goddess that he'd risked his life to please. Two books. Both had leather covers inlaid with any number of precious and semi-precious gems in intricate designs and bound with what looked to be a golden thread.

When he opened the first book's cover, Micah almost dropped it. The first page was without embellishment, simply stating *Temporal Power: Its Collection, Transfer, and Usage by Mursa, Goddess of Moon and Magic* in plain but legible writing. With shaking hands, he picked up the second book and opened it. The title was less shocking, but *Intermediate Daemon Summoning by Mursa, Goddess of Moon and Magic* was still a work that would likely be worth hundreds of points of attunement.

Micah flopped onto his back with a smile. Maybe there was a way forward that didn't involve going to the Royal Knights after all.

33

FORGING FORWARD

T his is a book that you should not be reading. The knowledge contained within is dangerous and forbidden for good reason. Summoning daemons from Elsewhere, while a potent art, cannot be done with any measure of exactitude. Even the most talented of ritualists could easily drain their entire life force by accident or fail in binding a daemon that they summon. For those brave enough to actually use this book, many of them will die at the hands of their own creations.

Nevertheless, the reason why you have received this book is simple. My path has always been one of discovery. My brother Luxos believes that mortal society will evolve together, slowly achieving the perfection needed to rise above the nursery that is Karell. Ankros believes that conflict is like a whetstone, sharpening the best amongst you. As you seek to overcome progressively more difficult challenges, eventually, you will grow past your humble beginnings and join us in the heavens.

For me, the answer has always been knowledge. Only through learning more about the world around them can a mortal purge their imperfect bodies and join us. Unfortunately, this is a project that by any rights should take several lifetimes if each mortal has to gather the necessary knowledge on their own.

This is where Luxos has the right of things. Society protects people, but it also protects knowledge, almost never for purely altruistic reasons. No, the rich hoard books to give them an advantage in their petty little games with their rivals, and spellcasters create esoteric traditions to curate and protect the handful of secrets they manage to wrench from the cosmos in their short lives. Still, it builds up over time as individual grains of sand gather to form a desert.

Ankros, on the other hand, makes his own compelling points. Luxos' pawns are too worried about their rules and games of power. They amass knowledge, but first, they ensure that it's safe, preventing anything with a modicum of risk from becoming publicly available. Without occasional existential threats to their very existence, most mortals would happily go about their everyday life without ever making major changes. That path is a dead end. If mortals are to make the leap beyond their station, they will need a kick. A reason to risk it all.

The path forward lies in giving mortals the tools they need to make something of themselves as well as the motive to use it. If you've received this book, it is because I foresee dark times ahead of you. Daemon summoning won't necessarily solve your problems—in fact, it might very well multiply them—but I suspect that you are running low on options.

Remember, no knowledge is truly forbidden. Feared and respected? Yes. You should fear and respect your magic just as your enemies fear and respect you. Forbidden? That is failing the fundamental task that we, Karell's Pantheon, have laid before you as mortals. You must learn and grow or die. Ultimately, stagnation is just as fatal as an arrow or disease.

-Mursa, Goddess of Moon and Magic

Micah closed the book thoughtfully. Even after reading it twice, he kept returning to the foreword. Both *Intermediate Daemon Summoning* and *Temporal Power* were very clear about what they were: a dangerous lifeline thrown to a drowning man.

He sighed. Theoretically, he should be grateful that Mursa was this blunt with him. Of course, that didn't change the fact that her "brutal honesty" was arriving in his third timeline. Maybe he'd give the fickle goddess more credit if she'd actually hinted at what was in store for him his first time through.

Of course, Micah thought as he massaged his temples and continued musing, he probably wouldn't have been desperate enough to use the books if she'd given them to him in his first or second iteration. Sometimes there was nothing to do but shake his head at the bright and cheerful version of himself that had joined the Lancers, sure that he was destined for an ordinary life full of ordinary adventures.

He'd been almost as naive when he threw himself at the mercy of the Golden Drakes. The implied promise of fame and security were all he'd needed to sign away his future, sight unseen, to a bunch of strangers that turned out to be calculating sociopaths. Even now, his reliance on the books provided by Mursa was probably the same brand of naiveté.

Through everything, his abilities were just too perfectly tailored to his circumstances. Hells, Mursa had laid it all out in her foreword. Her plan was to give him the power and knowledge he needed to succeed, and then force him into impossible circumstances until he surpassed them or broke.

The time travel, his affinities, the Ageless Folio—everything slotted together too neatly, like the brightly colored puzzles that woodworkers sold to children at the market. Mursa was giving him choices, but so many of them were such obvious dead ends that it would drive Micah to madness if he dwelt upon it.

He stood up and strolled out of the cave, pondering the books. Really, they were too good to be true. *Intermediate Daemon Summoning* contained the theory and basis for rituals summoning Brensen and Luoca, the fourth and third tiers of daemonkind, respectively. Before he'd acquired the book, he'd only heard rumors of the Brensen, great clawed vultures that tore through veteran adventurers with ease. The records didn't even mention Luoca beyond speculating that higher tiers of daemon likely existed.

As far as he could tell, each Onkert was more or less the equivalent of a level 20 human with a standard class. Brensens were roughly as powerful as a level 40 human, putting them around the level of most of the guildmasters in Basil's Cove. In theory, that meant that Luoca were as strong as a level 60 human, putting them on par with full Royal Knights.

Unfortunately, he wouldn't be summoning a Luoca anytime soon. Micah was skilled enough to summon an Onkert without too much difficulty, but the complexity and reagents needed for the higher-tiered castings were on another level entirely. Theoretically, he might be able to summon a Brensen, but he still wasn't entirely sure of the formula. Of course, the cost in life force to summon any of the higher-tiered daemons was astronomical.

That was where *Temporal Power* came in. Micah quickly learned that the temporal ritual that he'd used, steeped in years of experience transferring temporal power, was nothing more than the fumblings of a dabbler. The book contained no rituals or formulae itself, instead focusing on theory, but it opened doors to Micah that he hadn't even known existed.

All ritual magic tapped into another place, helpfully referred to in the texts as Elsewhere. Whatever Elsewhere was—besides the home of the daemons—the fundamental laws of magic and reality there differed greatly from those of Karell. Unlike Karell, where the deities created and regulated magic to make it safe for mortals to use, the magic of Elsewhere was borderline infinite. So long as you created the right spell form, you could theoretically do anything.

By carefully and methodically organizing and aligning Karell with Elsewhere inside a ritual circle, a caster could use primal energy to bridge the gap and use the untamed raw magic of Elsewhere. The trick was imbuing the circle with the right spell form, as any accidents could lead to dire side effects.

Apparently, the anima usually used in ritual casting was actually the primal energy of order and chaos. Temporal energy was similar enough to be used as a substitute, but a proper ritual utilizing temporal power would be designed to do so from the ground up.

In the week since he'd gotten the books, Micah had already

managed to increase the efficiency of the transference ritual fivefold. Even that increase just felt like a step along the path. He could almost sense further refinements, just out of reach, that could improve the ritual. With a little more effort, he could strain the ritual further, wrench a few more dregs of effectiveness out of it.

With a proper source, he'd be able to summon daemons that would exist for months or years at a time. Maybe Micah didn't have the power to stop the Durgh on his own, but with an army of daemons at his beck and call, he would bury them before they managed to crawl out of their holes.

Even if by doing so he made himself the marionette of a goddess, dancing at the ends of her unseen strings.

He sighed and exited his cave, carefully hiding both of the books. Given their value and the forbidden path they represented, he didn't dare keep them in Basil's Cove. Having his mother or sister find them while sweeping his room for risqué pictures or folios would be intolerable—both because it would spell the end to his plans and because it would simply be too ironic an end for him to bear contemplating.

The stag padded up to him, lowering its antlered head for him to scratch it behind the ears. Micah's hand sank into its fur while he pondered his next steps. Tonight was the night of his sixteenth birthday. Once he was done burning the midnight oil in his cave, he'd have to return to the city and make up some story about his blessing.

With a snort, the stag pushed its muzzle demandingly into his forearm. Chuckling, Micah turned the entirety of his focus on it, smoothing its white fur with both hands.

"You want me to pay attention to you and stop moping, eh?" He smiled as the soft fur tickled his fingers. "I have been brooding more than usual of late. You do have a point."

The stag chuffed in exasperation, pointedly lifting one hoof before tapping it on the ground. It turned its head theatrically and stared to the northeast.

"You want to visit the grove?" Micah questioned the stag, his fingers still rhythmically massaging its scalp. "We've been meaning to go there for a while, and tonight's as auspicious as any other time."

It nodded its head, leaning its broad shoulder into Micah's side. Once again, a smile flickered across his face. No matter how dark things got, the stag was always there. Sometimes supportive, sometimes insistent, it nevertheless provided a foil and counterpoint to his often morose reasoning.

"Let's head out, then." Micah picked up his spear and trekked away from the cave, the stag following him. "I've only got a couple of hours before I need to return home and get some sleep."

The stag snorted behind him.

"Of course I'll support you while you deal with the guardians," he replied without looking back at it. "You're getting close to your evolution and I want to see what you turn into as much as you do. Plus, I'm more in this for access to the trees. You're too young for me to safely draw temporal energy from you anymore. Those six old-growth trees have been there since before humans settled in these lands. I'd bet anything that I can draw enough temporal energy from them to power an army of daemons."

Micah glanced up at the stars as he walked. He was tired of repeating the same five years of his life. He was tired of playing into the divine hands of his patron. He was tired of the only real option laid out before him likely being a trap.

Even as he marched to summon the daemons he would need to fight back against the Durgh, he knew it was a poor choice. Mursa herself had warned against it. The ritual could go awry, shattering his mortal form. A slip of a word or a misplaced reagent and he could easily age himself to death as he tried to siphon the weight of time from the trees. Worse, the daemons could be summoned unbound. They'd eat him alive before murdering their way across the countryside.

Still, what choice had Mursa left him? He could try the summoning or he could pick death or slavery. There really only was one path forward.

34

EVOLUTION

Micah touched the craggy bark of the old-growth tree, his fingertips trailing across its rough and damp surface. Even without casting a spell, he could feel its age, the gravity, and presence behind the giant. Its branches spread out over a wide, mossy glade, practically touching those of its sisters. The six majestic giants towered over the clearing, only allowing a small amount of the sun's light through their leaves to dapple the moss and grass below.

He turned from the tree, sighing. The stag was trying in vain to wipe sap from a slain dryad on the forest floor, but the stubborn ichor clung to its antlers, staining them a brownish green. The bodies of a dozen dryads littered the clearing. Childlike creatures made of knotted wood and leaves, Micah had been loath to kill them. Each one of them reminded him of Esther, from their diminutive size to their playful mannerisms. Unfortunately, those mannerisms had manifested as they attacked impishly, giggling when they inflicted a wound or dodged an attack at the last second.

Still, there hadn't been much of a choice. If he'd been blessed as a fire mage, it would have been an easy battle. Instead, his only options were to compete with the dryads in his usage of Wood magic or try to use Air magic against the Wood-attuned creatures. Both were awful ideas. Air magic was notoriously weak against the Wood element; the spells just didn't work as well as they should in the same way that Fire magic was extra effective.

As for Wood magic? The dryads had been born to it and lived their entire lives using it in every facet of their day-to-day existence. One casting of *Plant Weave* was all Micah needed to know that their skill levels were at least a dozen points above his.

Instead, he'd simply fought with his spear alongside the stag and his summoned Onkert, occasionally healing them when the dryads made it through their defenses. Glancing over at the Onkert's shredded corpse, he pursed his lips. As soon as the dryads had hamstrung the daemon, they'd almost completely ignored Micah and the stag, focusing their efforts on tormenting the crippled creature. It gave them the opening they needed to pick off a couple of the shifty plants, turning the tide of the battle.

Without the Onkert, they clearly would have died. Even with the bonuses from the Thaumaturge class, Micah was only twice as strong and fast as the average human. The dryads, on the other hand, could literally merge with wood, making them as easy to fight in a forest as an individual wave in an ocean.

Almost every spear thrust was answered by one of the giggling dryads stepping sideways into the gigantic trees guarding the glade. Worse, the sweeping blows using the pole of the spear as a staff were simply ineffective. Micah had learned the hard way—at the cost of a bone-deep stab from a trio of wooden talons—that the wooden haft of his spear simply passed through the dryads.

Between healing the stag and himself frequently, and frantically fighting off the pesky creatures with his spear, they had barely managed to emerge victorious. The task had finally earned him the level-up he'd been waiting for since Mursa presented him with her challenge, but he was almost too exhausted to care. As for the stag? Micah glanced at it, a smile on his face. It had lain down and was beginning to glow, an aura of violet-and-gold lighting up the isolated glade.

He put his hand back on the tree, sinking his awareness deep beneath its bark. The stag would begin its evolution soon. There wasn't much to do but stand guard, and he might as well make use of that time to inspect the temporal energy stored over centuries in the massive plant.

The sap and pulp of the tree sang to him, whispering stories of bygone ages before humans had settled the frontier. After years of using temporal energy, he could almost see the tree as it had been, from a timid sapling to its current mammoth state. His fingers tingled as he all but tasted the potential of the tree.

For some reason, temporal energy wasn't just about time. Rocks were old, but they barely had any power in them. Same with people. You could take years from anyone, but with some people, their time just *meant* more than others. The important and famous people he'd met while working at the Royal Academy had been heavily laden with temporal energy, while an old peasant woman known by no one barely had enough to power a magelight.

These trees were important. Before humans settled the land, they'd been landmarks to the elves and beasts that dwelt in the forest. The elves had given the trees names and told tales of them to their young. He could feel their hands on his branches as they climbed above the canopy to survey the rest of the forest. Their voices whispered around him, giving thanks for his shelter from the elements. His roots touched those of his sisters, intertwining.

Micah pulled his hand off the tree, blinking rapidly. He took a deep breath and ran his hand through his leav—hair.

Trembling, he looked at his hands again. Covered in calluses and burns from constant exposure to the sun, they were still pink. Wonderfully pink. No brown at all.

He shuddered before returning his gaze to the tree with new respect. They were exactly what he was looking for, great batteries of temporal energy that could easily fuel dozens of great rituals. They were also a reminder. Once again, he was a child playing at understanding the games of adults. Rather than a grand match of false smiles and politics, Micah was tampering with the very forces of the cosmos itself.

For all of his mastery of ritual and Time magic, it was still a black box to Micah. He knew that when he changed some variables such as reagents, air pressure, and lunar phase, the results changed, but he didn't have the first inkling as to why. That lack of understanding meant that he could easily make an accidental misstep that could cost him everything without even knowing that he was walking down the wrong path.

In all likelihood, there was probably a good reason why the average wizard couldn't use temporal energy. It defied mortal comprehension and that made it dangerous. The tree had almost pulled Micah into its timestream and history. If he'd fallen deeper into its grasp, Micah had no idea if he would've been able to claw his way back out.

The scrape of a claw on bark in the otherwise silent clearing drew Micah's attention upward. Barely ten feet above him, a grayish-white form clung to the trunk of the tree, its large, luminous yellow eyes fixed upon him.

As soon as it met Micah's gaze, the monster let out an ear-splitting screech and revealed a pink maw studded with needlelike fangs. The world spun, the cotton gauze of vertigo wrapping itself around his thoughts.

Micah jumped backwards, stumbling and falling to the floor of the clearing as the ground lurched beneath him. The creature pounced and landed where he'd stood at the base of the tree just a second ago. He stared at it, dazed, his mind trying to make sense of the being as it stood on its hind legs and revealed a bipedal torso covered in gray bristles. It spread its arms wide, exposing the membrane connecting its torso to its arms.

The monster opened its mouth—a short, almost squashed snout— and let out a high-pitched chirping noise that stung Micah's ears and caused his vision to blur slightly more. Around him, a chorus of chirps responded.

"Oh fuck," Micah muttered, glancing to take in the creature's companions as they scampered down the other great trees of the grove. "Pack hunters."

They circled him, giving Micah a chance to plant his spear's butt in the soil to steady himself and clamber to his feet. He muttered the incantation to *Wind Shield*, hoping that its disruption of the airflow around him would be enough to deaden the creatures' sonic attacks.

With a distorted chirp, the monster in front of him leapt into the air and spread its clawed hands to glide toward him using its membrane. A cacophony of screeches assaulted Micah from behind. The *Wind Shield* did its work, and the dampened sound buffeted over him with little effect as Micah set his feet and plucked the creature from the sky with a well-timed *Gale Thrust*.

The spear stabbed clear through the creature, as its light and aero-dynamic body was not designed to absorb the mana-infused attack. With a spasmodic shudder, the monster died at the end of his weapon and a wave of distressed chirping erupted behind him.

Micah spun around to find another five of the monsters arrayed in a semi-circle around him, gesturing wildly. Without pausing, he cast *Root Spears* and watched as three of the creatures were impaled on stakes of wood that thrust up from the ground, shredding their thin and lightly muscled bodies.

The other two let out plaintive chirps, then hopped into the air and skimmed away from the area of the spell. Micah let them go. They were too fast for him to catch, and running into the forest after them on his own sounded like a tremendous way to get ambushed. Right now, the important thing was watching over the stag.

The next half-hour was spent pacing nervously, glancing into the darkness surrounding the clearing and hoping not to see the glint of a monster's eyes. All the while, the violet-gold aura surrounding the stag intensified until it was a veritable cocoon. Before long, it was so bright that Micah could no longer look at it. Even a glance robbed him of his night vision, and his situation was far too precarious to risk fighting blind.

Finally, with a bass rumble that rattled Micah's teeth, the light around the stag exploded outward in a burst of mana and wind. The blast almost knocked Micah from his feet, but after a quick step to recover, he turned to see his companion's new form.

It stood almost six feet tall at the shoulder, its lithe snow-white form brimming with barely restrained energy. The stag's horns now grew backward, a beautiful metallic array of thorny tines jutting from the main swept-back root. Micah caught his breath when he noticed the last and most significant of the changes: a pair of downy swan's wings folded against the creature's sides.

It approached Micah, and somewhat reverently, he put his hand on its pure white fur, feeling an almost-electric crackle as they made contact. Alien emotions suddenly filled his mind: pride, accomplishment, bemusement. Micah looked up, his mouth half-open, and noted the twinkle in the stag's eye.

Telivern. Its name was Telivern. Micah didn't question how he knew the name. It appeared in his mind fully formed yet disconnected the same way the emotions did.

"You can talk now?" Micah furrowed his brow, his fingers trailing through Telivern's fur. Mana in the fur crackled and sparked around his fingers, filling his nose with a faint whiff of ozone.

Amusement.

Micah smiled back at Telivern. "Well," he corrected himself, "maybe you can't speak, but this is close enough. All this time, I've felt like I could understand you, but now I finally can. That alone was worth risking my life against a bunch of terrifying wooden children and bat monsters."

Telivern glanced past Micah and took in the shredded bodies behind him. It brought its nose down and pressed the wetness of its muzzle against his cheek.

Gratitude. Affection.

"Come on," Micah responded, his hand still enmeshed in its soft fur, simply content to retain proximity to his friend. "We should head back to the cave. I need to teleport back to Basil's Cove and make up some sort of halfway-believable lie about my blessing."

Bemusement.

"I will say" —reluctantly, Micah removed his arm from Telivern's back—"of all my sixteenth birthdays, this one is my favorite."

It bumped its muzzle into the back of Micah's neck as he began walking from the clearing.

Confusion.

35

THE GROVE

Micah wasn't sure when turning sixteen and "revealing" his supernatural powers to his family had lost its charm, but it no longer interested him. He suspected that an entire timeline of enslavement and suffering due to the rarity of his "gifts" had something to do with it. Revealing some of his powers to his family was still necessary—after all, what sixteen-year-old wouldn't be excited about his new abilities? —but Micah just couldn't enjoy it anymore.

After some halfhearted bragging about his "Rare"-quality Blessing, Esther ran off, leaving him alone with his mother for the remainder of breakfast. He did his best to deflect her questions about his future, instead focusing on the need to "train his gift" before he made any long-lasting decisions.

He wasn't completely lying to her. Deceiving his mom via omission rather than an outright falsehood didn't do much to ease his conscience, but after his run with the Golden Drakes, Micah wasn't exactly enthused about the idea of trusting his fate to any outside organization. Even with the Lancers, a fairly honorable organization, Micah suspected that they'd bury him in training and low-risk combat for so long that he'd never get a chance to properly stop the Durgh threat.

As much as he might resist and look for another path, the goddess had provided him with a way forward. Using temporal energy to reach into Elsewhere and summon an army of daemons unseen outside the realm of legends wouldn't be an easy task, but with the help of the grove's trees, it wasn't an impossible one.

Despite everything, something inside Micah resisted his current course of action. He'd spent the previous timeline, isolated and almost friendless, performing the same dark rituals over and over again at the demand of those who'd taken him hostage. If he were to isolate himself in the grove for another two years to finish his task with no one but Telivern to keep him company, the solitude might literally drive him mad.

Of course, it didn't help that his plans involved engaging in the darkest of magics. As much as he might justify the rituals he planned to perform because they relied on temporal energy rather than literal blood sacrifices, he couldn't help but think of Mursa's preface. Tapping into Elsewhere could grant him great power, but the chances of horrifying side effects or outright death were much higher than he'd like to contemplate.

On the other hand, after having breakfast with his mother and Esther, what were Micah's choices? Neither of them would leave Basil's Cove, and even if they did, his entire family would be impoverished and at the mercy of the same callous and powerful individuals that had cursed his past life. Even if he had to risk death and sacrifice his sanity in order to enact the rituals needed to protect his home, it was a worthwhile risk. He might not have had the resolve to make this stand in a past life, but after watching the world fall apart and losing all trust in the powers that be, he'd discarded his former naiveté like a snake shedding its skin.

In his room, Micah cut his palm, letting blood drip onto the teleportation rune. It drank the red liquid, glowing dimly as the blood's essence seeped into it. He shivered slightly when a chill passed through his body and the ritual stole energy from him. Until he'd cast his first teleportation ritual, Micah had always wondered why they weren't more common. The ability to instantly translocate seemed incredibly useful.

The world flashed into a kaleidoscope of colors as he staggered into the cave, shivering and weak as a kitten. *That* was why. Quickly, he pulled together some tinder and lit it with shaking hands, starting a small fire. No teleportation could take place without drawing energy from the object transporting itself through Elsewhere. The amount of energy depended upon the distance and the quality of the beacon on the other end. If you tried to go too far... Well, not everyone exited a teleportation ritual safely.

Telivern walked into the cave, alerted by the noise of Micah starting the fire. Snorting, it walked up to him and lay down, curling around Micah. Its soft fur brushed up against his shaking body and warmed him.

Bemusement. Reassurance.

"I'm sure this is really funny for you, buddy." Micah's teeth chattered as he rubbed his arms. "Each and every time I hop out here, it's like running for an hour through a rainstorm after not sleeping the night before. You should be glad I like seeing you this much, because otherwise, I wouldn't put up with this crap each and every day."

Laughing accusation. Mirth.

"Okay"—Micah rolled his eyes at the mocking deer—"so I did this daily before I met you too. That doesn't mean it's fun. Teleporting is pretty miserable."

Patronizing reassurance.

"Yeah, yeah." Micah stood up, his hands tingling as the feeling slowly restored itself to them. "Thank you for the incredibly sincere sympathy. Look, Teli,"

The deer snorted at him, flicking its head.

"Telivern." Micah raised his hands palm-out in a placating gesture while rolling his eyes. "I need to go back to the grove. Your evolving is an important step, but we're both going to need to be a lot more capable if we want to achieve our goals. The grove has enough temporal energy for me to experiment. I learned some things in that last dungeon that could really help us in the weeks to come."

Telivern nuzzled him, burying its snout in his outstretched hand. Micah ran his free hand through its off-white fur, enjoying the thrills of energy that ran through him as small sparks fizzled off the deer in the wake of his fingers.

Acceptance. Reproach.

"I told you that I was sorry for leaving you behind." Micah smiled, flashes of electricity from Telivern's fur lighting the dim cave. "I didn't know how long I was going to be stuck in there or how much danger I was going to face. I would have brought you with, if I could."

Acceptance.

"It's been a couple of minutes since the ritual." Micah reached past Telivern and picked up his spear. "I'm ready to head out to the grove if you are."

Rather than respond through the strange tactile empathy they shared, Telivern just snorted and began walking out of the cave. Micah smiled as he followed it. Telivern might not be able to speak to him, but since its evolution, its communication had become noticeably clearer and quite a bit more sarcastic.

Following the deer out of the cave, Micah set out after it toward the grove. By now, most of the monsters and animals native to the area around his basecamp avoided him. In the past couple of months, he'd supplanted every predator in the area, slaying them for experience and the energy needed to power his rituals. Between Telivern and him, they'd clearly cemented themselves as the region's apex predators.

The grove itself hadn't changed much from yesterday. The bodies of the dryads and bat creatures remained where he'd stacked them at the foot of a nearby tree. The soil was still churned and scarred from the recent battle, most of the grass and bushes ripped up and destroyed from attacks that had missed the rapidly dodging dryads.

Sheepishly, Micah walked past the chaos and began assembling a ritual circle next to one of the six great trees, careful not to let himself sink into their temporal signature a second time. At first, Telivern watched on as Micah studiously carved the runes into the disheveled earth, but eventually, the deer grew bored and wandered off into the nearby woods.

Micah didn't let his focus slip as he continued his work. Periodically, he would pause from retrieving the rare and varied reagents he'd collected from his previous dungeon excursions to check his notes in the Folio.

Any time he conducted a new ritual, there was a high chance of failure. Given the complexity and power of this ritual, Micah wanted to make sure to double- and triple-check his calculations. Of course, the problem with a new ritual was that he didn't know yet what was truly important. For example, in a teleportation ritual, the phase of the moon mattered, but if your calculations were off by a day or two, it wouldn't become a dramatic problem. On the other hand, the number of days to the next solstice was a vital piece of information. The circumference of the crystal-dust circle changed with the passing of each day.

Micah *thought* he knew what he was doing, but anything from *Intermediate Daemon Summoning* was a risk. One footstep in the wrong spot or a mispronounced syllable could drain him of his life force or unleash a horror on the world.

Finally, the circle around the tree was complete. Micah cocked his head to the side, as if trying to view it from another angle. The reagents and runes all looked like they were in the right spot. He'd accounted for the position of the sun, phase of the moon, barometric pressure, and the position of every major constellation. All that remained was to hope that the position of a minor constellation, the temperature, or some other unknown variable didn't throw the ritual into disarray.

The circle was as complete as he'd ever be able to make it. At this point, any further embellishments were just Micah stalling for time and making excuses.

With a deep breath, he cut into his hand, drawing blood once more. Carefully, he stepped over the ritual circle and inscribed the final rune for the temporal transfer portion of the ritual on the tree. He shook his head to clear it of the tree's weight of purpose—the alien memories of leaves and roots, drinking water through the rich soil.

Slipping back over the circle, he squeezed his still-bleeding fist and allowed a dribble of blood to fall on the inscriptions. They began to glow dully, the unearthly light rapidly spreading around the outside of the intricately carved runes.

Micah withdrew the Folio and began the ritual, reciting the words written in its yellowed pages. His cadence and hand motions synchronized with his precise notes. Slowly, the spell built around him. First, he connected with the tree. His voice faltered as memories of growth and light filled him once again. For a second, he thought that he'd doomed himself with the misstep, but the ritual continued unhindered.

Then he felt another link. The ritual breached something invisible, ripping a hole into the very skein of reality. Just out of reach, he felt unlimited potential. A world of power and consequence without any definition or form beyond that created through a force of will. The hole resonated with the tree, drinking in the aged giant's history and temporal energy. Somehow, Micah knew that this portal was different. That all he needed to do was reach out his arm, and he could have the power of Elsewhere dancing at his fingertips.

He restrained himself—barely. The thirst for the power and the possibilities it represented burned at him, but common sense prevailed. Nothing good came from changing a ritual midway to completion.

The portal stabilized, growing in size. A skeletal claw the size of Micah's torso reached through, grabbing on to the border of the rip in reality and pulling itself through. Micah felt his Adam's apple bob as he stared at the creature, sweat dripping down his back. He focused every fiber of his being on ensuring that the transfer of more temporal energy from the tree to the daemon continued unabated.

It stood almost twice his height, a great vulture covered in ragged black feathers everywhere but its scaled head. It fixed its solitary red eye on Micah and squawked. He wasn't sure if it was a sonic attack, or just what passed for a greeting amongst daemons, but he stumbled, falling to his knees as the words to the ritual continued.

The monster spread its great skeletal arms and stared up at the night sky, breathing in Karell's air as more temporal energy flowed into it. Micah reached his limit and cut the connection between the daemon and the tree. The portal behind it fizzled, disappearing in a flash of mana and static.

Nothing happened immediately as the monster turned its gaze on Micah. He returned the favor, inspecting the creature with a smile growing on his face.

Despite the odds, he'd succeeded. A Brensen. The second tier of daemons, roughly as powerful as a level 40 adventurer. Unseen on Karell in almost a century, and with enough temporal energy powering its summoning ritual to keep it on this plane for five years. The weakness of summoning had always been the limited duration of the summons. It took too much energy to keep a being of any power on Karell for more than one or two battles.

Temporal energy allowed him to sidestep that problem. He might not be able to summon an entire army of daemons due to the cost in energy of each casting, but the grove would provide him with enough energy to make a very credible defense against the Durgh scourge.

Still, his mind flickered to the promise of power he'd felt when his mind reached through the portal to summon the Brensen. The possibilities were endless. He just needed to find the right ritual.

36

FATEFUL ENCOUNTER

Summoning the second Brensen pushed Micah to his limit, but it turned earning experience to level up into a joke. Each daemon was almost as powerful as Martin, a full Royal Knight, and fully capable of handling most of the dungeons around Basil's Cove on its own. With the addition of the second, even the Cavern of Rust—the highest-ranked dungeon in the surrounding area—wasn't a credible challenge.

The dungeons themselves were sorted by the average level of their inhabitants. Some encounters might involve a "mini boss" in the form of a solitary monster more powerful and higher-leveled than the dungeon's standard denizens. Others might be filled with swarms of weaker and lower-leveled creatures designed to overwhelm adventurers that lacked the capacity to attack a wide area.

Entrance into the low- and mid-level dungeons was strictly regulated, usually in the form of a strict queue only allowing one adventuring team to delve into the dungeon each day. Every guild in Basil's Cove wanted access to the level 5 through 20 dungeons. Between the attunement, physical rewards, and experience, they were a veritable font of resources for those able to safely and successfully loot them.

Even though higher-powered dungeons, in the level 20 to 30

range, weren't overflowing with applicants, the guilds would still raid them with some regularity. Considering that the average guild leader was between level 30 and 35, most struggled to put together a full team of the appropriate level to handle such a delve. Conventional wisdom was that a party should be at least two to three levels above the dungeon's level in order to ensure the survivability of the team. After all, delving adventurers regularly ran into at least ten to twenty-five normal encounters before fighting the boss. Challenging a dungeon at your own level was a great way to run out of resources before the final battle, greatly increasing the risk of lasting injury or death.

The Cavern of Rust was level 38 and posed a serious risk to the entire area. Only the Golden Drakes or a coalition of every other guild leader in Basil's Cove could credibly challenge it, and even then, only at great risk to themselves. Almost half of the losses amongst Basil's Cove's adventurers above level 25 came from the infrequent raids on the Cavern of Rust.

Only by paying a stiff price in attunement could the city ensure that the Cavern was regularly pruned of monsters. Of course, without regular raiding, there would almost certainly be a dungeon break of creatures at a level that Basil's Cove wasn't even close to prepared to handle.

Dungeon denizens respawned at least once daily. By some exercise of Ankros' will, new spawns and the old dungeon residents refused to coexist. Almost immediately upon spawning, they would fight to the death with the victors, gaining experience just like a blessed. If left alone long enough, monsters could gain levels or even evolve. While the increasing difficulty level of a dungeon over time was bad enough on its own, any dungeon-born creature that exceeded the dungeon's level by five or more would break free of the dungeon's control and attempt to escape.

In short, Micah rationalized to himself, by raiding the Cavern of Rust, he was almost providing a community service. Really, he was the good guy.

Micah threw himself to the side in an attempt to avoid a stream of metal quills stitching the ground toward his previous position. Digging the butt of his spear into the ground, Micah rolled to his feet, not even bothering to return fire with an offensive spell. Maybe if he were closer, *Sonic Bolt* would be able to do some damage, but the Cavern's boss monster, affectionately referred to as "The Decrepit Behemoth," was so far above Micah's level that directly attacking it was almost pointless.

The Behemoth glowed red as its internal flames stoked higher. It raised both of its metal-clad fists, swinging them futilely at one of the two Brensens as it swept past. The daemon's skeletal claws raked across the Behemoth's metal armor, digging deep and ripping great slivers of steel from them but failing to penetrate. At its feet, the other Brensen dug its claws into the joints of the armor covering one of the Behemoth's four knees. This time, the claws punched through the thinned armor, rewarding the Brensen with a fountain of boiling black ichor.

Micah tried to ignore the Behemoth, a monstrous metallic centaur with access to both Fire and Earth magic, as it towered over him. The dull red of its decaying armor appeared ominous in the flickering light emanating from the orb hovering between Telivern's antlers. It slammed a metal-clad hoof at the Brensen on the ground, but the daemon hopped away with a squawk and a flap of its dark wings.

The ground rocked beneath Micah's feet, dropping him to one knee and knocking Telivern to the floor entirely. Gritting his teeth against the heat and distractions, Micah mouthed the words to *Heal* as he routed his mana toward the two Brensen on the front line. Even though the agile monsters had managed to avoid every direct attack from the lumbering Behemoth, the boss was powered by potent Fire magic that raised the temperature around it to levels usually only found in a forge or blast furnace.

Unfortunately, his skill level with *Heal* wasn't high enough to fully mend the burns on both of the daemons, but it went a long way toward supplementing their natural regeneration. Silently, he cursed his level. Even with his advanced class, limited mana would restrict him to only casting the spell six to seven times in a row.

Another geyser of blood erupted from the Behemoth as the flying daemon landed on its lower back and began shredding its way through the heavily worn armor. The boss bellowed, trying unsuccessfully to reach behind itself and dislodge the Brensen from its back. Ordinarily, an attack of this nature wouldn't be possible. A normal human like Micah would ignite if they remained in close contact with the monster. Worse, the heat radiating from the Behemoth would quickly soften and melt any weapon to the point that it couldn't even scratch the creature's leathery skin, let alone its armor.

Micah cast *Heal* once more, targeting the daemon riding the bucking centaur. Instinctively, as the spell took hold, he could feel the damage from the heat aura accumulating on his summoned monster. Already, it'd lost more hit points than Micah even had.

He winced as another gush of blood from the Behemoth soaked the Brensen, the scalding liquid shaving off another fraction of its total hit points. Luckily, the daemons regenerated and were fairly resistant to environmental stressors such as extreme heat and corrosion. Without their resilience, the entire battle would have ended almost fifteen minutes ago and Micah would already be dead.

The Brensen at the Behemoth's feet ducked under the huge creature as it failed in its confusion, slashing its underbelly with both of its deceptively sharp bone claws. Micah hurried behind a boulder and began recovering his mana. The last thing he needed was for the Behemoth to fire another swarm of needles, any one of which could kill him in a single shot if they hit him cleanly.

There wasn't much he could do other than heal his daemons. Even though his Air magic held the advantage against the Earth magic that powered its rusty iron armor, *Air Knife* didn't pack enough of a punch to actually damage the boss. Of course, his Wood magic was completely pointless against it. The fire aura around it held the advantage, and any Wood spells he cast would be negated before he could even finish them.

That said, he wouldn't need to step in. Micah couldn't see the Behemoth's HP, but it was covered in wounds and visibly tired from the daemons' harassment. So long as he fulfilled his support role and kept healing the daemons, it was only a matter of time before they brought the creature down.

A bellow rang out as one of the Brensens did more damage to the Decrepit Behemoth. Micah smiled as Telivern walked over to him, lowering its head slightly. He ran his hand through its off-white fur.

Accomplishment.

"Almost, friend." He chuckled slightly. "The daemons have everything in hand. Pretty soon, all we'll have to do is collect the experience and rewards and then we can head back to the cave."

Discontent. Unnatural.

"I know you don't like the Brensens, buddy." He scratched Telivern behind the ear. "Just trust me that there isn't another way. Something big is coming, and they may be our only way to fight back."

Acceptance. Discomfort.

"I just wish I could control a couple more of them." Micah frowned slightly. "None of the books say anything about a maximum number of creatures that can be summoned at the same time, but I think that's because no one tried to summon daemons this powerful at a level as low as mine. I'm pretty sure that summoning is tied to my Mind attribute. Unless I do something drastic, I'm going to need to gain a fair number of levels before I can summon a third."

Confusion.

Before Micah could answer, the ground shook. Glancing over the boulder, he took in the Decrepit Behemoth, splayed out on the ground and soaked in its own steaming blood. One of the Brensens grasped the rusted-over iron plate surrounding the monster's throat and tore into it with its hooked beak. A couple of seconds later, his status updated, displaying the huge amount of experience he'd gained from his contribution to the boss's death.

Checking his status, he smiled grimly. One more level until he could learn his class specialty once again.

Micah Silver

Age 16 [ERROR] / 26
Class/Level Thaumaturge 19
XP 4,100/15,000
HP 355/390
Attributes
Body 10, Agility 10, Mind 33, Spirit 33
Attunement
Moon 13, Sun 2, Night 10
Mana
Moon 209/810, Sun 562/788, Night 503/804
Affinities
Time 10
Wood 6
Tier I - *Refresh* 10*, Mending* 9, *Plant Weave* 9
Tier II - *Augmented Mending* 10, *Root Spears* 11
Tier III - *Heal 6*
Air 5
Tier I - *Gale* 7, *Air Knife* 15, *Air Supply* 4
Tier II - *Wind Shield* 6, *Sonic Bolt* 8
Tier III - *Updraft* 2
Blessings
Mythic Blessing of Mursa - Blessed Return, Ageless Folio
Skills
Anatomy 7
Enchanting 11
Fishing 1
Herbalism 5
Librarian 5
Ritual Magic 17
Spear 11
-Wind Spear 8
Spellcasting 23

. . .

He chuckled. Thaumaturge really was a broken class. He wouldn't even need a ritual to cast *Foresight*. Between his incredibly high Mind attribute and level in Spellcasting, the spell would cost roughly half the mana it had when he was at the Academy. That fact, combined with his mana pools being roughly twice what they were the last time he hit level 20, would make the casting of the spell a trivial matter.

Micah stepped out from behind the boulder and walked over toward the altar to Ankros, where the reward for finishing the dungeon had appeared as soon as the boss expired. A book. He shrugged to himself. Books weren't uncommon, but usually, they just had introductory spell formulae, martial arts, or enchantment recipes. Valuable and powerful items, but not usually something that would benefit Micah at his current level.

He'd expected a bit more from the Cavern of Rust. His last couple of runs had earned him an enchanted suit of chainmail and a gem covered in indecipherable runes that could turn earth and metal into lava if he fed it enough mana. Unfortunately, without a Fire affinity, the process was slow and required an obscene amount of mana. In short, the rewards were usually powerful and valuable, even if he couldn't directly use all of them.

Micah picked up the book and turned it over in his hands. The book was simple, only adorned with the word "Haste" and the picture of an hourglass. The leather enveloping the wooden cover was old but well maintained. As Micah opened the book, a smile lit up his face.

The book's interior didn't contain any superfluous information. No page devoted to the scribe. No sheet on the author. Just the spell formula for a fifth-tier Time spell called *Haste*.

Quickly, he scanned it, not entirely able to commit the spell formula to memory but gaining a decent idea about its effect. The smile morphed into a full-on grin. *Haste* sped up the flow of time around a target, allowing them to move and act between 10 and 250% faster depending upon the level the caster achieved in the spell.

Packing the book away, Micah motioned to the Brensens. Both of them immediately looked up from the corpse of the Behemoth, their beaks soaked in its blood from their feast. He motioned to the exit of the boss's chamber as he began walking toward the exit. He'd need to drop them off at the grove before he returned to Basil's Cove to avoid suspicion. Even if the average person couldn't recognize a Brensen as a daemon, everything about them screamed both power and menace. They wouldn't just raise questions—a mob armed with torches and pitchforks was more likely.

Silently, he thanked both Mursa and Ankros. There was no way that spell had been awarded to him randomly. He wasn't sure which god, but one of them was looking out for him.

After hours of walking, the walls of Basil's Cove began growing on the horizon. It was a shame that he couldn't use his teleportation ritual every day, but given his registration as a solo adventurer, the guards would just assume he'd found a way to sneak in and out of the city and ask him questions about avoiding taxes. It was simpler to just pretend to be a normal adventurer two to three days a week to avoid suspicion.

Quickly, he joined the line to get into Basil's Cove, a long, winding thing at the end of the day filled with farmers, adventurers, and merchants waiting for their turn to be inspected and taxed. Just as he was about to pay his attunement and enter the city, a familiar voice jolted him from his musings on the new spell.

"Micah!" He looked up to see Trevor walking over to him, a big grin on the larger man's face. "I can't believe how busy you've been as a solo. Still, there's no excuses now. We're both done with adventuring for the day. Nothing to stop us from catching up over a drink."

"Sure," Micah replied, letting a genuine smile creep across his face. Trevor had a point. He'd spent every waking moment since the reset researching or adventuring. He needed to take a minute to relax every now and then or he'd lose his edge.

"Great." Trevor punched him on the shoulder and winked. "My new team and I are a bit behind you in line, but if you wait for us inside, we'll catch up with you."

"New team?" Micah asked, cocking his head.

"Apparently, I tried flirting with the guildmaster's daughter at a party." Trevor blushed, scratching the back of his head. "Although everyone but him was amused by it, I've been assigned to help protect a squad of new Lancers while they train up to the point that they can handle themselves."

"Anyone I'd know?" Micah replied, an uneasy feeling starting to settle in the pit of his stomach.

"Maybe?" Trevor shrugged. "Do you know a big guy with a cleaver, a guy that can turn to stone, or a pair of sisters? I don't think I've introduced them to you, but everyone but the stone guy has been around the guildhouse a couple times before, so you might have seen them around."

37

AN AWKWARD REUNION

"Come on, Micah." Trevor dragged him by his arm as Micah struggled weakly. "No one really cares that you're sixteen. As long as you have attunement to spend and I vouch for you, I'll be able to get you into the Lancers' guild bar."

"But—" Micah began, his eyes flicking back to Drekt, Jo, Sarah, and Will bemusedly following Trevor.

"Nonsense," Trevor continued, ignoring Micah's distress. "You can be a solo if you want, but I'm not letting my brother become an absolute loner and a shut-in. My new team are good people and they're around your age. Mom and Esther worry about you."

"Esther?" Micah asked, turning his head to Trevor in confusion.

"She may be young," Trevor said, smiling wryly, "but she notices a lot. She keeps asking where you are and saying that you look lonely. Whenever I tell her that you're training or going on adventures, she points out that I didn't work anywhere near as hard when I joined the Lancers. She's right, you know."

"I have my reasons for working hard," Micah demurred evasively. "Can't it just be enough that I want to raise my levels and skills as high as possible before I join a guild?"

"Don't worry about it too much." Trevor winked at Micah as he pulled him through the familiar front door to the Lancer guild. "Dad and I have always known that you're the studious one in the family. Ever since you started your apprenticeship at the library, you've kept long hours. None of us wanted to make a big deal out of it, but we saw the bags under your eyes and we knew how hard you were working."

Trevor chuckled. "Still, you don't have to be that mysterious about it. You haven't even told any of us what your blessing is."

"It's more than Common." Micah smiled, trying to keep his thoughts from straying to the previous timeline. As much as he might want to talk about his gifts with his family, Trevor was a drunk and his mother and sister were notorious gossips. Anything he said would find its way to those in power fairly quickly, and he had enough on his plate without some noble deciding that his refusal to join a guild with his level of blessing marked him as a malcontent or a threat.

He smiled to himself as he sat at a table in the small Lancer bar. Everything from the odd scents and distressing sticky spots to the initials carved in the wood of the benches was exactly the same as he'd remembered. Maybe Trevor was onto something. He'd spent most of the last couple days talking to a magical deer that probably understood him. He needed some normalcy to ground his life or he'd go insane.

Laughing at a joke from Drekt, Sarah and Jo sat down at the table with Micah. A moment later, they were followed by a confused Will.

"I still don't get what's funny, guys." Will's whining lilt immediately brought Micah back. Quickly, he raised his hand to scratch a cheek, concealing a smile. "I don't understand why the Duchess would be so upset about her chambermaid cheating on her in that story. She should've been mad at the Duke when he admitted that he slept with the chambermaid instead. It just doesn't make sense."

"It's a joke, Will." Micah put his hand back on the table and leaned back, finally relaxing slightly as the gentle murmur of the tavern lulled him into letting down his guard. "The point of it was that the Duchess doesn't give a crap about the Duke. She's only actually upset with the chambermaid for 'cheating' on her by sleeping with the Duke."

"But they're both girls?" Will asked, looking at Micah with an expression that resembled a duckling separated from its mother. "Two girls can't date. They don't have the right parts."

"Oh, don't worry," Jo cackled, positively shaking in her seat, "we have our ways. Ways that are often not nearly as quick, disappointing, and messy as other options."

"I don't understand?" Will turned back to Drekt, his face a rippling mass of confusion and furrows. "Why would two women date each other? They can't have babies and the Church of Luxos says that babies are the only reason for two people to date each other."

At that moment, Trevor returned to the table with a wooden plate covered with small metal cups. The unmistakable scent of juushk wafted toward Micah, causing him to pale. His eyes could barely make out the shit-eating grin on Trevor's face through the bar's murky lighting as he began to set a cup in front of everyone at the table.

"I got us the good stuff since we're meeting up with my kid brother." Trevor smiled as he pulled up the last remaining stool in their vicinity. "What'd I miss?"

"Drekt was about to explain the birds and the bees to Will." Jo giggled as she grabbed the mug of hard liquor. "Well, more specifically, the birds and the birds and the bees and the bees."

"Drekt." Trevor's eyebrows shot up. "I didn't know that you were…"

The big man grabbed his mug and downed it in one quaff with a grimace and a satisfied sigh. Almost gently, he put the metal receptacle down on the table.

"When you look as Durghish as me"—he shrugged, a flicker of distaste on his massive face—"it hardly matters if you're a deviant in one way or two. The same people would hate me for either. I do not advertise what I am, but I will not deny it."

"Wait." Jo put her cup back down. "We were just joking around with Will. I didn't realize that you were gay, Drekt."

"Not gay." Drekt looked wistfully into his empty cup while

Trevor's eyes fixed themselves upon him appraisingly. "Simply more free with who I am. I'm attracted to powerful personalities, and the gender of that person doesn't seem very relevant to me."

"Why are you so surprised, Jo?" Micah asked, glancing dubiously at his own cup before sliding it to Drekt. "Didn't you just say that you liked women?"

Jo blushed and quickly took a sip of her juushk, coughing as the acrid liquid hit the back of her throat.

"I just said that to mess with Will, not that it worked." She squinted, the flush from the alcohol already starting to hit her cheeks. "Wait, what's your name? I know you're Trevor's little brother, but how do you know my name? I don't think I ever introduced myself to you."

"He knew Will's name too," Sarah said, speaking for the first time and cutting Micah off before he could think up an excuse. "Has Trevor been talking about us?"

For a second, Micah was tempted to use Trevor as an easy out while Drekt distracted him. Ultimately, it wouldn't get him anywhere. At some point, Trevor would mention that Micah and him really hadn't had a chance to talk in months and everything would become unraveled.

He'd screwed up—it was time to make up a story and take his licks.

"I was, uh..." He struggled for words. Years of isolating himself in a cave reading books might help his level, but it really wasn't the most efficient method of developing social skills. "You guys were talking and telling jokes on the way to the bar. I overheard you mentioning each others' names. Sorry about that if it was a little weird."

Sarah squinted at him. Micah could feel the room warming around him as he tried to avoid her gaze. She didn't believe him. He could feel it.

"Give him a break, Sarah." Jo rolled her eyes as she took another sip of her juushk. "It's a little weird, but where else would he have heard our names? Nothing else actually makes sense."

"I will shoot him if I catch him trying to drink my bathwater or go through my soiled laundry." She leaned back in her chair, eyes still on Micah. "I've had to deal with that type before and it isn't a pleasant experience."

Micah turned beet red as Jo snickered at him. She still looked exactly as he remembered her, slim and pretty with a quirky smile tugging at the corner of her mouth. Everything about her brought him back to their months together, from the way she tilted her head to the clear chime of her laughter. It all crashed into him at once.

It might be the loneliness from more or less living in a hole with a magical buck, but he missed her. It'd been years of Micah's time since he'd seen her, but it didn't dull how he felt around her. His pulse still raced at her jokes and he had to make a conscious effort to not get lost in her smile.

In his first timeline, Micah might have convinced himself that he was okay with their breakup, but he wasn't. Intellectually, Jo was right—he wasn't self-assured enough to be in a relationship with her. Emotionally? Her dumping him had been devastating. Her sacrifice during the Durgh incursion had made everything worse.

Of course, she wasn't the same Jo that he knew. To her, this was their first time meeting and he was just the kid brother of her team leader. He winced thinking about Sarah's accusation, and amended his thoughts. The creepy and possibly stalker kid brother of her team leader.

A hand shook his arm. Micah looked over at Trevor. His brother rolled his eyes at him.

"Micah." Exasperation filled Trevor's voice. "You were dozing off there. I'm pretty sure I asked you the same question about four times."

"Sorry, Trevor," he replied, crossing his fingers under the table that no one had noticed his wistful bout of nostalgia. "I've been working myself to the bone lately and I must be more exhausted than I thought I was."

"Fair enough." Trevor took another sip of the juushk. "I was asking what your class, level, and blessing were. We have a slot reserved next weekend for a level 11 dungeon. Unfortunately, I think we're a little rough around the edges right now. We could probably take the dungeon on our own, but there might be casualties if we aren't careful. I know you're a spellcaster of some sort, and that's exactly what we're missing."

"Oh," Micah replied, suddenly noticing that everyone at the table had stopped drinking. He shifted in his seat, a bit uncomfortable with their attention. With everyone else, he'd long ago shed any vestige of self-consciousness, but with his former team... Well, there was just something that brought him back to his first days as a weak and inexperienced neophyte trying to find his way in the scary world of adventurers.

"I'm a Magi," he improvised. It was a rare enough class to get him attention, but not so rare as to be a danger to him. No one needed to know he was a Thaumaturge. That was just asking for the nobility to act. "My affinities are mostly related to healing and summoning, but I do have a few combat spells. As for my blessing and level? I don't think you have to worry about me in a level 11 dungeon. I'll let you know if we're near my limits."

"A little cocky, are we?" Sarah sniffed her juushk before pushing it away. "Unless you've been in a dungeon, you don't know how quickly things can go bad down there. One wrong matchup and suddenly even a foe weaker than you can leave you beaten and crippled."

"I summon daemons." Micah smiled faintly as Drekt promptly snagged and drank Sarah's mug. "I don't even know how to call up spirits or elementals. Onkerts are slightly stronger than Trevor."

For a second, no one responded. The only sound was Drekt's cough as the juushk burned his already-ravaged throat.

"Trust me." Micah shrugged. "I know how dungeons work. Being solo doesn't mean I can't go delving. It just means I don't usually have a team with me."

"Great!" Trevor slapped him on the back, while the rest of the team mulled over Micah's words. "Next weekend it is, then. Good to have you on board, Micah!"

38

SUMMONING SOMETHING LARGER THAN YOUR HEAD

Micah threw the reagents on the ground in frustration as the ritual fizzled once again, filling the air with an aurora of strange colors and smells before the circle burned itself out entirely. From the other end of the clearing, Telivern snorted at him.

"I'm sure this is funny for you, buddy." Micah rolled his eyes as he wiped the ash covering his hands off on his trousers. "You didn't brag about being some sort of incredibly powerful summoner only to have every fucking summoning ritual fail on you."

Telivern cocked its head and pawed the grass of the grove before pointing its horns at one of the two Brensens lounging in the shade of the trees.

"No." Micah ran a hand through his hair. "I can't use one of them. Onkert are already incredibly powerful for someone my age. If I show too much potential too early, the Golden Drakes or the Royal Family will either kill or enslave me. I'm not a big fan of either option."

He sighed. Unless there was a comet he hadn't spotted, Micah had performed the ritual perfectly. Four failures in a row wasn't an accident. Something was wrong.

Tracing his toe in the dirt, Micah went back through his steps.

and importance were drained from it. Micah
over the edge of the burning, hovering ring of
the touch, sending an electric tingle of power
d its potential.

be without limits. The Drakes and the Royal
beneath him as he became a being of intellect
esses of flesh, the weakness of Karell would
Without any further hesitation, Micah stepped
the crooning of his Brensens.

grated in a lightning strike of white-hot agony.
of Elsewhere tore him apart, leaving not even a
oth behind. For a fraction of a second, he was
cloud of dust before his mind expanded, shed-
to his previous form.

n, a new reality stretched past him. Instantly, he
of things. Physical form and distance were illu-
e slab of meat between his ears to try and assign
The mists of Elsewhere took whatever form his
changing shape in time with his thoughts and
could have anything he wanted so long as his

except intellect, time, and primal energy. Every-
his family, the Golden Drakes, even Jo—were all
the gods because they knew that humanity wasn't
Limits meant to guide wayward children down a
eld them from harming themselves in some care-

ed against his mind. In a fraction of a second, he
f thoughts with the creature, a daemon, tasting its
ement at the concept of mortality. Its confusion at
s, and why he would choose to be restricted to five
ould instead sample reality in millions of other

t, his mind shattered. Micah knew that he'd gone
ivable metric, but at the same time, those metrics

The only thing that had gone awry was the final step. As the temporal energy coursed through the reagents into the ritual circle, the sense of connection to Elsewhere had been off.

Rather than the boundless power he was used to, the ritual felt like he was trying to force a bucket of water through a straw. As much as he strained, only a trickle of the other plane came through, not nearly enough to complete the casting and open the portal.

The entire time, he could feel his connection to the two Brensens. Every time he tried to draw on the energy from Elsewhere, they stood in the way. Micah couldn't be sure, but it was seeming more and more likely that summoning had a maximum limit.

Still, he couldn't help but think of the tantalizing feeling that ran through his body both of the times he had summoned the Brensens. Like he was cracking open a door to peek into the splendor of Elsewhere. Something deep inside him whispered that the door didn't have to be cracked open. If he just pushed, he could open it completely.

Two Brensens wasn't enough to fight the Durgh. If that was his limit, as powerful as the daemons were, Micah might as well give up now.

He opened the Ageless Folio, flipping through his years of notes on ritual magic. Micah's face furrowed as he looked for an answer, anything that even discussed the problem.

Finally, he slammed the Folio shut in frustration. If anyone else had struggled with summoning too many daemons at once, they hadn't committed their problems to writing. Of course, given the cost in life energy for keeping a demon on Karell, it wasn't surprising that the limits of the magical discipline weren't properly explored.

Micah sighed and slumped against one of the large nearby trees. Only he had developed the ability to substitute temporal energy for life energy. If this problem were to be solved, it would be something he'd have to do on his own.

A wet snout pressed against his cheek. Without looking up, Micah reached out and ran his fingers through Telivern's fur.

Acceptance. Reassurance.

His mind flashed over everything he had. Another chance to rekindle his friendship with his old team. Telivern. His parents and Esther. Micah's breath came faster, in short and shallow gasps.

Things were finally going right. He'd now had a chance to avert the invasion and live his life happily until *this* happened. No one had ever said anything about ritual magic having upper limits. Hells, almost all the reading on the subject heavily implied that the only limits were his skill and ability to supply reagents or power.

He had too much to give up now. Micah closed his free hand into a fist while the fingers of his other rhythmically ran through Telivern's fur. Mursa hadn't set him down this path just for him to shrug and give up at the first sign of difficulty. He might fail, but he wouldn't give up without a fight.

Support. Reassurance.

"Thanks, Telivern." Micah looked up at the concerned deer. "I don't know what I'd do without you around to ground me and keep me sane. I think I have it sorted out now. It might not be easy, but I know what I need to do."

Micah pulled back both of his hands and opened the Ageless Folio once more. He opened the book to his notes on the Brensen summoning ritual and began jotting down his own annotations. He didn't need the full ritual, just the segment that opened a deeper and wider portal to Elsewhere.

Clearly, there was a limiter preventing him from drawing power directly from Elsewhere. That was his stumbling block, the only thing standing between him and an army of daemons warding off the Durgh incursion.

All he needed to do was cast the ritual so that he could stand before the doorway of power once more. This time, he wouldn't peer through or take a handful of the other plane's energy. He would step through himself. With the power of Elsewhere coursing through him, he would be able to anchor the daemons to himself.

Frantically, for almost six hours straight, Micah worked without rest, checking astrological charts and cross-referencing it with the

Folio's record c
Brensen ritual, n

Finally, almo
from stress and l
of the clearing. H
nerves as he finis

Quietly, he be
materials around
squawked at him
in its soft brown e
centered on the rit

It would work.
from Elsewhere si
flashed, lit by the in

Micah slapped
breath.

He reached forw
grove. For a second, t
Then the ritual began.
words from his spider
circle as an unnatural
the Brensens perked up

Micah closed his
and flow of energy sv
like suns flanking the
used for the summon
threads of energy, guid
the skill of a maestro co

The Brensens flap
vortex of energy *conn*
potential of Elsewhere f
his hair as a mad smile e

He stepped forward,
song of Elsewhere echo

visibly as its history
lovingly ran his hand
energy. It was cool to
up his hand as he taste

There, he would
Family would be ants
and will. The weakn
only hold him back.
through, heralded by

His body disinte
The roiling energies
scrap of blood or cl
nothing more than a
ding any connection

The pain forgott
recognized the *truth*
sions, invented by t
meaning to chaos.
will assigned them
emotions. Here, he
mind could shape it

Nothing existed
thing else—Karell,
a lie. A lie told by
ready for the truth.
path that would sh
less mistake.

An entity brush
shared a lifetime
curiosity. Its amus
Micah's limitation
senses when he
ways.

In that momen
mad by any conc

were meaningless. A shackle holding him back. His mind expanded as he observed the cosmos as it truly was.

A gentle hand reached out of the mists, its solid yet feminine shape a shock in the formless mists of Elsewhere. It brushed the entity he conversed wordlessly with aside. Softly, it touched Micah, a cool rag against the burning coals of his madness.

Bit by bit, he came back to himself. Concepts such as family, the Durgh, and Jo regained meaning. His goals and ambitions began to solidify and grow once more.

Silently, the hand withdrew, its work done. Micah took in Elsewhere once more. Its beauty and untapped potential still called to him, but he wasn't ready. He knew that now. One day, he might join the ageless entities that lurked here, but for now, there were mortal hopes and ambitions that he could not set aside.

With a flicker of will, his former body condensed from the mist. He merged back into it and willed himself through the portal as it guttered out.

Micah fell to the grass of the grove, gasping for breath as he tried to frantically fill his empty lungs. Marveling, he looked at his hands, not even noticing that the great tree that he'd used to power the ritual was nothing more than a sapling. They were without blemish. Every scar and stain was gone. He'd been born anew by his own hand.

He closed his eyes, a smile spread across his baby-smooth face. In the darkness, he glowed just as bright with the power of elsewhere as the Brensens. Instinctively, he knew that his summoning would no longer be limited. He was no longer just an entity of Karell. He existed with a foot in both worlds.

39

BEING SOCIAL

The Onkert slammed one of the scale wolves against the dungeon wall. Micah lashed out with his spear, willing mana into it to make it wrap around the wolf on top of Will. The monster clawed and bit ineffectually at Will's stone face and throat while the portly man screamed in panic. It wouldn't be able to harm Will through his blessing until he ran out of mana, but Micah was getting a headache from the man's shrill yells.

He yanked the wolf closer to him with his right arm, taking advantage of his increased Body attribute to overpower the burly animal. With his left, Micah cast *Paralytic Sting* and jabbed his fingers into the soft spot in its scales right under its right foreleg.

The green glow flowed from his hand into the rust-colored monster, stunning it. Micah flicked his wrist, releasing the wolf from the spear entangling it, and kicked the limp beast over onto its back. Planting his foot on its chest, he thrust the spear into its throat. The wolf shuddered and kicked twice before it went still.

Micah glanced over to the rest of the party. Trevor was holding one of the wolves at bay with a series of lightning-fast jabs from his spear, drawing its attention while Drekt stepped into position with practiced ease, his cleaver raised to finish the creature off. Jo danced back and forth, darting in and out of the shadows to drag her short-swords across the fourth monster's flanks. Meanwhile, Sarah put arrow after arrow into any wolf that presented her with an opening, with smooth efficiency.

He reached down and helped Will to his feet, grunting and struggling against Will's weight. The man wasn't light in any form, but turning his skin to stone didn't help matters. Will reached down and picked up his hammer, his lower lip vibrating as he tried to calm himself.

"Micah, it—it—" Will blubbered at him.

"I saw," Micah replied, his eyes on the other fights just in case another party member needed emergency intervention or a quick heal. "You have to watch out for the tail on scale wolves. They're heavily muscled and prehensile. Not enough to harm someone wearing proper armor, but more than enough to loop around an ankle and pull you to the ground. That's a useful blessing you have there—it saved you a fair amount of bleeding and pain today."

The Onkert leaned forward, ripping the wolf's throat out before dropping the limp body to the dungeon's floor. Drekt slammed his cleaver down to a startled yelp as he nearly bisected the animal. Micah frowned slightly and thrust forward with his spear, slamming a spike of wind into the final monster's haunch and disrupting a knee-high sweep of its tail that likely would have caught Jo.

An arrow sprouted from the back of the stunned creature's neck as Sarah shot it again. The wolf twisted around to snap at the attack, exposing itself to another pair of slashes from Jo. It flopped to the ground, the tendon in both forelegs severed by her sudden attack.

"—bit my throat, Micah!" He tuned back in to Will's breathy rambling. Micah knew he should be annoyed, but for some reason, the man's panicked account was endearing after his years of solitude. "I was stronger than it, but it just kept squirming away from me. I did everything I could, but it kept just biting me. If it wasn't for my blessing, I would have died, Micah!"

"I would have healed you in time, Will." Micah smiled at him.

"Don't get me wrong, it would have hurt like all of the hells at once, and the feeling of the flesh of your throat magically knitting shut while your breath whistles out of you isn't something you'd forget easily, but other than that, you'd be fine."

The rest of the party began to circle around Will and Micah, their eyes straying to where the Onkert crunched and chewed its way through the scale wolf. As far as Micah could tell, the daemons didn't actually need to eat. For them, it was more a matter of pleasure. They enjoyed the taste of blood and flesh, the act of taking life.

"Thanks for the save on Will, Micah." Trevor grinned at him before crouching down next to the corpse of the scale wolf that Micah had paralyzed and slain. "That's a clean stab there. How'd you manage it?"

"His spear bent around it." Sarah frowned slightly as she looked from the Onkert to Micah. "He pulled it off of Will in one quick motion before he stunned it and killed it."

"What she said." Micah chuckled weakly. "He looked like he was having a bit of a rough go of it, so I stepped in just in case."

Drekt frowned and picked up the corpse with some difficulty. Jo whistled as the big man's biceps bulged with effort.

"What level are you again, Micah?" Trevor asked a bit uneasily as he looked from Drekt to Micah. "Hells, how did you find a spell-casting class that improves your physical attributes? I thought you were just bragging earlier, but it looks like you have the levels to back it up."

"Summoning isn't really a class thing." Micah scratched the back of his neck. "It's more a matter of studying and research. My class is more of a healing and support caster. Usually, I just go into a dungeon with one or two daemons and let them do the hard work while I keep them in fighting shape."

Micah shrugged. "As for my attributes, there are rituals that let you fortify them. They're hard to pull off, but you know me. I always have my nose in one book or another. If you put in enough work, it's not that crazy to augment yourself. As far as I can tell, most nobles have the rituals cast on them just after they receive their blessings."

"Leave it to you to find a way to end up in better shape than me just from reading some books." Trevor burst out laughing. "I knew I should have tried to get an apprenticeship with Keeper Ansom."

"Did you say that you've been hitting dungeons on your own?" Drekt asked, dropping the monster corpse he'd been struggling with. "That sounds fairly dangerous, even with the strength of that daemon you've displayed for us. If you get outnumbered badly enough, something could slip past your summon and an accident could still happen."

"I've had to heal myself a couple of times," Micah replied, chuckling. There was some truth to that. Admittedly, it'd only happened in very high-level dungeons, but an area-of-effect attack that would just scratch a Brensen might cripple him.

Had crippled him. His conversation with Will about healing a torn throat wasn't a matter of speculation. He vividly remembered the moment. A monster had shattered a nearby boulder and he'd taken a face full of shrapnel. He still had nightmares about having to hold his throat together, the blood pumping out of him, as he struggled to push enough oxygen past his vocal cords to croak out the words to *Augmented Mending*.

"That sounds traumatic," Drekt rumbled, wiping some of the viscera from his cleaver. "It also sounds needlessly lonely and dangerous. Why not join a guild? You're clearly powerful enough to warrant special treatment."

"There's special treatment"—Micah smiled halfheartedly—"and then there's too special of treatment. I don't want to be treated with kid gloves. It would make me soft and prone to mistakes." Micah's eye settled on Will as the large man whined animatedly to Sarah.

"Plus," Micah continued, "if you reveal a blessing past a certain level, people take notice. Sometimes it makes them want to be your friend, and sometimes it makes powerful people think that you'll grow into a threat. The nobility aren't dumb. They won't let a potential problem turn into an actual problem. Potential problems have a tendency to die of fortuitous accidents."

"Wait." Trevor's eyes widened. "Is that why you're always so cagey about your blessing and level?"

"Maybe I just like being a man of mystery," Micah said, winking back at Trevor. "Didn't you tell me that the ladies were into men who kept them guessing?"

"How is that working for you?" Jo asked, her voice barely concealing a smirk. "As far as I can tell, Trevor's idea of being mysterious is to keep a girl guessing as to whether he's cheating on her with her best friend or her neighbor."

"You wound me to the quick, madame," Trevor gasped and grabbed his chest. "To hear my honor so openly impugned, I don't know if I will ever recover fully."

"I'm pretty sure the answer is both," Micah snorted. "I don't remember how many times he forced his 'cute brother and sister' to run interference with a jilted lover while he escaped out his bedroom window."

Jo burst into laughter, a clear tinkling of bells that filled the dungeon. A second later, both Trevor and Micah joined her. Drekt even managed to crack a smile.

This was what he'd been missing. The camaraderie, the mutual aid, a cure for the loneliness. As great as Telivern was, it couldn't fill the emptiness that Micah had carried around with him since he'd joined the Golden Drakes in his last life.

"But seriously," Jo said, intruding upon his thoughts. Micah's breath caught in his throat as he realized how close to him she was standing. Maybe it was her stealth skills, maybe it was her blessing, or maybe it was just good old-fashioned inattentiveness on his part, but at some point, she'd approached within a hair's breadth of him. "How is that man of mystery thing working out for you? You're attractive, powerful, and not attached to any of the guilds. It sounds to me like you should be beating off the ladies with a stick."

"That's our Jo." Drekt chuckled. "If she sees something she wants, she just goes ahead and takes it."

"Could you at least try to avoid picking up my brother in front of me?" Trevor groaned. "Or, I don't know, at least wait until we're out of the dungeon? It just seems so wrong to try and pick up boys in a dungeon."

Micah opened his mouth to reply, but just blushed instead.

40

LEGION

The five Brensens flitted about the Decrepit Behemoth, digging their skeletal claws into dark red armor and ripping it off piece by piece. The gigantic monster tried to swipe at its assailants, but they easily hopped out of the clumsy monster's way with a series of angry squawks.

The flames powering the beast stoked higher, bringing the temperature in the room to a sweltering level. The daemons didn't seem to notice as yet another plate of armor clanged to the ground, hints of the Behemoth's blood visible where the plate had been bolted to the creature's bone.

It screamed, more out of frustration than pain. Surely the Behemoth was in pain, but more than anything, the humiliation angered it. It was supposed to be the master of the Cavern of Rust, apex predator and feared by everything it saw. Even if something were capable of defeating it, the battle would be dangerous and the victor wouldn't emerge unscathed.

Instead, the daemons were toying with it. Piece by piece, they ripped off its armor, taking chunks of bone and flesh with it. Periodically, they would pause their torment to swoop at the Behemoth and rip another furrow in its comparatively thin flesh, but it was clear to everyone in the room that they were enjoying themselves.

Micah knew that he should be troubled by the Brensens' blood-thirsty nature, but truth be told, it barely bothered him. He could feel their excitement as they inflicted pain on the creature. He could almost taste the rich copper of its blood wetting his beak.

He shook his head briefly. Ever since his excursion to Elsewhere, he'd found himself becoming more and more in tune with the daemons. They were far from being able to converse with each other, but Micah found their alien emotions and senses bleeding over into his own more often.

Strangely, when he picked up feedback from the daemons, it wasn't anywhere near as disruptive as it should be. Seeing flashes of an object from five different directions simultaneously, festooned in purples and reds that shouldn't be visible to the human, should've turned him into a gibbering wreck. At a minimum, he should be suffering from migraines.

Instead, his feelings were more paternal. He disapproved of the Brensens' actions. There wasn't really any reason to torment the Behemoth like this. That said, the daemons and he walked a very solitary path. Blowing off steam every now and again wasn't the worst thing on Karell.

Telivern grunted worriedly, pushing its head against Micah's shoulder.

Discontent. Wrongness.

"Okay," Micah responded, not looking away from the battle. "I get it, buddy. I'll tell them to hurry it up so we can get back to the grove."

Micah took a deep breath and centered himself before casting *Haste* on his daemons. Even after selecting Chronomancer as his level 20 class specialty, the fifth-tier spell drained almost a third of his reserves.

Even so, it was worth it. A smile blossomed onto Micah's face as the daemons blurred into motion. Their strikes came faster and harder, ripping great gouts of flesh and ichor from the Behemoth as it tried to defend itself by spitting a stream of metal quills. The Brensens easily flapped and jumped aside, squawking and cackling at the boss while their brethren continued to tear deeper and deeper.

Finally, the Behemoth slumped to the ground, spilling its life into the dungeon floor. Almost immediately the Brensens began wetting their beaks as they ripped off and devoured strips of its flesh. Turning away from the grisly buffet, Micah tried to ignore the slimy taste of the dungeon boss in the back of his throat.

Disgust. Repulsion.

"I know, buddy," Micah replied as he walked toward the dungeon's altar, eager to see what he'd receive this time. For the past couple of weeks, they'd raided the Cavern of Rust every other day. Not every reward was useful to Micah, but he'd gained experience and a handful of higher-tier spells. He still wasn't a Battlemage by any extent, but another third-tier spell and a pair of fourth-tier spells certainly helped round out his repertoire.

Telivern snorted behind Micah. He looked back at the deer. It stood tall in the dirty chamber, pure white and glowing faintly, a halo of energy rippling around its horns. It cocked its head slightly, concern in its large black eyes.

"I'm sorry," Micah replied, running a hand through his hair. "There's just so much going on right now between the level-ups, the summoning, and dating Jo, I just haven't had the same sort of free time as before. I swear we'll have a chance to hang out soon. Just you and me, like the old days."

It snorted, pawing the dungeon floor with its hoof before it looked back up at Micah.

"I don't like the Brensens that much either." Micah leaned against his spear, making eye contact with the deer. "It's just that we need them. There's a storm coming. Monsters by the hundreds, if not the thousands. If we don't stop them, they're going to overrun everything. What they don't kill, they'll warp and twist into mindless abominations of magic and fell alchemy."

He sighed. "I don't have the power on my own to fight them. Even with the Brensens, it probably won't be enough. I'm going to need more of them. Hells"—he shifted slightly—"I'm probably going to need to up the ante and summon a Luoca. Maybe two or three. I just don't know if I have it in me to tackle the ritual. A couple more levels and my Mind attribute should be sufficient."

Telivern walked toward Micah. Its hooves clattered against the dungeon floor, the steady *click-click* of its measured pace the only sound audible over the wet tearing and cracking of the Brensens devouring the Decrepit Behemoth. Micah closed his eyes as Telivern approached.

The five daemons shone like stars, orange and red with tethers of ephemeral fire connected to Micah himself. He willed his perception downward, to the small, swirling portal of energy and flame deep within his chest. The chains of power flowed directly into it and back into Elsewhere itself.

The deer stepped into the range of his mind's eye. Unlike the daemons, it shone a gentle green and blue. Slowly, it swam forward in the inky darkness until its snout was in his hand once more. Looking down, he winced. He glowed a dim orange. A smoldering coal next to the bonfire of the daemons, but it would be a lie and an excuse to deny his senses.

There was no doubt that the ritual had changed him on a deep level. Something more than just the night terrors that interrupted his sleep as he felt the fingers of a great and unfathomable mind reach out to mark him. The taint of Elsewhere was upon him. Otherwise, Micah would be completely incapable of maintaining more than a handful of simultaneous summons.

Concern. Discontent.

"I'm worried too, Telivern," he said quietly, running his free hand through his friend's fur. "I'm changing and I know it, but I can't find any another way. The levels I've gained are beyond anything I could possibly earn on my own. This power I'm borrowing from Elsewhere isn't without cost. I know it. You know it."

Tears began to flow down his face as his hand balled in Telivern's fur.

"I keep trying to tell myself that everything is normal." He buried his face in the great buck's fur. "I keep saying that I've faced down problems beyond mortal comprehension. That I've been broken down time and time again only to come out whole. But this is different. I can feel my humanity starting to slip away."

Comfort. Worry.

"You don't understand, Telivern." He let out a shuddering breath as he tried to calm himself. "I can understand them. Their motives, their desires... it's all beginning to make sense to me, and that shouldn't be the case. I feel like... something human is fading away from me."

Comfort.

"But I can't stop." He smiled weakly. "As much as this scares me, as much as I can feel myself taking steps down a path that I might not be able to come back from, I have to keep going. People like Jo and Esther deserve a chance to live and grow in peace. If I'm to be the sacrifice that earns them another decade or so of peace, that's a sacrifice I am obligated to make."

Acceptance. Friendship.

"Thank you." Micah wiped the tears from his face as he took a step back from Telivern. "I'm not sure if any of my friends or family would understand, but you do. It kills me to not be able to talk about this with Jo. I've known her for years, and yet to her, it's just been a couple of weeks."

He painted a faint smile onto his face. "Well, let's see what today's spoils are."

He turned back to the altar. There was a book sitting upon it, brown and made of twisted reeds. Micah rested his hand on the cover, running his fingers gently over its cool surface. Flipping the cover open, he found a spell formula. *Poison Fog*, a tier-four Wood spell that created a vast bank of toxic mist.

Micah flipped through the book, consigning its writing to the Folio for future use. Quietly, he put the book into his satchel. Even if he wouldn't be using it directly, it would be a valuable addition to his collection.

He opened his status screen.

. . .

Micah Silver

Age 16 [ERROR] / 26

Class/Level Thaumaturge 21

XP 3,400/19,000

HP 430/430

Class Specialty

Chronomancer

Attributes

Body 10, Agility 10, Mind 36, Spirit 36

Attunement

Moon 13, Sun 2, Night 11

Mana

Moon 350/971, Sun949/949, Night 967/967

Affinities

Time 10

Tier V - *Foresight* 2, *Time Echoes* 1, *Temporal Transfer* 2, *Haste* 2

Wood 6

Tier I - *Refresh* 10*, Mending* 9, *Plant Weave* 9

Tier II - *Augmented Mending* 10, *Root Spears* 11

Tier III - *Heal* 6, *Paralytic Sting* 3

Tier IV - *Regeneration* 2, *Healing Wave* 3

Air 5

Tier I - *Gale* 7, *Air Knife* 15, *Air Supply* 4

Tier II - *Wind Shield* 6, *Sonic Bolt* 8

Tier III - *Updraft* 2, *Pressure Spear* 2

Tier IV - *Flight* 1

Blessings

Mythic Blessing of Mursa - Blessed Return, Ageless Folio

Skills

Anatomy 7

Arcana 3

Enchanting 11

Fishing 1

Herbalism 5

Librarian 5
Ritual Magic 19
Spear 11
-Wind Spear 8
Spellcasting 24

Two levels in two weeks, including one in the last ten minutes. More than anyone could reasonably expect, but still not enough. The new spells were useful, but not any sort of gamechanger. *Flight* allowed Micah or one of his summoned daemons to fly. Not terribly useful for a Brensen, but amusing to say the least when applied to an Onkert.

Pressure Spear was little more than an upgraded version of *Air Knife*, a thin jet of ultra-pressurized air that could punch through all but the thickest of armor. *Regeneration,* on the other hand, was a powerful supportive spell. It lasted for almost an hour with each casting, and greatly improved the rate at which its recipients recovered from wounds, almost to the point that the injuries would visibly close during combat.

The Arcana skill was a tougher addition to explain. He still didn't know what it did. None of the books he'd read in any of his three lifetimes even touched upon it. All he knew was that it had appeared on his status screen once he returned from Elsewhere.

Micah sighed. The boosts to his Mind attribute from the new level would have to be enough. Even a dozen more levels wouldn't be enough for him to stop the Durgh on his own. He needed more daemons. A Luoca or two would go a long way toward evening the odds.

He walked toward the exit to the boss chamber, whistling to grab the Brensens' attention. Their heads snapped up from the twisted wreckage of the Behemoth. Chirping back at him, they fell into step behind him. He needed to return to the grove. He had a lot of research to do.

41

A NIGHT ON THE TOWN

Jo's laughter filled the night as she ran out of the bar with a crumpled hat in her hand. Micah pursued her, trying to keep a smile from his face. Behind the two of them, three burly men and a sunburnt woman sprinted down the dark street, livid expressions darkening their complexions.

A pair of daggers coated in flame soared past Micah, lighting up the moonless night as they guttered out on the cobblestones of Basil's Cove. Jo spun around in a graceful pirouette, then bowed and placed the crumpled hat on her head in one smooth motion before she resumed her flight.

"All of this over a cap?" Micah puffed as he barely kept up with Jo. He'd used the free points from the Thaumaturge class to fortify his Body and Agility attribute, but at the end of the day, Jo had a speed-oriented physical class, and pacing her was a challenge.

"You can't wear a hat that ugly around me and get away with it," Jo cackled. "It's a sin against the senses of both god and man. I'm doing him a favor. Without my intervention, a god would likely strike him down for inflicting that fashion travesty on the masses."

"Then why in the name of the Sixteen are you wearing it?" Micah asked as he cast *Wind Shield* just in time to deflect an arrow. He frowned slightly. How in the hells did someone manage to shoot an arrow at him while running? One of their pursuers must have a blessing that let them fire a bow one-handed. It was the only explanation he could think of.

Jo's only response was another peal of laughter as she slid to a stop in front of a nondescript house and sprinted off into an alley. Micah rolled his eyes as he followed her, barely arresting his momentum in time to avoid slamming into the next building over.

Behind them, their pursuers shouted something indistinct. Micah frantically mouthed the words to *Updraft* as he sprinted and squirmed past the refuse littering the narrow path between the houses. Just as the spell was triggering, he grabbed Jo's arm and jumped, carrying both of them onto the roof of a nearby home before the spell fizzled out under their combined weight.

Micah flopped onto his back, breathing heavily and staring up at the stars as he began to come down from the adrenaline of the chase. Next to him, Jo whipped off the hat and put her hand in her mouth, biting down to muffle the laughter that rocked her body. He glanced over at her and smiled.

Even without the moon, Jo was beautiful in the starlight. The past two months had been magical. He'd raided a dungeon with the Lancers once a week, handling the Cavern of Rust on his own, but the rest of his time was devoted to these stolen moments with Jo.

A night of mischief here, and a nice dinner there, and the years melted away. It was almost like he was back in the first time loop again, basking in the glow as the candle of Jo's energy burned at both ends.

"Did you see the look on his face when I grabbed his hat?" Jo hissed, her teeth faintly visible as she smiled at the stars above. "I couldn't believe how big the oaf was. By the Sixteen, I swear that he was half Durgh and half Muskox."

"You know he's down in the alley right now?" Micah whispered back, shaking his head slightly. "If we make enough noise, they'll figure out we're hiding up here."

"Oh, come on." Jo stuck her tongue out at him. "I've seen you fight. Between the two of us, we could wipe the cobblestones with these yahoos."

"And then we'd have to explain what happened to the town guard." Micah lay back against the rooftop, panting slightly. "Let's save the adrenaline for killing monsters. I have enough problems without picking a fight with every minor guild in Basil's Cove."

For a second, there wasn't any noise but the muffled voices of their drunken pursuers, stumbling through the trash-filled alleyway. Jo propped herself up on her elbow, her eyes flashing as they hungrily traveled up and down Micah's exhausted body.

"If you aren't going to let me talk"—she smirked slightly in the night air before crawling over to Micah—"I'm sure I can find something else we can do."

"Jo." Micah's eyes went wide. "There are five drunk people down there looking to skin us alive, if we're—"

His hushed words were stolen as her lips pressed against his. Micah briefly tried to struggle, but her hands were on his shoulder and his hair, the warm weight of her body pressing him into the shingles of the roof.

Hours later, Micah stared at the stars once more. Jo had fallen asleep almost immediately. Rest didn't come so easily to Micah.

He chuckled quietly, trying not to wake Jo, while he remembered his first sixteenth birthday. Nerves had kept him awake almost the entire night. No matter how much he'd wanted to sleep, he couldn't force it. The anxious energy had filled his mind with concerns and worries that paralyzed him for most of the night.

Jo, on the other hand, managed to fall asleep while angry drunken adventurers tore up the dock quarter looking for her. It was something that he envied about her. She lived her life hard and without regrets. He might worry about whether he was taking the right course of action, but Jo would just *do* it and worry about the consequences later.

Tonight was a great example. He honestly didn't know whether he was still awake because he was nervous about the angry adventurers or because he was still trying to find a way to talk to her about his future.

Of course, it might be the series of rituals he'd used to restrict his need to sleep. Even after he'd stopped casting the rituals, energy flooded his body from the portal humming in his chest. Every night, he slept less and less, and although he tried to avoid thinking about it, Micah couldn't help but worry that his humanity was slipping through his fingers.

It was true that he was becoming something greater. A mere human couldn't gain levels or control the number of daemons like he did, but at the same time, he didn't know exactly where his path ended. Hells, he didn't know if it actually ended at all.

He closed his eyes. Immediately, the darkness was lit up by the threads of fire extending from his chest toward the grove in the distance. Fifteen of them now. He ran his finger over the tethers. His hand wasn't quite as red as the strings of fire yet, but it was noticeably darker than in the Cavern of Rust.

Next to him, Jo glowed with the same quiet blue-and-green light as Telivern. Much dimmer than the deer, but given that no other human he knew glowed, something worth noting.

He sighed and opened his eyes. Jo had her secrets. Everyone did. In three lifetimes, he'd seen nothing but consistency from her. There was no need to pry just because of his new senses. Plus, they'd have plenty to talk about come morning anyway.

He closed his eyes again, following the chains of flame binding him to his daemons once more. Micah had hours to kill before sunrise and he might as well spend them on something useful, like trying to probe the nature of the tethers and the portal. Right now, all he knew was that they connected to Elsewhere and that they were changing him. An uncertain and worrying prospect.

The hours flew by as he focused on each inch of the fiery bindings. Before too long, he found himself able to dimly sense the thrum of otherworldly energy passing through them. After drawing his attention deeper, Micah began to see the shapes of the daemons' minds. He couldn't touch on much more than their rawest and most primal of emotions, but even that experience gave him a blinding headache as he tried to make sense of their alien minds and desires.

A slim hand grabbed his shoulder and shook gently. Micah blinked awake to Jo smiling contentedly down at him in the early dawn light. She'd propped herself up, hand holding the side of her head as her elbow rested on the cheap shingles of the roof.

"Good morning, sleepyhead." Her voice was soft, barely audible over the sound of Basil's Cove waking itself.

"I wasn't asleep," Micah replied, sitting up and shifting himself so his back pressed up against the house's chimney. "You know I barely sleep."

"Well, thank you for protecting me all night, then." She laughed, a quick peal of chimes, before she continued. "What were you worrying about this time? As great as you are, that's your one problem. You're always worried about what troubles tomorrow might bring. You never fully relax and enjoy the moment."

"What if I know exactly what problems tomorrow might bring?" Micah asked, a half-smile on his face. "If I knew what was coming, it wouldn't exactly be irrational of me to worry about it."

"Nice try, Silver." She blew a lock of her hair off her face. "Even if you know what plan the gods have in store for us, worrying about it won't change anything. We're grains of sand on a beach, afraid of the tide coming in. At the end of the day, we're tiny, insignificant, and the forces that move around us are capable of shaking the cosmos itself."

For a moment, neither of them spoke, just resting in the quiet murmur of the city.

"Did I ever tell you about Sarah's and my childhood?" she asked, cocking her head with a slightly wistful look on her face. When Micah shook his head, she continued. "Our mother was an elf. I'd appreciate it if you didn't spread that around. Elves aren't the same kind of social pariahs that the Durgh are, but that doesn't mean that the Church of Luxos makes it easy for us."

Her voice lowered slightly. "Anyway, Mother was a kind soul. Too kind. After our father died of pneumonia, she took pity on a trapper that lost his way in a blizzard and got lost in the deep forest. He fell ill and she nursed him back to health. We spent almost four months with him while he recovered, but come spring, he was well enough to return to his community. He came back, though." Briefly, Jo looked like she'd bitten into something sour. "While we'd been caring for him, he'd noticed the moonstone jewelry that all of us wore. That summer, he returned with a large party of adventurers. They killed most of our warriors, robbed our tribe, and drove us off of our land. For years after that, we were nothing more than refugees, preyed upon in every human kingdom we came across. Sometimes..."

She looked away from Micah for a second before resuming her story. "Sometimes I wish that I'd killed that trapper. It would have been as simple as crushing up some bloodroot and silver ivy leaves and putting them in his tea. He'd have gone to sleep and never woken up."

Her eyes came back to Micah, laden with sadness. "It wouldn't have mattered, though. I carried that anger around with me for years before I learned that humans had slowly been encroaching further and further into the deep forest. The trapper might have hastened the attack on our tribe by months or even a couple years, but the raid was inevitable.

"Sarah's sort of like you." Jo crawled over to Micah and laid her head on his shoulder, watching the sun rise with him. "She's convinced that if she becomes powerful enough, she'll be able to stop something like that from happening to us again. That's why she tries to play all of these games. I mean, she's even flirting with that pork-ball Will. He's ugly, clumsy, and acts like a child, but with his blessing, he's meant for greatness. For Sarah? That's enough."

"What about you?" Micah asked, running his fingers through her hair. "How do you make sense of all the awfulness in the world?"

"I don't." She shifted slightly against him. "What will be, will be. I'll fight what I think is wrong, but I'm not planning on getting myself killed struggling against some impossible fate. We're all doomed to die anyway. Some of us are just more efficient about that process than others. My goal is just to make the best out of the meantime."

For almost a minute, they sat in silence as the sun crested the horizon and began to cast its warm rays down on Basil's Cove. Finally, Micah interrupted the sounds of the city stirring.

"I can't say how"—his fingers stopped flowing through her hair, cradling her gently against his shoulder—"talking about it will only make things worse, but I know what's coming, Jo. You're going to die. Trevor's going to die. My parents and my kid sister are going to die. Basil's Cove is going to be destroyed. Unless I can stop it, the best-case scenario is that everyone we know and love will survive as refugees, and even that is a stretch."

She glanced up at Micah from his shoulder, her eyes seeking his as she looked for a sign of deceit or mockery. She pursed her lips.

"For the sake of argument" —her voice was contemplative— "let's say I believe you. How in the name of the Sixteen would you be able to stop it? You're incredibly powerful for your age, don't get me wrong, but anything capable of sacking Basil's Cove is beyond any one person."

"You've only seen the weakest of my daemons." Micah bit his lower lip. "I can summon even more after that. I've finally raised my level high enough that I can cast a ritual that I've been struggling with. I'm not sure it'll be enough to protect Basil's Cove, but it will at least give me a fighting chance. This is it, Jo." He shifted, cupping her face with his hand so that their eyes met. "I finally have a real chance at saving us. At saving everyone."

"How?" she asked, confusion lacing the word. "What are we supposed to do to stop whatever it is you've seen?"

"I have to summon daemons." Micah smiled, but there wasn't much mirth in his eyes. "I have to summon a lot of daemons. Then I have to bring them to the Great Depths and fight an army of Durgh amassing to attack Westmarch and Basil's Cove. I don't even really have to win, just do enough damage to make them think twice about attacking the surface."

"You're serious, aren't you?" she asked, a hint of a smile teasing the corners of her mouth upward. "By the Sixteen, whatever this vision was, you believe it enough to risk the Depths."

Micah just nodded.

"Well." She smiled back, her eyes flashing like gems in the early morning sunlight. "Just tell me when we're heading down. That's not an adventure I'm going to miss."

"Jo," Micah said, frowning, "I don't know exact levels, but the average Durgh are around level 20. The daemons can fight them, but you'll get torn apart. I've literally already seen you die once. I'm not willing to do it again."

"Micah," she replied, her voice snippy as she crossed her arms, "we're more than just friends. If you think that I'm going to just let you run off into danger to 'save' me from the unknown, you have another think coming."

He frowned. "Jo."

"I'm not some sort of damsel in distress, Micah." Her tone rose as her eyes flared. "I've been taking care of myself for years before I met you. I can handle fighting and hardship just as well as you."

"*Jo*," he implored her, "if I go, I might die. If you go, you *will* die. I can't take that again. Worse, I'll be so worried about your safety that I'll be distracted. I won't even be able to fight properly."

She frowned, opening her mouth to respond before closing it again. Finally, she turned her back to Micah and stood up. Tiptoeing to the edge of the roof, she glanced backwards briefly from the precipice.

"Fine." Her voice was a mélange of bitterness and sadness. "Have fun on your adventure. I'm glad I could at least send you off in style."

She jumped off the edge, catching a windowsill on her way down to slow her fall.

"Jo—" The word was torn from Micah's lips, but it was too late. Micah scurried to the edge where she'd disappeared. He glanced up and down the alley, but she was already gone.

He sighed, running his hand through his hair. No matter how

many lifetimes he spent with Jo, he felt that he'd never actually understand her.

Micah pulled up his status screen as he began to cast *Updraft* to slow his own descent. Frowning, he stopped the spell. Where in the hells had that skill point in Arcana come from?

42

DO NOT GO GENTLE INTO THAT GOOD NIGHT

Micah sighed, taking in the collection of saplings that used to be the grove. Every dreg of temporal energy had been siphoned from the old-growth trees and into his collection of daemons. Dozens of Onkerts milled about, snarling and whining at each other as ten Brensens lounged indolently in the shade just outside the bounds of the grove.

Next to Micah, the two Luocas—cicadas the size of an ox with the head of a man and the tail of a scorpion—stood silently, observing his forces with him. Each had taken an entire tree's worth of temporal energy to summon them, and they chilled him to the core. Unlike the rest of the more bestial daemons, the Luocas could reason. When they weren't under orders, he could hear them conversing in low, hissing voices that he couldn't quite make out.

As much as they disturbed them, he'd seen their speed and power. Even better, reality itself seemed to shy away from them. Their wings and tail seemed to soften or even melt matter that they came into contact with. Not enough to destroy what they touched, at least not immediately, but they certainly weakened anything they were striking. Micah didn't really have a frame of reference for how powerful a level 60 Blessed was, but at least according to the book he'd received from Mursa, the Luocas were more or less their match.

He reached down and ran his fingers through the dirt. Micah didn't know if it was the act of tapping temporal energy from the great trees guarding the grove or some other effect, but the rich soil of the clearing had slowly transformed into lifeless sand. All around him, ferns and grass struggled to take root in the loose and nutrient-free earth.

They'd starved. Soon, the clearing would be devoid of all plant life, a brown-and-gray smear in the verdant green of the forest. After that, it was only a matter of time before the rest of the nearby ecosystem avoided the grove.

It pained him to see what had been more or less his second home after Telivern and he moved out of the cave wither away, especially given his role in its destruction. Of course, that didn't mean that Micah regretted his actions. Although his "army" numbered less than fifty daemons, it could almost certainly level Basil's Cove on its own. Especially with him supplying support spells to his minions.

That was another pleasant discovery of the last couple of weeks. He could cast spells that normally needed physical contact through the tethers that bound him to the daemons. It wasn't entirely pleasant to think of the implications of that piece of information—that the daemons were inexorably linked to his soul—but every time he closed his eyes, his body illuminated the darkness like a bonfire. He barely slept or ate anymore, and when he rested, he could almost hear the daemons speaking to each other, like voices whispering just around the corner. Whatever was happening to Micah, he suspected it was irreversible at this point.

With a whistle, he called the attention of the daemons. It didn't really matter. His home was ash and he wasn't entirely sure if he still counted as human, but Micah had successfully marshalled an army that could challenge the Durgh. If the price to save his friends and family was turning his back on everything that made Micah who he was, that was a bargain.

The daemons stopped their activities and turned to Micah. Row after row of dully glowing eyes set in bestial faces, all waiting expectantly.

"I don't know how much you can understand," Micah began, rapidly feeling sheepish about speaking to a collection of summoned creatures but too embarrassed to admit his mistake, even to himself. "I don't know how, but I think I'm beginning to understand you. At least a little. You hunger for destruction. Unmaking what the gods have created. I haven't summoned you without reason. Today we set out to destroy a great many beings that would otherwise hurt me."

Silence filled the clearing. Other than a disinterested snort from Telivern, none of the creatures responded. Despite that, Micah knew that they understood. Maybe it was the way the Onkerts panted or the gleam in the Brensens' cyclopean eyes, but they knew that their moment was fast approaching. That soon, Micah would let them off of their leashes to destroy.

With a motion of his hand, he began walking through the woods toward the road to Westmarch. Once they arrived at the road, Micah directed the daemons to stay in the woods, just out of sight while Telivern and he walked toward the citadel. After an hour or so of silence, the buck lowered its nose and nuzzled Micah.

Tension. Illness. Worry.

"It'll all be over soon, buddy." Micah smiled slightly as he reached up to scratch the back of the deer's neck. "I don't know if we have enough daemons, but we're out of temporal energy. If this isn't enough, well... It'll end one way or another soon." He pursed his lips. "Tomorrow's my eighteenth birthday. For better or worse, we've run out of time to prepare. Unless we act now, we have maybe four months until Westmarch falls."

Confusion. Worry.

"In just over three months, the Durgh are going to march forth from the Great Depths and lay waste to the countryside," Micah replied. "We're going to beat them to the punch. We'll descend into the Depths and do enough damage to their forces that the Durgh can't even think of an attack."

Grudging Acceptance.

With that last exchange of thoughts, Telivern stepped away and they kept walking, only stopping when the deer needed sleep. Micah either kept watch or hunted with the daemons, quickly and easily finding rabbits or other small game to fill his meager food requirements.

Finally, they reached Westmarch. A great tower, unimpressive after the architecture of Bitollan but an achievement in and of itself, surrounded by a great wall. Even from a distance, Micah could see the siege equipment stuffing the upper levels of the tower, their impressive height giving them a commanding advantage when attacking anything encroaching on the small hill that the citadel was built upon.

He didn't even bother. Micah had the attunement to go into town and shop, but it would just be a matter of procrastination and he knew it. His fate, for good or ill, lay under the nearby mountains.

They followed the road further, this time not even trying to hide the daemons. Without the forest, it would be impossible anyway. Luckily, they didn't meet too many people, just a handful of intrepid merchants that braved the Great Depths to trade food and surface medicine to the Durgh in exchange for their superior metalworking.

The quiet trade between human lands and the Durgh clans had never really made sense to Micah. While not explicitly evil, almost no civilization actually liked the Durgh. Their tendency to suddenly attack neighbors and allies without warning in order to fulfill Ankros' mandate didn't exactly earn them many friends.

Even if the clans were peaceful, the Great Depths themselves were as dangerous as any dungeon. Expeditions needed to be large and well-equipped to fend off the various horrors that dwelt in the shadows long enough to even reach the Durgh.

They reached the guard post protecting the yawning cavern without incident. Not much more than a walled fort with a couple of huts in it to house the soldiers that worked the outpost, Micah made to simply walk past it into the Depths themselves.

His brow furrowed slightly as a soldier hesitantly left the guard encampment to meet him—a nervous woman in her forties, her knuckles white around the halberd she carried. Behind her, the other three or four troops on duty quietly snuck into the fort.

Micah stopped, allowing her to approach. By the time she reached him, her companions were watching silently from the outpost's walls.

"In the name of King Gosswood and the Pereston Kingdom, I—" She paused for a second, her voice cracking slightly just before she licked her dry lips. "I request that you stop."

"I'm stopped," Micah replied, trying not to laugh as the soldier almost jumped out of her skin when an Onkert whined plaintively at her. He couldn't help but wonder what her thoughts would be if she could feel even the barest hint of the daemon's hunger—not for her flesh, but for the very primal essence that made her a coherent entity.

"Thank you." She gave Micah a pained smile. "I know that you don't have to humor me, but I appreciate it. I've seen Onkerts before and I know that four of five of them is more than enough to tear down our entire outpost. I can't recognize the other daemons, but every instinct in my body is telling me to throw down my weapon and run away right now."

"You have good instincts," Micah chuckled. "Now, if you could let me know what this is about, I have places to go and things to kill."

"I'm required to stop every party venturing into the Great Depths to ensure that they can handle themselves and to ascertain their purpose." She paled at Micah's words but did her best to continue normally. "Now, for you, I know that this is a formality, but could you tell me your class, level, and goal in the Great Depths?"

Micah opened his status screen. Ever since his entourage had grown, his levels had started growing at an exponential rate. It helped that for experience purposes, the tethers turned the daemons into extensions of himself. Even without Micah present, his summons cleared every dungeon that wasn't regularly raided by Basil's Cove on a daily basis.

Micah Silver
Age 17 [ERROR] / 27

Class/Level Thaumaturge 32

XP 17,250/40,000

HP 650/650

Class Specialty

Chronomancer

Attributes

Body 10, Agility 10, Mind 53, Spirit 52

Attunement

Moon 16, Sun 2, Night 15

Mana

Moon 2112/2112Sun2084/2084Night 2110/2110

Affinities

Time 10

Tier V - *Foresight* 4, *Time Echoes* 1, *Temporal Transfer* 2, *Haste* 5

Wood 6

Tier I - *Refresh* 10, *Mending* 9, *Plant Weave* 9

Tier II - *Augmented Mending* 12, *Root Spears* 11

Tier III - *Heal* 8, *Paralytic Sting* 3

Tier IV - *Regeneration* 4, *Healing Wave* 6

Air5

Tier I - *Gale* 7, *Air Knife* 15, *Air Supply* 4

Tier II - *Wind Shield* 6, *Sonic Bolt* 11

Tier III - *Updraft* 2, *Pressure Spear* 5

Tier IV - *Flight* 2

Blessings

Mythic Blessing of Mursa - Blessed Return, Ageless Folio

Skills

Anatomy 7

Arcana 7

Enchanting 11

Fishing 1

Herbalism 5

Librarian 5

Ritual Magic 23

Spear 11
-Wind Spear 8
Spellcasting 25

The Thaumaturge class was finally beginning to show its strength. The constant advancement to his Spirit attribute had over doubled his mana totals since level 20. When combined with his incredibly high Mind attribute, which increased the power of his spells as well as decreasing their mana cost, Micah could cast his fifth-tier Time spells dozens of times before exhaustion. Hells, if he could get his hands on a sixth-tier Time spell, he could probably cast that as well.

Of course, his Air and Wood magic were much less than half as effective. Each rank in an affinity represented a major shift in power. Even his Wood spells, at affinity 6, cost an average of 30% less than his Air spells at affinity 5.

Micah returned his attention to the quaking soldier. She'd obviously misinterpreted his moment of silence, and now he could practically see her knees rattling through her greaves.

"As for my class" —Micah just laughed—"I'm a spellcaster. I'm level 32 and my goal is to prune the Durgh clans before they can rise up and attack Westmarch. One of my dungeon rewards alerted me that they planned an attack before the end of the year, and I consider this my patriotic duty."

"But," she sputtered, her eyes wide as she took in the ranks of daemons, "Pereston has a peace treaty with the Durgh. If you attack them, you'd break that treaty and they'd be fully justified in starting a war."

"I plan on honoring that treaty just as much as the Durgh do," Micah replied, rolling his eyes. "Look, I realize that I am venturing into the unknown and attacking a vastly superior foe, but I am out of time. If I'm not strong enough, well. That is what it is, but I'm not going to sit around cowering behind a wall and waiting for someone else to save me."

Micah's voice took a bitter turn. "I have seen what is coming to pass. No one takes the invasion seriously, and the powerful flee, leaving the rest of us to our fates. Eventually, the Royal Knights retake the land and we start over. Even if averting that tragedy seems impossible, I still have to try. No one is coming to help."

He looked her dead in the eye. "I am your last hope. If I fall, you die. Westmarch dies. Basil's Cove dies. Tens of thousands up and down the Horn Coast will be butchered or enslaved."

43

OLD AGE SHOULD RAVE AND BURN AT THE CLOSE OF DAY

The Durgh sentries died quickly. Brensens dropped from the ceiling of the great cavern on top of them, their bony claws ripping through the guards like a boulder through paper. Only their warbeasts—great chitin-hovered hounds with fangs the size of Micah's forearms—survived the initial surprise attack. They didn't survive the daemons' follow-up.

The sliver of light that marked the entrance to the Great Depths had long since disappeared behind Micah, assigning the expedition a sense of finality. Intellectually, he understood the magnitude of his task, but as the last of the day's light disappeared behind him, the truth of the matter set in. He was single-handedly challenging a small nation, and there was no room to return home a failure. Either he succeeded or the tunnels and caverns of the Great Depths would be his tomb.

Luckily, whatever the rituals were changing in Micah's body extended to his eyes, allowing him to see in the dark without pause or trouble. Although Telivern could glow softly and illuminate the heavy darkness of the Great Depths, it would be as good as announcing their presence to every subterranean creature they came across.

Micah didn't even spare a look in the direction of the dead

Durgh. Although the soldiers were strong by human standards, roughly between levels 15 and 20, they were merely an appetizer for the battle to come.

The next group of scouts spotted his party from afar. They managed to fire a volley of bone arrows at Micah before the Brensens reached them. With a wave of his hand and a word or two of power, a *Wind Shield* sprang into being. The arrows—with heads molded from strange alloys that bit into the stone itself—clattered to the ground around him ineffectually.

Screams of alarm echoed through the cave as the Durgh quickly found out how outmatched they were. They tried to resist, swinging axes and mauls at the daemons, but the Brensens were too fast and their claws too sharp to be denied. In a flurry of motion, limbs and blood littered the cave's floor.

Ahead, voices began to echo through the empty caves. Even if Micah had spoken the harsh and guttural Durgh tongue, he wouldn't be able to understand them, but the content of their words hardly mattered. He wasn't here to parley, just to eliminate the threat that the tribes posed. The only significance the voices had to Micah was as an indication that he'd been noticed.

A shame, but not really unexpected. He'd only be able to get so close to the nearest Durgh encampment without being spotted. An army of almost fifty hulking daemons with glowing eyes was more or less the opposite of a stealthy approach, after all.

Ten minutes later, Micah approached a gate made of dark bone and bound with finely crafted clasps of metal spanning the mouth of a cavern. Within, lights of flame and magic illuminated buildings and humanoid shapes, but blocking his way were two Durgh, much larger than even their oversized brethren.

"Human." The male of the two stepped forward, a glaive over his massive shoulder. "You stand before the Rokdur clan at the head of a great host. Your creatures' claws are stained with the blood of our clansfolk. Tell me, why should I let you pass?"

Micah looked the massive, musclebound Durgh up and down and shrugged.

"You shouldn't, really," he replied dismissively. "I know that the Durgh are amassing an army. That in a couple of months, you will spill out of your caves and invade the surface. I'm here to thin your numbers enough that your invasion never comes to pass. I fully plan on killing every warrior in your clan."

"I don't know where you've heard such slander," the female Durgh cut in, "but our clan isn't making any such preparations. If you attack us, we would welcome the challenge. Your blood will make our warriors stronger, after all. There is no need for conflict today. Turn around, manling. Return to your safe wooden homes in the placid overworld. Be thankful that today the Durgh Host does not need your life."

The entire time she spoke, Micah's eyes never left the male Durgh. He refused to meet Micah's eyes as he shifted his weight from leg to leg nervously. The Durgh's hand grasped the bone haft of the glaive so hard that his dark knuckles began to turn white from lack of blood.

"Your friend may not have corrected you," Micah answered blandly, "but his actions are as obvious as any words. He may as well be shouting the truth at me."

"She doesn't know," the male Durgh interjected. "The Khan demanded that the clan heads keep our preparations secret until the last moment to preserve the element of surprise."

Micah nodded slowly, ignoring the look of shock on the female Durgh's face. She stepped forward, lips flaring around her tusks, and grabbed the male's massive forearm.

"Horrl," she bit out, "I am your prime wife and the clan's lead warrior. What is the meaning of this?"

"You heard the human," Horrl said shakily. "I am not sure how he learned of the Khan's plans, but the edict is clear. His discovery is our failure. Honor demands a duel to silence him."

Horrl smiled ruefully. "I apologize. As much as I enjoy a good fight, this feels too much like subterfuge and dishonor to me. I know my duty, but I am uncomfortable performing it."

"I understand." Micah smiled slightly in return. "It feels like another lifetime, but I was a scholar of sorts. I am well aware of your people's honor and how it binds you. Do what you need to do."

"Human." The giant Durgh turned to Micah, slamming the butt of his glaive onto the cavern floor with a deafening crash. "I stand before you, Horrl of Clan Rokdur, head of that clan. I challenge you or your representative to a duel of honor. If I win, I only ask that you turn back from your mission. If you win, I ask that the noncombatants in my clan be allowed to evacuate before your attack."

"Noncombatants?" Micah cocked his head as he motioned with a free hand toward one of the two Luocas.

Horrl shied backward as the great daemon approached, leering at him from its human face. "Those without blessings." The Durgh's eyes were fixed on the Luoca. "Children too young to receive them and their caretakers, those passed over by Ankros in his wisdom."

Telivern grunted beside Micah. He reached up without turning around and ran his hand through the deer's fur.

"I was thinking the same thing, buddy." Micah smiled slightly before turning back to the Durgh, his face returning to its previous severe expression. "Your deal is acceptable. I will warn you that you do not stand a chance in this duel. I would ask that you begin the evacuation now. Your survivors may let your Khan know that I am coming. My goal is not to destroy your civilization, just to stop this war before it spills over onto the service."

Relief flowed into Micah's hand from Telivern.

"I thank you for your honor and mercy." Horrl inclined his head slightly toward Micah before turning to the female Durgh. "Chuth, gather the Unblessed and the children and prepare them for the journey to the Khanmoot. Make sure that they tell the Khan that a human has come to thwart him, and—"

The Durgh's voice caught slightly. He shook his head before continuing.

"Make sure they know that Clan Rokdur died on its feet on the field of honor." He smiled slightly at the other Durgh, his tusks reflecting the distant light of the village. "There is no need for vengeance or a blood feud in an affair of honor. They must not seek out this stranger. If he survives his attack on the Khanmoot, he is well beyond any of the little ones. I would not have them throw their lives away."

"Horrl." Chuth's voice was incredulous. "How can you be so sure of our failure? I've seen you take down two cave skulkers, bare-chested and unarmed. The fight has not yet happened. It is not our way to surrender before the first blow has landed."

"Chuth." Horrl's voice betrayed a definite note of sorrow. "My blessing gives me the senses and reflexes of a predator. I can see and smell what others cannot. Despite his size, that human over there is a vortex of energy and danger. I might prevail against him, but my odds are not good. The creature he has selected as his champion is so far beyond me that I would be lucky to land a single blow before it ends me. I have accepted my fate and I shall face it with honor." He motioned back toward the clan gate. "Now go—you and the other warriors have work to do before it is your turn to face your destinies."

Chuth paused for a moment, obviously wanting to disobey her clan leader's orders. Eventually, duty got the better of her and she turned back to the gate. She pressed her hand against one of the ornate metal clasps, which glowed brightly for a second before it swung open and allowed her to pass.

"Thank you, human." Horrl inclined his head once more. "May I ask your name before we begin this duel?"

"Micah Silver," he said, his voice quiet but reaching every corner of the absolutely silent chamber.

"You honor me, Micah Silver." Horrl lifted his glaive and spun the weapon with practiced ease. "Now watch, Micah Silver. It may be my time to die, but I die on my feet."

Horrl sprinted forward, the glaive held right-handed in a low guard while his left hand grabbed and threw three needlelike daggers at the Luoca with methodical precision.

It didn't move, observing him indolently. A flick of its wing deflected the daggers, sending them skittering into the distant corners of the cavern, where they hissed and melted from their brief contact with the daemon's caustic essence.

With a blur that Micah could barely discern, the Luoca's tail erased Horrl's head. One minute, he was every inch the powerful Durgh warrior, charging forward with his back straight and fire in his eyes. The next, he was a torso tumbling to the ground while a spatter of *something* painted the wall distantly behind him.

Telivern shook slightly under Micah's stroking fingers.

Unease. Illness.

"We did what we could, buddy." Micah sighed, his hand still combing through the buck's soft fur as he sought some comfort in its depths. "We're walking down a dark road, and our hands are going to get more than a little dirty before we come out the other end, but in the end, we weren't really given another choice."

Ten minutes later, the rest of the Rokdur exited their home cavern. Chuth gently closed the gate behind them and sealed it by pressing her hand against the metal latch. It glowed briefly, sealing their home against predators and scavengers.

"Clan Head Horrl has fallen in honorable combat," Chuth bellowed, her back to Micah and his daemons as they waited patiently. "This human has challenged our clan, but he is not without honor."

She paused. Micah could see her hand quivering slightly as it gripped her great bone warclub.

"Noncombatants to the east tunnel." She motioned with the club. A collection of Durgh wearing simple brown robes led hundreds of children away. Chuth turned to the remaining warriors and raised her club above her head. "As for the rest of us, it may be our time to die."

"But we will die on our feet!" they thundered in response, almost four hundred Durgh charging as one.

The robed Durgh led the children in a hymn, a wordless dirge of lament. The entire procession of noncombatants stopped just far enough away to mark themselves as outside the conflict. One and all they clasped their hands together, witnessing the final moments of their clan.

Micah motioned with his free hand, sending his daemons surging forward to meet the charging Durgh. He cast *Root Spears*. Despite its low tier, Micah's high Mind attribute and skill in the spell were enough to slow and injure most of the advancing clan.

Before the Durgh could respond to his spell, Micah followed up by casting *Haste*, touching the threads connected to his Brensens as they swooped down onto the stalled charge. Their claws extended and snicked through corded muscles and spines, beheading a Durgh with each swipe.

He cast *Regeneration*, this time on the Onkerts that formed a rough line as they advanced. Although powerful, the Durgh were capable of injuring or killing the big gorillas. Most of them would need healing before the battle was done, so Micah pre-empted their needs.

Then the two Luocas tore into the Durgh battle line, their human faces howling and snarling as their insect wings tore through the enemy warriors. Limbs flopped to the cavern floor, melting around the edges due to the daemons' otherworldly energy eating away at them.

Quickly, the Durgh tried to flow around the Luocas, recognizing Micah as the real threat and sacrificing lives in droves to slip past the tearing wings and piercing tails of the great daemons. The survivors charged onward, harried by the flying Brensens until they hit the crowd of Onkerts.

Noting their strategy, Micah nodded to himself. It might be futile, but he couldn't fault the Durgh for their bravery or intelligence. He began casting *Haste* on himself. The Onkerts would do their best, but against a determined foe that didn't care if it lived or died, their power had limits.

After a moment of fighting, Chuth and two other Durgh made it past, leaving their weaker brethren to occupy Micah's daemons. Telivern stepped away from Micah. Wordlessly, one of the Durgh accompanying Chuth broke off to fight the buck.

Micah removed the spear from his shoulder and shifted it to a guard position. First and foremost, he was a spellcaster, but even after all of the timelines, the spear was still Micah's primary tool and weapon. He nodded to the two Durgh as he quickly mouthed the words to *Foresight*.

They moved quickly, trying to catch Micah in a pincer, the male armed with a huge two-handed sword coming from his right while Chuth tried to slip into his blind spot on the left to deliver a killing blow.

It wasn't fast enough.

The spell took hold, and rainbow afterimages of probability stretched out from both of his opponents. Ten seconds. That was what his Mind attribute, skill levels, and Chronomancer specialization bought him. It would be enough.

He leaned slightly to the side, letting the male's sword rush past him as he rapidly cast *Paralytic Sting*. Just as the blade hit the ground, the warrior's hands stood still for a fraction of a second before he could withdraw his swing. Micah's hand, covered in a sickly green glow, snaked out and tapped the warrior on the wrist.

Micah flowed forward, the warclub missing him by an eyelash, only to slam into the Durghish sword planted in the ground, shattering it. In a second, he was behind the twitching and frothing male Durgh. Micah whipped the butt of his spear into the back of his reeling opponent's knee, causing the man to fall over backward.

He quickly planted his spear against the cavern floor, using the massive weight of the warrior's limp body to do what his limited Body stat could not: punch through the Durgh's thick skin, pierce its neck, and skewer up into the falling man's brain.

"But you're a spellcaster," Chuth spoke in slow motion, her eyes widening in shock at a glacial pace.

He'd used four seconds. Plenty of time.

Micah unleashed the *Pressure Spear* he'd been casting while Chuth wasted time talking. The jet of air punctured her hand, forcing her to drop the club. Micah strolled forward, shifting his weight slightly to dodge the frantic barehanded swing from the Durgh, once again mouthing the words to *Paralytic Sting*.

He tapped her wrist, and Chuth's eyes rolled up into her head. Methodically, Micah kicked out her knees, bringing the Durgh down to his level, and scurried onto her chest. He knew that he barely had a second left before the powerful warrior shook off the effects of his spell.

Touching his thumbs to each of her eyes and his forefingers to her sensitive ears, he cast *Sonic Bolt*. *Paralytic Sting* wore off, but the sonic attack had scrambled Chuth's senses too much for her to resist properly.

Micah shifted his body perfectly with her struggles, moving in sync with her to avoid being unseated. He cast *Sonic Bolt* again and her body stiffened. He cast it a third time. A fourth.

The rainbow blur around her faded. There were no more potential actions for Chuth to take as her body breathed its last under the weight of a severely hemorrhaging brain.

He stood and took in the struggle between the final Durgh and Telivern as the prismatic display of probabilities began to fade. Both were covered in wounds from the quick and vicious fight.

Micah cast *Heal* on his friend, closing its injuries. The Durgh glanced backward at the two corpses and became frantic, struggling harder against Telivern. It activated a blessing, its ribs bursting from its back into skeletal, bladed spider legs.

A *Pressure Spear* took it through the hamstring, rupturing the muscle in a spray of gore. It stumbled, using the new limbs growing from its back to catch itself before it could fall entirely, but the distraction was enough.

Telivern lunged forward and thrust its glowing antlers into the Durgh's throat. Blood slickened the floor as the light left the warrior's eyes. He slumped, still suspended from the bone legs planted into the stone of the cavern.

Micah walked to the first Durgh, twisting his spear and kicking the massive corpse off of his weapon in order to retrieve it. Finally, spear in hand, he turned back to the battle.

Fundamentally, it was over. One or two Durgh warriors remained, but the Brensens were more or less hunting them for sport. Three of the Onkerts had been slain in the clash, but the rest were recovering rapidly. He nodded.

Next time, he'd need to be more careful. He'd won, but Chuth had been under level 35. The next time he was challenged to hand-to-hand combat, he might not be so lucky. Even with the help of *Foresight*, he was still primarily a spellcaster.

The final Durgh fell, a Luoca's tail punching a fist-sized hole in its chest. Suddenly, the song of the noncombatants stopped. For a moment, all of them inclined their heads in a disconcerting, choreographed moment. Then, wordlessly, they filed out of the cavern.

Micah sighed, rubbing his gore-covered spear on the breeches of the Durgh he'd killed with it. He glanced up as Telivern plodded over.

"Almost done, buddy," he said, slinging the spear back over his shoulder. "We just have to go and break up the Khanmoot. Then we can rest."

44

RAGE, RAGE AGAINST THE DYING OF THE LIGHT

The cavern was gigantic, more than large enough to house Basil's Cove in it. More than that, it was gorgeous. Every cliff face and stalactite was covered in intricate carvings and inlaid with metal filigree. Even the ceiling was inlaid with a vivid tile mosaic, displaying great battles of old in intricate detail.

Micah sighed and looked at the enemy—almost two thousand Durgh warriors standing behind rows of slavering warbeasts. Past them, the Khanmoot itself—a bastion of civilization in the wilds of the Great Depth—rose out of the rock floor. None of the buildings were more than three stories tall, but each of them was covered with a colorful array of metal-and-bone ornamentation.

Two Durgh stepped away from the armed and ready band of warriors and began walking toward Micah and his daemons. One stood almost twice his height, a towering monster of a man wearing armored fashioned from what appeared to be human bones. Over his shoulder, he held a handle attached by a finely crafted chain that ran across his back to the large, spiked metal head of a flail.

The other Durgh was much smaller, even shorter than Micah, and unarmed. He followed the warrior, trailing almost ten paces behind him and playing a steady beat in time with the larger Durgh's steps on a pair of drums. The drums were simple, little more than hollow wooden cylinders with skin stretched over them, and each blow from the smaller Durgh's hands took the entirety of his focus.

Micah stepped forward and walked a good ten paces from his daemons, enough that he could politely meet with the Durgh at a symbolic distance from his forces to match the two Durghs' example, but not so far that his summoned creatures wouldn't be on hand to aid him if the apparent parley turned violent.

Abruptly, with no outside sign, the leading Durgh and his drummer stopped simultaneously. Up close, Micah could see that the warrior's thighs were as big around as his torso, corded muscle rippling under his thick black skin. He craned his head upward, only to notice the Durgh taking him in as well, dissecting him under his intense gaze.

"I stand before you, Krosst, Khan of the Southern Caverns." The Durgh's voice boomed out—clearly, he wanted to be heard by his own soldiers as he spoke to Micah. "The survivors of the Rokdur say that your champion bested their leader in a duel, and then you defeated their warriors in honorable combat. If it were not for the peace treaty between our races, I would raise a mug to honor your valor, but your King and I have a treaty. Tell me, human, why do you travel the Great Depths and make war upon our people?"

Even from a distance, Micah could hear the sounds of shuffling and talking from the Durgh lines as they took in Krosst's words.

"In about four months, you will invade the surface anyway," Micah responded blandly. "Without warning or formal declaration, you'll overrun the surrounding areas, putting entire towns to the sword."

The drummer drew in breath with a hiss. Behind Krosst, his soldiers stopped whispering. An electric tension filled the air. Apparently, Micah's words were some sort of dramatic faux pas. He couldn't bring himself to care.

Then Krosst let loose a great, booming laugh, his free hand slapping his chest as he struggled with his mirth.

"So I will, human!" Krosst reached up to wipe tears from his face. "You have courage. No one has called me a liar to my face in a decade. If you weren't so small and pink, I'd suspect that you had some proper Durgh blood in you. Nevertheless, Ankros has called us to the glory of battle." Krosst smiled, revealing a pair of rune-encrusted tusks. "Our youth must test themselves and win honor. It is the way of things."

"My brother will die in that battle," Micah replied, his voice steady despite the thunder of his heart beating in his ears. "After Westmarch falls, you will march on Basil's Cove, killing many people that I care for."

"I'm sure I will," Krosst agreed cheerfully. "It will be a glorious raid."

"I can't let that happen," Micah finished, struggling to maintain his calm facade. While Krosst wasn't as powerful as Archmagus Ikanthar, the energy coming off of him was comparable to some of the most famous of the Royal Knights that he'd operated upon. There was no way to know Krosst's exact level, but Micah would bet his last point of attunement that the Durgh had passed level 60 years ago.

"I admire your sentiments, human." Krosst shook his head, a grin exposing his tusks once again. "Unfortunately, a god disagrees with you. Ankros has commanded that we test our youth in combat, and it is not my place to argue with the Lord of Night and Struggle."

"It was worth a try." Micah smiled back wryly. "I don't suppose you'll let me return to the surface and try this all again later? I seem to have miscalculated your numbers when I was putting together my little war party."

"Of course not!" Krosst chuckled. "It would ruin the surprise of our raid if we simply let you return. Plus, it would be a shame for us to waste the opportunity to test our youth against a warrior as valiant as you. I'm sure your death will be one for the skalds to recite around the fires for decades to come.

"Monloff"—Krosst gently kicked the drummer—"that means you. I expect a proper poem about this young man's nobility and valor for the feast tomorrow night."

"Yes, my Khan," the drummer replied in a musical baritone that seemed out of place coming from his tiny frame.

"Shit," Micah replied, his eyes flowing over the army arrayed before him. "Well"—he shrugged at Krosst—"what's that line your people say? 'It might be my time to die, but by the Sixteen, I'll die on my feet?'"

Micah slung his spear over his shoulder and turned to walk back to his daemons, already trying to calculate how to get away from the Durgh for long enough to teleport back to the cave outside of Basil's Cove. It would take almost all of his mana given the distance, but it was theoretically possible. After that, it looked like it was time to lay low until *Blessed Return* came off of cooldown.

He wasn't terribly excited with the idea of reverting to his thirteenth birthday once again, but after looking at the forces arrayed before him, this timeline appeared to be a dead end. The concept was good, but his skills were still lacking.

"Wait," Krosst called out, halting Micah. "Human, what is your name?"

"Micah Silver," he replied, pausing his slow walk back to his summons to turn and face the gigantic Durgh.

"Micah." Krosst tasted the word. "You're facing death with the demeanor of a Durgh rather than a human, so I thought it only fair to give you the advice I would give a Durgh warrior: You aren't without options." Krosst smiled, tusks winking in the dim light of the scattered patches of phosphorescent fungus. "All sapients have the sacrosanct right to challenge the local Durgh Khan to single combat. If you win, you may make one request or undo one edict of that Khan. In this case, you could stop the invasion of the surface."

Micah snorted. "Khan Krosst, unless I'm very wrong, you're higher than level 60 and I'm sure you're aware that I'm below level 40. I don't suppose that you'd let me use a champion?"

"That isn't how the old laws work." Krosst shook his head sadly. "However, I do see your point. Let us make this sporting. We do not wish to declare war on Pereston; simply blood our soldiers. If you and your... companions can survive a half-hour of battle with my men and their beasts, you will have served our purpose. There will be no need to invade the surface and harm your friends. Does that seem 'fair,' Micah Silver?"

"It certainly seems like a better bet than fighting you," Micah answered, turning and walking to his waiting daemons. "I look forward to entertaining your army."

"And I look forward to ripping the wings off of one of your giant bugs." Krosst nodded cheerfully. "Come, Monloff, we must let Micah Silver make his peace with Ankros."

With that, the two of them walked away, leaving Micah to his thoughts. Telivern's hooves clicked against the stone as it approached him through the mob of restless daemons. Unconsciously, his fingers twined themselves in its fur.

It was all coming down to this. The days of training. Almost a decade of not spending time with his friends and family, frantically trying to raise his skills and the swarm of daemons he would need. The sleepless nights, haunted by those he had to leave behind in each abandoned timeline.

Despite everything, he was outnumbered and outmatched. The Royal Knights had never mentioned how many Knights they sent to quell the Durgh, just that it had happened. Given the numbers before Micah, it must have been a decent portion of the order.

He removed his hand from Telivern's fur and took the spear from his shoulder. He might be outmatched, but Krosst had given him an out. Even if the Durgh considered it a favor to a doomed man, it was only because they didn't know his abilities.

There was only a moment before Krosst started the attack to decide. Fight, or run and hide long enough to reset. His gaze flickered over the assembled daemons.

Anger flowed through him. He was fucking tired of being kicked around. Of being a plaything of the nobles or the gods. Of being tossed from one disaster to another, only surviving by hiding like a roach wedged beneath a piece of furniture long enough to trigger his reset.

Trevor and Jo had died because he was weak. Bart had died because he was weak. But this time, he wasn't weak. Maybe he wasn't strong enough, but he certainly wasn't weak. Maybe he didn't have any options before, but he had them now.

Telivern's nose pressed against his arm.

Worry. Danger. Escape.

"Not this time, buddy." Micah brushed the buck aside. "I can't promise that I'll make it through this, but I won't bring you down with me. Go to the entrance of the cavern. If I don't meet up with you in three hours, you've been a solitary light in a bleak stretch of my life. You're family to me, and I've seen too many family members die."

The nose pressed back against Micah forcefully, pushing him slightly off balance.

Denial. Support.

"No." His voice caught in his throat and his eyes burned as he turned to Telivern. The deer's eyes were plaintive, asking him questions beyond just the emotions and simple thoughts that could be transferred by contact. Questions that Micah didn't want to answer. "I need you to go, buddy. This fight is beyond me, but it sure as hell is beyond you. I can't protect you and fight all of them. If you stay, I'll die trying to keep you safe."

SUPPORT.

"I know." Micah blinked, fighting back the tears that he'd been holding at bay since he turned down Jo. "But the only way you can help me is by waiting for me. Please. I know it's hard, but I need you to do this for me, buddy."

Telivern snorted angrily at him before turning and walking away, Micah's eyes on its back as it receded towards the cavern's entrance. Then a horn blew, shattering the moment.

With a roar, the Durgh began to sprint across the cave toward Micah and his daemons, and there wasn't any more time for self-doubt.

45

THOUGH WISE MEN KNOW AT THE END
THAT DARK IS RIGHT

As they charged, Micah cast *Wind Shield* and *Flight*. The last battle had shown that even if his minions were more powerful than their opponents, it wasn't impossible for the weight of numbers to overwhelm them. Earth magic might have let him make a shield of rocks, and Fire magic would let Micah ring himself in flames, but he simply didn't have access to proper defensive magics. All he could do was fly and protect himself from arrows, forcing the battle into the air.

The Brensens and the Luocas could fly with him, swooping down to kill or maim Durgh while drawing the battle out. As for the Onkerts? Micah didn't hold out much hope that they'd survive the battle, even if everything went perfectly.

As it was, heavily outnumbered and with high-leveled Durgh such as the Khan thrown into the mix, the Onkerts were dead, and his only real chance was to keep flying. The Durgh would have some way to attack him—a group of blessed that size surely would—but if he remained on the ground, they would overwhelm his small group with sheer numbers in a matter of minutes. At least in the air, he had a better chance at limiting the size of the engagement.

Micah leapt and the wind caught him. Soaring up amongst the finely carved stalactites, he ignored the barrage of arrows and javelins that followed him, trusting in the *Wind Shield* to deflect the projectiles. Seconds later, the flying daemons joined him as he began casting *Haste*, his mind's eye touching the tethers binding him to the Brensens.

A ball of flame struck the stalactite next to him, reducing it to half molten shrapnel, easily deflected by his *Wind Shield*. He finished the spell and frowned down upon the small army of Durgh.

The Brensens swooped downward, *Haste* speeding their descent as they struck like hawks. They squawked happily and slashed their skeletal claws through victims before returning to the cavern's roof. Near him, the two Luocas flapped amidst the crags of the roof lazily, waiting for Micah to finish their casting of *Haste* so that they could join their siblings.

The spell completed, settling over the Luocas just as a pair of Durgh rose from the column with their blessings' batlike wings sprouting from their backs. Almost casually, one of the Luocas darted forward, its wings blurring through the aggressors, bisecting them and letting their dissolving bodies fall onto the Durgh below.

Micah winced as half of the chains binding his Onkerts to him snapped before withering away. He glanced down at the battlefield. It was as he'd suspected. The Onkerts had managed to bring down a single careless Durgh before the higher-levels amongst their numbers disabled them with a series of spells and blessings long enough for those on the front lines to dispatch them.

Even as he watched, a great cylinder of stone carved from Earth magic fell from the ceiling onto the daemons, crushing and instantly killing another two. Again, he felt the connection between them sever.

His attention snapped back to his situation as a silver harpoon simply ignored his *Wind Shield* and slammed into his leg. For a second, his mind went white as the weapon shattered his thigh.

The barbs bit into his flesh and pulled him toward the ground with an overpowering jerk. He screamed. Despite his agony, Micah's vision was drawn to the Durgh holding the chain. A giant like all of his subterranean race, his mouth was wide with laughter, exhibiting his tusks and sharp teeth. Around him, the other Durgh cheered him on, one clapping him on the back, congratulating him for spearing Micah.

Without thinking, Micah touched the invisible chains binding his Luocas. One blurred past him, too fast for Micah's eyes even as he knew it was coming. Its wing dipped slightly in the air before it sliced through the harpoon's chain. The other slammed into the ground in the middle of the Durgh formation, killing a handful with its bulk before lashing out with its wings and tail.

Micah blinked back tears, taking some small satisfaction in watching the Durgh that had skewered him vomit from the backlash as his Luoca shattered the chain of his blessing. The other interposed its body in front of him, intercepting a volley of spells and blessings that lit the dark cave up in a pyrotechnic display.

He hissed in relief as *Augmented Mending* deadened his nerves and knit the bone back together. Micah's HP had dropped dangerously; any lower, and the harpoon would have killed him outright without any need to reel him to the ground.

Another volley of spells struck the Luoca while Micah recast his spell. It whined slightly, the repeated attacks finally beginning to chip away at the great daemon's prodigious health. The minute Micah's calf muscle knit back together and his hit points crested above 80%, he released the daemon mentally, sending it to vent its frustration on the swarm of Durgh.

It veered away from Micah, preparing to dive toward the column of soldiers only for the gigantic head of a flame-wreathed flail to slam into it and drive it into the cavern ceiling.

With a thought, Micah flowed to the side, frowning at the reddened and newly hairless skin of his forearms where the heat from the flail had seared him. The ball of the flail itself continued rotating, grinding the Luoca against sheer rock. His eyes trailed back along the chain, a series of glowing red links that illuminated the otherwise dimly lit cave, to find Krosst.

The Khan met his gaze. Where he was once twice Micah's height, he now stood at least four, maybe five times as tall, his body the dull orange of molten rock. Magma hissed as it dripped from the creases in his body, leaving a trail of dim lights behind him. Unsurprisingly, none of the Durgh came within a dozen paces of him, unable to bear the heat radiating off his gigantic body.

The flail head rocketed back toward Krosst at speeds that left a dull afterimage in Micah's vision. The Durgh caught it in his left hand, and a feral grin twisted across his burning face as the Luoca emerged from a crater in the ceiling, its human head screaming incoherent defiance.

Krosst wordlessly dropped the head of the flail to the cavern floor, the impact knocking several of the nearby Durgh off balance. Without breaking eye contact with the Luoca, he extended his left hand and flicked his fingers toward himself to beckon silently.

Micah began casting *Haste* on his Luocas. As powerful as they were, he didn't have any confidence that they could beat the Khan quickly without his help.

Orange and red flashed across Micah's vision as Krosst threw a glob of magma at the Luoca with enough force to knock it almost ten paces to the side.

Mentally, he amended his assessment from "quickly" to "at all."

Haste let the Luoca correct its course, narrowly dodging the chain of Krosst's flail as it whipped by. Micah switched to his Sun mana pool in an effort to give his Moon mana a moment to replenish itself and began casting *Regeneration*. Given the heat mirages rising off of the gigantic Durgh, even if his daemon fought the battle perfectly and struck the Khan, it would suffer damage. *Foresight* could come next, but for now, it needed staying power.

Micah wove through the stalactites on the ceiling, using the carved pillars of stone as cover against the javelins and magic of the Durgh as he finished his spells. Just as he completed *Foresight,* a jet of pressurized air shattered the cavern next to him, spraying Micah with shards of stone that his *Wind Shield* barely deflected.

He glanced down and frowned—almost twenty Durgh flew toward him under the influence of spells similar to *Flight* or under the power of some blessing. One of them held a great metal apparatus similar to a blacksmith's bellows and, as Micah watched, she pushed down on the accordion. Sigils and glyphs running up and down the spout of the device glowed briefly, and a spear of pressurized gas roared past him once again.

A handful of rapid thrusts from Micah's spear sent the Durgh scattering as one of their numbers fell to the ground, bleeding from a series of holes drilled in him by the spears' enchantments. Micah turned his attention back to his daemons while weaving through the air, taking advantage of his flight to throw off the aim of the Durgh on the floor.

The Brensens dove in and out of the swarm, leaving grievous wounds or claiming heads entirely. Of course, despite their power and magical reinforcement, the Brensens didn't operate with impunity. The Durgh were far from defenseless, and each swoop into their ranks triggered attempts to rob them of their aerial advantage. Although this took the form of nets and spells, more often than not, it resulted in Durgh, drunk on the potential honor of bringing down such an illustrious foe, attempting to tackle or bear-hug a daemon.

It didn't take long, only a moment to disrupt a Brensen's momentum, and the rest of the mob would swarm upon it like ants attacking scraps of food at a picnic. Sometimes the Durgh in the area wouldn't be strong enough to hold the great daemons down, and seconds later, the Brensens would flap away from a charnel scene of blood and limbs.

At least once, however, a Brensen had been tackled by a high-level Durgh with a clan leader nearby. Even though this Durgh was only slightly more powerful than the daemon, she was able to prevent the summon from fleeing with a series of rapid attacks while her kinsfolk ripped it to shreds.

Taking in the multiple open wounds on his surviving Brensen, Micah began casting *Healing Wave*. He'd need to resist the urge to support the second-tier daemons further with mana-intensive Time spells. Despite the damage they were dealing, the Durgh army stretched deep into the cavern. He held no illusions about winning the battle conventionally. Instead, he needed to survive twenty-eight more minutes. If he were to see the light of day again, Micah would need to conserve both his mana and his stamina.

The Luocas, on the other hand, fared much better. One of the duo rampaged through the Durgh, its very steps warping and melting the reality of the rocks it stepped upon as its wings and tail sheared through even the thickest of armor. Shamans did their best to restrict its motions, creating cages of stone and prisons of ice. None of them did much. The aura of Elsewhere weakened the magic, made the bonds frail and brittle enough for the Luoca's wings to cut them apart with ease.

Krosst gave a much better account of himself. Micah's Luoca used the power of *Foresight* and the speed of *Haste* to dodge each attack by the barest of margins. The moment the Khan overextended himself, the daemon's tail would lash out, already knowing from *Foresight* that its attack would succeed. Each blow struck a weak point, sinking shoulder-deep into the magma of a knee or shoulder.

Through his connection to the daemon, Micah could feel the stifling heat burning away at the Luoca's HP. By the same token, each blow from its tail fundamentally changed some of the molten rock that composed the Durgh Khan. Joints hardened and became brittle, and blow by blow, he began to move slower as the magic of his transformation was eroded and morphed by the essence of Elsewhere.

Micah frowned at his mana reserves and began casting *Foresight* once again. The spell was expensive, but he needed Krosst eliminated if he was going to survive. Already the Durgh were calling up warbeasts specialized for their specific situation: giant, twisted arachnids capable of spitting webs into the air to trap and bring down the evasive Brensens and mutated bats, likely to hunt Micah himself.

Renewing *Foresight* on the Luoca, Micah quickly recalled two of the Brensens from their attack runs with a thought. The flying Durgh were regrouping, and it would only be a matter of time before the flying warbeasts rallied to their aid.

Hovering, juking, and dodging far above the battlefield might put him out of reach of his average opponent, but that wasn't a situation that could last forever. Even if the Durgh were focusing on the daemons directly attacking them, Micah's summons were too heavily outnumbered to draw all of his enemies' focus. In the end, they would notice him, and just one or two powerful melee combatants within spear range would force Micah to spend mana on defensive spells that he could ill afford to lose.

The bats and Durgh rose toward Micah, the warbeasts screening the more powerful warriors from Micah's attacks. With a shrug, he dipped into his mana once more and cast *Sonic Bolt*.

The spell's biggest weakness was its range. Despite its name, sound didn't stick to a "bolt" format naturally. More than a couple paces out, it began to disperse and spread. In reality, it was more of a "sonic cone." Against powerful opponents, that meant closing to point-blank range in order to ensure penetration. Against bats that used their sensitive hearing to echolocate prey?

Half of the warbeasts dropped from the sky bonelessly, their large ears leaking blood. It didn't really matter whether the spell killed or disabled them—the hard stone of the cavern floor equalized everything in the end. The other half swerved wildly, their direction and control compromised by the sudden assault.

The two Brensens protecting Micah dove into the confusion, their claws scattering and killing the remaining bats. At their best, the warbeasts might have slowed the cyclopean vultures gleefully scything through their ranks, but damaged and confused, they didn't stand a chance.

The Durgh behind them fired a volley of javelins and magic into the bats' ranks to try and slow the daemons down, using blades of water, fist-sized rocks that detonated into shrapnel, fireballs that left Micah blinking away afterimages, and, of course, the large air-pressure cannon. It worked, after a fashion—the Brensens emerged from the mass of bats riddled with small cuts, their wings smoldering from fire-based attacks.

Micah simply cast *Augmented Mending* again, circumventing the spell's lack of ranged effect by touching both of the daemons' tethers. Through their eyes, he saw the recognition dawn on the flying contingent of Durgh as the wounds closed. He released his mental grip on the Brensens' bindings when they lunged forward with dizzying speed, claws outstretched to tear through the suddenly undefended and inexperienced fliers.

Below, another Brensen died, the pop of its tether severing drawing Micah's attention as he hid himself behind another outcropping of rock on the ceiling. One of the great spider warbeasts had caught the daemon in a net made of webbing and reeled it back to the cavern floor before it could escape. The daemon performed well, however, tearing the legs from the arachnid with its claws even as the webbing bound its wings together.

By the time it finally collapsed, three bone spears piercing its body, almost a dozen Durgh corpses surrounded the daemon. With a shudder, the arachnid stopped moving.

For a fraction of a second, Micah considered recalling his Brensens. They weren't as robust as the Luoca and their injuries were beginning to add up. But scanning the chaos of the battlefield, he realized he couldn't.

There were too many Durgh. If they weren't under constant pressure from the swooping daemons, the enemy would have a moment to think. Micah had a sinking sensation that any planning by the Durgh would involve "focusing fire on the squishy pink summoner." Even if constant action meant taking losses, he needed to keep the Durgh off balance long enough to avoid that outcome.

Touching the connection to his Luocas, Micah grit his teeth and began casting *Foresight* once again. The spell was powerful, insanely so, but its short duration almost made it a liability in an endurance battle like this. Almost.

Krosst was slowing. The angry orange of his body dimmed to a dull yellow as tail strike after tail strike from the Luoca warped and twisted the magma that made his gigantic battle form. Thanks to the *Haste* and repeated castings of *Foresight*, Krosst hadn't struck the Luoca again after the first surprise attack with his flail. The daemon still had just over half of its health, a natural outcome when combat forced it to jam an appendage into magma.

The ground around the Khan was soaked in glowing yellow-and-orange liquid, the molten rock refusing to harden even as it cooled. Then Krosst stumbled, his right knee giving out slightly. As he fell, the Luoca's tail slashed across his throat, the serrated appendage already in motion before the Durgh even began moving.

Magma sprayed across the nearby Durgh that had formed a circle around the two of them to protect the sanctity of their duel. It wasn't quite enough to kill any of the veteran warriors that made up the Khan's honor guard, but more than one burst into flames as the superheated rock touched the dry cloth and leather that padded their armor.

Krosst's form blackened, the heat disappearing in an instant. The Luoca screeched defiance and lunged forward, its wings shattering the hollow statue. Inside the rubble of his defeated combat form lay Krosst's normal body, naked and gasping for breath.

Before anyone could react, the Luoca's tail darted forward and impaled the Khan. The tail extended, holding the body high above the battlefield. The entire conflict settled into a lull as the eyes of every Durgh not actively fighting a daemon focused on their crippled Khan.

Krosst twitched, his hands—each the size of Micah's head—reaching for the tail lodged in his chest. They grasped at the limb as he tried to pull himself free.

Then the Khan started to dissolve. His hands. His torso around the wound. Great drops of flesh and refuse dribbled from them as they seemed to melt.

Krosst looked up and opened his mouth as if to say something, true fear in his eyes for the first time. Instead, his mouth remained slack as the light left his gaze.

The Luoca bellowed an incoherent sound of triumph and challenge. It smashed the still form of the Durgh leader into the stone, crushing the lifeless body into a paste of meat and bone.

The Durgh surged in rage. Where before they'd attacked joyously but cautiously, now they struck out with abandon, uncaring as they wasted their lives and mana in an attempt to bring down Micah's daemons.

His summons responded to their ferocity in kind, ignoring their injuries and counting on Micah's hasty castings of *Regeneration* to keep them in fighting shape as they reaped life after life.

A Brensen fell, its lower body encased in stone after a shaman summoned a great hand of rock to pluck it from the air. Tens of Durgh lay injured or dead around it before a glaive finally clove the great vulture's skull from its shoulders.

Then another. Micah had to change positions as an Earth spell-caster turned the ceiling next to him into a great fanged maw that snapped at him. Without even looking, he directed a Luoca to the caster and a pair of insect wings bisected the man.

He began to lose track of time. A spell or attack would wound him, Micah would heal. A spell would run out on his daemons and he would renew it. The world became a blur of action as Durgh and daemon alike fell, bathing the dark battlefield in blood.

Finally, a horn blew from the Khanmoot itself. The remaining Durgh began to extricate themselves from combat. With a tired thought, Micah called back his daemons. What remained of them anyway.

One Luoca and three Brensens had survived, all well below half health. The Luoca that had defeated the Khan was targeted almost immediately by the Durgh. Even though it out-leveled everything around it, the unending string of attacks eventually ripped the wings from its back, crippling the daemon. That battle had drawn the attention of the Durgh host's elite for almost fifteen minutes.

Without its sacrifice, Micah tiredly realized that he would have died. Even if the Luocas were more powerful than any of the Durgh other than the Khan himself, quantity had a quality of its own. That monomaniacal focus on their leader's killer had allowed the rest of his daemons to regenerate enough hit points with the aid of his magic to survive to the end of the battle.

In a half-hour, his summons had managed to kill just over fifteen hundred of the Durgh. Not even half of the host. Another five to ten minutes, and his skull would've joined his Luoca's on the cavern floor.

A large Durgh stepped forward from the army as his soldiers claimed trophies from the fallen on both sides.

"Micah Silver!" the Durgh's voice boomed forth over the background noise of the crowd. "You have fought honorably for a half-hour, and I would parley with you."

Reluctant but exhausted, Micah flew down from the ceiling of the cavern, his clothes burned and torn to shreds. Each hole and tear was a testament to a deep wound that he'd healed in the heat of combat.

The floor was cold under his single bare foot. He'd lost it entirely to a Durgh warrior whose blessing let him throw a spinning blade that would boomerang effortlessly back to him. *Regeneration* had regrown the limb, but it still felt strange and new as Micah put his weight on it for the first time.

"I stand before you, Laghra, Khan Candidate and third in command for Khan Krosst." The Durgh nodded pleasantly at Micah, his face devoid of hostility. "You fought well today."

"As did you," Micah replied tiredly, the accumulated stress of combat dulling and clouding his perception like great puffs of cotton. "I am sorry about Krosst; he seemed to be a good man."

"He was," Laghra agreed, "but he also died well under the approving gaze of Ankros. No Durgh could ask for more. Now" — Laghra nodded at Micah—"Krosst made a deal with you, that you might request a cessation to our hostilities and preparations to invade the surface if you survived a half-hour of open combat. Do you make that request?"

"I do," Micah replied, unable to put any energy behind the words.

"Very good." Laghra nodded. "Congratulations on your victory, human. The next time we meet, the Durgh will be better prepared."

Without a further word, the Durgh turned and walked away, attempting to organize the chaos of the post-combat cleanup.

Micah began walking away, his daemons trailing after him. Each step took his entire focus as he tried to line one foot in front of the other. Micah's vision faded and flickered, transforming his journey into a vignette of carved rock and darkness.

Finally, he came upon Telivern, a shining white beacon in the heavy night of the Great Depths. Not knowing how, where, or why he came upon his friend, Micah stumbled forward, tripping and collapsing into the deer's soft white fur.

46

VICTORY

Micah opened his eyes in the cave, his body covered in mostly healed bruises and cuts that he barely remembered. Telivern lay curled against him, its fur having warmed and cushioned him through the long night.

"Congratulations, Blessed." The voice Micah had come to associate with class selection and growth spoke from nowhere. "You've reached your second milestone and are eligible for a class specialty. A series of options have been presented to you based upon your affinities and skill levels. This message has repeated two hundred and sixty-four times without response. Please make a selection."

The voice continued its even tone and measured cadence, unfazed by Micah's wry amusement. "For your achievements in learning the martial art Wind Spear, you may upgrade the martial art to Uncommon rarity, increasing the effectiveness of all abilities associated with that martial art. Due to your increased physical fitness, you may specialize as an athlete and gain additional hit points upon each level-up. For following The Path of the Spear, you may specialize as a spear adept, making you more effective in many small ways with a spear. For your achievements in Wind magic, you may specialize as an Aeromancer, decreasing the mana cost and increasing the effectiveness of your Wind magic. For your achievements in Wood magic, you may specialize as a Healer, decreasing the mana cost and increasing the effectiveness of your Wood magic. For your achievements in Time magic, you may specialize again as a Chronomancer, decreasing the mana cost and increasing the effectiveness of your Time magic. For your knowledge and achievements in ritual magic, you may specialize as an Occultist. For your knowledge and achievements in enchanting, you may specialize as an Enchanter. For your knowledge of Elsewhere, you may specialize as an Arcanist, increasing your understanding of, and chances of surviving direct contact with, the corrosive mists of that plane."

The rocky ceiling of his cave stared back at Micah as he pondered his options. After everything he'd done, the risks he'd taken, the timelines he'd abandoned, it was all over.

Micah didn't hold any illusions. Someone with his level of power would be forced to fight again. Karell simply wasn't the sort of peaceful place where he'd be allowed to retire and rest on his laurels.

Still, Micah had earned himself a moment of peace. For once, his decisions didn't need to be focused on the next moment, on grabbing every last mote of power that he could. The all-consuming threat of the Durgh invasion was gone. He had the luxury of picking something that he truly wanted to do.

Everything he'd done, every sacrifice he'd made, ran through Micah's mind. The friends he had watched fall only to see them standing and joking again in the next timeline. The moral quandaries he'd ignored, sure that the ends would justify his means.

Hells, that put him closer to the Royal Knights than he'd like. He kept telling himself that he'd never sunk to the same lows as his former mentors, but it was a thin distinction. He'd trafficked in blood and time to save his friends and family, and there was no doubt in Micah's mind that he'd do it again, if necessary.

He raised his hand up. Even with his eyes open, it glowed slightly red with the light of Elsewhere. He curled his fingers into a fist.

For now, he could relax. He could afford to live a normal life for a time, to recover from wounds both physical and spiritual.

"Congratulations, Blessed," the voice repeated itself. "You've reached your second milestone and are eligible for a class specialty. A series of options have been presented to you based upon your affinities and skill levels. This message has repeated two hundred and sixty-five times without response. Please make a selection."

"Enchanter." Micah spoke the word aloud, waking Telivern with his voice. Beside him, the deer stirred, lifting its head to look at Micah with concern.

He wouldn't live the rest of his life as a craftsman, but it would give Micah a chance to relax and focus on his research.

"It's fine, buddy." Micah patted Telivern's flank. "I don't know if it's all over, but it's over for now. It was a close thing, but we did it."

Relief. Wrongness. Sick.

Micah stood up and walked out into the clearing beyond the cave. He put his hand to his forehead, shielding himself from the sun after his time in the Great Depths. Birds chirped nearby and a pair of squirrels chased each other from branch to branch.

He'd have to get used to the cave again. The grove was gone, one of the many sacrifices he'd made to gain the power needed to save Basil's Cove. Still, it was nostalgic in its own way.

Micah called up his status.

Micah Silver
  Age 18 [ERROR] / 28
  Class/Level Thaumaturge 40
  XP 31,200/150,000
  HP 785/810
  Class Specialty
  Chronomancer, Enchanter
  Attributes
  Body 10, Agility 10, Mind 65, Spirit 64
  Attunement
  Moon 17, Sun 2, Night 23
  Mana

Moon 3224/3224, Sun 3204/3204, Night 3246/3246

Affinities

Time 10

Tier V - *Foresight* 6, *Time Echoes* 1, *Temporal Transfer* 2, *Haste* 7

Wood 6

Tier I - *Refresh* 10*, Mending* 9, *Plant Weave* 9

Tier II - *Augmented Mending* 13, *Root Spears* 11

Tier III - *Heal* 8, *Paralytic Sting* 3

Tier IV - *Regeneration* 5, *Healing Wave* 6

Air5

Tier I - *Gale* 7, *Air Knife* 15, *Air Supply* 4

Tier II - *Wind Shield* 6, *Sonic Bolt* 11

Tier III - *Updraft* 2, *Pressure Spear* 6

Tier IV - *Flight* 3

Blessings

Mythic Blessing of Mursa - Blessed Return, Ageless Folio

Skills

Anatomy 7

Arcana 8

Enchanting 11

Fishing 1

Herbalism 5

Librarian 5

Ritual Magic 23

Spear 11

Wind Spear 8

Spellcasting 27

Telivern followed Micah out, resplendent in the sunshine. He turned to the deer and leaned against it after it approached him, its fur soft against the side of his face. Micah smiled as the bristles tickled his cheek. He wanted to see his family. He didn't even know how long it had been since he'd had a moment to actually sit down and talk with them.

Support. Concern. Frailty.

"I suppose they are a weakness of mine," Micah said with a chuckle. "There's plenty that I need to protect in this world. You and they are at the front of the list."

The walk back to Basil's Cove was a dream. Even his bare feet didn't really bother him. Stones dug into him, but he barely even felt the pain. 800 hit points had toughened him beyond what Micah would ordinarily consider human.

The gate to the city barely slowed him. The guards took pity on Micah based upon his ragged appearance and waved him in without forcing him to pay the toll.

Internally, he chuckled. His clothes were grimy, burnt, and filled with holes. Half of his hair was missing, burned from his head by a near miss. Even his spear was covered with divots and burns from the shrapnel and spells that had targeted him during his battle with the Durgh. To all the world, he looked like nothing more than an adventurer returning after biting off more than he could chew.

Inside Basil's Cove, he took in the regular day-to-day bustle of the city as he walked toward his parents' house. Merchants shouted the virtues of their wares in the marketplace while day laborers told jokes as they worked. Occasionally, a messenger would run by, a hand on their satchel as they darted through the crowds in an attempt to ward off thieves or interception.

Micah smiled. This was what he was protecting. The chaos and beautiful normalcy of a city going about its business, entirely unaware how close it had come to complete destruction.

Finally, he arrived at the front door to his parents' house. Next door, his father's shop bustled as the assistants—all forgotten that his parents were trying to aid—helped clients with their fittings. His dad would be busy with work until after sundown, but Mother would be home, likely tutoring Esther or preparing dinner.

He knocked on the door. Inside, his mother shouted something indistinct at Esther before he heard the sound of footsteps leading to the door. It opened.

Before Micah could say anything, he was wrapped up in a hug.

"Micah!" Esther shouted from inside. "Momma, did you know that Micah was coming home?"

"Hush, poppet," his mother replied, tears sparkling in her eyes as she looked up at him. "Trevor said you ran off on some sort of big mission. You disappeared for a week. Seven whole days without any news. I know you're an adult, Micah, but you can't do that to your parents. You need to stop by now and again, or we'll worry about you. It's what your father and I do."

"I'm sorry, Mom." Micah's voice caught in his throat. "You won't have to worry about it again. I have all the time in the world now. Before, something came up that threatened the entire city. I was the only one that could do something about it. If I didn't, everyone would have gotten hurt. I just couldn't stand by and let that happen."

"Esther" —she turned to her daughter—"get your father and Trevor. Let them both know that Micah's back and that I expect both of them here for supper. We're having a family dinner tonight no matter what. Tell them that I won't forgive them if they're even ten minutes late."

Esther scampered past the two of them, pausing briefly to look back at Micah before she ran over to the clothing shop. Micah's mother looked him up and down and clucked her tongue before pulling him into the house.

"Look at you, Micah Silver." She shook her head. "You look like someone dragged you on a rope through all of the hells, one after another. I'm not sure I even want to know how you managed to let your clothing get to that state."

"It feels like it, Mom," Micah chuckled, "and honestly, I'm not sure you'd believe me if I told you."

"Well," she continued, pulling him into the kitchen and motioning for Micah to sit at the table, "it doesn't matter. You're back, and you're going to eat dinner with the family for the first time in years. That's what matters."

Dinner was perfect. The years spent mostly in the forest or under the thumb of the Royal Knights faded into an unpleasant memory as

Trevor complimented their mother on the dinner rolls and Esther hung on to Micah's and Trevor's words as they described their various adventures.

As dinner came to close, Micah's mother sent Esther to the washroom to get ready for bed and his father brought out a bottle of the good port. Usually, the fortified wine was reserved for big sales, such as an entire line of blouses to a noblewoman or a contract to exclusively make the suit jackets for a major noble house's servants. Today, his father beamed as he poured four large glasses of the expensive amber liquid.

"Micah" —the older man held up his glass—"no matter how old or strong you may grow, this will always be where you belong. To always returning home again."

Micah drank a sip along with his parents and brother, savoring the sweet burn of the liquid. By the Sixteen, there was no way that he'd ever touch juushk again.

"So, Micah." His father sat down, a slight flush on his cheeks. "Now that you've accomplished whatever your mysterious goal was, do you have any plans? From the way Trevor talked about it, you probably have enough attunement to retire, but that sounds like an awfully boring path to take when you're only eighteen."

"It's not anything exciting." Micah's face twisted into a wry smile. "Certainly not anything as harrowing as how I've spent the last couple of months, but I've learned a thing or two about enchanting. I'll still probably raid a dungeon now and then, but I'd really like to buy a little shop up by the market and start selling things to adventurers. I know how useful those sorts of things can be during a tough run, and if I could save a couple lives by ensuring that some of Trevor's guildmates have what they need, that seems like a more than worthwhile pastime to me."

"If you're any good at it, you'll make a killing," his father said, beaming back. "Just make sure to pay your dues to the artisan guilds and they'll smooth things over with the city. I'll introduce you to someone tomorrow and we'll have you up and running in no time."

"What about Jo?" Trevor cut into the cheer. "I know she misses you, but she was really upset with how you stormed off. I think she wanted to be there with you on whatever your big final mission was. I really think the two of you should try and patch things up."

"Wait." His mother's head whipped around to squint at Micah. "Jo? The Jo in Trevor's squad? How come I didn't know that my little boy had a girlfriend?" She snorted and tossed her head toward Trevor. "I can't count on this one to settle down with any one girl. He's always looking for something that he can't quite find. That said, if I have a chance at grandkids, I need to know."

"Veronica." Micah's father shook his head. "By the unending grace of the Sixteen…"

47

AN EPILOGUE OF SORTS

The bell jangled on the door to Micah's shop, causing him to look up from the Folio. He'd spent most of the afternoon working on the design for a pendant that would increase its bearer's strength. It was an interesting combination of ritual and Wood magic he'd been worrying over for the past two days without any real results.

Closing his book, Micah searched the small store for his customer. Simple wooden shelves contained some of his earlier works, and placards detailing their effects covered the walls. A pair of windows let in light, illuminating three pots with different flowers in them, colorful against the dark wood of their surroundings.

Nobody.

A voice giggled beneath the counter. Micah smiled and stood up, walking around the edge of the wooden table.

"There you are, Esther." He reached out and tousled her hair. "What are you doing here? I thought Mom wanted you helping her around the house with chores."

"Chores are boring." She pouted, scrunching her nose. "Mom just makes me clean the house over and over again. As soon as I'm done, she tries to teach me how to read."

"Don't underestimate reading." Micah smiled down at her.

"Pretty much everything I know I learned from a book. The rest? Well, I'm not sure you need to know it."

"But, *Micaaaaah*." Esther ran to one of the walls, picking up a wooden flute enchanted to put low-level monsters to sleep. "I don't like reading. It's slow and the words are too big. Why can't you just tell me what I need to know? Then we get to spend time together and I can grow up to be big and strong like you and Trevor!"

Micah snatched the flute from her hands, quickly snagging an ivory carving of a dog and placing it in Esther's grasp. He'd been meaning to enchant the carving later, but for now, it found a higher calling as a knickknack to keep his sister's nimble fingers occupied.

"I can teach you some things," Micah replied, casting *Plant Weave* with a motion of his hand. After enough skill levels, the spells incantation had shortened. Years of repeatedly using his spells in combat situations meant he didn't even need his words for a first-tier spell.

A leaf extended from one of the flowers, growing rapidly on a thin stem from the window until it reached Micah's hand. Gently, he plucked it. In his hand, it twisted into the figure of a young woman made of vine and sap. She began dancing, twisting and swaying to unheard music while Micah smiled on.

"Wooow!" Esther exclaimed, her eyes wide as she clapped her hands, the dog figurine forgotten. "Teach me how to do that! I want to be a magician when I get blessed too!"

"I can teach you the words to the spell," Micah chuckled at her, extending his arm to allow the figure to prance and twirl its way toward Esther, "but past a certain point, you'll need to study what they mean. How they interact with each other and the rest of the world. At some point, you're going to need to read to solve the riddles I don't have the answers to."

The leafling jumped from the end of Micah's hand onto Esther's shoulder. It spun toward her before grabbing on to her hair and climbing atop her head. Esther giggled, reaching for the leafling. With a wiggle of Micah's fingers, the construct dodged past her hand and jumped onto Esther's other shoulder.

"Are you ready to go home and do your chores now, Esther?" Micah asked, a smile on his face as he watched her shriek and try to collect the dodging plant golem. "Mom is going to worry if she can't find you."

"No." Esther grabbed the leafling just as the spell ran out and it reverted into inert vegetable matter. "I can learn to read later. I didn't get to play with you for almost two years, and then when you came back to the city, you started spending all of your time at this shop. I'm playing with you today."

"I need to watch the shop in case a customer shows up," Micah said, trying to deflect her earnest energy.

"There's nobody here." Esther furrowed her brow as she glanced back and forth. "Actually, it doesn't look like there's been anybody here for a while."

"Fine." Micah chuckled, reaching out to touch a crimson string that stretched into the back of the shop. "If you want to play, we're going to go and do something actually fun. There's no point in hanging around an empty shop all day hoping for a customer."

Esther squealed and ran out of the store into the busy market district of Basil's Cove. Micah followed her, pausing briefly to bar the door and make eye contact with the Onkert that slipped out of the back room to guard his shop.

Outside the shop, he closed the shutters on both windows as a pair of horses clopped by. No need to advertise the presence of a daemon to the entire downtown. The Church of Luxos was already trying to make trouble for him, constantly asking nosy questions about where he'd acquired his wares.

"Micaaaah." Esther's hand on his shirt brought Micah back to the crowded street outside of his store. "You said we were going to do something fun. Where are we going?"

"We're going to tell Mom that you're tagging along with me for the day first." Micah scooped Esther up and put her on his shoulders.

"I don't want to go home," Esther said, trying unsuccessfully to struggle free as Micah held her in place with his enhanced strength.

"Mom will yell at me for not cleaning my room or washing the dishes."

"You can clean and wash later." Micah began walking toward their home at a steady clip, weaving in and out of the busy market-place foot traffic. "I just know better than to let you spend an entire day hiding from your chores with me without telling Mom. She'll get worried and yell at me until her face turns red."

Above him, Esther's tiny frame shook as she laughed, squirming against his shoulders. Micah smiled.

"Sure," he said, feigning outrage, "it might seem fun to you. You're not the one getting yelled at for helping his kid sister run off without saying anything."

The walk home was relatively uneventful. At one point, Micah and Esther had to step out of the street to allow a carriage to pass, but other than that, there was no damper on their cheerful banter. After alerting their mother and quieting her concerns, Micah brought Esther to the city gates.

A quick chat with the guards later, and they were on their way toward the cave, Micah barely able to hold Esther's attention as her wide eyes took in the countryside. Eventually, he just gave up trying to talk to her and let her run back and forth, pointing out squirrels and birds.

After ten or so minutes, the excitement began to fade, and Esther stopped chasing every small and cute animal. Before too long, she began nagging Micah, complaining about the distance of their walk. Finally, they reached the cave.

"We're here." Micah set Esther down after carrying her for the last half of the journey to quiet her complaints. "This is where I come in my spare time. It's easier for me to get work done out here away from the bustle of the city."

"Is it like a fort?" Esther perked up, the boring walk forgotten once she saw the signs of Micah's campsite. "This is where you came to play while we were working?"

"I don't know about playing." Micah chuckled, watching Esther run over to the cave. "It was actually brutally hard work."

Micah glanced up at the snap of a twig from the forest. Telivern walked into the clearing, slowly chewing on a mouthful of moss.

Esther squealed. Turning from the empty firepit, she sprinted toward the great white deer. Almost before Micah could say anything, she grasped onto its fur and pulled herself up onto Telivern's back with the agility of a monkey.

The deer looked at Micah with mournful eyes, cocking its antlered head to the side in a silent question.

"Esther," he laughed, "this is my good friend Telivern. Telivern, this is my sister Esther. She was curious about how I'd been living my life, so we took a little trip out here to meet you."

"Wow!" Esther's eyes were wide. "It's like it can talk to me, but only in feelings. It just keeps saying 'confusion' and 'amusement'."

"That seems like a fair emotional response to a little girl climbing on your back to me." Micah shook his head, smiling at the two of them. "I suppose it's better than Esther being terrified of you, but it was hardly the reaction that I expected."

Telivern snorted back at Micah before lowering its head to eat some grass near the edge of the clearing around the cave. Maybe it was the fairly constant campfire that he kept lit when he traveled out to the cave to inscribe his enchantments, but the grass was yellow and patchy. Whatever was in the soot had twisted and killed the plants.

Someone coughed gently, prompting Micah to spin, an *Air Knife* half-formed in his hand before he recognized Jo at the woodline. She averted her gaze, spending a solid second looking at the firepit and the cave before looking back at Micah as he watched her silently.

"Gods." Jo smiled weakly. "This is a lot harder than I imagined it."

Micah sighed, trying to clear the memory of her jumping off that roof in Basil's Cove from his mind. It'd only been a month ago, but after his war with the Durgh and establishing his new peaceful existence, it seemed like a lifetime. He'd seen her a couple of times since then, but each time, she'd managed to avoid him, ducking out of social gatherings and disappearing into the night before he could track her down.

"How did you imagine it?" The question didn't come how Micah had intended it. Instead of carrying the confidence and swagger that he'd tried to cultivate, the words were quiet. Almost scared.

"Well." Jo looked back at him for the first time. "I imagined secretly following you out here to whatever secret base you had and giving you a piece of my mind, for one. I thought we were something more than a quick f—"

Her eyes flicked to Esther playing with a visibly suffering Telivern, and her sentence ended abruptly in a fit of coughing.

"I thought that things were heading in a more serious direction," she finished, slightly flatly with just a hint of a blush coloring her cheeks. "But now, none of that really seems to matter. If we're going to be something more, I can't have any more of this 'hero-complex man of mystery' crap. It was cute at first, but that isn't something you base a relationship off of."

Micah smiled back at her.

"Before you ran off last time, I was going to tell you everything." As he spoke, he walked toward her, his voice quieting so that Esther couldn't hear. "I fought most of the Durgh army in this area. They were going to attack, wipe Westmarch and Basil's Cove off the map. I had a couple dozen daemons around level 20. They didn't even last a full minute in the final battle."

"Micah," she said, her voice as quiet as his, "I never really asked, but what level are you?"

"40," he replied, a slight smile on his face. "My class is a bit different, though. I gain 3 attribute points per level and I can maintain a lot of powerful summons at once."

"Fo—" Jo burst out laughing. "My class gives me 3 attribute points every four levels. You're literally getting more than twice as many attributes per level as me. By the Sixteen, you're probably more powerful than the guildmaster and you're not even eighteen!"

"I am," Micah responded evenly. "In the final battle, I had two summons that were the equivalent of a level 60 warrior, and about a dozen that were the equivalent of a level 40. Well, over half of them died and I barely escaped. If you'd come with me, you would have died. I can guarantee that."

"Gods." She stared at him in silence for almost five seconds before continuing. "No wonder you didn't want people to know what you could do. No one would ever leave you alone if they knew."

"Or worse," Micah agreed, a shadow flashing by his eyes despite his slight smile.

"So," she sighed, not quite able to meet his eyes, "I guess you did have a good reason to warn me off before you went on your adventure? It wasn't really some sort of masculine bravado?"

"Jo." Micah shook his head. "I'd never do something to hurt you. I sent Telivern away at the end. I don't actually think there's anyone in Basil's Cove that could have properly stood with me in that final battle. I really just couldn't bear to see someone I loved die in front of me while I looked on, helpless. Again."

"Lo—" Jo blushed. "I. Uh."

"Look." Micah smiled at her, taking both of her hands into his. "We don't have to be fast about this. Why don't we just start things over again? This go around, I have all the time in the world for you."

The afternoon went quickly. Micah, Telivern, Esther, and Jo played tag in the woods, much to Esther's delight despite Jo always winning. When his sister grew bored, they searched for herbs that Micah's mother had requested until the sun began to go down.

After walking both Esther and Jo home, Micah walked back to his shop whistling. Now that he had his own business, it wasn't appropriate for him to spend every night at his parents' house.

Unbarring the door, he walked in, a cheerful smile on his face as he sent the Onkert back to the small chamber it lived in behind the storefront proper.

Micah hardly even noticed that all three of the plants in his window were wilted and yellow as he climbed the ladder to his lofted bedroom, as crisp and lifeless as the grass in the clearing.

48

THE SETTING SUN

The next morning, Micah got out of bed early to work in the shop. It was a stretch to say that he woke, given that he barely slept an hour a night, but even so, he found it refreshing to spend at least a couple hours in bed with his eyes closed going over the events of the day.

Business was sedate as usual. Few people could afford the luxury of enchanted items, but those that could were willing to pay. Shortly after sunrise, a merchant stopped in to commission a set of crystal bottles that could maintain the freshness of their contents with Wood magic.

That project kept Micah occupied for at least an hour or two, at which point a noblewoman's servant came in to pick up her purchase from a week ago. The project wasn't anything all that taxing for Micah. Just a pair of hairpins that would tighten skin and prevent wrinkles. Exactly the sort of thing to keep him occupied during his semiretirement.

Checking the time, Micah smiled and dismissed the Folio. He'd almost completed his design for the enchantments on the bottle, but it was time for lunch.

Walking out of the store, he plucked the thread leading to the guard Onkert, summoning it from its hiding spot as he barred the door and shuttered the windows. Briefly, he frowned at the dead plants. He was unsure when exactly they'd grown brittle and yellow, but ultimately dismissed the passing thought.

He'd have to hurry back to his parents' house if he wanted to make it in time for lunch. He'd only gotten his mother to agree with his kidnapping Esther for the entire afternoon by agreeing to a family meal, and he was pretty sure that she'd track him down and beat him black and blue despite his levels if he tried to back out of his agreement.

The walk back was brisk and uneventful. He spent most of his time halfheartedly thinking of the days before his sojourn into the Great Depths. He'd never had moments like this back then. No time to enjoy fresh air for its own sake or try to earn an honest living while enchanting mundane things.

True, he couldn't help but wonder about more combat-oriented enchantments. In the past month or two, he'd had a couple of ideas about ways to imbue Time enchantments into armor and weapons. The idea was borderline intoxicating. An adventurer armed with bracers of *Haste* and a helmet that could grant brief flashes of *Foresight* would be incredible.

Even someone as weak physically as Micah was able to kill a pair of elite Durgh warriors under the influence of those spells. In the hands of trained warriors? Well, it wouldn't be as impressive as the Luoca fighting at the Khanmoot, but it would make a mockery of an opponent's levels. Even if someone was more powerful, moving faster than them and being able to see their next move was a hell of an advantage in a life-or-death struggle.

Of course, there was no real need for weapons like that. Basil's Cove didn't face any real threats. Other than the Cavern of Rust, adventurers could face every other challenge at their own pace. They might buy a sharper sword or armor that could repair itself, but beyond that, most of the adventurers were content with whatever low-tier enchanted weapons they could dredge out of the dungeons.

Despite enjoying the period of peace, Micah couldn't help but feel like something was wrong. His entire existence was predicated on perfecting himself, always preparing for the next challenge recklessly, disregarding his own physical and emotional health. Spending his time crafting peacefully or relaxing with Telivern just felt wrong. Like something terrible was hiding just out of sight, waiting around the corner for him to let down his guard for a second.

It wasn't like Micah stopped training altogether. He still raided dungeons with Telivern and his daemons late at night, working on his spells, skills, and experience. Still, one or two runs a week was a far cry from his daily fights. No matter how he tried to assure himself that he was moving in the right direction, that taking a moment for himself wasn't wrong, Micah couldn't help but feel like he was missing something.

Finally, he arrived at his parents' house in a rather pensive mood. Micah barely managed one knock before his mother opened the door, sweeping him inside. Trevor was already there, chatting with their father about a new line of doublets he was working on.

Before Micah could introduce himself, he stumbled forward from an impact to his lower back. Esther's tiny hands wrapped his torso in a hug.

"Well, hello to you too." He chuckled, awkwardly reaching behind himself to ruffle her hair. "You're awfully eager to see me for someone that just spent the entire day with me."

"I told Mommy and Daddy about your deer!" she responded cheerfully, her tiny fingers digging into Micah's stomach. "They said that they wanted to meet him too!"

"Micah!" Trevor's eyes lit up, noticing Micah after Esther's unprovoked assault. "Jo seemed a lot happier this morning, and Sarah was able to drag it out of her that you two made up. Of course, Sarah was peeved, but then again, she's sour about everything. Now, tell me, what's the story with Jo and this 'magical deer' that Esther is so wound up about?"

"Sit down first." Their mother bustled by, shooing them toward the table. "The rolls are already out. I'll have the fruit, jam, and cured meats out in a second. You can talk about girls or work all you want, but at least do it while sitting down and eating. I know how busy everyone is and I don't want you showing up late to your next appointment and then using that as an excuse to avoid a family get-together next time."

Micah chuckled and pulled out a chair, the worn wood of the seat scraping noisily against the freshly sanded planks of the floor. Everything was just as he remembered it. The kitchen was small and filled with shadows, lit by the orange glow of the hearth. The smell of fresh bread filled the air, and the faint scent of meat and herbs toyed with the edges of his senses.

It was the same thing every time he went back. The sounds, smells, and bustle of home. Now that he had a moment away from the constant stress and challenge of bettering himself, Micah began to realize how much he missed it.

A wave of nostalgia washed over him as Trevor and Esther fought good-naturedly for the bread, their mother interrupting them to place a plate of jam on the table. Micah's father quietly ate a roll, a smile on his face as he watched the playful bickering.

"Now, honey." Micah's mother rested a hand on his shoulder as she leaned past him to set down a plate of cured meats. "Esther said that you let her play with some sort of dangerous wild animal? I certainly don't recall you running that idea past me when you stopped over here, but maybe my memory isn't working that well in my old age."

Micah shrank back from her touch as she sat next to him, deftly making herself a sandwich of fresh bread and cured pork. If it wasn't for the faint smile dancing across the tips of her mouth, he'd have been truly frightened. No matter how many loops he lived, her ire wasn't something that Micah was prepared to take lightly.

"That was my friend Telivern." He grabbed a glass of water and drank, trying to cover his nervousness over the situation. "I met Telivern when it was just an ordinary buck. We had our share of adventures, and eventually, it evolved. We've been through a lot together and I trust it with my life. Frankly, I trust it more than any human not in this room."

"What about Jo?" Trevor asked, winking at Micah.

He scowled back at his brother, feeling his mother's gaze boring into his side as her full attention returned to him.

"Yes," his mother followed up, her eyes narrowed to slits, "what about Jo? Trevor says that you've had a little bit of a fling with a girl in his squad. I do have to ask, Micah. Why is it that I'm only finding out important facts about my little boy's life from Trevor? Is there something about this trollop that you're trying to hide from me?"

"Trollop?" Micah put his hands up, leaning back in the chair. "That's hardly fair—you don't even know her. Jo's a lot of fun, but we didn't really know if it was going to be anything more than that until recently. Now that we're planning on making things official, I'd have brought her around... sooner or later. Probably much later," he mumbled under his breath.

"Oh, so you were 'just having fun' with some poor girl, then?" His mother's expression changed in a moment. "I thought I raised you better than that." She turned to his father. "Jon, tell Micah that I raised him better than that."

"Veronica." He shook his head, reaching for another roll. "There is no way in any of the hells that I would get involved with this. If you want to torment the boy, go ahead, but the way I figure? He's eighteen. The boy is entitled to a couple of secrets. Gods know I had my share when I was his age."

"Trevor"—Esther turned her overly large eyes on Micah's brother —"is it bad if Micah had a lot of fun with Jo? I was there and they looked like they had loads of fun!"

Micah turned redder than the strawberry jam on the table as Trevor literally fell out of his chair laughing. His father let out a startled guffaw before he managed to silence himself with the fresh-baked bread. Even his mother had a hard time keeping a smile from her face as she restrained a laugh.

"We're just teasing Micah," his mother intervened, studiously ignoring Trevor's rolling and crying form on the kitchen floor. "You really don't need to know what that means yet."

"Or ever," his father chimed in, having recovered from his

sudden need to eat. "You're my little girl, and I think it would be just fine if you never bothered to pick up that habit of Trevor's."

"Dad!" Trevor sat up from the floor, wiping tears from his face. "It's not my fault that the ladies love me. I'd try beating them back with a stick, but you and Mom have raised me to never beat a woman. It's just not in my nature."

Micah rolled his eyes and snagged some of the cured meat for his sandwich. Trevor could go on for hours if given the chance. Depending upon the moment, the man was either a braggart or the most sincere friend one could have.

Quickly finishing the roll, Micah washed it down with a glass of water, a smile on his face as he watched Trevor banter with his father. This was what he'd been missing over all of those years. Sure, he'd gotten stronger, but he'd never gotten a chance to live a proper childhood and develop honest friendships. The closest he'd had was his relationship with his squad in the first timeline. Ever since then, he'd been adrift, disconnected from the realities that he floated through.

"Mommy," Esther said in a quiet voice. Micah frowned. She was much paler than usual. "I really don't feel that good, Mommy. I think my tummy is upset."

His mother put the back of her hand against Esther's forehead and frowned. Even from where he sat, Micah could see the beginning of cold sweat accumulating on her pallid skin.

"How about I get you a tonic, honey?" His mother stood up and took a step toward a nearby cabinet where she kept the powders and herbal remedies that the family made do with. They weren't poor, but the services of a proper healer were expensive, only for nobles or a real emergency.

"Let me, Mom." Micah placed his hand on Esther's arm and mouthed the handful of words to *Augmented Healing*. "At some point, I became a healer. Looking after Esther is the least that I could do."

He barely registered his mother's nod as the spell sank into his sister. He frowned. There was nothing wrong, yet everything was working incorrectly.

Usually, the spell worked in conjunction with his Anatomy skill to identify internal problems in the patient so that it could magically fix them. With Esther, he couldn't pinpoint a virus, wound, or mana imbalance that was afflicting her. By all rights, she should be doing perfectly.

The spell revealed a different story. There wasn't anything specific wrong, but everything about her was off. Her temperature was much hotter than was healthy, her blood moved slower than it should, and her very cells almost seemed to reject the energy that was transmitted to them by what blood did reach them.

He cast *Regeneration* on her instead, hoping that the fourth-tier spell could fix what his second-tier casting couldn't identify. Nothing changed.

Micah's frown deepened. Almost in horror, a thought came to him. He looked down at his hands on her forearm, glowing faintly red.

Slowly, he closed his eyes. The red light was no longer content to just remain in his body. A corona of Elsewhere's energy shone off of him as waves of thrumming power filled an area about two arm's lengths from him.

Without opening his eyes, he turned his sightless gaze to Esther. She was visible in his pitch-black world, the faint red glow of Elsewhere clinging to her slight form, attaching to every cell.

"Oh no," Micah whispered, his eyes jolting open as images from yesterday ran through his mind. Esther on his back. Him holding Esther's hand. Climbing up a tree with Esther under the crook of his arm and placing her on a branch.

"Oh gods, no." His eyes widened as he remembered the sandy soil and dead grass outside the cave. He looked down at Esther. Her skin showed just the faintest hints of yellow. The same yellow of the crisp, dead plants just inside his shop windows.

49

THE COST

The Brensen lifted another rock to the top of the formation that housed Micah's cave. Above him, the three Onkerts that he'd summoned after his return from the Great Depths chipped the boulders into rough bricks and piled them atop each other. Already the base of a structure was beginning to take shape.

Micah sighed as he looked around the clearing. The grass was completely dead. Over the week or so since Esther had fallen ill, the aura surrounding him had grown in both size and intensity. When he closed his eyes, he could already see the field spreading almost five body lengths from his outstretched hands.

Forty days. Forty days until the cooldown on *Blessed Return* ran down. He closed his hand. He'd told Trevor not to follow him and sent Telivern away. He couldn't stomach the idea of his mere presence hurting another person he loved.

Almost worse than anything was how easy the Onkerts were to summon. He barely even needed a touch of temporal energy to bring them over for two months. Communing with Elsewhere was as natural as breathing to him now, and the prospect scared him. With each ritual he used, Micah could feel the mists on the other side calling to him.

It was becoming harder to resist. Every time he opened a

portal, his blood sang and, through the tethers, his daemons responded back. Their voices rose in a glorious chorus of chaos and unmaking. He could almost understand them. The whines of the Onkerts, the squawks of the Brensens, and the hiss of the Luocas—they were like words spoken in another room. Micah felt like he only needed to concentrate and their meaning would be clear to him.

It was a line he shouldn't cross. Somehow he knew that actually speaking with the daemons would cost him something vital. No amount of Arcana gain would be worth what he'd have to leave behind.

Instead, the solution was isolation. Set himself up far enough from Basil's Cove that the aura surrounding him wouldn't harm anyone and wait out the cooldown. The only downside was that solitude and worry were already driving him mad. Every day, there was nothing to do but read through the books he'd copied into the Ageless Folio from the Academy library and worry about Esther.

If he was honest with himself, his stir craziness was the reason he'd decided to build the tower. He'd spent days coming up with excuses: it would give him a better view of the area, it would suspend Micah high in the air and prevent his energy from harming the local ecosystem any more than it already had, and even just that it would look cool.

Deep down, Micah knew that he needed a project. As much as he liked going over the books in the Folio and research, he was struggling emotionally. During his brief periods of sleep, he still dreamt about the Royal Knights, waking with a start and covered in sweat.

Sending Telivern away had hit him harder than he expected. There was something about the stag's presence that comforted him; it created an island of placidity in the raging ocean of his ambitions. Now? He had nothing but time and no one to spend it with. It was enough to drive a man mad, and Micah knew that he was closer to crossing that bridge than he'd like.

Micah turned, his hand reaching for his spear as he heard a twig snapping in the woods. Mentally he probed for the threads connecting him to the daemons, only to relax when he recognized Jo and Trevor walking out of the forest, their faces grim.

He closed his eyes, watching Jo's dim, glowing form approach his corona of fire. Just as she approached the edge, he opened his eyes and raised a hand, halting their advance.

"That's close enough." He smiled slightly. "After the incident with Esther opened my eyes to what was going on, I've explored its limits. Right now, you're as close as you can safely approach."

"We're almost twenty paces from you, Micah." Trevor frowned. "What's happening? You just ran off after Esther fell ill and we haven't seen you in days. I was only able to find out about this place after talking with Jo."

"Did Jo tell you that I've seen the future?" Micah asked, cocking his head toward her. Jo shook her head, frowning back at him. "I don't suppose there's any harm now." Micah chuckled slightly. "My blessing is a Mythic gift from Mursa. It lets me travel into the past."

"I thought you got a book?" Trevor asked, confusion evident in his voice. "I know you've been secretive about your gift, but I've seen the book. I don't know how you could have faked it."

"I do have a book." Micah summoned the Folio and paged to a description of Bitollan. "It records everything I see or do and helps me learn skills and spells. It also tracks what I've learned in my previous lives."

"This is a lot to take in, Micah." Trevor glanced from Jo back to him. "It also doesn't explain what happened to Esther or why you're hiding in the woods with an army of daemons."

"In my first life"—Micah turned back to the rock formation, watching the daemons continue their construction—"I lived normally. I joined the Lancers and became a member of Jo's team. With a healer, they never bothered to assign you, Trevor."

"Wait," Jo cut in, her brow furrowing slightly. "You never told me about this. That we were teammates in the past. What else is there?"

"Just let me finish." Micah directed a Brensen to continue carrying another large boulder to the top of the other rocks. "We adventured and grew close. We dated for a time." He smiled slightly, his face still turned from Jo and Trevor. "It didn't work out, but that was for the best. I was young and timid. What did happen"—Micah turned back to them, his face grim as he began reliving the memories that still occasionally haunted his infrequent dreams—"is that the Durgh attacked. Westmarch must have violated their rules of honor, ignored the results of a duel or something. We were dispatched to investigate the rumors of their attack. They attacked from ambush and killed almost the entirety of our group."

He pointed at them. "Both of you died to save me. I had to watch Jo take her last breath. Even that was robbed of me with Trevor's death. He carried me from the battle and was wounded too badly to continue. Drekt carried me the rest of the way, leaving Trevor behind."

For a second, no one spoke. Jo shifted slightly, uncharacteristic anxiety on her face. Trevor scratched at his chin silently, the only sound being the thud of the Onkert placing bricks atop the boulder.

"Hypothetically"—Trevor waved a hand—"let's say that this is true. What does it even mean? How does it explain you sequestering yourself out here?"

"I've lived a life since then." Micah smiled slightly. "I'm almost thirty now. I tried to solve the problem of the invasion by asking for help, and I failed. This time, I tried to solve the problem on my own."

"What happened?" Jo asked, interrupting Micah's monologue with worry in her eyes. "You disappeared and came back. You told me that everything was fine, that we had time to grow together. Now you isolate yourself from everyone and you're speaking like the protagonist from a bard's tragedy."

"A tragic protagonist." Micah laughed blackly. "That fits, I suppose. This time, I won, but the cost was too high."

"Seriously," Trevor said, looking back and forth between Micah and Jo, "what in the Sixteen is happening? You were always a serious kid, Micah, but Jo's right. You've caught a serious case of the melodrama."

"I needed power and I needed it fast." Micah shrugged, turning back to the daemons. "Ritual magic and daemon summoning provided that power. Unfortunately, I didn't heed the warnings in the grimoire I learned the ritual from. I took too much power too quickly and it changed me. I barely sleep and eat. At some point, I began to emit the same energy as the daemons. Simply being in my presence harms living things. That's the reason why this clearing is a wasteland, and that's the reason that Esther got sick. I am dangerous to be around."

"You'll find a cure, Micah," Jo said hopefully from behind him. "Seriously, you may be the smartest person I know. If anyone can come up with a ritual to undo whatever this is, it's you."

"Yeah," Trevor chimed in. "I don't know half of the stuff you're saying right now, and it all sounds kinda like mopey navel-gazing to me, but if there's a problem, you should just fix it. Less whining, more studying. That's the Micah I know."

"It'll fix itself," Micah replied, watching the ongoing construction. "My blessing can be used again in forty days. Just over a month"—he turned back—"and this will all be a dream. I'll be thirteen again, trying to find a solution to the invasion that won't involve my enslavement or mass death. For a fourth time, we'll grow up together. Maybe next time, I'll be as smart as you seem to think I am and actually solve this dilemma."

"What will happen to us?" Jo frowned. "You go back, but what about those of us left behind?"

"Honestly?" Micah shrugged. "I don't really know. Maybe I disappear and you just go on with your lives. Maybe you fade away like a half-remembered dream, and when I'm done, all of this has never happened. I really hope you fade away." Micah paused, emotions warring within him. "I've... made a lot of mistakes. Some things are better off having never existed."

"Micah." Jo bit her lip, then opened her mouth to say something more before catching herself. Instead, she just stared at him, her gaze hooded. "Basil's Cove sent us to bring you back." She sighed. "After you left, your parents took Esther to the Church of Luxos. They were barely able to treat her, but after hearing your parents' story, they accused you of practicing forbidden magic and demanded that you return to the city for questioning."

"Well," Micah chuckled darkly, "they're right. I did practice forbidden magic, and right now, I'm paying the price. Of course, having me come back to the city is a terrible idea. My very presence will kill people, but even if it didn't, I suspect that the Church wouldn't let the matter drop. No, just tell them to wait for forty days and the problem will go away on its own. Forgive me for sounding morose, but I realize that my current self is a blight on Karell. I will leave as soon as I can."

"They told us to use force." Trevor frowned. "Even if that could work, neither of us would lay a hand on you, Micah. We'll try and warn them off, but you know the Church. They aren't the type to listen to reason when sudden and violent action will do the trick."

"Thank you," Micah said, nodding at the two of them. "It really was good to see the both of you. Staying out here has been awfully lonely, and it was nice to see some friendly faces before I once more resume my march back through time."

"Maybe next time." Jo smiled weakly. "I'm sure you know all the moves to pull on me by now. Make sure to sweep me off my feet."

"I'll be honest." Briefly, a flash of light illuminated his eyes. "I still haven't figured you out entirely. Hopefully, we fare better this time than our last couple of attempts."

"Say," Trevor interjected, awkwardly scratching the back of his neck, "if you're really traveling back in time, it'd probably be helpful for me to tell you something that only your future self would know. You know, to convince the other me that you're from the future."

He squared his shoulders, struggling for words as he stared Micah down. "Micah, I don't know how to say this. It's a secret that's always hung over me. For years, I've wanted to come clean. Just get it off my chest, but each time I get ready to start, I just can't." He smiled weakly at Micah. "Me, the guy who always stands in the front line fighting off monsters with little more than a spear and a smile, a coward."

"Look," Micah said, smiling back, "you're bisexual, Trevor. You told me in a previous timeline. Once you said the words, it all made sense. Gods above, you can't stop yourself from hitting on Drekt anytime you get a cup of juushk in you."

"What?" Trevor's eyes bugged out. "No! I mean, I am, but... I was going to tell you that when you were ten, our neighbor Becky and I were the ones that stole all of Mom's peppers and put them in your clothes. Remember how you ended up itching and crying for days? I know the mystery of it drove you crazy for years."

"You piece of shit." Micah shook his head, but there were tears in his eyes and a smile on his face.

"See you on the other side, Micah." Trevor waved at him as he and Jo disappeared into the forest.

50

A PROPER DISPLAY OF GRATITUDE

"Come down and be judged for your crimes, heretic," the priest, a severe and skinny man with a freshly shorn skull, shouted up at Micah. The man's voice was relayed to him by the ears of a Brensen flying overhead. "We have it on good authority that you've engaged in dark and corrupt rituals. If you're innocent, the truth will come out and we will cleanse your name. If you're guilty, we will cleanse your soul."

"It sure sounds to me like you've already decided that I'm guilty," Micah shouted back, not looking up from the Folio from where he sat on the third story of the outcropping's stone tower. "You're going to need a much better pitch or more people if you plan on actually forcing me back to Basil's Cove."

"Karell itself rejects your corruption, blasphemer," the man called back. "The grass and trees curl and die around you. Even now, I can feel the darkness pouring off of you."

"Brian," the man next to him hissed, "I've never seen daemons like that, and this guy's tower is giving me a serious case of the willies. He sure seems to think that he can take all of us at once. Maybe he isn't bluffing."

"Refer to me as Brother Gage in front of the heretic, Sir Melvin."

The priest wheeled on his companion, zeal and madness flashing in his eyes. "Your informality will only embolden him."

Micah returned the Folio to the mark on his wrist with a sigh and walked to the tower's window. Below him, a motley crowd uneasily surrounded what had been his cave, the priest and Sir Melvin standing a couple of paces in front of the rest.

"What in the name of the Sixteen is this about?" Micah cast *Wind Shield* with a wave of his hand and a muttered word as he hung out the window and frowned at the assembly. "I'm trying to live peacefully in the forest away from society. Out of nowhere, what looks like a raid party shows up on my doorsteps issuing threats and accusing me of a crime. Hells, if I performed dark magic, at least tell me what spells and rituals I'm accused of performing."

"You know *exactly* what we're accusing you of." Brother Gage pointed a finger at him. "The proof flies about your fortress on fell wings even as we speak. Luxos forbids the use of all summoning rituals. Only those imbued with Elementalist and Spiritualist classes through the intervention of the Church may use summoning magic. No pious human would've created those... *things*." He spat the last word.

"My goddess is Mursa." Micah shrugged. "I have a book from her up here where she pretty much explicitly told me to summon them. Theologically, I'm almost certain I'm in the clear. Regardless, as the follower of a different Major Deity, I'm pretty sure I am outside of your jurisdiction unless I harm a follower of Luxos. Come back with a priestess of Mursa—they'll verify my words and refuse to take part in this sham."

"Sham?" Gage's eyes bulged and his finger shook. "*Sham*?! An infidel like you dares to call—"

"Brian." Melvin grabbed the priest's arm, silencing him. "The man is right. The Church of Mursa is independent and coequal. So long as he's telling the truth, there's nothing we can legally do to touch him without a priestess of Mursa's involvement."

"Do you even know why I summoned the daemons?" Micah asked lazily, still hanging partially out the window, his view only slightly impeded by the blur of the *Wind Shield*. "The Durgh were going to attack and murder everyone in Basil's Cove. I needed the help to fight their entire army to a standstill. I literally fought a challenge of honor with them to save everyone present's life."

"It doesn't *matter*!" Gage screamed, pulling his arm from Melvin. "The Code of Luxos is clear. Ritual summoning without using the Church is a sin punishable by death. Even if everything you said is the truth, you still summoned daemons."

"Brother Gage," a tall man with dark hair contrasting with his paper-white skin interrupted. Absently, he reached back and stroked the handle of the massive cleaver—almost the size of his own body —that lay strapped across his back. "I have to say, I think it matters if he summoned the daemons to save all of our lives. I've seen plenty of priests summon elementals or daemons before. I mean, sure, they're often used for evil, but if the man actually used them to help us, how is that different from the Church summoning them?"

"Because it is only legal if the Church summons them." Gage glanced around at the various adventurers behind him. A man with a broadsword and a peg leg nodded slowly. Another man, as big as an ox and leaning against a glaive, frowned at the priest. In the rear of the formation, a man and a woman wearing the apparel of combat spellcasters looked on incredulously.

"Why are you all looking at me like that?" Gage asked, wheeling around to face the adventurers. "Without the intervention of the Church, how can we know that the summoning would be safe? A spellcaster could easily screw up the formula and open a portal into the screaming void, dooming us all. It may seem harsh, but only by severely and publicly punishing those who perform unsanctioned acts can we create an incentive to stop future castings."

The priest waved in Micah's direction. "It may have worked for him, but that doesn't mean that what he did was safe or a good idea. He risked all of our lives with a dangerous ritual. These rules are in place for a reason. Without them, we're no better than the Durgh."

"The only reason you're alive is that the Durgh follow rules," Micah chimed in helpfully. "They aren't the same as those preached by the Church of Luxos, but they take affairs of honor seriously. I won an honor duel. Even though I stained the caves of the Great Depths with their own blood, they simply thanked me, sent me on my way, and honored the terms of their agreement."

"Fine." Gage threw both of his hands up in the air before pointing at each adventurer with him in turn. "Let's make this simple. You shall honor the terms of your agreements. You have been rewarded with attunement. You are under contract, and each and every one of you will do your best to help me subdue this miscreant."

"Look," the man with the glaive said, scratching the back of his head with his free hand, "I don't want to get arrested later for breaking the law, and I'm not keen on getting into some sort of pissing match between the three big churches. As long as you can prove that he's harmed someone that follows Luxos, you have jurisdiction. If you can show that, a contract is a contract."

"He's hurting me right now, Flavicus." The priest put his hand on his chest. "Can't you see the way his aura attacks all of you? The way it invades your body? Even if you can't see it, surely you can feel it. That itch under your skin. The cold sweat on the back of your neck. That's him."

Gage's eyes were wild as he walked up to the man with the peg leg and put his hand on the warrior's chest. "Even as we speak, Jonah, he is sapping the very form, definition, and meaning from you. Simply standing in this clearing is taking years off of our lives. Every one of us will grow sick more easily, suffer abnormally from the cold, and recover from wounds and illness more slowly." Gage grabbed the wrist of the huge man holding the glaive. "He is a sickness, Flavicus. A tumor growing out of the surface of Karell. Just look at the dead grass we're standing on. He kills everything he touches."

The adventurers shifted uneasily as they took in the dead clearing. All of the grass was little more than dust, and most of the trees within sight had already lost their leaves. Brittle branches littered the ground beneath the dead and dying trees.

They looked back to Micah, hanging indolently out of the

window of his tower. Before they could respond, all of them ducked and clutched their weapons as a Brensen swooped overhead. The male spellcaster looked up at it in trepidation, mumbling to himself as he edged slowly back toward the treeline.

"Steady, Gongo." Melvin raised a hand at the caster. "We have a job to do and a couple of summons won't stop us. He didn't know we were coming, so these must be long-term summons. That means that he either used a stupendous amount of life energy, or they're weak. He probably just used them to build that tower he's living in."

Micah snorted. Through the daemons, he could practically taste their fear. Melvin and Gage might be putting on a good show, but every other adventurer was somewhere between uncertain and terrified.

The daemons were exultant. Their joy echoed through the tethers and rattled around inside Micah's chest. The fear excited them, aroused their hunger. Energy pulsed up the fire chains that linked them to Micah, indicating their readiness and soundlessly asking a question. They were asking permission, and after the priest's pompous zeal, a dark part of him wanted to grant it.

He shook his head, an answer for both the daemons and himself. He'd solved too many problems with isolation and violence. Even if he'd be leaving this timeline shortly, he wasn't the sort of person to just kill a crowd for annoying him.

The daemons were influencing him. He knew that for sure now. Ever since he'd crossed over to Elsewhere, he'd become more irritable. Less empathetic. Bloodthirsty.

He closed his eyes and exhaled as they continued to argue.

"Maybe I can make this easy for everyone," Micah interrupted. "I'm going to disappear and never bother Basil's Cove in eighteen days. Literally, I'm planning on leaving Karell. If you come back in twenty days, I'll either be gone forever or I'll voluntarily return with you."

"That seems like a pretty good deal," the retreating mage spoke soothingly, trying to placate Brother Gage. "He goes away and we don't have to fight those daemons. Everyone wins."

"No." The priest shook his head, staring at the spellcaster incredulously. "The only reason we are out here is to punish him for his crimes. If we let him walk away solely because he's powerful, what example would that set for others? Should we just amend the law? 'Summoning one daemon is punishable by death, but summoning five will make the punishment squads nervous, so you will be let off with a stern warning?' The law is the law, Gongo!"

"To be clear"—Micah stepped away from his window and back into the upper floor of his tower—"I could kill all of you in a matter of moments. I'm only negotiating with you to avoid staining my conscience with your blood."

"Even now he threatens us!" The priest rounded on the rest of the uncertain party. "Your duty to humanity and the Church is clear. He will never come down from that tower on his own."

Micah shook his head, reopening the Folio to study some bits of spell theory from a grimoire that he'd copied in the Royal Knights' library. If they tried anything, the daemons would handle them. He'd given the self-righteous fools a chance.

"Melvin"—Micah heard the female spellcaster through one of the circling Brensen—"I've checked. During the course of the conversation, the sphere of corruption around the tower has expanded by another two paces. If we leave him alone for too long, who knows how far the blight will spread?"

"And who knows what he will summon!" the angry priest cut in. "I cannot believe that you're seriously considering leaving a *ritual* caster alone for twenty days. He could cast anything in that time. When we return, he would be even more prepared. Who knows what he could do to us then? Curse our bloodlines? Pluck the sun from the sky and rain its fire upon us?"

"Fine," Melvin, the swordsman that appeared to be leading the rest of the adventurer troupe, replied with a sigh. "We'll do it your way, Brian. Send Jonah and Alan to fetch the deer. We'll force him to come down."

Micah closed the Folio with a frown.

51

AN UNWELCOME FINALE

Micah returned to the window, casting *Flight* as he walked. At the precipice, he simply stepped out onto empty air and continued at his former pace, mimicking an ordinary stroll while he scowled down at the crowd of adventurers.

"Oh shit," Gongo hissed, his eyes going wide. "That's a tier-four Air spell."

"What's that supposed to mean?" Flavicus asked quietly, his eyes never leaving Micah as he gripped his halberd tightly.

The one-legged swordsman the priest had called Jonah spat on the ground before drawing his thin rapier. His gaze returned to where Micah stood impassively in the sky.

"It means," Jonah grumbled, "that this guy isn't bluffing. Fourth tier usually means level 30 or so. Even then, Blessed of that level usually use it as more of a finishing move. They take so much mana that even the guild leaders can only cast them eight or nine times in a row."

"Oh gods, oh gods." Gongo's mumbling was picked up by the circling daemons as the man's fingers fiddled with the hem of his robe.

"Gage," Melvin said as he turned to the priest, frowning, "You never said anything about the target being on par with a guild leader. This doesn't seem like a terribly good idea to me."

"Adventurers"—Brother Gage threw up his hands angrily—"I paid you to fight a threat to our realm, not to argue with me. He is connected with the stag. Luxos' seers have seen it. If you can capture the beast, he'll surrender."

Micah motioned with his left hand, tapping the chains of fire that bound his daemons to him. A handful of the newer Onkerts exited the cave while the surviving Luoca and Brensens soared lower until they were circling him.

"It doesn't look like he plans on surrendering, Brother Gage." Melvin shifted his stance, raising himself up onto the balls of his feet as he lowered his center of gravity. A wise change that would let him spring into action at a moment's notice. It wouldn't be enough.

Micah's eyes took in every move, the circling Brensens providing a panoramic view of the nervous adventurers. He probably should've been disturbed by his ability to process input from a dozen eyes at once without being confused and dazzled, but he wasn't. Not much disturbed him anymore. All he wanted was to be left alone, to read his books until the cooldown on his ability ran out.

The adventuring party shifted uneasily, gripping weapons tighter and muttering to each other as the creatures grew closer. Micah stopped, a handful of paces in front of them and more than a dozen up in the air.

"The offer for you to leave is still on the table." He motioned with his spear at the party before pointing to the woods from which they'd come. "Do not bother Telivern. The stag is under my protection. If you harm it, I will send the daemons after you, and that will only end in blood and viscera."

Before Melvin or the rest of his adventuring party could reply, Brother Gage screamed incoherently in frustration and pointed a hand at Micah. Briefly, the priest's outstretched hand glowed with the light of the rising sun before a beam of energy pulsed out from it, striking Micah in the stomach.

Micah doubled over, the smell of burning flesh filling his nostrils as his HP dropped by a quarter. The beam stopped, leaving a dagger of fire and pain lodged in his gut. Without even thinking, Micah's pain and anger merged with his tethers.

He wasn't sure if he subconsciously ordered the daemons to act, or if they moved in response to the emotional outburst. Regardless of the action that set them in motion, they rushed toward the adventurers with a terrible momentum while Micah frantically cast *Augmented Mending* on his burn.

Gage was the first to die. In the midst of casting a spell, the Luoca landed on him, pinning him to the ground with an insectoid leg. For a brief second, all of the adventurers stared in shock at their impaled leader. Then the scorpion tail streaked downward, gouging a hole through his chest.

The man began to melt. The definition on his extremities blurred together as the corrosive aura of Elsewhere entered his body through the stinger. It pumped into the gasping man like venom as it reduced his lungs and organs to a puddle of semi-organic sludge in moments.

"Brian!" Melvin's shout broke the clearing's silence.

Gongo and the female caster both targeted spells at the Luoca. A hand made of earth reached toward the daemon while a series of ice shards slammed into it from the other side. Flavicus and Alan, the two heavily built warriors of the party, charged toward the creature, their sword and glaive poised to strike.

The Luoca didn't even notice. It whipped its stinger from the priest, spraying the two charging warriors with his still-warm blood. Gongo blanched, his hands trembling as he began mumbling to himself and backed from the fight.

A Brensen dove from the sky toward Melvin. The fighter tucked himself into a roll, barely escaping the vulture's skeletal claws as they dug furrows in the dead earth where he'd been standing.

Jonah hopped forward with a grunt, his wooden leg sinking deep into the loose dirt. Extending his rapier, he swiped it through the air, firing *Air Knife* after *Air Anife* from the blade at the daemon.

Micah squinted. The visual distortion created by the spells were small, tight, and fast. Quickly, Jonah wove a web of mana-infused air, slapping and battering the more powerful daemon long enough for Melvin to escape. Clearly, Jonah had all but mastered the spell. The speed, efficiency, and power of his casting were too much for any other explanation.

Taking advantage of his distraction, a pair of Onkerts slammed into Jonah, knocking him to the ground. With an agility that belied his crippled appearance, he rolled to the side and rose up from the ground on a burst of Air mana.

His rapier flashed, taking an eye from one of the daemons while Melvin sprinted under a wild swing from the creature, his sword slashing across its hamstring. It stumbled forward as its legs suddenly lost the ability to support its weight. Jonah landed on the daemon, cracking his peg leg into its collarbone. With a quick pivot, he drew his sword across the monster's throat.

Micah winced as the tether connecting him to the Onkert snapped in tandem with *Augmented Mending* restoring his last missing hit point. He thrust with his spear, triggering the enchantments and firing a spike of air pressure at Jonah. Using the breathing room created by distracting the spellblade, Micah prepared himself to cast a more powerful spell.

The man's rapier blurred as Jonah coated it in the high pressure of an *Air Knife* and intercepted Micah's attack. Micah's eyebrows went up when the spell absorbed his attack in a display of pinpoint control over both mana and air pressure.

The other Onkert took advantage of Jonah's distraction to kick Melvin. The warrior's mouth transformed into an "O" of surprise as the blow knocked the breath from him and sent the man flying across the clearing.

Micah finished casting *Poison Fog*, grimacing at the unfamiliar feel of the spell. A billowing cloud of greenish-yellow smoke appeared around him and began to descend on the clearing, obscuring his view of the invaders. One of the adventurers screamed in alarm—Micah couldn't quite make out which one, but it hardly mattered.

He closed his eyes, relying upon the sight of the daemons as they pursued the humans through the opaque mist. Micah's senses filled the Luoca as it chased after the two warriors that had rushed to Brother Gage's rescue. Both of their weapons—Alan's gigantic sword and Flavicus' glaive—lay on the ground, bisected by the daemon's wings.

The men choked and stumbled as they ran, their high Body attributes letting them resist but not ignore the fog. Micah frowned sightly when the Luoca slowed—like a hound savoring the chase, it sought to prolong its pursuit. He pursed his lips. Honestly? That was probably why they were still alive. He doubted that either of the men could have stopped the wing strokes that had destroyed their weapons from cutting deeper. It easily could have slashed them in half with the same motion.

Flavicus slammed his foot into a rock and gasped in pain, taking in a lungful of the gas. Almost immediately, he fell to the ground, hands clawing at his throat. Without slowing, the Luoca thrust its tail out and speared the huge man through the chest.

It continued after Alan, moving at a leisurely lope. On the ground nearby lay Melvin's corpse, his face bloated and lips blue. The man's Agility-based build might have been useful against the ponderous Onkert, but his slight frame was unable to fight off the heavy toxic clouds.

Alan veered to the side. Lying on the ground was the female caster, her chest barely moving. Her robe was ripped, exposing her bare legs to the stalking daemon.

Micah nodded as he saw the source of the rip: a strip of cloth covering her mouth, soaked in an indeterminate liquid. Quick thinking on the caster's part. Without some sort of filter, there was no way she could survive the roiling clouds of miasma that filled the clearing.

The huge man reached down and slung the woman over his shoulder while the Luoca looked on in amusement. Micah shook his head as he paced them in the air above the cloud.

"Quit playing with your food," he muttered, reaching out and touching the burning chain that connected him to the daemon. "I can't have witnesses, but you don't need to drag it out. Kill them and be quick about it."

The Luoca snorted and pounced forward, its human face locked in a sneer as its two front legs punched through Alan's calves and into the ground beneath. The man screamed, his abruptly halted momentum sending the caster flying. Her body landed ten or so paces ahead of the Luoca.

"Fuck," the man said, his eyes wide as he twisted his torso to take in the monster that had doomed him.

The daemon casually removed Alan's head with a wing before walking over to the spellcaster's unconscious body. With a single thrust of its tail, it caved in the back of her skull. Unhurriedly, it continued strolling out of the mist, following the sound of the other spellcaster, Gongo, panting and stumbling as he ran.

Pain erupted from Micah's throat. He blinked, returning his vision to his own body. Jonah Baird, the crippled spellblade, stood just outside the poison fog, a blurred sphere around his head from the *Air Supply* spell proof of the resourceful man's survival. In his hand, another *Air Knife* hovered, prepared to finish the job if the first had failed.

Micah's hand came away from his throat, covered in his own blood. He tried to pull in a breath, only to be rewarded with a wet, whistling noise from his wrecked windpipe. A mortal wound. Panic threatened to overwhelm him, but Micah fought it down, instead reaching for a ring he kept on his right hand.

"And so he falls," Jonah said darkly, mainly to himself but loud enough for Micah to hear. "A formidable daemonlord to be sure, but in the end, he was as human as the rest of us. One targeted spell is all it takes to bring down a caster. Without his breath, he can't cast spells. If you catch them unaware, even a daemonlord in his tower will die just as easily as the rest of us."

Micah brushed the tethers connecting him to the surviving Brensen as he poured mana into the ring, causing the enchantments inscribed in the chip of amethyst to glow. His vision narrowed and his body screamed for oxygen, but Micah didn't let it distract him.

He'd suffered too much and come too far. He'd defeated men much greater than this motley band of adventurers. There was too much left to do.

His vision dimmed.

Micah redoubled the mana flow into the ring. The inscriptions grew hot as he overwhelmed them, but the onslaught of magic did its job. The pain in his throat dulled. More than anything, it *itched* as the skin and tissue began to reknit itself.

This battlefield would not be his grave.

Next time, he would save them all. Next time, Esther would live. Next time, he and Jo would actually be able to make something together without misunderstandings or interruptions.

Next time.

The ring shattered on his hand, cutting and scarring him, but the spell was finished. His throat was still ragged and bloody, but air passed through it once more.

Immediately, Micah cast *Augmented Mending* on himself. The emergency enchanted ring had limited power, but it was perfect for situations like the one that the spellblade had forced him into. Many tried to injure or silence casters first. The ability to cast a robust healing spell on yourself without speaking or moving was an essential survival tool.

The remaining Brensen descended upon Jonah. Without both of his legs, he didn't have the mobility to escape. Three slashes of their claws later, his shredded body adorned the clearing floor.

Gongo's wet, gurgling scream in the forest marked his end as the Luoca caught up with him. Micah sighed and entered his tower once more.

He'd have to leave. They'd found him here once; it was entirely possible they could do it again. Next time, they might bring a higher-level subjugation team or hostages. His very presence was putting Telivern and his family at risk.

After a couple hours of packing his meager belongings, Micah mounted the Luoca and directed it to fly. He didn't give it particular directions. Just a general idea. North.

The aura of Elsewhere pouring off of the daemon almost comforted him, cradling his tired and injured body as the daemon's great wings flapped and they covered a day's march each hour of flight. At some point, he went to sleep, only waking up when they were deep in the mountains.

A flick of his eyes and a touch of the tether and they were beneath a rock overhang near a waterfall. It would be as good a place as any to practice his spells and wait for the timer to run down.

The days passed swiftly. At first, some predators approached his hiding spot, but the aura around him and his daemons quickly dissuaded them. After a short amount of time, the vegetation around him died and all of the creatures in the valley learned to avoid him.

The silence suited Micah as he cast spell after spell in an attempt to push up his skill and spell levels for the next iteration. Before long, the walls of his overhang were scarred from constant magical abuse as he spent days at a time without the sleep or food he no longer really needed, practicing his skills all the while.

Finally, the day came. In relief, he invoked *Blessed Return*, eager to escape the doomed timeline and try again.

The magic took hold of him, and he began retracing his steps faster and faster, his actions and surroundings a blur as he moved backwards through both his successes and mistakes.

Then he stopped. Micah and his surroundings were frozen. Bugs trapped in amber on the empty plains of Elsewhere.

The mist around him roiled and backed away from Micah as a great hand reached out from nothingness toward him. He remembered this moment. It was when he'd been broken, body and mind, after he'd foolishly thrown himself into Elsewhere.

He watched, unmoving, as the hand grasped him about the torso and pulled. His vision erupted in a kaleidoscope and the world spun. Then the sensations were gone. He was sitting in a gaudy and slightly overstuffed chair.

"Micah Silver," a strangely familiar feminine voice spoke behind him. "You've bumbled back and forth through time aimlessly three times now. I think it's only fair that you and I have a little chat. I'm sure you have plenty of questions that you think need answers."

52

CONVERSATION OVER TEA

"Oh, sit down." Her voice was pleasant and disarming, but with an undertone of command as it halted Micah's half-rise from the chair.

A woman in her early thirties entered his vision from the side. The first thing Micah noticed was that she glowed faintly. Her shoulder-length silver hair framed pleasant, if nondescript, features as she carried a tray laden with an intricately painted porcelain teapot and four cups.

She was slightly taller than Micah, her face filled with a matronly smile that looked out of place on her younger features. Humming quietly to herself, she set the tray down on the short table in front of Micah and began pouring the steaming brown liquid into each of the four cups. One by one, she put the cups in front of the slightly tacky and overdecorated chairs.

"What's going on?" Micah asked the woman as she took a seat to his right. The room was rather large but spartan. The walls were wood and the floor was covered with carpet, but beyond those details, there was little else of note. It was lit, but from no obvious source, and the only entrance was an archway that revealed nothing but foreboding mist and darkness.

There wasn't even any furniture other than the table and the chairs. The more Micah looked around the room, the more it appeared to exist for no other reason than to serve as a comfortable but bare meeting place.

The woman picked up the teacup with both hands and brought it to her mouth, blowing on the steaming liquid before taking a sip. A moment later, a look of absolute joy blossomed on her face. She set the cup back down before answering Micah.

"I think you've guessed who I am," she said, smiling at him slightly.

"Mursa," Micah responded, the word a statement rather than a question. Between her appearance and the strangeness of the encounter, there couldn't be any other explanation.

"Very good!" Her laughter was like a clear chime. Beautiful, but at the same time, Micah couldn't help but notice the slightly condescending tone to her voice. Like he was a prized pet that had just performed a particularly clever trick.

"See, Ankros?" she called out to the empty archway. "I told you that he was one of mine."

Micah turned to look at the entryway. Something stepped through. The breath was knocked out of him as Micah tried to comprehend the terrible power roiling off the being that suddenly shared the room with them.

For a brief moment, it was like staring into the heart of a star. Energy flashed and writhed chaotically, constantly changing yet older than mana itself. The air seemed to leave the room as the entity poured itself inside. The liquid fire flowed around Micah and pressed him into his seat before coalescing into the form of a large, well-muscled man.

Micah let out the breath that he hadn't realized he'd been holding. Sweat covered his body as he tried to draw air in with ragged gasps. The man tossed his head, a mop of dark, unruly hair fluttering slightly in some unseen wind.

"Mursa," Ankros' deep voice rumbled as he walked across the empty room with great and purposeful strides, "my choices are not stupid. They just seek to prove themselves in combat. The stupid ones take on challenges above their skill. They don't last long." The god nodded at Micah as he took a seat to his left. "Micah." A great dark hand reached out and brought the teacup to his lips. A moment later, he sighed in appreciation.

"Even if this was only an excuse to get us all to incorporate"—he flashed a smile of startlingly white teeth at the goddess—"I have to say that I approve. It's easy to lose yourself in the mists and forget about simple pleasures like a cup of jasmine tea."

"Drink your tea, Micah." Mursa smiled his way as she picked up her own cup. "We still have to wait for my other brother before we can begin, and he's been a bit ornery lately. I wouldn't be surprised if he leaves us waiting on purpose."

"I am not ornery," a clipped and annoyed voice said from the entryway. "I am simply precisely on time. It is not my fault that neither of you can keep a schedule."

Micah turned in his chair to look at the newcomer. A tall, thin blonde man wearing an immaculate suit walked to the open chair. Much like Mursa, he seemed to glow from within. Unlike her, he didn't carry an ounce of warmth or cheer.

"Ankros," the man said, shaking his head at the other god, "your aura is leaking again. You're probably suffocating the poor mortal you're inflicting this entire charade upon."

"It builds character," the huge black god said as he grinned back. "Plus, he's already been to Elsewhere and back. A couple glimpses of little old me isn't going to shatter his psyche. He's a big boy."

"Now that Luxos is here"—Mursa smiled at the two men before turning back to Micah—"I think it's about time we explained things to Mr. Silver. He's made it much further than any of us expected, and it only seems fair that we let him know the rules of the game he's playing."

"Wait." Micah frowned, looking at the three most powerful gods of Karell as they bantered lightly. "You didn't expect me to make it this far? What did you think was going to happen?"

"I thought you were going to die in the first invasion," Ankros responded flippantly as he took another sip of tea. He turned to

Mursa. "You know, Mursa"—he gestured at the teacup, tiny in his huge hand—"this is delicious, but I can't help but feel like we need some food to complement it. Maybe like those little sandwiches you brought last time."

"Fine." Mursa rolled her eyes and reached her hand to the side. Micah's breath froze in his throat as reality itself rippled and her hand passed into mists and darkness.

Except it wasn't her hand. It was a tendril covered in thousands of fronds made from soft silver light that positively thrummed with power. The ribbon of power twisted and squirmed through the mist, grasping at something indeterminate before pulsing brightly enough that Micah was forced to blink repeatedly to prevent his vision from being damaged.

Her hand returned and Micah let out a shuddering breath, the impossible shapes and angles of her appendage seared into his memory. She put another tray on the table, this one covered in small sandwiches. Their crusts were cut off.

"Cucumber and watercress sandwiches just for you, Ankros," she told her brother with an easy smile. "And yes," she continued, turning to Micah, "I expected you to fail when that awful Martin character forced you to cast rituals far above your level in high-stress situations. I truly thought you were going to rip a hole into Elsewhere or get yourself possessed. You were only a slight inflection of your voice away from some truly interesting possibilities."

"And I am a pessimist," Luxos cut in dourly. "I thought you were going to die in each timeline before you managed to use the return, yet you managed to prove me wrong every time. Good for you, I guess."

The god didn't even look at him while speaking, instead reaching out and picking up a sandwich before delicately putting it on the saucer next to his teacup. He took a sip of the tea before returning it to its plate. Quietly, the deity produced a napkin from his suit's pocket and laid it on his lap before he began nibbling on the sandwich.

"Regardless," Mursa said, smiling at him cheerfully, "you've succeeded where thousands before you have failed, and I think that warrants a small celebration and an explanation."

"Succeeded?" Micah asked incredulously, a hint of anger in his voice. "I've fallen from one failure to another. I've been enslaved and tortured by others for years at a time. Even this last time, my victory was short-lived and hollow. The tools that you gave me to fight back made me into a monster. I was barely even human at the end. Obviously, I exuded toxic energy that destroyed everything I touched, but even my emotions weren't my own. I was quicker to anger, less likely to empathize with other humans. You're the deities. By what metric is that a success?"

Luxos snorted, but he kept eating his sandwich. Mursa just smiled at him.

"By the only metric that matters, Micah." She took another sip of the tea. "You've seen and done things that have hardened and developed your soul to the point that you can directly handle the essence of Elsewhere. You're the first mortal in almost a millennium that has made it this far. Our last candidate was much more promising than you, and she failed right before the final step."

"Dakkora." Luxos spat the word angrily. "At least this new one has a shred of common sense. She didn't even notice the energies from Elsewhere changing her. Decades of manipulating events and training disappearing in an instant because our pet megalomaniac decided to try and summon a Prince of Elsewhere onto Karell. Of course the ritual didn't work. The Princes are almost as powerful as lesser gods. The energy needed to bind them would rip a mortal apart."

"Admit it, Brother." Ankros erupted into laughter. "You just didn't like her because she tried to tear your church down. Frankly? I thought the girl had spunk. Trying to set herself up as the dark queen of the mountains and take on all comers. I just wish I'd thought to give her a blessing rather than our sister. That's the kind of attitude I can get behind."

"That certainly didn't endear her to me." Luxos sniffed before taking another sip of tea. "At least this one has the right instincts.

Protect his homeland and his family from marauding hordes. Now if we could just speed things along, I would appreciate it greatly."

"Dakkora?" Micah asked, looking at each of the deities with wild eyes. "Karin Dakkora? I was told that she went against the teachings of the gods and had to be destroyed?"

"Hardly." Mursa set down her teacup and steepled her fingers. "Luxos' followers are a bit liberal with the truth when it serves their benefit."

"She was a madwoman, and the people needed to be protected," Luxos bit back, eyes flaring like stars as a pulse of energy pushed Micah back into his seat. "Even your pet here"—the god waved vaguely in Micah's direction—"was almost destroyed by the fragments of her work that the two of you forced me to leave lingering on Karell. Without your intervention, Sister, he'd be little more than another discorporate consciousness floating about in the mists of Elsewhere."

"He has a point." Micah acknowledged the God of Light grudgingly. "I fucked up the last time. I performed the ritual, but it almost shattered my mind. I'm pretty sure it would have without your help."

"You did exactly as well as I'd hoped," Mursa corrected him. "For you to take the next step, it was necessary that you connect with Elsewhere directly. It's true that there were some... side effects, but those were hardly unexpected. But, Micah"—she shook her head sadly—"no mortal is going to survive direct contact with Elsewhere without scars. The magic you've been learning has expanded your soul and mind to the point where I could intervene to save you, but compared to what could have happened, you emerged all but unscathed. We might look all powerful, but matters of the soul are one of the few places where the gods are truly limited."

"After all," Ankros interjected between bites of sandwich, "if we knew how to manipulate souls, there really wouldn't be much need for Karell and all the experiments."

"What does he mean?" Micah asked, his eyes widening. Luxos simply smirked at him, but at least Mursa had enough character to look abashed.

"We created Karell because we're lonely." Mursa's voice was hesitant for the first time. Embarrassed. "Between the Void and Elsewhere, there were the sixteen of us, a handful of mindless spirits, and the Princes of Elsewhere. The Princes are boorish and awful." The goddess's face wrinkled as if she'd eaten something sour as she continued speaking. "They spend all of their time plotting against each other and us. All they can talk about is absorbing the Void into Elsewhere and conquering the mists. They might be our cousins, but the Princes are absolutely terrible company. So we created a new world."

She smiled wistfully. "A nursery for the wisps and fragments of souls we skimmed from Elsewhere to acclimate them to the Void and let them grow in a safe environment without the higher orders of daemons and the Princes feeding upon them. That's the goal of Blessings." Her voice filled Micah's ears as he felt his stomach dropping out beneath him. "The souls that can handle more power are given it. Those that can't live out a life are reincarnated into a new body to grow stronger until they, too, can accept a Blessing."

The goddess smiled bitterly. "Unfortunately, souls lose some of their vibrancy upon death. That is why we've provided the status sheets to mortals. They create an incentive for you to push yourself in each life and expand your souls to the point where you can accept greater and greater Blessings after reincarnation. The final steps are what we call Candidates." Mursa picked up her cup of tea, swirling it briefly before she finished speaking. "Having a strong enough soul is important, but the conscious mind attached to that soul needs to be developed too. You need to know enough of the workings of the universe, either through spellcasting, ritual magic, or martial arts. Also, you need to be able to touch the very source of magic, the mists, and remain both whole and sane. After your experiences, you now have met both requirements. Micah Silver, you are now officially a Candidate."

Micah looked around the circle of deities in confusion. Ankros and Mursa gazed back, expectant looks on their faces. Luxos simply drank his tea.

"A candidate for what?" he asked, frowning slightly. "You just said a whole lot of words about your grand design and plan, but it doesn't mean anything to me. What is the point of all this?"

Ankros burst out laughing, leaning back in his chair to slap his knee.

"That's what I like so much about Micah, Mursa." He forced the words out between deep belly chortles. "You talk for minutes without saying anything and he just points it out. The boy has the heart of a warrior in him after all."

The goddess pursed her lips, maintaining a stern facade for a handful of seconds before she smiled as well.

"Fair enough," she replied, a hint of amusement to her voice. "You haven't spent eons playing these games, so everything is new to you. I shouldn't speak to you like you're one of our cousins when there is so much you don't know. From this day forward"—her voice took on a formal tone, lending the words an aura of finality—"you will only have one class available to you, Micah Silver: Candidate. Just like tributaries inevitably must converge on a river or lake, all martial and magical paths on Karell merge as well."

A hint of amusement entered her gray eyes. "You asked me what you are a candidate for. You are a candidate to join us. To make the Sixteen into seventeen. Young Micah Silver, if you continue to survive and grow, one day, you will ascend above Karell and become a god."

THANK YOU FOR READING BLESSED TIME, BOOK ONE

We hope you enjoyed it as much as we enjoyed bringing it to you. We just wanted to take a moment to encourage you to review the book. Follow this link: Blessed Time Book One to be directed to the book's Amazon product page to leave your review.

Every review helps further the author's reach and, ultimately, helps them continue writing fantastic books for us all to enjoy.

WHAT'S NEXT IN THE SERIES?

BLESSED TIME:

BOOK ONE

BOOK TWO

Want to discuss our books with other readers and even the authors like Shirtaloon, Zogarth, Cale Plamann, Noret Flood (Puddles4263) and so many more?

Join our Discord server today and be a part of the Aethon community.

Facebook

Instagram

Twitter

Website

You can also join our non-spam mailing list by visiting www.subscribepage.com/AethonReadersGroup and never miss out on future releases. You'll also receive three full books completely Free as our thanks to you.

Looking for more great LitRPG?

Jeff Driscoll becomes the only active Game Master for the VRMMORPG Infinite Worlds after a rogue patch turns the game into a buggy, dangerous mess. Can he fix it on his own and save the players?

GET MANUFACTURING MAGIC NOW!

When Hall is trapped inside of Sky Realms Online, he loses everything. His level, his stats, his real world life. Even worse, nobody knows the new rules. What's next, permadeath?

GET GRAYHOLD TODAY!

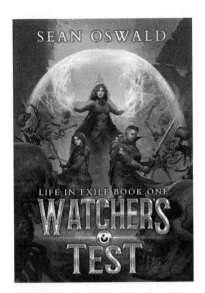

When lifelong gamer Dave is portaled into a game-world called Eloria with no way out, he thinks all his dreams have come true. However, in none of those dreams did his wife and daughter ever accompany him. Can he keep them safe in this strange new world?

GET WATCHER'S TEST NOW!

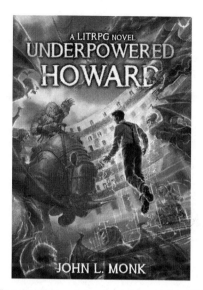

When there's no way to win, cheat, and cheat BIG. Howard, desperate to save his friends and countless innocents, hatches a plan to fix things. Using his deep knowledge of game mechanics, he'll start again as a level 0 necromancer and exploit his way to power.

GET UNDERPOWERED HOWARD NOW!

I was in my garage when the space elves addressed the whole world. They didn't call themselves space elves, of course. Most humans struggled to pronounce Khjurhnalva, so we opted for the easier version. They had a message for us: forces that had eradicated their species' males were now heading for Earth. Hungry for our resources, the alien hordes annihilate everything that stands in their way. The space elves offered us access to the System and asked for very little in return. After all, cooperation was vital to the survival of both our species. I, Mathew Alexander Dunphy, know all of the above is bullshit. I saw the truth with my own eyes and heard it from their beautiful, delicate, deceitful mouths. No one believes me, though. They call me mad. What reason could the space elves have to lie? Planet-wide survival reality show? Ridiculous.

GET THEY CALLED ME MAD NOW!

For all our LitRPG books, visit our website.

SOCIAL MEDIA

If you enjoy what you read, please make sure to visit my website or reach out to me on twitter (where I talk about writing amongst other things) or join my discord where I almost exclusively talk about my existing books/what I'm currently writing.

https://www.caleplamann-author.com/

https://discord.gg/xzgycqtFNe

https://twitter.com/WritesCoco

https://www.patreon.com/CoCo_P

GLOSSARY

Affinity

The connection a blessed has with a school of elemental magic. The higher their connection the more powerful the spells (and the lower the mana cost)

Air Knife

A first tier air spell that fires a sharp shard of high speed air at a target.

Air Supply

A first tier air spell that creates a sphere of oxygen around the target's head, negating gas attacks and allowing operation in airless spaces.

Ankros

The God of Darkness and Struggle. He is the patron of the Durgh and the primary source of Night attunement/mana. His church focuses on darwinian struggles to bring out the best in individuals and cultures.

Attunement

A combination of currency and magical power, only those with blessings can actually check their status sheets to know their attunement levels. Attunement is granted directly by the gods for achievements and can be tranferred directly via physical contact.

Augmented Mending
A second tier wood spell that requires physical contact but allows the healing of serious wounds.

Basil's Cove
Micah's home, a coastal city and regional trade hub. A mid-sized city, it isn't anywhere near as cosmopolitan as larger cities sucha as Bitollan

Bitollan
Capital of Pereston, famed for its soaring architecture that incorporates both magic and blessings it is known as the City of Lights due to its almost constant magical illumination.

Brensen
The second tier of Daemons, roughly equivalent to a level 40 blessed. They resemble bipedal vultures with long skeletal claws.

Chronomancer
A specialization that increases the mana efficiency and power of time based spells drastically.

Drekt Garrul
A part Durgh warrior. Users a heavy cleaver/single bladed sword with a dull reverse end.

Durgh
A subterranean race of large musclebound humanoids with tusks and a dark complexion. They were created by and traditionally worship Ankros. The Durghd are known for being master crafts-

men/metalworkers in addition to their overtly warlike demeanor. Durgh culture is focused around rigid rules of honor and respect, often tied into the concept of ritual combat.

Elementalist

A spellcasting class that limits the caster to just one element where they receive a modest bonus in power.

Elves

An almost extinct race that used to dwell in Karell's forests, focusing primarily on magical growth and knowledge over the course of their unnaturally long lives. They were originally created by and primarily worship Mursa.

Esther Silver

Micah's younger sister, precocious and a notorious gossip.

Flight

A fourth tier air spell that lets the caster fly.

Foresight

A fourth tier time spell that allows the caster to see events a couple seconds into the future.

Gale

A first tier air spell that buffets a target with a high speed gust of wind, potentially knocking it off course or into hazards.

Great Depths

A series of connected caves stretching deep into the earth. Home to many of Karell's more dangerous monsters as well as the Durgh Khanates.

Haste

A fourth tier time spell that lets the caster speed the movement and perceptions of the recipient.

Heal

A third tier wood spell that functions as 'augmented mending' healing serious wounds but at range.

Healing Wave

A fourth tier wood spell that heals a large number of targets at range.

Humans

The primary race of Karell, Humans dominate the planet's surface and primarily worship Luxos.

Jo Redflower

A partially elvish scout with a wild streak to her, Micah's on and off love interest. She's Sarah's younger sister.

Karell

The planet/domain created by the sixteen deities. The location where all mortals dwell.

Karin Dakkora

Legendary spellcaster and researcher that sought the answers to forbidden questions, earning the enemity of most of the world.

Kingdom of Pereston

The Kingdom containing Basil's Cove and Bitollan. Micah has lived his entire life in Pereston

Luoca

The third tier of Daemons, roughly equivalent to a level 60 blessed. They resemble locusts the size of a bull with the head of a human and the tail of a scorpion.

Luxos

The God of Sun and Growth. He is the patron of Humans and the primary source of Sun attunement/mana. His church contains most humans and focuses on cultural conformity and raising standards of living in an attempt to improve humanity as a whole.

Magi

A class that requires more than five levels in spellcasting, two or more affinities, and one level in ritual casting. Magi gain one point in Mind and Spirit per level.

Mending

A first tier wood spell that allows the caster to heal light wounds.

Mursa

The Goddess of Moon and Magic. She is the patron of the Elves and the primary source of Moon attunement/mana. Her church is diffuse and disorganized but it focuses on the accumulation of knowledge and research as a path to self-improvement.

Onkert

The first tier of Daemons, roughly equivalent to a level 20 blessed. They resemble gorillas with the heads of wolves.

Paralytic Sting

A third tier wood spell that requires physical contact. It magically induces paralysis in its target.

Plant Weave

A first tier wood spell that allows the caster to control simple plants, turning vines or grass into barriers or snares.

Pressure Spear

A third tier air spell that drastically improves upon air knife, dealing modest ranged piercing damage.

Refresh

A first tier wood spell that cleanses and detoxifies the recipient, curing modest fatigue.

Regeneration

A fourth tier wood spell that steadily heals a target over time.

Root Spears

A second tier wood spell that spurs the growth of roots/underground plants and turns them into a series of spikes that jut out of the ground, attacking a wide area.

Sarah Redflower

A partially elvish archer. Jo's older sister. Very cold, but protective of her sister.

Sonic Bolt

A second tier air spell that attacks using soundwaves. It has short range but generally ignores armor.

Telivern

An albino enlightened stag. Capable of tactile empathy, for a long stretch of time Telivern is Micah's only friend.

Temporal Transfer

A fourth tier time spell that lets the caster transfer temporal energy from one target ot another.

Thaumaturge

A class that requires three or more affinities, and ten skill points each in spellcasting, enchanting, and ritual casting. It grants one point in Mind and Spirit per level as well as one 'free' point that could be assigned anywhere.

Time Echos

A fourth tier time spell that allows the caster to see recent past events that took place at a location.

Trevor Silver

Micah's older brother, a spear wielder with a bit of a drinking problem.

Updraft

A third tier air spell that aids jumps or climbing by creating an upward gust of wind.

Westmarch

A fortress/citadel in Pereston guarding the main entrance/exit to the Great Depths.

Will Grantly

A human warrior with a rare blessing, thrust into combat situations over his head due to the power of his blessing.

Wind Shield

A second tier air spell that creates a barrier made out of buffeting wind. Useful for stopping ranged attacks.

Wind Spear

Micah's common tier spear art.

Wizard

A class that requires one level in spellcasting and more than one affinity, grants one ability point per level (split evenly between mind and spirit)

GROUPS

Don't forget to join LitRPG Addicts and come hang out with me!

I'm also very active and thankful for LitRPG Books and GameLit Society

Also, check out www.amazon.com/litrpg for more books in the genre!

To learn more about LitRPG, talk to authors including myself, and just have an awesome time, please join the LitRPG Group